1

Thanks for the Memories

A Novel of the SW Pacific Air War July-September 1942

By

Tom Burkhalter

COPYRIGHT NOTICE

Thanks for the Memories: a Novel of the SW Pacific Air War July-September 1942

This is a work of fiction, based on historical events and the technology as it existed at the time. Any resemblance to living persons is coincidental and unintentional.

Cover art by Tom Burkhalter

Sketch Maps and Photos contained herein are from material in the public domain.

Cover Photo Credit: US Air Force.

Acknowledgments

For me there seems to be a point in producing a new book where I suffer doubts. I understand this is normal. I also understand that it's probably rooted in baseless anxiety. Whatever, it feeds on the desire that everything be, if not perfect, then *right*.

So permit me to comment upon the importance of *sharing* these doubts with your peers and fellow writers. When you share doubts with others you are able to see your own doubts in a more objective manner. Which, of course, sometimes keeps you from making a major mistake like publishing too early or without adequate editing.

Thanks for the Memories suffered from all of that, just like my previous three forays in the Pacific air war. Only now there's the future.

Jack Davis appears in the next novel, *The New Kids*, along with some new characters.There are other novels in the pipeline, some of which have considerable text written, especially *POINTBLANK*. Some others have bits and pieces, like *Nos Credimus*, *CARTWHEEL*, *Unto the Final Hour*, and *No Merciful War*. No hints other than the title what they're about or who's in them.

The acknowledgments go to the usual suspects: first, of course, Rama Donepudi and Brad Kurlancheek, and beyond them the members of my writer's group, the CVKAWG. I can't tell you what the letters stand for. I'd blush. But that includes Igor Kudyakov, Nikolai Vitsyn, and Richard Hites.

5

Also can't go any further without mentioning Marianne J. Dyson, writer, scholar, and mother, whose passion for space is always inspirational.

Diana, who shares my life, well, I couldn't get along without you and I don't want to. Love ya, babe.

The Flight So Far

By July 1, 1942, the United States has been fighting in the Pacific for nearly seven months. The Japanese advance halted west of Australia at the island of Timor, and from Timor the Japanese stage bombing raids on Darwin. In the north, the Japanese hold the former Australian possessions of New Ireland and New Britain, including the town of Rabaul in the north of New Britain. Holding Rabaul gives the Japanese possession of Simpson Harbor, a deep-water port that the Japanese turn into a formidable forward base, swarming with Zeros and antiaircraft weapons. Rabaul begins to earn an evil reputation among the bomber crews of the USAAF and RAAF who fly there.

In May the Japanese tried to take Port Moresby, the Allied base on the south coast of Papua New Guinea. They were turned back at the Battle of the Coral Sea. In June, the Japanese were soundly defeated at the Battle of Midway in the north Pacific. Both sides suffered losses but neither the Empire of Japan nor the Allies were close to being beaten. East of Salamaua and Lae on the western end of the Huon Gulf, the north coast of Papua New Guinea is a no-man's land.

Jack Davis has been sent home, and Jimmy Ardana takes his place as Boxcar Red Leader. Charlie Davis and his crew continue flying missions in their increasingly worn and patched B-17E, *Bronco Buster II*.

Everywhere in the world there is savage fighting. The Japanese are fighting in Burma against the British and in China against the Chinese. The Germans are fighting the Soviets on a front from the Baltic to the Black Sea, and in Stalingrad the Wehrmacht and the Red Army slaughter each other for possession of a city being bombed and shelled into rubble. The Afrika Korps is fighting the British 8th Army in Libya. The British supply line to Malta and the eastern Mediterranean is under constant attack by the navy and air forces of Italy and Germany. In the North Atlantic the Kriegsmarine's U-boats are sinking freighters and tankers at a rate that may choke off Great Britain's war effort. In England, the fledgling US 8th Air Force flies its first mission on July 4, 1942, with airplanes borrowed from the RAF. In the United States the mobilization of the economy to produce tanks, airplanes, and warships is only beginning, as is the training of the men to take those weapons to war.

In the South Pacific there is a lull, but in that lull the Japanese continue to stage air raids on Port Moresby and Seven-Mile Drome, and the Allies continue to bomb Rabaul and Simpson Harbor.

Turn the page. Step back in time.

Chapter One

Starlight, Searchlights, Rabaul

Al Stern stepped down from the astrodome and transferred the results of his star sights onto his position log. The log was headed 3 JULY 1942. Opposite the time entry of 1403 GMT the comment column bore the notation "TAKEOFF." A glance at the chronometer showed it was now 1700 Greenwich, which translated to 0300 local time. A few minutes of addition and subtraction, a consultation with gyrocompass, airspeed indicator, and thermometer, and he had the bomber's position and new heading worked out.

"Pilot, navigator," he said over the intercom.

"Go ahead, Al."

"Charlie, come right of present heading to 060."

"Understand 060."

"Affirmative. We're thirty minutes from Rabaul on that heading."

"Understood, Al, thanks."

The navigator felt the deck shift under him as Charlie banked the B-17 bomber onto its new heading and leveled out. Al checked the gyrocompass, which read 060, and nodded to himself.

Not that he expected Charlie would do anything else, not after the last seven months of flying with Charlie Davis over oceans, thunderstorms, flak, and Jap Zeros to bomb places he'd mostly never heard of until they came out here to the South Pacific. But checking and double-checking was part of his job. Al knew Charlie relied on him to figure out where they were and which way they needed to go, and Al relied on Charlie and their current copilot to fly them there. And, of course, on the bombardier, Bob Frye, to drop his bombs on the target, and on the gunners to keep the Zeros off them.

Al scooted forward four feet to peer over the bombardier's shoulder. Frye turned to look at him, face mostly hidden by his oxygen mask. Frye nodded ahead of them, in the direction of Rabaul.

As Al looked lightning flickered in the distance, lighting up the insides of thunderclouds like so many gargantuan Chinese lanterns strung for a party by the great Jehovah. He watched the lightning display for a minute, clapped Frye in the shoulder, and scooted back to his plotting table.

The chart showed their track and last position, penciled in with neat lines and x's. Al figured the line of thunderstorms was between their bomber, *Bronco Buster II*, and their target, the town of Rabaul on the west shore of Simpson Harbor on the northern end of the island of New Britain. It was a night bombing raid combined with a photo-recon mission.

Plus a little something extra, hatched over beer in Townsville with the RAAF.

Charlie and Al were in the RAAF Officer's Mess when Wing Commander Dobbie came in with a couple of his pilots. After they were served they sat down, and Dobbie smiled benevolently at Charlie and Al while his own pilots sipped their beer.

11

"Understand you blokes are headed up north first thing in the morning," Dobbie said. "And you should know I have this from your Colonel Connor, who spoke to my Group Captain."

Al looked at Charlie, who shrugged. "Rabaul," Charlie said.

The Aussies nodded. Rabaul. That one word was all that needed to be said, because Rabaul was the biggest Jap base in the area. Rabaul had one of the best natural harbors in the world, certainly the best in this part of the South Pacific. Rabaul was a sore point with the Aussies, since Rabaul and the island of New Britain were owned by Australia until the Japs kicked them out back last January.

The Japs knew a good thing when they saw it, too, because they moved in troops, airplanes, and warships until Rabaul and Simpson Harbor were thoroughly fortified and virtually unassailable by land. The Jap Navy staged out of Rabaul when they tried to invade Port Moresby last May. They hadn't succeeded, but Al imagined they were still sitting up there, sharpening their bayonets and sabers and brooding over the problem of taking Port Moresby and using it to cut off Australia's supply lines from the US.

General MacArthur and the Bataan Bunch, down in Brisbane, were doubtless concerned with this same idea, although from a different perspective. The Allies had to defend Port Moresby, which meant that information about what the Japs were doing up at Rabaul was of vital importance, and the only way to get that was to fly over and take pictures. They'd done a lot of that over the last month, only this mission they were going to do it at night, using a photoflash bomb as an experiment, coupled with two of the more normal parachute flares, and eight five-hundred-pound bombs for "targets of opportunity."

"Rabaul," agreed Wing Commander Dobbie. He took a sip of his beer and gestured expansively at the five pilots who came in with him. "This is Ian, an' Davie, an' Ben, Adam, an' Joe. We're headed up to Rabaul ourselves and thought maybe we could come up with a joint plan, you know, cooperation between gallant allies and all that sort of tosh."

"Tosh?" said the one called Ian. "Tosh, my bloody oath. Spent too long with the Poms, you did, Winco."

"Behave, Ian, or I shall send you to North Africa."

Ian snorted and drank his beer. He muttered something to Davie that made them both chuckle.

"The lot of you, then," Dobbie said severely. "I know people in RAF Bomber Command, I do, and you could wind up flying bombers over Germany."

The pilots pretended to shake in fear. Al shook his head. Charlie grinned. "Gallant allies, eh? Now I know you blokes want something. What's your idea?"

While Charlie and Dobbie discussed the notion of a cooperative raid on Rabaul, Al looked over Dobbie's pilots. They were short guys and tall guys and stocky and slender with blonde hair and brown hair and blue, brown, or grey eyes, and every single one of them, despite grins or other expressions of devil-may-care, had that deadly serious air of men who knew they were headed for, well, Rabaul, and its blast furnace of flak and searchlights.

"So, you blokes like to come in high, eh?" asked Dobbie.

"We'll be at 23,000 feet this mission," Charlie said.

"How 'bout this, then," said Dobbie. "You lot go in a bit ahead of us, say ten minutes or so, drop your flares or whatever, get everyone looking up…"

"With every searchlight and gun they've got," Charlie observed drily.

"Yes, but you were going in alone anyway, eh? So your flares burn out, the Nips are searching for you in the starry heavens, we'll dodge in over the waves and catch them looking in the wrong direction."

Dobbie sat back, grinned again, and drank his beer.

Charlie looked at Al, who shrugged. "We were going it alone anyway, all right."

That conversation was thirty-six hours in the past. Al checked the chronometer over his desk. It was set to Greenwich time and read 1710, which 0310 local time.

Bronco Buster II would be over Simpson Harbor at 1730 Greenwich, coming in from the southwest. Dobbie and his lads flew Hudsons, a fast twin-engined light bomber that couldn't carry much in the way of a bombload, not and have the fuel to get from Seven-Mile Drome to Rabaul and return.

When Charlie commented on the bombload, Dobbie smiled and said, "Well, you know, a Nip here, a Nip there, it's all to the good, eh?"

Al looked at the thunderstorms ahead of them and keyed the intercom. "Pilot, navigator."

"Al, you see those thunderstorms up ahead?"

"Yeah. Tops look like they're below us, except for a couple. Thread your way around those, and I'll keep track of the course deviations."

"OK."

So, it was all to the good and now here they were, winding their way among thunderstorms that lit themselves from within, one here, one there, three at once and then darkness until lightning arced from one cloud to another, lighting *Bronco Buster II's* nose compartment in silver and shadows, showing the bombardier, Bob Frye, silhouetted in front of his Norden bombsight.

Al wanted to ask Bob how he planned to see anything other than darkness through the bombsight's telescope, but he'd served with Frye since before the war began and knew the bombardier was resourceful.

They flew on in silence for ten minutes. They passed through the line of thunderstorms into clear sky. Al updated his dead-reckoning position and got onto the intercom.

"Pilot, navigator."

"Go ahead, Al."

"Charlie, we're about twenty-five miles southwest of Rabaul."

"OK, thanks, Al."

"Pilot, bombardier. We'll be over the IP in a minute. I'll open bomb bay doors then."

"OK, Bob."

Charlie looked over the nose of *Bronco Buster II.* Ahead of them columns of white light speared up into the sky over Simpson Harbor, weaving slowly back and forth. These were searchlights, the first Charlie had seen since the war began. It looked like a Hollywood premiere Charlie saw once before the war, flying past Los Angeles into March Field in California. When they got closer Charlie figured they'd see flak burst in winking pinpoints of red and yellow light dotting the sky in a tight hemisphere around the searchlights.

"Radio operator, pilot."

"Go ahead, Skipper."

"Send Nelson in the clear."

"Roger."

The code word "Nelson" meant *Bronco Buster II* was on its bomb run over the harbor. The RAAF Hudsons, according to the plan, were somewhere over Blanche Bay east of Simpson Harbor, hopefully undetected by the Japs.

"Bombardier, pilot, can you see the target?"

"Pilot, bombardier, roger. Well, I can see all those damned searchlights anyway. Bomb bay doors opening."

Charlie nodded to himself. He could see bursting flak amid the weaving searchlights. The flak looked like it was at their altitude, more or less, so maybe this much of the joint plan would work.

"Pilot, bombardier."

"Go ahead, Bob."

"Skipper, I'm going to drop on that searchlight battery to the left. I can see that through the bombsight."

"Okey-doke."

"Yeah, okay. Give me ten degrees left so I can line up on those bastards."

Charlie looked over at his copilot, some kid named Simmons who came aboard the day before at Townsville.

"Simmons, you be sure to follow through with me on the controls."

"Yes, sir, but why?"

"Well, if the Japs get lucky and take me out, someone's got to fly the airplane. That lucky someone is you. So, put your hands on the controls and try and remember how to fly."

"Yes, sir," the kid said. His voice was a little more than a squeak.

Charlie might have felt bad for Simmons, but the bomb bay doors were open and the target was just ahead. Looked like the flak was intensifying, and another battery of searchlights blinked on and pointed into the sky, looking to illuminate intruders.

"Pilot, bombardier, keep it steady. Five minutes."

There was a push on the wheel. Charlie pulled back against it, keeping the bomber level, and looked at Simmons. The kid was craning up in his seat, peering over the nose at the searchlights over Rabaul. When he felt Charlie pull on the controls he turned guiltily to Charlie and let go of the controls.

"Stay on it, Simmons," Charlie said, using his dead-level, no-nonsense voice.

"Steady, pilot," said Frye. "One minute."

"Roger, one minute."

Charlie looked at Simmons, then looked away. The copilot still strained forward, as much as his seat belt allowed, anyway, and in the soft ultraviolet glow from the instrument panel Charlie could see his eyes were huge and staring.

"OK," said Frye. "OK, steady, steady...steady...bombs gone, flares gone, closing bomb bay doors."

Charlie felt the lift of the bomber as it shed four thousand pounds of weight in five seconds. He eased forward gently on the controls.

Below them there was a burst of light as the photoflash bomb went off, illuminating the extent of Simpson Harbor for a split-second in harsh relief, showing hills and shore and volcanoes and the warships and transports in the harbor, brighter even than the searchlight beams.

"OK, pilot, bombardier, the camera's running, keep it steady until the flares pop."

WHAM! WHAMWHAM!

Flak burst in a line down the left side, three shells exploding with sudden, freakish accuracy. Shrapnel zinged through the flight deck, starring the windows ahead of Charlie and slashing through the instrument panel. Wind screamed through the holes in the Plexiglas.

Simmons gave a startled *uhhh!* and went limp, falling forward on the controls.

"Copilot's hit," said Charlie. "Crew, sound off."

"Bombardier OK."

"Navigator OK."

"Top turret OK."

"Radio operator OK."

"Right waist OK."

"Left waist OK."

18

"Tail gun OK."

"All right. Smith, get down here and help me with Simmons. Sparks, send a message to Seven Mile, bombed the target, returning to base."

Charlie swept the control panel and engine instruments.

Nothing, no sign of trouble anywhere. Three flak shells exploding that close together and that close to the airplane, and the only real damage was to Simmons.

Holy jumping Jehosophat.

"Bombardier, pilot, you got the pictures from the flares?"

"Yeah, roger, skipper. It's in the can."

"Charlie, it's Al. Make your heading 132 for Seven-Mile. I'm coming up."

"OK, thanks, Al."

Smith came down from the upper turret and felt Simmons' neck for a pulse. Charlie looked over at the flight engineer, who shook his head grimly. Al Stern came up the tunnel from the nose compartment and helped Smith pull Simmons' body from the co-pilot's seat. Charlie put the bomber on autopilot and looked over his shoulder. Al had the kid's coveralls loosened at the neck, and, like Smith, tried to find a pulse. Charlie turned back to the instruments and looked around the panel. Al was the unofficial medic for the crew. If anything could be done for Simmons, on the narrow flight deck of a bomber flying in the cold thin air of the lower stratosphere, Al Stern would do it.

In a moment the navigator climbed into the copilot's seat and strapped in. That told Charlie everything he needed to know.

"OK, Al, you reckon you remember how to navigate from up here?"

The navigator gestured around the bomber. Thunderstorms were strewn liberally across their path and in the area around them.

"We're still on dead reckoning and pilotage, Charlie, at least until we get clear of this mess."

"OK. Anything we can do for Simmons?"

"No."

"Yeah. Crew, pilot, let's double-check. Anyone else get hit? Any damage to the airplane?"

There was a chorus of negatives over the intercom. Charlie shook his head. That poor damned kid. Some Jap gunner must've put Simmons' name on those shells.

"Pilot, tail gunner."

"Go ahead, Em."

"Skipper, all of a sudden those searchlights flipped down over the water. Hell of a lot of flak bursting at low level."

"OK, thanks. Radio operator, pilot."

"Go ahead, skipper."

"Sparks, check and see if there's anything on voice from the RAAF."

"Yes, sir. Just a sec. OK, switching now." There was a click on the line, and the hiss of static. Then, weakly, a babble of voices and static.

"...(*skee!*)ight, Ian, left away from that great bugger..." A crackle of machine-gun fire and an explosion. Then a different voice spoke. "Skipper, got a hit ...*ssss!crack!*...left, breaking left. Searchlights from that   bastter,   God,   that's

20

bright...sksshshskssss!....Adam! Jesus! Adam! Holy Christ he's....*rrrrrssskkkkkkkkkkkkkss!*...Steady on, Joe, steady, watch that *WHAM!* … left and...*krkrkrkrsss*...Aaaahh!....Skipper, that's Joe...Right, Bill, right, right, that's bombs gone...Right, lads, time to go...All right, that's it, let's go."

There was silence over the intercom for a moment.

"Pilot, radio operator. That's it, skipper, they went back to radio silence."

"OK, thanks, Sparks. Tail gunner, pilot, Em, could you see if we hit anything?"

"Looked like a big fire and a little fire, skipper. Our bombs hit in a string across some searchlights. You could see the bombs going off and about half that searchlight battery went dark. Some sort of secondary at the tag end of all that."

"Ball turret, you see anything?"

"'Bout like Em said, skipper. There's a big fire, might be a ship out in the harbor. Thought Ah saw masts or somethin' like 'em, silhouetted, you know. And we did knock a couple searchlights galley-west."

"OK. Thanks, Johnny, thanks, Em."

Charlie relaxed and settled back against his seat, scanned the flight and engine instruments, and took a deep breath of oxygen.

"Al, I'm setting us up for a 500 feet-per-minute rate of descent," Charlie told the navigator. "We'll level out around 15,000."

"Why are you telling me? You're the boss."

"I don't know, Al, I guess I'm just used to you."

"Softie," the navigator scoffed.

21

Charlie shook his head, grinning under his oxygen mask, as the bomber descended between the thunderstorms on the way home.

Bronco Buster II landed at Seven-Mile as the sun came up. On approach the gunners stayed at their stations, watching for Zeros. Kim Smith stayed in the upper turret until Charlie swung the bomber around in front of their revetment and shut down the engines.

An ambulance met them at the revetment. A captain got out of the ambulance with the corpsmen, who unfolded a stretcher and approached the airplane.

There really wasn't a good way to get a dead man out of a B-17. Pulling Simmons' body out the narrow, confined passageway under the flight deck to the nose hatch still meant pulling the limp and uncooperative body along the passageway and lowering it from the nose hatch. The alternative route required maneuvering the body past the upper turret turntable and through the hatch to the catwalk leading through the bomb bay. It wasn't the first time the corpsmen had to do it, and Charlie waited while the men maneuvered the copilot's body off the flight deck to the radio compartment, past the ball turret assembly and down the waist to the door on the right side of the bomber.

Only then did Charlie and Al get out of their seats. "I'll secure my gear," Al said quietly.

Charlie nodded. Al crawled down through the passage to the nose. The pilot followed him and exited the airplane via the nose hatch. He leaned against the left main gear, wishing for the millionth time that he could stand to smoke. His gunners gathered outside the revetment, lighting up, and staring blankly off into the scrub brush and trees on the side of the runway.

"I see you lost Simmons."

Charlie turned and looked at the man who spoke. It was the captain who got out of the ambulance, Captain Don Yellin, another pilot in the 19th Bomb Group. They shook hands.

"Morning, Don. Yeah, Simmons. Too bad. What are you doing up here?"

"Same as you. Soon as we gas up we're headed up to Rabaul to take some pictures."

The two pilots talked about Rabaul and fighter opposition and flak batteries for a few minutes. Then Yellin asked, "How was it at night?"

Charlie shook his head. "No fighters, but some Jap gunners got lucky. That's how Simmons got it. Three flak bursts, almost right on us."

Al Stern swung down from the nose with his navigator's bag. He nodded to Captain Yellin.

"Morning," he said. "You guys headed up north?"

"Sure thing, Stern. You mind talking to my navigator about the route?"

"Sure. Where is he?"

"At the ops shack."

"Let's all go," said Charlie. "We've got to make our reports anyway."

They walked out of the revetment and down the foot path to the ops shack. Stern yawned.

"Oh, hell, Stern, don't start that," said Yellin. "I'll start yawning and my boys will catch it from me and that's all we'll do from here to Rabaul and back."

Stern yawned again. "Sorry. Long night."

"I bet."

"Wonder how the RAAF did?" Stern mused.

"Guess we'll find out."

"You're doing a lot of guessing, Charlie."

"Every second of every day, and more often when we're flying, pal."

"Swell."

They found Wing Commander Dobbie waiting for them at the ops shack, nursing a cup of coffee.

"Morning, chaps," said the RAAF officer. "Heard you lost a bloke. Hard luck."

Charlie nodded. "We think you hit something," he told the WinCo. "Saw two fires burning, one of 'em pretty big."

Austin nodded slowly. He took a slow sip of coffee. "The other was probably B-for-Burton," he said quietly. "Joe Morton's kite. They went in burning and for some reason didn't sink right away."

"Sorry to hear it," said Charlie.

"Yes," said Dobbie. He looked at Captain Yellin. "You and your lads on your way north, then?"

"Within the hour."

"Don't need to tell you to be careful of those bloody little men," said the WinCo. A savage, angry gleam crossed his eyes, there and gone in an instant. "But some pictures of Simpson Harbor would be useful."

"We'll bring 'em back," Yellin promised.

Stern came in with another navigator, who went up to Captain Yellin.

"Sir, I've got the weather from Al, here, and Sgt. Keller tells me they're topping off our tanks right now."

"OK, thanks, Graham." Yellin stuck his hand out. Charlie shook it.

"See you back at Townsville," said Yellin casually. He walked out with his navigator.

Charlie watched them go. He'd been over Rabaul in daylight. Flak, fighters, more flak, and more fighters. Even if Yellin climbed to 27,000 feet, the Zeros could reach them in fifteen minutes from takeoff.

"Hope we didn't stir up a hornet's nest for that bloke," said Austin. He took a last gulp of coffee and set the cup down. "Well, we're off for Townsville. See you around, Charlie."

"Good-oh," Charlie said. The Aussie grinned briefly and walked out of the ops shack.

"You know, Charlie, we've got a bit of a problem," Al said.

"Oh? What's that, Al?"

"We're short a copilot, and we're supposed to go back to Townsville ourselves in an hour. You going to fly the airplane alone?"

Charlie blinked. It hadn't occurred to him. "Jehosophat, Al, you're as good a copilot as any of these so-called pilots we're getting from the States."

"True, but the weather over the Coral Sea between here and Townsville isn't good. You might need me to navigate."

Charlie thought about it. Al, by force of accident and circumstance, had acquired the rudiments of a copilot's job, at least to the extent of setting the autopilot, lowering or raising flaps and landing gear, and handling the throttles. Kim Smith, the flight engineer, could handle the engines but he was slow with everything else.

"Well, damn," Charlie said.

"Maybe I can help," said a new voice, that seemed familiar.

Al Stern looked over Charlie's shoulder and grinned. "Damn, Charlie, we've been invaded."

Charlie turned to look.

A young man, medium height and build except for something broad in his shoulders, stood in the doorway. He was a first lieutenant and he wore a long-barreled Colt revolver in an odd holster that hung just above and inside his left hip.

Charlie grinned and walked forward. "Well, great Jehosophat, if it isn't Jimmy the Kid. What you doing over here in bomber country, Jimmy?"

The two men shook hands.

"Looking for a ride," said Jimmy Ardana. "Col. Wagner told me to take a week off."

Charlie nodded slowly. "So, you need a ride to Australia. Think you can pull your weight?"

"You mean, can I fly as your copilot? Hell, it's just an airplane."

Charlie smothered another grin. He remembered his brother Jack, who had been Jimmy's flight leader before being transferred back to the States, believed Jimmy Ardana was one of the best natural pilots he'd ever seen. Jimmy flew P-39 Airacobras with the 8th Fighter Group across the field.

The four Jap flags painted on Jimmy's P-39 said he was pretty good, and lucky, too.

"Come on, then," Charlie said. "Let's see if you can handle a real airplane instead of one of those little toy kites."

Jimmy Ardana looked around the cockpit of the B-17E.

"Damn, Charlie, you guys have a lot of room in here," he said.

Charlie grinned. "Only someone who flies a P-39 would think so," he replied. "Have a seat."

Jimmy eased himself into the copilot's seat. He reached out to touch the controls, one hand on the control wheel, both feet on the rudder pedals, left hand on the throttle and mixture controls. He leaned out the window.

"How do you guys see out of this thing?" Jimmy asked.

"I've got six gunners, a bombardier and a navigator for that. All you have to do is keep an eye out ahead and watch the instruments."

"You make it sound easy."

"Well, hell, Jimmy, like you said, it's just an airplane."

The pursuit pilot smiled. "So it is. Just kind of a big airplane when you're used to flying a P-39."

"So what d'you think? Want a ride down to Townsville with us?"

"Sure. Otherwise I'll have to ride out in a Catalina or something."

"At 90 miles an hour. Jehosophat, the Wright Brothers flew faster than that."

Jimmy laughed. "So, when are you leaving?"

"Did you bring your bags?"

"Yeah."

"Load 'em up. As soon as Al and the rest of the guys get here we'll head for Oz."

The bomber swayed a little as someone climbed in through the nose hatch. In a moment, Al Stern poked his head up from the nose compartment and grinned up at Jimmy. "You ready to get the hell out of Seven-Mile?"

"Hell, yes. You sure you can find Townsville? Kind of the opposite direction for you, isn't it?"

Al frowned at the pursuit pilot. "*Et tu,* Jimmy? Charlie, don't let this guy get too aggressive with this airplane. You know I get airsick."

"Al, I'm going to let Jimmy fly the whole way and catch up on my sleep. You'll have to take your chances."

Al shook his head and withdrew down the tunnel. A snorted word that sounded suspiciously like "Pilots," floated up from the nose.

"Here's the checklist, Jimmy. Call 'em out for me."

Jimmy took the proffered document. "Pilot's duties in red, copilot's duties in black. Holy Hannah, how many steps in this checklist?"

"To get to the After Takeoff part? Forty-two."

"Damn. OK, I hope you did the preflight and the Form 1A. Fuel transfer valves and switch to OFF."

An hour later the B-17E leveled out at eight thousand feet, on a heading of 180 and an ETA Townsville, as Al Stern cheerfully announced, of two and a half hours. That brought a chorus of approval and cheers from the crew over the intercom.

Jimmy looked over at Charlie. As soon as they reached cruise altitude Charlie set the autopilot.

"When was the last time you were in Townsville?" Charlie asked.

Jimmy smiled. "When Jack and I stole a couple of P-39s," he said.

"First I've heard about that."

"You guys were on leave at the time. But we didn't exactly steal them, Charlie. We were supposed to pick up a couple of P-39s from the depot there, and the guys at the depot didn't want to let us have them. Something about being in the middle of taking inventory."

"You're kidding me."

"Swear to God."

"What did you guys do?"

"Let's just say we persuaded them that we really, really needed those airplanes to shoot Japs with. We also persuaded them we needed a couple of cases of beer apiece."

"How'd that go over?"

"It took a little bit more persuasion than the verbal."

"Jehosophat. How'd you guys get away with that?" Charlie eyed Jimmy's revolver. "Don't tell me. Maybe I don't want to know."

Jimmy laughed. "Aw, I didn't shoot anybody, regardless of some of the rumors I heard later. You know how a good story gets embroidered."

"Jungle-happy pilots let loose on innocent rear-echelon types?"

"War is hell," Jimmy said sagely.

"Yeah, but still..."

"It didn't hurt that we shot down a couple of Zeros on the way home, and that Jack had his orders waiting when we got back. Speaking of which, have you heard anything from him?"

"Jack? I didn't know he was gone until I got back from leave. By now I expect he's married and enjoying life."

"Good. If you hear from him, let me know, will you?"

"Sure thing. You got plans for Brisbane, Jimmy?"

"Aside from seeing the sights and finding out what kind of fun Australia offers? No, not really."

"Al and I have reservations at Lennon's Hotel. Why don't you tag along with us?"

"You aren't afraid I'll ruin your social standing? You know, bomber guys hanging out with pursuit guys?"

"Hey, pal, if it don't bother you it don't bother us. We're broad-minded in the 19th Bomb Group."

"Count me in, then. It's not like I know anyone in Brisbane."

"Swell. You being loyal to a girl back home?"

"I have a pen pal back in Montana, but that's it."

"Good! Then we'll see what's what."

"Pilot, radio operator."

"Go ahead, Sparks."

"Boss, I've got Garbutt Field on the horn. They're expecting us."

"OK, great. Thanks, Sparks." Charlie turned to his copilot and grinned. "You know that flying is only the second greatest adventure known to man, right?"

"Yeah? I'm almost afraid to ask what's the first."

30

"Landing, Jimmy my boy, landing. Let's see what you've got. I'll handle the checklist, you're going to put her down. Think you can handle it?"

Jimmy scoffed. "It's just an airplane."

"OK, hotshot, we'll see."

Charlie coached Jimmy on taxiing the B-17 after they landed at Garbutt Field, following a beat-up Ford truck to a parking area where a dozen B-17s in various stages of damage and disrepair were parked. One had its No. 2 engine removed, and a sheet-metal crew was hard at work on the nacelle and the wing behind it.

The truck dropped them off in front of the apron and an airman waved them in to a parking spot, finally giving them the "cut" signal. Charlie read the shut-down checklist to Jimmy, which mostly dealt with shutting down the four Wright engines and the electrical and hydraulic systems.

A jeep drove up as the crew gathered on the tarmac apron, with an older officer in the passenger's seat.

"Guys," said Charlie.

The crew looked at the jeep and hurried to line up on Charlie, who pulled Jimmy next to him.

"What's up?" Jimmy whispered from the corner of his mouth. "The brass?"

"Yeah," said Charlie. "My boss. Colonel Connally, the group commander."

"Gotcha."

As the colonel got out of the jeep Charlie barked, "Atten-HUT!"

His crew came to attention. Jimmy followed suit.

Colonel Connally walked up and returned Charlie's salute.

"Rest, gentlemen," said the Colonel. "Welcome home."

The colonel's eye traveled over the crew and stopped on Jimmy. The colonel frowned and looked at him.

"You aren't Simmons," said the colonel.

"No, sir. Ardana, James T., first lieutenant, 8th Fighter Group."

The colonel turned an inquiring eye on Charlie.

"Simmons was killed over Rabaul, sir. Flak."

The colonel grimaced and nodded slowly. "Yeah," he said. He indicated Jimmy's revolver.

"Reckon you didn't kidnap this fellow, Charlie," the colonel said drily. "How'd you end up with a pursuit pilot in the right seat?"

"Colonel, Jimmy's on leave and needed a ride. I've known him awhile. He was in my brother's flight up at Seven-Mile. In fact, he took over the flight when Jack went home last month."

"I see." The colonel turned back to Jimmy. "How do you like the B-17, lieutenant?"

"A lot bigger than what I'm used to, sir."

"I'll bet. First time in a multi-engine airplane?"

"No, sir. I had the chance to fly a Hudson, once."

Charlie rolled his eyes. "Jimmy's being modest, Colonel."

"Oh? Well, you might have a shot at the big leagues, then. After all, bombardment is where we separate the men from the boys in the Air Corps."

32

"Yes, sir," said Jimmy innocently. "I've heard it takes a ... oof!"

Jimmy looked accusingly at Charlie and rubbed his shoulder where Charlie elbowed him.

The colonel laughed. "Sorry, lieutenant. Couldn't resist. Just wanted to be sure you were a real pursuit pilot."

"Oh, Jimmy's OK, colonel," Charlie said. "He shot a Zero off our tail back last May."

The colonel nodded. "Good work."

Colonel Connally turned to Charlie. "You and your boys are headed to Brisbane this afternoon?"

"Yes, sir."

"Fine. Come up to HQ when you're done with your airplane, will you, Charlie? I need a few moments of your time."

"Of course, sir."

The colonel nodded, exchanged salutes with Charlie, and drove off in his jeep.

Charlie turned on Jimmy and shook his head. "I guess Jack rubbed off on you in more ways than one," he told the pursuit pilot.

Jimmy smiled. "He taught me everything I know. Well, almost everything."

"Great Jehosophat. Well, come on, you can help us for a bit, and then we'll cadge a ride down to Brisbane. The RAAF almost always has something headed that way."

Charlie was ushered in to see the colonel almost at once. The colonel offered coffee, which Charlie declined.

33

Connally leaned back in his chair. "Your navigator's been with you awhile."

"Came out from the States with me."

"Good navigator?"

"You trying to steal him, Colonel?"

Connally shook his head. "Your whole crew has been together for a long time."

"Yes, sir."

"But you aren't so lucky with copilots."

Charlie recognized the change in the colonel's tone. *This is what he's really after*, Charlie thought. *But why does he care about my copilots?*

"No, sir," Charlie said.

"Here's the thing, Charlie. It's too bad you lost Simmons over Rabaul, because we're fresh out of copilots. Normally we could tap the RAAF for copilots, but they have their own problems right now."

"I see, sir."

"Charlie, I have to ask. You've been out here a long time. You and your boys have been through a lot. Are you OK?"

Charlie frowned. "What kind of question is that, Colonel?"

"A lot of the old-timers are acting tired, so I think it's reasonable enough. Not that you seem tired, Charlie."

"I'm not going Asiatic on you, if that's what you're asking."

"I hope not. Squadron commanders aren't any easier to replace than copilots."

"Squadron commanders?"

"Don't be stupid, Charlie. We've had captains as squadron commanders, and you were promoted to major a little early. The intent was to put you in command of a squadron."

Charlie frowned. "Colonel, respectfully, that was two months ago. I've been bouncing around filling in for squadron commanders and the group operations officer ever since."

"I know." Connally waved his hand and frowned himself. "It's been one thing after another, and, truth is, Charlie, you've been damned useful to me like that. And there's something else."

Charlie kept silent. Connally looked down at his desk and then back up.

"Within the next couple of months the group will rotate home. That's what I hear from Brisbane, anyway. When that happens you won't be a squadron commander anymore, and you'll probably go to one of the bomb groups they're training back in the States. You might start as group operations officer, but you'll have your own bomb group pretty soon. And then, lucky lad, they'll send you across the pond to fight the Krauts. That's not something you need to spread around, by the way."

Charlie nodded.

Connally took a sip from the cup on his desk and grimaced. "Wish we could get some decent coffee out here."

"That was one thing about Java. At least we had good coffee."

"Japs have all that now," the colonel observed.

"Yeah."

"Maybe you can get a decent cup of coffee in Brisbane, Charlie. So, you and your boys, go down to Brisbane, raise some hell, drink some beer, chase some sheilas. By the time you get back we should have some replacements."

Charlie nodded. "Yes, sir."

Chapter Two

A Good Scotch

Jimmy stopped cold inside the door of the RAAF Hudson taking them to Brisbane.

It was the smell of dried blood and shit in the enclosed space of the Hudson's fuselage that hit him like a fist. It took him back to another Hudson, being shot to hell by Zeros, the day he first flew into Seven-Mile Drome.

"You OK, Jimmy?" asked Charlie.

The young pilot shook himself. "Yeah. Yes, sir."

Jimmy moved into the fuselage, put his B4 bag down beside one of the jump seats, and sat down. Charlie Davis sat next to him, and Al Stern sat down on the other side of the fuselage.

"What's the matter, Al?" Charlie asked. "You too good to sit with us?"

"I'm three feet away, Charlie, and looking at your ugly face."

"I am *not* ugly," said Charlie with dignity. "I'm ruggedly handsome."

The exchange snapped Jimmy out of the image in his mind of two pilots, messy dead in the seats across from him. He took a deep breath and blinked.

Charlie looked at him and looked across the aisle at Stern. Jimmy saw their eyes meet.

"I'm OK," he said. "The smell caught me by surprise, that's all."

The older pilot nodded. "That was your first trip up, with Jack?"

Jimmy shook his head. "Oh, yeah."

Charlie looked at the unmanned gun turret and sighed. "Goddamned kid brothers," he said softly.

Steps sounded on the stairs into the fuselage and the RAAF crew boarded the airplane.

"Hello, Yanks," said the man in the lead, wearing RAAF pilot's wings. "Headed for Brisbane?"

Charlie recognized the pilot. "You're Adam, right? One of Dobbie's pilots."

"That's me. Dawkins, Adam Dawkins. You're Charlie and Al, eh? Cadging a lift to Brisbane?"

"Too right," said Al. "You *are* going to Brisbane, aren't you?"

"Oh, ay," said the pilot. "Lucky for us it's just down the coast a bit. Shouldn't be hard to find."

Jimmy asked, "You wouldn't know a guy named Tiny Harris, would you?"

"Tiny? Sure. He's just out of hospital. Why do you ask?"

"I met him, a couple of months ago."

The RAAF pilot looked speculatively at Jimmy. "A couple of months ago, is it?"

"That's right."

"You wouldn't be the lad that pulled Tiny out of his seat?"

Jimmy nodded. The RAAF pilot put out his hand.

"Tiny's a cobber of mine," he said. "I'll shout for the beer when we get to Brisbane."

"Thanks," said Jimmy. He shook the man's hand. "This is Charlie Davis, and his navigator, Al Stern."

Dawkins turned back to Charlie. "We saw you in the searchlights while we were over the west end of Blanche Bay."

"How'd the plan work?"

"To keep the flak up high? Worked a treat, except for the light cannon. That Jap 25mm stuff is murder. We figure that's what did for Joe Miller and his crew."

There was silence for a moment.

"Well!" said Dawkins. "Right bit of fun, that was. What d'you reckon you hit?"

"Clobbered some searchlights. Maybe something else. My tail gunner saw a secondary in the town."

"Good-oh. As WinCo says, the odd Nip here and there adds up, eh?"

Charlie nodded.

Jimmy said, "Tommy, you mind if I come up front after we get off the ground? I'd like to see how one of these things flies when I'm not getting shot at."

Dawkins grinned. "Sure. I hear you made a pretty good landing."

The pilot sketched a brief salute and walked up front.

"Small war," said Al. "Who's Tiny Harris?"

"He was pilot on the Hudson that brought us up to Seven Mile last May."

"When you got jumped by Zeros?" Charlie asked. He looked at the gun turret.

Jimmy followed his look. "Yeah. Jack got into the turret, but you know that. Kept the Zeros off us."

The port engine's starter whined and the propeller began to rotate, slowly, then faster until the engine caught with a roar and a plume of white smoke that dissipated in the wind.

Al Stern relaxed after takeoff and looked at Jimmy and Charlie with a sardonic grin. The two pilots were casting looks around the airplane. Jimmy looked forward to the flight deck, and Charlie looked aft at the gun turret.

"Why don't you just hop on up?" Al asked Charlie. He jerked his head at the gun turret. "Don't mind me. I've seen a machine gun."

Charlie snorted, but he released his seat belt and walked aft to the step of the turret. He looked up into it, studying the layout, and climbed up.

The visibility from the gun turret was amazing. There was an all-around panorama, the view of the whole plan of the airplane from one wingtip to the other and, as you rotated the turret, the twin fins of the vertical stabilizers. The Hudson was still climbing, but as Charlie looked aft he saw the elevator go down, which brought the nose of the airplane down as it leveled out.

Charlie had been under fire often enough to imagine what it had been like for Jack, had enough Zeros make passes at his B-17 that he could see it in his mind's eye, had heard bullets zing and snap through his flight deck and had the cockpit glass shatter in front of him. So, he knew what it was like, but Charlie himself had always been busy flying his airplane.

It suddenly came to Charlie that, for all his experience, he'd never actually fired a gun in anger. It seemed strange to him, rotating slowly in the Hudson's turret and watching the clouds, with the triggers of the twin .303 machine guns under his hands, that he'd never so much as fired a shot during any of the missions he'd flown or any of the air raids he'd endured.

It wasn't necessarily an officer's job to fire guns himself, but to direct the fire of the men under his command.

At that, Charlie figured, he was pretty good.

Al watched Charlie climb into the turret. Jimmy went forward, which left Al alone in the fuselage, looking around at the holes punched in the aluminum skin of the airplane.

He closed his eyes and listened. There were all the familiar sorts of sounds, the muted roar of the engines and the slipstream over the fuselage, the vibration in the seat of his pants, the smells of aluminum and burned aviation fuel and hot electrical wiring, overlaid with scents he was also all too familiar with, the stink of blood and other human smells associated with combat in an airplane. Not to mention the whistle and sigh of the slipstream over shrapnel holes.

He couldn't remember the last time he'd flown and wasn't part of the crew, responsible for guiding them to a target or a destination, and doing whatever else needed doing, like firing machine guns or bandaging the wounded.

Or closing the eyes of the dead.

Al took a deep, slow breath.

He opened his eyes and looked at his hands. He rotated them slightly, watching the fingers.

Steady, not the least tremor.

The hands of a surgeon, if that's the kind of doctor he finally wanted to be.

The navigator leaned back and closed his eyes. He was sure the RAAF guy was a good pilot, but even if he wasn't two of the best pilots in the Air Corps were with him. If anyone could handle a problem in an airplane, those two could.

In three breaths, he was asleep.

"Here you go, chum," said Dawkins. "She's on autopilot, so slip right in and I'll show you the ropes."

Jimmy slid into the pilot's seat of the Hudson and strapped in. Dawkins leaned on the edge of the armored seat back.

"Right, on the controls, then."

Jimmy nodded. He put his feet on the rudder pedals and took the wheel in his hands.

Dawkins grinned and flipped off the autopilot.

It was an odd sensation. One second the wheel felt stiff and unresponsive, and in the next it came alive under his hands.

He looked around the airplane through the canopy. Around him white cotton-ball clouds floated by, and ahead, on the right, was the coast of Queensland, and on the left the shades of blue of the Coral Sea.

Jimmy flexed his fingers on the wheel and settled into the seat. He could feel the airplane soaking into him. It was familiar, reassuring. He became the airplane, on a beautiful sunny morning, flying along on two good engines without a care in the world, in easy gliding distance of at least two possible landing spots if both those engines quit.

"Nice day, innit?" said Dawkins. "You know which instruments are what?"

Jimmy pointed to and named the flight and engine instruments, touched the cowl flap levers, and the wing flaps and landing gear.

"Good enough, chum. I'm going to take a nap. I'll be right behind you. Sing out if you run into any trouble."

Jimmy nodded, looking at the blue sky and the horizon ahead. Out of habit he scanned the sky around them, warily, looking for company, even if it wasn't the company of Zeros.

A collision with a perfectly friendly airplane could ruin your day just as fast.

Charlie came down out of the turret to find Al fast asleep in his seat. He went forward to the flight deck, grinning a little to see the RAAF pilot, Dawkins, propped up against the bulkhead next to the radio operator and sound asleep. No, not a radio operator but a W/T operator, he corrected himself. After all the man flew with the RAAF.

The W/T operator grinned at him.

"All right, Yank?" the man asked.

"Who's flying this bucket?" Charlie asked.

"The bloke you brought with you," said the Aussie. "He's been up there for an hour now. Good pilot."

"Thanks," said Charlie.

He poked his head around the entrance to the cockpit and stood next to Jimmy.

"Thought you were a single-engine type," he said.

"Mostly. I fly up to Rabaul with the B-26 guys when they need a copilot."

"Jehosophat, Jimmy. Thought you had more sense than that."

"At least as much as any of you bomber guys."

"Yeah? You know, I had a beer with Bob Zeamer, you remember him?"

"Sure. I fly copilot with him in his B-26 sometimes."

"Bob said you're a certifiable lunatic."

"Ha. He's the one that makes a living flying a heavy airplane with two postage stamps for wings."

Charlie grinned. "He also said you were a pretty good stick, for a pursuit guy."

"Gosh, how sweet. Maybe I'll bring him a box of chocolates. But he's a pretty good stick, too. For a bomber guy, anyway."

"Gee, thanks, Jimmy."

"No problem, Charlie. You're not bad yourself. Must be hereditary."

"Funny. You know, my Pops was pretty much a single-engine guy himself."

"Maybe you're a variant on the mutation."

"What?"

"Sorry. My cow-country genetics course showing through."

"How do you figure, mutation?"

"Oh, it's a silly theory of mine."

"Spill. You're among friends."

"Why do mutations have to be genetic? I mean, just genetic?"

"OK, I'll bite. Why?"

"My theory, well, hypothesis, really, is that changes in external circumstances bring out changes in internal circumstances. It's pretty much Darwin's theory in action."

"External circumstances?"

Jimmy waved his right hand. "Well, flying isn't exactly a natural act, is it? Not in the usual sense of the phrase. So along come Orville and Wilbur, and redefine what's natural. And hey, presto, the world changes, and latent possibilities come to the forefront."

"Holy Jehosophat, Jimmy, and here I thought you were just another pretty face."

Jimmy laughed. "It's only an idea. I was drinking beer one night with some buddies at school and we came up with that."

"Who were your friends? Biology professors?"

"Not hardly. We were all pilots, sort of, I mean, my flying time back then was bootleg, but the rest of the guys were in the Civilian Pilot Training Program, hoping to be Air Cadets someday. We got to arguing about Darwin and evolution, and flying being such a sudden shift in human abilities, it came to me to claim it was a mutation. Mostly the beer talking. You know how that goes."

"Jimmy, I've done a lot of talking over beer with pals, but the only genetics we discussed involved willing females."

"Oh, yeah? Maybe it was that all-male school you went to. Not having women around would do things to a man."

"Absence makes the heart grow fonder, as they say." Charlie looked at the engine instruments. The Hudson and the B-17s used the same engines, the Wright R-1820 Cyclone.

"See anything?" Jimmy asked.

"Looks like they're running fine," said Charlie. "Want me to take it?"

"No, I'm OK."

"Busman's holiday?"

"It's the aviator gene. I can't help myself."

"I haven't seen many of you guys from the 8th headed south on leave. So what's the scoop here, Jimmy?"

The younger pilot scowled. "Yeah, well, I got into trouble with Colonel Wagner the other day. You heard about that air raid last week?"

"Which one? Monday, Tuesday, Wednesday, or Thursday?"

"Wednesday, smart guy."

Charlie smothered a grin. "Go on."

"Me and my element leader, Slim Atkins, were up with a couple of new guys. We were up around 15,000 doing some formation work when we got a raid warning. Jap bombers, fifteen minutes out, so we start climbing, one eye out for Japs and the other eye on the fuel gauge. We staggered up to 21,000 feet, and saw the Jap bombers, on their way in to Seven-Mile, but what we didn't see were Zeros. You can imagine we looked."

"And looked again, and kept looking."

"That's right. So I sent Slim and his wingman after the bombers while my wingman and I kept climbing."

Charlie looked at Jimmy quizzically. "You stayed up to cover your boys instead of going after the bombers yourself? Don't you want that fifth flag?"

"Charlie, I could smell the Zeros, even if I couldn't see them. I could've told Slim to stay up top or I could've taken the whole flight down, but..."

"But you could smell the Zeros," Charlie said. He know what Jimmy meant.

"And they came out of nowhere. All of a sudden there were twelve of the bastards, swarming all over us. All my wingman and I could do was go into a diving spiral. Slim and his wingman made a pass through the bombers. They got some hits, and made another pass, more hits and smoke and one of the Bettys fell back. Next thing you know there's this beautiful plume of fire and black smoke. And me and Roman were pulling five or six gees in the turn, diving to keep our speed up, so the Japs can't pull lead on us in the turn."

"I don't understand, Jimmy. Sounds like you did the right thing. At least your flight got a kill, and if you weren't keeping the Zeros occupied that might not have happened."

Jimmy scowled again. "That's kind of what Wagner told me. Then he had some choice comments on what I did next."

"Oh."

"Yeah. Long story short, I tried to mix it with those Zeros, and I got some hits on two of them, but Roman and I got shot up pretty bad. Finally we dove out of the fight, which is what Wagner said we should've done in the first place, outnumbered the way we were."

"What? I thought he was a big believer in aggressiveness."

"Kind of what I told him. He looked at me and said, aggressiveness was fine, right up to the point where you get your ass shot off, and a good pursuit pilot knows where to draw the line."

"Sounds like something Jack would say."

"Probably where Jack heard it first."

"So why did Wagner send you on leave?"

"The Colonel said I was probably a little tired and needed a break. So he told me to go drink some beer and chase some sheilas and be back in two weeks."

Charlie reflected, not for the first time, that Boyd Wagner was a first-class leader. Looking at Jimmy's profile, Charlie reflected Wagner was probably right. There were fine lines at the corners of Jimmy's mouth and something in the narrowing of his eyes that looked like a man who was maybe under a little too much strain.

"Sounds like a plan," Charlie said, careful to put no emphasis in his voice. "Don't feel too bad, Jimmy. My boss told me pretty much the same thing."

"Yeah?"

"Seems he thinks I'm getting a little tired, and I might strain my luck one time too often."

"Damn. Not exactly what they taught us in flight school."

"Nor at West Point, but Jimmy, you know the best steel has a breaking point."

"I guess that's so."

"So maybe we both need to relax a little."

They flew for two hours until Dawkins woke up and genially kicked Jimmy out of the pilot's seat.

Jimmy looked out the fuselage window of the Hudson. The Hudson was on downwind approaching RAAF Archerfield near Brisbane.

"Charlie, wake up. We're getting ready to land."

Charlie yawned and sat up a little straighter, blinking. "Brisbane already?"

"Yep."

Charlie reached across the aisle and shook Al's shoulder.

"Wake up, Al. We're there."

Al Stern repeated Charlie's motions, except he added a stretch after the yawn.

By then the Hudson turned onto the crosswind leg of the approach. The engines changed note as the pilot throttled back. Wheels and flaps came down.

Jimmy could see Brisbane in the distance as the airplane lost altitude. The skyline looked like any American city of a decent size, with ten-story office buildings and long streets and bridges over a curving river. Smoke curled up from factory chimneys. Cars and trucks were visible on the highways below.

The Hudson turned on final approach and Brisbane slid out of sight. The horizon sank down, the ground was closer, they flew over the fence at the end of the runway. The pilot cut power to the engines, and a second later the wheels *chirruped* as the airplane touched the runway, running along tail high as the speed bled away.

It took Jimmy a moment to realize why he felt there was something wrong with the landing, something off, and then he knew that the runway was smooth civilized concrete and not the rough surface of the runway up at Seven-Mile with its part-dirt part-macadam surface and the uneven spaces where the bomb craters were filled in.

Charlie Davis saw the look on Jimmy's face and grinned. "Civilization, eh? Takes some getting used to."

"Guess you guys get down here a little more often."

"Not really. Usually no further south than Townsville."

There was a roar that sounded as if it was within inches of the top of the fuselage, which shook and swayed. Jimmy darted to the window and looked out.

A P-39 flew down the taxiway, barely ten feet over the tarmac, and pulled up into a slow roll. Three other P-39s were in front of it, considerably higher.

"Son of a bitch," Jimmy said. "Look at that, Charlie!"

"Yeah, I see him. I wonder if the flight leader knows what his No. 4 is doing."

"Can't believe I'm saying this, but ..."

"But you'd burn his ass if he were in your flight?"

"Something like that," Jimmy said.

"Careful, Jimmy. You might grow up into a first-class flight commander, and then they'll give you a squadron."

"Oh, hell. Don't know if I'm ready for that."

Charlie laughed. "You *do* sound a lot like Jack."

The Hudson taxied up to the ramp. Dawkins swiveled the plane around, revved up the engines to clear the plugs, and shut down.

The radio operator came down the fuselage and opened the door.

He turned and said, "Welcome to Amberley Field, gents," he said.

Dawkins and the radio operator came down from the front of the airplane.

"Who were those blokes that buzzed us?" Dawkins asked.

"Don't know," said Jimmy. "I think the 35th Fighter Group is still down here. Probably with them."

"Well, that one fellow ought to do pretty well strafing troops," Dawkins said drily. "Hope he saves some of that for the Nips."

They got out and stood on the tarmac, stretching again. Jimmy watched the P-39s peel off to land and shook his head.

It was the usual story. The lead pilot looked as if he knew what he was doing, mostly, but No. 2 and No. 3 stumbled down the approach any old way, alternately too high and too low and holding too much power on final, chopping it off way early, and falling the last ten feet onto the runway, bouncing and jerking, with their wingtips bobbling from one side to the other and always too damned close to the runway until more speed bled off.

That brought Jimmy back to No. 4, the buzz king, who was already on downwind when Jimmy looked back at him. Watching the P-39 turn on to final, with flaps and gear coming down and the power audibly reducing, Jimmy concluded the pilot was almost as good as that buzz job said he thought he was. The landing was a little hard, judging from the smoke puffing out behind the main gear, but the pilot planted the airplane solidly on the runway. It didn't bounce, and the power came off the engine just before touchdown.

All in all, it was a passable performance, better than some guys Jimmy knew who'd been flying the P-39 for two months.

"Why do you think that joker is flying No. 4?" Charlie asked. "He looks better than his element leader.'

Jimmy frowned at the P-39s turning off onto the taxiway. "You're right. He's at least as good a pilot as his flight leader, and better than his element lead. That buzz job, at least on a field like this one, shows he might be kind of impulsive."

"Could be," said Charlie. "But I understand that's not a quality unknown in you pursuit types."

"Yeah?"

"I heard the pursuit boys who first came back here from the Philippines were prone to some wild flying. There was one story about them flying down Main Street here in Brisbane, waving to the office workers on the second floor."

"Jack did that?"

Charlie shook his head. "I doubt it. The way I heard it Jack was released from hospital in Darwin, flew here, and within two or three days he was headed north with a gaggle of newies learning to fly P-40s on their way into combat."

Jimmy shook his head. "So, you're saying this could be a guy with some experience who has a discipline problem?"

"Why, Jimmy, I'm surprised to hear you have a word like 'discipline' in your vocabulary."

The younger pilot snorted.

"But, all kidding aside, I think you put your finger on it," said Charlie. "Good on the stick and light in the brain."

Al looked at them. "Well, if class is over for the day, maybe we should find a ride into Brisbane."

Dawkins looked back from the baggage compartment of the Hudson.

"You blokes have a place to stay?" he asked.

Al pointed to Charlie. "My pilot here says he's got a room for us at some place called Lennon's."

"Oh, ay, Lennon's, is it? You're related to General MacArthur, then, Major?"

"No. Why?"

"Well, he stays there along with a lot of other brass hats in your Army. You're sure of your reservation? I've got a place you're welcome to stay, if you don't mind fellows who like their grog."

Charlie grinned. "Dawkins, if it turns out they've lost my reservation, I'll take you up on that. In the meantime, why don't you come with us? Even if they don't have a room I'll bet we can drink at the bar."

"Good-oh, then."

Lennon's was an eight-story building on George Street, not far from the river. Charlie thought it looked like some of the art-deco buildings he knew from Los

Angeles, with straight lines and pronounced ledges and a row of cars in front that were either limousines or taxicabs like the one that dropped them in front of the hotel.

"Nice," said Jimmy. He craned back to look at the upper stories. "Which one d'you suppose MacArthur lives in?"

"He likes penthouses, so probably up on the top floor," said Charlie. "That's where he lived in Manila, anyway, on the top floor of the Manila Hotel."

"Yeah? You were in the Philippines, too, that's right."

"Twice, actually. Jack and I went out before the war with my Pops. We met MacArthur, just to shake hands and say hello, back in 1937."

"No kidding," said Jimmy. "1937. That was the year I went on my first cattle drive."

"No kidding?" said Al. "You never told me you were a for-real cowboy, Jimmy."

"Cattle drive?" said Dawkins. "You're a ringer, then?"

"Ringer? Is that what you Aussies call a cowboy?"

"Oh, ay. At least if you can take your Hollywood movies seriously about what a cattle drover does. And my word, I doubt anyone carries so many firearms here in Australia."

Jimmy laughed. "No self-respecting cowpoke would carry less than a Colt revolver and a Winchester carbine, back in Montana."

The hotel lobby was crowded with men in a variety of uniforms from at least three different countries and their respective armies, navies, and air forces. A loud hum of conversation filled the air along with a gray cloud of cigar and cigarette smoke.

It took a minute to get to the reception desk, where a harried, elderly clerk asked what he could do for them.

"Major Charles Davis," Charlie said, producing his ID card. "And guests. I have a reservation."

"Reservation?" The clerk frowned and produced a ledger. He flipped it open and ran his finger down a page. The frown cleared into a smile. "Ah, yes, here we are. The Davis suite, 402 and 404. And, I believe, one moment..."

The clerk turned to the cubbyholes behind the desk. He took a key below one of the cubbyholes and extracted an envelope from the cubbyhole itself.

The clerk handed both items to Charlie. "And the gentlemen with you, sir?"

Charlie took the key and the envelope and gestured the others forward. While they showed their ID cards to the clerk Charlie opened the envelope.

It was a note from Jack.

Hi, Charlie,

I had some dough left over from a poker game, so here's a present for you. And just to show you the goodness of my heart, I gave the sommelier, a guy by the name of Horace Wilson, $50 American to keep two honest-to-God bottles of Scotch as well. Figured there'd be plenty where I'm going, and it seems to be running short around here. Enjoy it, and if you *run into any of the guys from my flight, give them my regards.*

Jack

Charlie grinned. "Horace Wilson still work here?" he asked the clerk.

"He does, sir. I believe he's on duty now. And..."

The clerk snapped his fingers. An elderly bell-boy turned and walked to the desk.

"Yes?"

"Joey, please ask Mr. Sabin to come to the front desk. I believe he has something for Major Davis."

"Right," said the bell-boy, who walked towards an inconspicuous door, with an equally inconspicuous brass plate reading "Manager".

A short, slender, middle-aged man in a tuxedo emerged from the manager's office. He had pomaded hair slicked back from his forehead, and a pencil-thin moustache that reminded Charlie of the one his Pops sported. The bell-boy ushered him up to Charlie.

"Morton Sabin," the man said, holding out his hand to Charlie. "Major Charles Davis, I presume."

"That's me," said Charlie.

"Ah. If now is a convenient time, may I ask that you come with me?"

"Sure," Charlie replied. He turned to Al.

"We'll wait in the bar," said Al. Jimmy and Dawkins nodded.

"Or, if I might suggest, perhaps Simonds here could conduct you to your suite?" Sabin said. He snapped his finger, and another elderly bell-boy appeared.

Al shrugged and surrendered his bag to one of the bell-boys. The others followed suit.

"This way, please," said the bell-boy.

Charlie watched, a little amused, as the bell-boys ushered Al, Jimmy, and Dawkins to the elevator, which swallowed them and whisked them upstairs.

At his elbow, Sabin cleared his throat. "Major?"

"Sure, Mr. Sabin. What's this all about, anyway?"

"If you would," Sabin said.

The manager ushered Charlie into his office, sat him in a comfortable leather armchair next to a desk, and turned to a wall safe.

"I understand you have the note from Captain Davis," Sabin said as he turned the dial of the safe. "You saw he left you what he refers to as 'a little something.'"

Charlie blinked. "Yes."

"Americans don't generally possess the English gift for understatement," Sabin said. "Ah. Here we are."

Sabin opened the door to the safe. He reached in and pulled out a large envelope.

"We have connections, or had connections, I should say, with the more established hotels in Manila and Soerabaja," said Sabin. "Before they were occupied by those odious Nipponese, they managed to transfer much of the items in their safes to us. For the duration, as one might say."

Sabin handed the envelope to Charlie, who opened it curiously. Inside was a thick stack of greenbacks, and another note.

Charlie,

*I got lucky in more than one poker game,
so I'm leaving some of that luck for you. Make
sure you spread it around for the benefit of the
Air Corps!*

Jack

*PS – it should be about ten thou. When I
said lucky I meant it.*

"Jehosophat," said Charlie reverently. "Thank you,
Mr. Sabin."

"It's my pleasure, Major. Now, how may I be of
further service to you?"

Charlie weighed the envelope in his hand. "We'll
be here a week. I doubt I'll spend all of this or even
most of it. Would you care to recommend a good
bank?"

Jimmy opened the doors onto the balcony of Room
404. It was a good view, spanning George Street and
the Brisbane River. He could see boats and barges on
the river, and following them downstream recognized
the masts of freighters and, he thought, a couple of
warships.

Al and Dawkins joined him on the balcony.

"Dawkins, are you from Brisbane?" Jimmy asked.

"Not I. I come from a sheep station northeast of
Melbourne named Gloomarra."

"Gloomarra? What kind of name is that?"

"Couldn't say," Dawkins cheerfully replied. "Always been called that, far as I know."

"You didn't tell me you were a sheepman."

"Why?"

Jimmy explained the difficulties cattlemen and sheepmen had coexisting with each other in Montana.

"My word," Dawkins said.

"Well, it was fifty years ago, anyway," said Jimmy. "No one pays much attention, now. Usually. So, you don't know much about Brisbane?"

"Didn't say that, chum. I know a couple of good grog shops, and if you're looking for a certain sort of female companionship, well, I don't care for that myself, not condemning those who do, mind you, but I can point you in the right direction."

"That's a friendly offer, Dawkins, but I feel like you do. Not exactly saving it for the girl back home, but..."

At that moment Jimmy was assailed by an image of Linda Sue Gibbons, back home in Choteau, at the high school dance the year before he went off to college.

He came back to the present to see Dawkins grinning at him.

"No girl back home, eh?" said Dawkins.

Al said, "Now me, I don't have a girl back home. But maybe you could tell me where a man might find a good chocolate milkshake. That's what I've been missing."

Dawkins blinked and looked puzzled. "A what? A milkshake? Never heard of it, but I can tell you where to find a dairy bar. They'll have ice cream, anyway."

"That's a start."

Jimmy suspected Al of deliberately deflecting Dawkins from the subject of girls back home, and the first chance he got he winked at the diminutive navigator, who nodded minutely and smiled.

The door opened and Charlie came in. He was followed by one of the elderly Lennon's bell-boys pushing a cart. The cart bore a bucket of ice, glasses, and a brown paper bag. There was a tray of sliced fruit and sliced bread and butter on the cart as well.

"Put it right over there, Eldridge," Charlie said. He handed the bellman a folded bill.

"Thank you, sir," said Eldridge, and bowed his way out of the room.

"Dawkins, it's a good thing you're one of the noblest of our noble Australian allies," Charlie said.

"Oh? How's that, Charlie?"

For answer, Charlie opened the paper bag to reveal two bottles of Scotch whisky.

"My sweet Lord," Dawkins whispered.

"Wow," said Jimmy. "Is that real Scotch?"

"We're about to find out. Ice, or neat?"

They took glasses. Charlie, Jimmy, and Al put ice in theirs, but Dawkins scorned any such, claiming it spoiled the taste of the whisky.

Charlie poured.

"A toast," he said. "One I heard my Pops use, years ago."

"Let's have it," Al said.

Charlie raised his glass. "Here's to us," he said. "Who's like us? Damned few, and they're all dead. Drink!"

Jimmy had had good Scotch once, in San Francisco, waiting to ship out. Before that he thought of himself as a bourbon man, and he reckoned bourbon good enough for most purposes. But the rich, peaty flavor of Scotch was something else again, and it flowed across the tongue and down the throat into his stomach, where it begat a gentle warmth that spread well-being from his toes to his curly black hair.

"Now that," said Dawkins. "That is why so many great men come from Scotland."

"Glad you like it," Charlie replied. "Have another."

Chapter Three

"There's this place called Buna"

When Jimmy got to Townsville, returning from leave, he wasn't lucky enough to find a B-17 or a Hudson headed to Seven-Mile. He finally caught a lift with an RAAF Catalina crew and churned north across the Coral Sea at 90 mph.

Slow the big seaplane might be, but flying at 1000 feet over the ocean was an interesting experience. He spent the flight yarning with the RAAF gunners and scanning the ocean for the periscopes of Jap submarines, until finally the Owen Stanleys rose above the horizon.

Jimmy watched the New Guinea coast approach. The water below changed color from the deep blue whitecap-dappled Coral Sea to a lighter blue. As the depth of the water decreased the lighter blue changed to turquoise and light green, and a long low island appeared off the wing. Jimmy recognized Daugo Island, where he and the other P-39 pilots practiced air-to-ground gunnery.

The engines throttled back as the Catalina descended. The retracted pontoons on the wing tips folded down and locked into place.

"Hold on, Yank," said the gunner. "Be a bit of a bump when we land."

The landing lived up to the gunner's warning. The water was smooth and calm in the harbor, but the deceleration was abrupt. Jimmy felt the pilot come back on the elevator to raise the nose and keep it from digging in. The seaplane slowed and steadied except for a rocking motion as the pilot gave the engines a bit of throttle to taxi across the harbor.

The gunner unlocked the blister and retracted it. Hot humid air redolent with the smells of rotting vegetation and rotten fish and salt water wafted in, mixed with the aroma of spilled oil and scorched metal from bombed-out ships.

"Ah," said Jimmy. "Home."

The gunner grinned. "We'll tie up to a buoy here, Yank, an' a launch'll take us to the dock. From there you can find your way out to Seven-Mile?"

"Reckon so."

They were on the launch near the dock when the air-raid sirens howled. The helmsman laid them alongside. Jimmy and the Catalina crew piled out, and Jimmy followed them to an air raid shelter.

The Japs were after the harbor, and the bombs marched and countermarched near and not so near but always too damned close. Jimmy, crowded in with a bunch of Aussies in Army and RAAF and Navy uniforms, gritted his teeth and put his hands over his ears when the bombs get too close. Someone started screaming. Jimmy looked up to see an Army guy shaking, eyes screwed tightly shut, mouth open. Another soldier held him, talking to him, as the bombs marched closer and marched away.

The explosions quit except for the *Crack!Crack!* of antiaircraft guns. Then they stopped firing and it was quiet.

The soldier kept screaming until his mate shook him and said, "Oi! Calm yourself down, chum, it's over!"

The soldier stopped screaming abruptly and looked around, blinking. He took a deep breath and patted his friend on the shoulder.

"Right, all right, then, Stu. I'm all right."

"About bloody time. Get your thumb out, we've work to do."

Jimmy watched them hurry out the entrance. He let out a breath and turned to the RAAF gunner who took shelter with them.

"You seen those guys around before?" Jimmy asked.

"Yeah, last time we had to run in here. That fellow's name is Jones. Seems like he always does that. Starts screaming, and chops it off cold when it's over."

"Guess you do what you can with what you have," said Jimmy.

"Too right, chum. Come on. Let's find you a ride."

A dilapidated army truck dropped Jimmy off near the operations shack. He walked up the path to the same grass-roofed hut with woven palm-frond walls he saw his first day at Seven-Mile. Over the doorway was a hand-lettered sign: 8TH FIGHTER GROUP OPERATIONS.

He stood inside the doorway, looking around. Inside were the same desks improvised from 55-gallon drums and sawn planks. A corporal pecked unenthusiastically at a typewriter. An orderly dozed by the entrance. A sergeant looked up from his paperwork and stood.

"May I help you, lieutenant?"

Jimmy handed the sergeant his orders. "Where's the officer of the day?" he asked.

"Captain Dolan is, ah, out of the office at the moment, sir," the sergeant said. "But Colonel Wagner is expecting you."

Jimmy nodded. "Is he in?"

Yes, sir. This way, please.

Jimmy followed the sergeant to a back room. It was the same office Colonel Boyd Wagner, Director of Fighter Operations for the Port Moresby area, had occupied since last

April. The only difference between then and now was the electric fan on Wagner's desk.

"Sir, Lieutenant Ardana," said the sergeant.

Wagner looked up and smiled. "Hiya, Jimmy," he said casually. "How was Brisbane?"

"Crowded. Expensive."

Wagner looked at the sergeant. "Thanks, sergeant, that's all."

"Yes, sir."

Wagner waved Jimmy to a seat. "You and Charlie ever find any Scotch?"

"Jack had two bottles of Glenlivet salted away for us, but I'm afraid we drank that."

"Did he? And you drank it all without thinking of me? I'm hurt, Jimmy."

"Well, don't be too hurt. I brought you a consolation prize."

"Oh? You try it out?"

"Extensively. We only tried it because the bartender at Lennon's swore on his sainted grandmother's grave the stuff was Scotch. I think it was doctored-up firewater, but we drank it anyway. I bought a couple of bottles for luck."

Wagner laughed. "Thanks. Meet any interesting women?"

"Aw, Colonel, all those Aussie girls are pretty interesting, but I think they're getting bored with compliments from Yanks."

"I'll bet. Thousands of horny young American servicemen loose in the cities of Australia with time on their hands and money to spend? I'm sure those gals have heard every line in the book and a few invented on the spot."

"Looked like it to me, sir," Jimmy said.

"Well, I hope you got some rest along with all that recreation."

"I did sleep a couple of hours on the Catalina coming back."

"Good! You should be all rested up and ready for anything, and that's good. I've got a little problem, Jimmy, and I'm going to need your help with it."

"Oh? Is this the point where I run like hell?"

"Only if you had good sense."

"Ma always said I never had any sense. What's the job, sir?"

"First, Jimmy, how are you feeling? Any dysentery, malaria, or dengue fever?"

"Not so far."

"You're lucky or tough or both. I'm losing more pilots to tropical bugs than to the Japs. Which brings me to my first point. By the end of July, FEAF will replace the 8th Fighter Group with the 35th. The airplanes will all stay here, though. My question for you is, do you want to stay with the 8th?"

"Are you asking if I'll stay up here at Seven-Mile with the 35th?"

"Yes."

Jimmy frowned. "I'll stick around."

"Good. Jimmy, Steve Wolchek and I talked things over and we've made some changes. While you were gone I had Slim Atkins take over your flight, and that's going to be permanent."

Jimmy blinked. He felt like Wagner punched him in the gut. "Colonel..."

"Hold up, Jimmy. Don't get upset, this isn't a demotion or anything of the sort. Hear me out."

Jimmy nodded.

Wagner took a couple of puffs on his pipe, staring at the ceiling. "Slim's taking over your flight because he's ready to go on flight lead status and needs the seasoning. You, my impetuous young friend, are one of the best flight leaders I've got, even if you are a little excitable."

Jimmy sat quietly and clamped down on his temper. It must have been obvious to Wagner, who grinned at him through the wreaths of pipe smoke surrounding him.

"What do you think about your last fight? Now you've had time to think a little?"

"If we'd had different breaks, it could've gone either way. So maybe I counted on luck a little too much."

"Maybe. Were you too aggressive?"

"Aw, Colonel…"

"I know. There you were, pulling hard on the stick and all that blood headed to your toes, trying to move your head and track the Japs against all those gees, and you've got some kid with you and you have no idea what he can do but at least he's sticking with you, right? That about sum it up?"

"That, and I really wanted to shoot at least one of those bastards down."

"For that fifth flag?"

"Maybe, Colonel, but mostly I just wanted the kill."

"Good! Nothing wrong with a pursuit pilot being bloodthirsty. So, how do you suppose Jack Davis felt, that first time you and he were up against those Jap bombers?"

Jimmy blinked. "I hadn't actually thought about it."

"I know you've got a least two brain cells between your ears, Jimmy, so rub 'em together and tell me what happens."

Jimmy did think about it, and for the first time from Jack's perspective. He wondered how Jack really felt that day, knowing Jimmy was not only new to combat but had less than five hours flying the P-39. Then he remembered Jack's voice over the radio.

"Were you the one who asked if we were in a position to attack?" Jimmy asked.

"I was."

"What I'll never forget is how Jack didn't even hesitate. You asked if we could attack. Jack radioed back, Affirmative."

"I remember."

Jimmy shook his head slowly. "I was scared spitless."

"So was Jack, but not so much for himself. He knew the risks. What scared him was having to take you into a fight when you were in no way ready."

"Yeah? No offense, sir, but how do you know?"

"Oh, Jack let me know about it." Wagner smiled. "He presumed on long acquaintance and the fact that we'd saved each other's asses back in the Philippines to let me know just how it felt to take some wet-behind-the-ears kid into a fight."

Jimmy blinked in surprise. "He did?"

"Jack needed to blow off some steam. And he didn't mean any disrespect. That's kind of my point. There's maybe a handful of guys out here who have any notion of what they're doing, fighting the Japs, and two of them are sitting in this room. Now don't get bashful on me, cowboy. Here's where the roof falls in."

Jimmy looked warily at Wagner, who grinned and put his pipe aside.

"I'm told there's this place called Buna, up on the north coast. Tomorrow morning I'm going up there with the Aussies and some engineers to look for a place to build an airfield. We'll need an escort, because we'll be flying up there in a couple of RAAF Catalinas."

Jimmy nodded.

"I want you to work with Captain Groves and Major Wolchek. They're putting together an escort plan to keep two flights of P-39s over us while we stooge around along the beach up there. One flight up high, one flight down low, staggered arrivals so we've always got someone close by with enough gas to fight. Get the idea?"

Jimmy could see it in his mind: the clouds, the green jungle below, the white beach and the blue ocean, the cross-shaped PBYs tiny with distance, thousands of feet below. Orbiting around at max conserve to keep the short-legged P-39s on station as long as possible.

"Yes, sir."

"Fine. Keep your eyes and ears open with Wolchek. I want you to start learning things besides flying an airplane."

"Sir?"

Wagner smiled. "That's all, Jimmy. Dismissed."

Wolchek grinned at Jimmy. "The Colonel putting you to work, is he?"

"I guess so, Steve."

"Look, there's not much to it. Ed will fill you in."

"Aw, Steve, if there's not much to it, why don't you teach Jimmy here how it's done?"

"Because me squadron commander, you operations officer. I only jump in if you make a mistake."

Groves rolled his eyes. "Swell. OK, Jimmy, here it is."

The Ops officer pulled out a ragged sheet of paper and a pencil. He tested the pencil point, scowled, and whittled a new point with a pocket knife.

"So let's not worry about what the coast looks like too far west or east, right?" Groves sketched rapidly on the paper. Groves drew two lines on the sketch, widening to the west and narrowing to the east. Between them he drew a series of chevrons, and on the north coast a dot, and on the south coast another. He tapped the dot on the south coast. "That's us, here at Seven-Mile. Up here on the north coast, that's Buna, call it one hundred miles away on a compass heading of zero-five-three. The hash-marks here, those are the mountains, and in this area they aren't so high, maybe eight thousand feet, give or take. Most of this you know already."

Groves looked at Jimmy, who nodded. He remembered Buna from covering the rescue of a crashed B-17 crew, not far from there. He pointed to Buna.

"That's where that major from the 19th crash-landed his B-17, first part of June," he said. "I've been there, at least."

71

"Right. Well, I hear the Aussies had a crappy little airstrip in the marshes here, near the coast. There's some kind of bay and a peninsula, and that's Buna Mission. There's a river to the west a couple miles. No one's been up there since the Japs took Lae and Rabaul, because no one's been interested."

"Why are we interested?" Jimmy asked.

"FEAF wants to put an airstrip up there," Groves replied. "I gather the Aussies weren't too encouraging about flying P-39s or anything much bigger than a Piper Cub out of this airstrip they had. So the Colonel will probably look for something not too far inland."

Jimmy nodded. "This base is going to be a lightning-rod, isn't it?"

"What do you mean?"

Jimmy tapped the sketch. "The Japs at Rabaul and Lae will be closer to any field we put at Buna. So it'll be worse than this lousy hole for air raids, plus the Japs can land troops on the coast up there whenever they want. We put an airstrip there and we'll stir up a real hornet's nest."

"So?"

"So I understand we're going to put two squadrons up there. How long d'you think they'll last, even if the Japs don't land troops and try to take the place away from us?"

"I guess FEAF thinks we have to try."

"I don't disagree. But the supply situation is bad enough here. Do we have enough C-47s to fly gas, ammo, and spare parts up to Buna?"

Wolchek exchanged glances with Groves. "Go on, Jimmy."

Jimmy gestured to the flight line, dispersed in among the trees. "Well, take this escort mission tomorrow. How many flyable airplanes do we have? If we want two flights over Buna on staggered intervals, we're committing sixteen airplanes to this mission. That's assuming no aborts and no losses."

Wolchek nodded. "It's going to be a strain, but it's important."

"I understand, skipper. I wasn't saying we shouldn't do it."

"I know. You were just wondering how much further down we can scrape the barrel." Wolchek grimaced. "So, back to tomorrow's mission. High element goes up first, the low element a half-hour later, about the time the Catalinas come on station. The high element gets replaced, then the low element. Got it?"

"Stagger the time so there's always someone with plenty of fuel on station."

"That's right. No sense in having everyone run out of gas all at once. I'd hate to lose Boyd Wagner in a Catalina just because we couldn't get our timing straight."

Jimmy nodded slowly. It was pretty straightforward, and like the scene over Buna he visualized in Wagner's office, he could see this in his head, too: mostly the gas and the oil that had to be readily available for a quick turn-around, the rendezvous times and radio recognition signals had to be agreed-upon, all the bits and pieces he'd taken for granted during mission briefings now acquired an extra dimension, because *someone* had to decide those things and plan to make the mission happen.

"You've got a kind of far-off look in your eye, Jimmy," Wolchek observed. "All this staff work a bit too much for you?"

"No, sir. I was just thinking things through." Jimmy turned to Groves. "Ed, is there a form of some kind the orders go on? Like to the fuel dump and the ammo guys?"

"Sure is."

"And someone has to talk to the RAAF mob, make sure we all know what's going on."

"That's right."

Wolchek said, "Ed, walk Jimmy through all this. Let him carry the load, but make sure he's doing it right."

Jimmy looked from Wolchek to Groves. "You guys know something I don't?"

"Bloody wars and sickly seasons, Jimmy me boy," Wolchek said expansively. "You never know when you might get promoted. If you do, you'd better know what you're doing. Think of this as on-the-job training."

Jimmy nodded slowly.

The field telephone on Wolchek's desk rang. Ed Groves answered. "28th Squadron Operations, Captain Groves speaking."

Groves listened for a moment. "Right. Got it."

He put the phone down and looked at Major Wolchek.

"There's three flights of P-39s inbound from the 35th Fighter Group. They're up here to get familiar with the area. Wagner wants us to watch them land and check their technique."

"OK. What's their ETA?"

"Fifteen minutes."

Wolchek nodded. "Jimmy and I will do that, then we'll go check in with the RAAF."

Jimmy sat in a jeep with his squadron commander and watched as the first flight of P-39s entered the pattern.

"What are their radio call signs?" Jimmy asked.

"This squadron is the Corncobs."

"Corncob? And I thought Boxcar was bad."

Wolchek laughed without taking his eyes off the P-39s. "What, you don't like the idea of being Corncob Yellow Leader?"

Jimmy shuddered theatrically and Wolchek laughed again.

The first flight of P-39s crossed the field and peeled off, one by one, following the flight leader onto the downwind leg of the landing pattern.

It was that first turn from downwind to base Jimmy wanted to see.

The flight leader's turn was sharp and well-coordinated, gear and flaps coming down, and his wingman and the element lead looked pretty good too. Looking sharp and flying well-coordinated in the landing pattern was part of the game, part of the way the pilots and their squadron were assessed in terms of skill.

It was the number-four airplane that both of them watched suddenly, and at the same moment, when the pilot made his turn. The P-39 was sensitive on the controls, prone to enter an accelerated stall, especially in tight turns at the lower airspeeds in the approach. The Number Four pulled too tight in the entry, recovered abruptly by pushing forward on the stick, then back again, producing a wobbling, bobbing sort of turn that only damped out when the P-39 was on base.

Wolchek let his breath out. Jimmy discovered he'd been holding his breath, too.

The first P-39 landed with a puff of dust on the mains as the pilot pulled back on the throttle. His wingman was right behind him, a little wobbly but acceptable, and touched down as the element leader finished his turn onto final. The second flight roared overhead, entering the break.

"Looks like they think they're on approach to Kelly Field," Wolchek said. He didn't take his eyes off the P-39 on final. "They'll need to speed things up, keep it fast and tight."

"Oh, hell," said Jimmy.

Number 4 turned on final too high and too slow. The P-39 stalled and stopped flying ten feet above the runway. Jimmy winced but didn't look away. The P-39 bounced hard into the air, came down on one wheel as the pilot applied power a second too late, then wobbled from one wheel to the other, yawing as the pilot over-controlled on the rudder, throwing up a rooster tail of dirt. The engine power made the airplane accelerate, and for some reason the pilot came in with right rudder. The P-39 lifted back into the air at an angle, shuddering, then the pilot brought all the power off the engine.

"Aw, hell," said Wolchek in disgust.

The P-39 came down on one wheel and a wingtip. The wingtip dug in and the P-39 cartwheeled, shedding bits and pieces as it went.

Behind them came a roar of engines as the next flight on approach applied power to go around. Jimmy glanced over his shoulder at the flight after that. They were continuing on final. The lead P-39 slipped adroitly to one side to avoid the P-39 on the runway. When Jimmy looked back the P-39 was at rest in a cloud of dust. The pilot opened the door and stumbled onto the wing, falling to the ground in time to avoid the P-39 landing almost on top of him.

Wolchek whipped the jeep into gear and turned to race down the side of the runway. He skidded to a stop opposite the wreck. Jimmy jumped out, grabbed the pilot, and pulled him to the side of the runway as other P-39s landed. Wolchek got out and helped Jimmy pull the man into the jeep before racing clear of the runway. Jimmy looked at the pilot. Blood crept from under his leather helmet and one lens of his goggles were cracked.

The man muttered something, inaudible over the burbling roar of the landing P-39s.

"You got him?" Wolchek asked.

"Yeah. Here comes the ambulance."

Wolchek nodded.

The truck with the red cross painted on its side stopped next to them. A pair of medics got out.

"What happened to him?" One asked.

"Cracked up and jumped out. Looks like he banged his head pretty hard."

"Right, then, we've got him."

He and the other medic got the injured pilot into the ambulance and drove off.

Jimmy sat down in the jeep. Wolchek watched the third flight of the P-39s land and taxi to dispersal.

The noise of airplane engines died away. A truck drove up with a trio of mechanics in it, pulling up alongside the wrecked P-39.

Wolchek waved at the mechanics, who waved back as they jumped off and started stripping parts from the P-39. Another truck drove up with three more mechanics. A brief shouting match ensued between the two parties, but quickly resolved itself.

Wolchek put the jeep in gear and drove off. Jimmy looked around as they wound up the rutted dirt road, flashing past a junk pile of debris that had once been airplanes and a line of tents where the pilots and mechanics of the 8th lived.

"Jimmy, stick with me a minute, will you?" Wolchek asked.

"Sure thing, Skipper."

They walked into the operations tent, which, if not exactly cool, was at least out of the sun. Before he went in Jimmy looked to the mountains in the north. The usual afternoon thunderstorms gathered around the peaks of the Owen Stanley mountains. Jimmy judged it would start raining like hell in the next hour.

Wolchek waved him to a seat.

"Jimmy, that kid that cracked up today. How many landings did you see out there that could have ended up the same way?"

"Three, maybe four."

"Agreed. Although the flight leaders looked pretty good."

"Yes, sir."

Wolchek nodded. "I want you to go to the hospital and check on that kid we pulled off the field. See what you think about him."

Jimmy blinked in surprise.

"Humor me, Jimmy. I have an idea."

It was sweltering inside the ramshackle tin-roofed Australian hospital. Like the rest of Port Moresby, if it wasn't built of grass, palm fronds or canvas, it was wood with a tin roof. In theory, a tin roof reflected the sunlight, helping cool the building. Jimmy thought it was a good theory, but didn't work that well. Or maybe it was so damned hot this close to the equator that a little reflected sunlight made no difference.

Jimmy knew from previous experience that most of the patients were there for tropical diseases. New Guinea hosted unknown bugs and microbes of a variety to gladden the hearts of doctors who studied such things.

It was different after an air raid.

For bad wounds, the Aussie medics usually gave their patients a grain of morphine to ease the pain, then started on the wounds. The morphine didn't always work. Someone in a screened-off ward was screaming at the top of his lungs, a scream that ate into Jimmy's nerves and caught at his throat. It lasted for one of those eternal seconds before tapering off into whooping sobs.

A group of men more or less superficially torn and bloody sat in the shade of the hospital veranda. Jimmy saw the pilot he and Wolchek pulled off the runway being treated by a medic. The medic was swabbing gently at the wound on the pilot's scalp. As Jimmy walked closer the medic finished cleaning the wound, then felt the underlying skull with his fingertips. After a moment the medic nodded, satisfied, and put a dressing on the wound.

"You'll be right, mate," the medic said. "Sit here for a few minutes an' rest up a bit before you try to walk home. If you feel queasy in the morning pop round and we'll have another look at you."

"Thanks," the pilot said.

The medic nodded and moved on to the next man.

Jimmy leaned on the railing and looked at the pilot. His coveralls were dirty. He held his flying helmet in one hand and still wore his Mae West. The butt of a .45 automatic protruded from a shoulder holster.

"Rough day?" Jimmy asked sardonically.

The kid opened an eye and looked up at Jimmy. "Who the hell are you?" he asked.

"Name's Jimmy Ardana. Who are you?"

"David Kellerman. Why?"

"Nothing. Just wanted to be sure you were OK."

"Why?"

"Because I pulled your ass off the runway after you almost walked into a prop, that's why. Jesus, Kellerman, where did you learn to fly?"

Kellerman opened the other eye and scowled at Jimmy. "Look. I don't know you, and you aren't in my squadron. I guess my flight leader will gig me good for cracking up that P-39, but it just got away from me."

"Oh, bullshit. There's no such thing as it just got away from you. You didn't know what you were doing."

"OK, fine. I made a dumb mistake. You happy now, Jimmy Ardana?"

They stared at each other for a second. Then Kellerman's face went pale. Jimmy moved quickly aside as Kellerman vomited forcefully on the ground in front of him.

The medic looked over from the man he was treating. "That's not a good sign, mate. Is that all you have or you think you might chunder again?"

"Chunder?" Kellerman gasped.

"Puke," Jimmy supplied.

"My head hurts."

"I'll bet."

The medic looked at Kellerman, who wiped his mouth, spit, and leaned back against the wall with a sigh. Some color came back to Kellerman's face. The medic looked at Jimmy.

"You know this bloke?" the medic asked.

"No, but I'll look after him if he decides he can walk."

"Right, then."

The medic went back to work. Jimmy looked around.

An ambulance roared up. The medics jumped out of the back and carefully pulled a stretcher from the rear.

It struck Jimmy how careful the medics were, hauling stretchers around. They hurried along and wasted no time. Even so it looked like they were walking on eggshells, trying their best not to jar or bump the torn and bleeding men they tended.

"Hey."

Jimmy looked down. Kellerman leaned forward gingerly and stood up, waving back Jimmy's offer of a supporting hand. Kellerman stood, wobbled a little, and blinked his eyes.

"You OK?" Jimmy asked.

"I think so."

"Reckon you can walk?"

"Yeah."

"We'll take it slow."

There was a pile of discarded equipment by the side door of the hospital. Jimmy saw a couple of web belts with canteens on them. He snagged them, shook the canteens, and filled them from the bottle of purified water at the side of the hospital building. Kellerman waited, blinking in the sun.

Jimmy offered him a canteen. "Here. Rinse your mouth out and see if you can drink a little. If you keep that down we'll head for home."

Kellerman took the canteen and did as Jimmy directed. One cautious swallow prompted another, greedier swallow, and then a dozen more.

"Better?"

"Yeah."

Jimmy refilled the canteen. He handed it back to Kellerman.

"Why'd you do that?" Kellerman asked.

"What?"

"Refill the canteen. It's still half full."

"Old habit. I grew up in ranch country. You come across fresh water, you fill your canteen."

"Where you from?"

"Montana."

"Jeez. You aren't kidding, ranch country."

"Been there?"

"No. Only stories and pictures."

Jimmy nodded. "Come on."

They walked slowly down the road. It was thick with dust hanging in the air from the passing of trucks and ambulances coming down from the airfield. Kellerman looked at a spot a few feet ahead of him as he walked.

Jimmy looked up at the mountains. The clouds were darker and uglier but hadn't started to come down the slopes yet.

"Nasty looking clouds," Kellerman said.

"Today's your first day at Seven-Mile?"

"Yeah."

"Well, it's going to rain like billy-hell within the hour. See if you can speed it up. We don't want to be caught in the downpour."

Kellerman nodded and picked up the pace.

By the time the clouds started downslope they reached the tent city.

"Where are you billeted?" Jimmy asked.

"Damned if I know. I thought we'd be assigned when we reported in."

"OK. You report in to Operations. Right up the hill there, see it."

"Jez, that grass shack is Operations?"

"Sure is. Sergeant Holmwood is the man you ask for. Think you can make it on your own?"

Kellerman nodded. "Thanks."

Jimmy said. "Sure thing. Look, you start feeling nauseous or dizzy, have one of your mates go fetch a flight surgeon, you got it? You sure you were conscious the whole time?"

"Yeah. It got kind of wobbly for bit, but I remember jumping out the door and you pulling me off the airstrip."

"OK. Well, take care of yourself."

"You too. Thanks again. I remember looking at a wingtip right in front of my nose just before you grabbed me."

Kellerman turned and walked towards Operations. Jimmy watched him go. The pilot's walk looked steady if a little weak.

Jimmy started back to the 18th Squadron's area.

Tent 7 had been home for two months now. Jimmy looked at the tent, built on a raised wooden floor. That tent was full of ghosts and memories after only two months. He wondered what it would be like in six months.

Inside the tent Slim Atkins snored on his bunk. The bunk was shrouded in mosquito netting.

The other occupant of the tent, Chris Lightman, was an element leader in Yellow Flight. The fourth bunk was stripped down to the mattress.

"What happened to Schrader?" Jimmy asked.

"You mean George?" asked Lightman.

"Hellfire. You lost two guys while I was gone? Who's George, anyway?"

Lightman shrugged. "He pitched his stuff on the bunk, introduced himself, we went on a mission, he didn't come back. Don't even remember his last name."

"What about Schrader?"

"Engine failed on takeoff. Too low."

Jimmy nodded. He looked out of the tent entrance, towards the mountains.

"Gonna rain," Jimmy said.

Lightman looked up. "Hey, Jimmy. How was Brisbane?"

"Crowded. Expensive. Anything else happen while I was gone?"

"Oh, you know. Air raids. Heat. Humidity. Rain."

"The usual, then. Anyone collect a scalp?"

"No. The Brickbats lost two guys, but not to the Japs. One got into a spin and couldn't get out. The other one had engine failure on takeoff."

Jimmy winced. Engine failure on takeoff could make enough of a drain on skill that luck was required to survive.

"How high was the guy that spun in?" Jimmy asked.

"Don't know exactly. I didn't see it. I heard he had plenty of altitude, but the dumb bastard didn't have the spin recovery down."

"Well, hell."

"Yeah."

Thunder cracked in the distance.

"Never saw a place like this for rain," Lightman said. "This gonna be another gully-washer?"

"Looks like it."

"Good. Done with flying for the day, then."

"Looks like it."

Lightman shook his head. "You got a real way with words, Ardana."

"Looks like it."

Atkins stopped snoring. "Stop provoking him, Lightman. You don't know how far he can take that crap."

"Were you just pretending to snore?" Jimmy asked.

Atkins grimaced. "Hellfire, Jimmy. I wasn't sure how you'd take it, me moving into the lead slot in Red flight."

"I'm broad-minded. Anyway, Wagner says he has another job for me. How do you like flying as Lead?"

Atkins grinned ruefully. "Being Boxcar Red Leader is sort of different from being Boxcar Red Three."

"Yeah. Tell me."

Outside the thunder cracked and roared again, even closer.

Atkins looked at Lightman. "Hey, anybody else say anything about the engines?"

"Engines?"

"Seems like I can only turn up about 2900 RPM for takeoff. If we can't get better airplanes maybe we could at least get some new engines," Atkins said. "Those trees at the end of the runway looked awful close when I went over them."

"What do you expect?" Lightman replied. "My crew chief and his boys do the best they can, but hell, all these airplanes have been rode hard and put up wet. Especially the engines. You go jockeying the throttle while you're jockeying around with Tojo's finest, that's hard on an engine."

"Add the heat and humidity," Atkins said. "Hell on men and worse on Allison engines."

"Who the hell would fight a war in New Guinea anyway?" asked Lightman. "Talk about the ass end of nowhere."

"Aw, bitch, bitch, bitch," said Jimmy. "You guys don't know when you've got it good. You've got all the Aussie M&V you can choke down, all the flies and mosquitoes you can swat, a hole in the ground for when you've got the runs, and if you get tired of the tropical sun there's always the tropical rain. If its variety you want you've got it, and if you want excitement, hell, there's always tomorrow's air raid."

"You're a regular ray of sunshine, Jimmy," said Lightman. "You bucking for morale officer?"

"Nah. That's Slim's job. He's the one whining about his engine not working."

Atkins laughed. "You'd have done more than whine with the end of the runway coming up and not enough airspeed."

Lighman snorted. "Whine? I'd be too busy cussing."

"Or praying," agreed Jimmy.

There was a crack of thunder, sounding almost as if it exploded right over their heads. Violet light flickered through the entrance of the tent. On the heels of the lightning came the rain.

"Forgot to tell you, there's a package for you under your bunk. Too heavy to be cookies and too small to be a cake, so we left it alone," said Atkins.

Jimmy hefted the package. It was oddly heavy. "Thanks, Slim."

Jimmy studied the package for a moment. It was also heavily wrapped, with a return address for the Teton County Sheriff's Office, Choteau, Montana. That was a little odd. Obviously it was from his Dad, but why not use the home address? He shrugged and opened the package.

The first thing revealed were two boxes, olive drab, with MONTANA NATIONAL GUARD .45 ACP

BALL AMMUNITION stenciled on them. Jimmy frowned, because the boxes were too big for .45 ACP cartridges. When he opened one of the boxes, he found fifty .45 Long Colt cartridges, which accounted for the weight. Jimmy smiled. So far he'd only fired two rounds out of his Colt revolver, but, as his father and grandfather said, you can never have too much ammunition, only too little.

There was another item, heavily wrapped in butcher's paper. Jimmy hefted it, puzzled.

"Whatcha got there, Jimmy?" Slim asked.

"Don't know."

"Well, unwrap it. You're killing me with suspense over here."

Jimmy tore at the paper.

The first thing revealed was a bone handle, a bit worn, that seemed familiar. Jimmy finished unwrapping.

"Holy jumped-up Hanna," said Slim.

"Jehosophat," Jimmy agreed.

In his hand he held a Bowie knife, and not just any Bowie knife, but one that belonged to his grandfather, Tom Ardana. Jimmy couldn't remember seeing the knife in years. Curious, he took it out of the leather sheath.

"Christ Almighty," said Lightman. "Now that's what I call a toad-sticker."

Jimmy remembered helping to skin an elk using this very knife on his first hunting trip up into the mountains. The knife's hilt was too big to use comfortably for his fourteen-year-old hands, but he remembered the way that knife sliced into the tough hide of the elk, and the blood that flowed along the blade.

"More'n elk blood on that blade, as I recall," his Dad said to Grandpa Tom.

Jimmy adjusted his grip on the hilt until it felt right. He flipped it between his right and left hands a couple of times, to bring back the feel of it, the way Grandpa taught him, and hefted the blade again.

Jimmy liked the feel of the Bowie knife. The blade was a foot long, closer to a short sword than a knife, with a brass guard and a bone handle. The Bowie was a comforting weight in the hand, the same way a Colt revolver felt comfortable. He looked along the dull steel of the blade and realized, looking at the edge, that the blade had been cleaned and polished and the edge sharpened. He pulled the blade over the hairs of his forearm. The edge shaved like a razor.

"Damn," said Slim. "That looks old, but it doesn't cut like it's old."

"German steel from the 1870s, or so I was told," Jimmy said. "My grandpa got this from a knifemaker down in New Braunfels, in Texas, before he came north to Montana."

"Do you mind?" asked Slim.

Jimmy shrugged. "Don't cut yourself."

Slim took the knife and tried to imitate Jimmy's shift from right hand to left. He dropped the blade, which embedded itself point first in the tent's wooden floor.

"Sorry," said Slim.

"If I'd'a known you were that much of a tenderfoot, Slim, I wouldn't have let you try it," said

Jimmy. He pulled the knife out of the floor. "The blade is weighted a little to the front, so you have to allow for that when you shift. Here, I'll show you."

Jimmy demonstrated the hand motion, a bit of an upward twist to the throwing hand to keep the hilt level when it contacted the receiving hand.

"Now, you try it, but take it easy until you get used to it."

Slim tried and promptly missed the toss. The knife tore through the canvas tent wall.

"Jehosophat," said Jimmy in disgust. "It's a good thing you can fly, Slim. Don't know that you're cut out to be a knife fighter."

"Sorry," said Slim.

Jimmy shook his head and picked up the knife, wiping it with his bandana. Then he put it into the sheath, and noticed something strange. The sheath had a belt loop and two leather straps. The straps, Jimmy realized, were about the right size to go around a man's leg, over his coveralls. The leather sheath and straps were brand new, and the sheath had a pocket with a whetstone and a small compass.

Then he noticed the envelope full of letters.

Dear Son, the first one began.

Reading between the lines of your last letter I see you've had to use your pistol. It's not Army issue, so I'm sure ammunition is scarce. I hereby enclose two boxes of same. I sincerely hope, though, that you'll do most of your shooting in the air.

I also understand there's jungle where you are. We're mostly prairie and mountain folk, and I don't like the thought of a jungle. Your grandmother recollected where your grandpa left his favorite Bowie knife, so your Uncle Kurt and I worked on it a bit and got it right and made you this sheath. Uncle Kurt says it should stay on even if you have to hit the silk. Which I hope you'll understand I pray you never do.

I know you aren't in a safe line of work, son, so I'll just remind you what your Grandpa taught us both about weighing the situation, and how sometimes what looks safe isn't. Let us hear from you. Your mother treasures your letters.

Jimmy looked up from the letter at the letterhead; it was on official stationery, which made him smile, and the quick, angular handwriting made him think his Dad dashed the note off in a hurry before heading down the street to the post office.

The next letter was from his mother, and what made it special was his mother wrote about nothing in particular. It was warm back home, and the flowers were out, and the riders were rounding up cattle, and his grandmother still insisted on having the buckboard hitched up from time to time, to ride down to his grandfather's grave.

He let his mind linger on that for a moment and turned to the third letter. It was wrapped around a picture of Laura Sue Gibbons, standing in front of the drug store on Main Street, smiling and waving. Laura Sue wore a light-colored knee-length dress and even in the black-and-white photo the sun caught glints in her hair.

Hi, Jimmy,

Got your letter from Somewhere Out There and I hope you don't mind, but I read parts of it to the gang here at the drug store. Thought the girls would swoon and all the boys got this look in their eyes that was kind of scary. Two of them went right on down to the recruiting station, mumbling something about joining the Air Corps. Don't know if they can qualify for pilot training, but I reckon they might try. Sammy Collings and Dan Blanton, you remember them?

Well, we're just pen pals, but I'm going to worry about you anyway, like I worry about all the boys we grew up with, and now some of the girls are joining up too, mostly to be Army nurses. I'll be twenty-one next month. I'd like to do something about the war, something a little more solid than raising War Bonds. We hear all sorts of news and behind the cheerful stories I see years waiting, when every hand will be needed to win this war.

So, write me some more about Evarra the witch doctor, and if you can slip in a few hints about where you are and what you're doing I'll give you a few hints about me.

To be continued!

Laura Sue

PS:

Hope you don't think I send pictures to just anyone, Jimmy Ardana, but I liked this photo and I hope you will too. A smile from the home front with best wishes!

Chapter Four

PROVIDENCE

It was a bit much to call Colonel Wagner's office a briefing room, but the three squadron commanders and their operations officers crowded into it for a briefing nonetheless. Jimmy tried to make himself inconspicuous and wondered why Steve Wolchek, standing next to him, wanted him here instead of Ed Groves.

"Gentlemen, tomorrow morning I'm going on a trip," Wagner said. "As you've heard, FEAF wants to put an airstrip on the north coast, so I'm going up there with some Army engineers and Australian army officers to find a site. This is the first step in Operation PROVIDENCE." Wagner spoke for five minutes, laying out the basic steps of PROVIDENCE, which would end with the development of an airfield, perhaps several airfields, near two villages called Popondetta and Dobodura, a few miles inland from Buna Mission on the north coast.

The site didn't sound particularly attractive to Jimmy, but at least no worse than Seven-Mile. The airfield sites were reasonably flat areas near rivers, with a trail up to the village of Kokoda in the highlands. Another trail led from Kokoda up into the mountains, where, from what Jimmy had seen flying over them, the terrain went up and down like the teeth of a saw and was overgrown with triple-canopy jungle.

"And make no mistake, gentlemen, when I use the word 'trail' I mean exactly that. The local Aussies assure me that when they say trail they mean it's a foot path. Men and mules can use it, but not vehicles," Wagner said. "The Aussies have two companies of infantry they're getting ready to send up the Kokoda Track to Buna as an advance party. They'll set up defenses at the airfield sites, cut away the kunai grass, and we can start bringing in engineers in C-47s to do the rest. We should be ready to fly in two squadrons of P-39s by the middle of August, along with more infantry and heavy weapons."

This forward base on the north coast would bring the Japs out. Jimmy was sure of that. The only question would be how hard and how fast they'd come. You didn't need to be Ulysses S. Grant or Robert E. Lee to figure out how the Japs were likely to react to an Allied base that close to their own. Jimmy wondered why he'd agreed to go up into the roughest kind of Indian country. He knew it had a lot to do with the fact that it was Wagner who asked. That made Jimmy wonder if he'd ever be that kind of leader. Wagner had been in the war from day one, and Jimmy knew he'd risked his own skin and that of others. Too often, at least for the others, the risks caught up with them. He wondered how Wagner stood it. Volunteering to lead a flight of P-39s from another airstrip hacked out of the New Guinea jungle, Jimmy realized he might come to understand Wagner very quickly indeed.

As he reached that conclusion the air-raid sirens went off, almost immediately followed by the crack-boom of heavy antiaircraft guns.

"Gentlemen, if I needed better proof of the necessity of this operation, the Japs just handed it to me. If you don't know where the slit trench is, follow me."

Jimmy rushed out of the Ops shack with the rest of them as the first bombs burst nearby. *Twenty minutes, hell*, he thought. Twenty minutes was luck. This time it was the air raid sirens and the whistle of bombs already falling.

Damn! They really needed closer slit trenches!

Charlie wanted to go back to sleep. He was awake, and he'd been asleep. All he wanted to do was go back to sleep, and whoever was shaking him was keeping him from that.

"Charlie! Wake up."

"Go away, Al. I just got to sleep."

"Well, that's too bad, Charlie, because the Colonel wants to see you."

"All right. All right." Charlie blinked and opened his eyes, focusing on the face of Al Stern, who grinned at him.

"How the hell can you be so chipper, Al?"

"I'm lucky that way. Also, I slept on the flight down from Seven-Mile."

Charlie shook his head. "If you got that much shut-eye when did you find time to navigate?" He sat up.

"From Seven-Mile to Mareeba? I could find this place in my sleep."

"We just moved here."

"All you do is fly to Townsville and turn right. Piece of cake."

Stern handed him a cup of coffee. Charlie took it and sipped.

95

"Jehosophat, Al. Where'd you get this mud?"

"It's what they had in the mess tent. Talk to the cook."

Charlie took another sip and grimaced. "Well, it's hot."

"You're welcome."

"What does the Colonel want?"

"Don't know. He didn't say. The idea was I should get you and meet him at Operations."

"Something's up."

"Something's always up, but yeah."

"Hand me my boots."

"Do I look like your orderly? I already brought you coffee."

"Then you might as well keep up the act."

Al scoffed and handed Charlie his boots by dropping them nearly on his toes.

"Gee, thanks, Al," said Charlie. "I didn't need those toes, anyway."

Al grinned. "I'll wait for you outside."

"OK."

Charlie sipped some more of the muddy coffee and stuffed his feet into his boots, stomped his feet to settle them in, and stood up. He'd gone to sleep with his uniform on, too tired for anything else, so now he unbuttoned his trousers, tucked his shirt in, and rebuttoned. Years at West Point made checking the line of his fly, belt buckle and blouse buttons an automatic gesture. He took his cap from the peg and settled it on his head. His fingers rasped against the stubble of beard on his face.

He stepped out of the tent, narrowing his eyes against the glare of the Australian afternoon sun. The tents were in the shade of some trees, but the tent was hot and outside it was even hotter, without a breath of wind.

Charlie yawned and blinked again.

"Damn, Charlie, are you tired already?"

"Aren't you tired?"

"Me? I never sleep. Don't need it."

"Good for you, Al. Bottle some of that and sell it if you have any extra." Charlie yawned again. "Heard anything about a new co-pilot?"

"No. Probably the usual infant fresh off the boat from the States."

"Jehosophat. Once, just once I'd like to have someone who's at least looked at a B-17 before he sits in the right seat."

"Oh, quit complaining, Skipper, it's unlike you." Stern stopped and looked at Charlie. "It really is unlike you. You okay?"

"I'm half-awake, Al. Look, let's just go find out what the Colonel wants while I can still keep my eyes open."

"You sure you're all right?"

"Yeah, yeah, I'm fine. Come on."

Stern looked at Charlie a moment longer before nodding and falling back into step.

Charlie took one last sip of the coffee in his cup, tossed the rest out, and put the cup down on the wooden steps of the Ops shack. He walked in.

The sergeant at the desk looked up. "Morning, Major. Colonel Carmichael said to send you right on back."

"Thanks, sergeant."

Charlie and Al walked to the back of the shack. Charlie knocked on the door.

"Charlie, is that you? Come in."

Charlie came in and stood in front of Carmichael's desk. Carmichael waved the two of them into seats.

There was another man in the room, a big-framed second lieutenant whose uniform looked too loose for him, as if he had recently lost a lot of weight. The man's face was gaunt and hollow-cheeked, the skin pale, with a yellowish tinge. He looked vaguely familiar to Charlie.

"Charlie, I'm sorry to get you up, but I need you to take your squadron to Seven-Mile this evening."

Charlie blinked. "My squadron?"

"That's right. You're now the commander of the 82nd Bomb Squadron. Congratulations."

"Yes, sir," said Charlie. "What's the job?"

"We'll get to that in a moment. How many operational airplanes are ready to go with you from your squadron?"

Charlie thought about it. He was familiar with both the 18th and the 82nd Bomb Squadrons, having pinch-hit as squadron commander of both.

"Three, Colonel, including mine."

Carmichael nodded. "OK. Go to Seven-Mile tonight. First thing in the morning, refuel, and bomb the Jap airfield at Lae. Stay up there a couple of days and concentrate your attention on Lae and Salamaua. We'll arrange to get some bombs up there for you. FEAF wants Tojo's finest preoccupied for a while."

"Any particular reason?"

"FEAF is scouting a location for a forward air base on the northern New Guinea coast. General Brett figures if we can keep the Japs busy filling in bomb craters and putting out fires it'll keep their attention off the scouts."

"OK." Charlie exchanged a glance with Al. As he did so his eyes fell on the haggard-looking second lieutenant.

Carmichael said, "Which brings us to another issue. You need a copilot. Meet Lt. Danny Evans."

The vaguely-familiar lieutenant stood up and walked forward, holding his hand out to Charlie. "Danny Evans, Major Davis. We met once, up at Seven-Mile."

Charlie took the man's hand and shook it, and the name and the voice brought the memory back. Evans had crawled out of a shot-up RAAF Hudson, spattered with another man's blood. Only Evans had been a lot beefier then.

"Yes, Evans. I remember you. Weren't you with the 8th, flying P-39s?"

Evans winced a little but kept his eyes on Charlie's. "Yes, sir."

"Yeah. You were in my brother's flight, but you cracked up an airplane and got hurt pretty bad. You don't want to go back to the 8th?"

"No, sir."

"Not cut out to be a pursuit pilot?"

"I had a lot of time to think it over in the hospital, sir, and I remembered some of the things your brother – Captain Davis, I mean – told me. So, no, sir, I'm not so sure about that, and if you aren't sure about it..."

Evans trailed off. Charlie nodded. "You've got to believe, and you don't."

"Not that way."

"You feel like you can handle a B-17?"

"Yes, sir."

"For someone who doesn't believe you seem pretty sure of yourself."

"I believe I can fly a B-17, sir. Better than a P-39, anyway."

"OK. We'll see."

"Good!" said Carmichael. He stood up. "Lt. Stern, why don't you take Lt. Evans here up to your ship? I want to talk to Charlie for a few minutes."

"Yes, sir," Stern said. He and Evans came to attention, saluted, and left the room.

Charlie looked at Carmichael.

"Have a good time in Brisbane, Charlie?" the Colonel asked.

"Yes, sir." Charlie knew his reply sounded cautious. Carmichael grinned.

"Relax. The MPs didn't call me and I'm pretty sure you didn't have to get any of your crew out of jail. I'm more concerned about you."

Charlie's eyes narrowed. "Colonel..."

Carmichael held up a conciliatory hand. "Charlie, how many planes should a full-strength B-17 squadron be able to field?"

Charlie raised an eyebrow at the elementary question. "Twelve, Colonel."

"And you have three operational B-17s. The rest are waiting for maintenance, repairs, spare parts, crew replacements. Just like the other squadrons in the group." Carmichael scowled at his desk. "So, in terms of operational airplanes, you're a flight leader and I'm a squadron commander. And how I see you reacting to it is this lone-wolf bit you seem to like. You fly too many solo missions, Charlie. You've hung a lot of Jap flags and mission markers on your airplane, and that's great. I want my leaders to be aggressive. I want them to lead from the front. But I don't want you to keep betting your life, and the lives of your crew, on this one-plane air force of yours."

Charlie said nothing. Carmichael drummed his fingers on his desk.

"What's with you Davis boys?" Carmichael asked quietly.

"Beg pardon, Colonel?"

"Jesus Henry Howling Christ, Charlie. I hear your brother is an ace, and so far the Air Corps only has a handful of those. Your navigator has the DSC, I don't even know how many DFCs and Silver Stars and Purple Hearts you and your boys have split up between you, and from some of the things I've heard there should probably have been a Congressional Medal of Honor and a couple more DSCs thrown in for some of the missions you guys pulled off. And your brother? Hell, seven Japs?" Carmichael shook his head. "Charlie, sooner or later they're going to send us home. We'll rest for a little bit and then we'll get shuffled off to bomb groups going to Europe. I think I've heard once or twice that it's going to be a long war. We have to pace ourselves. Your experience makes you valuable to the Air Corps."

Charlie frowned and stood up. "May I be dismissed, Colonel?"

Carmichael studied him for a moment. "When you tell me what I said that pissed you off."

"Permission to speak freely, sir?"

"Sure," said Carmichael.

"Back last February there was a tendency in the 19th to, ah, conserve the lives of the valuable men, was the phrase I heard. I never understood what that meant." Charlie hesitated.

"Go on," said Carmichael.

"We got a lot of half-trained crews, and because the valuable men were being conserved, there wasn't anyone else to send. The losses were ..." Charlie paused.

"Go on," Carmichael said gently. "Weren't you a valuable man?"

"Every single man on my crew is valuable, Colonel. Every one. Just like every poor bastard who dies out here doing the best he can."

"I didn't mean it otherwise."

Charlie nodded. "As if the losses weren't enough, we got our asses kicked out of Java. We're Americans, Colonel. We aren't used to losing. It makes us mad. And the only value I have, or anyone else out here has, is whether or not we can take the fight to those little yellow bastards, and maybe pass on to the new guys what we've learned about how to survive. That's what makes us valuable."

Carmichael sighed and nodded.

"So my boys and I fly a lot of missions," Charlie replied. "We aren't the only ones. And all of us who keep going have learned one thing."

"Don't keep me in suspense, Charlie. What's that?"

"Jehosophat, Colonel. It's trust. My crew and I trust each other to do our jobs. We believe in each other. We have to. No one else does."

"Jesus, Charlie." Carmichael looked down at his desk. Then he looked back up. "For what it's worth, I trust you and I believe in you."

Charlie nodded.

"Now take off, and good luck."

Charlie nodded, did an about face, and left the room. Charlie took the path to the flight line. He stood at the edge of the trees, looking at the B-17s in their revetments. Scattered around the flight line and the revetments around the runway were maybe twenty B-17s in various states of repair.

Spare parts for the engines and airframes were arriving from the States in a trickle. That was according to their own supply people, but after talking to Jimmy Ardana about his little adventure in Townsville back in May, he wondered about that. All Charlie could say for sure was that the spare parts weren't available for the 19th BG.

Replacements were a joke. Charlie was glad enough to have him, but Danny Evans wasn't even a multi-engine pilot. His time was all in single-engine airplanes, and he was probably more experienced than the handful of replacement pilots and copilots that reached the 19th. Gunners? Jehosophat, that was a worse joke than the copilot situation, because as far as Charlie knew there still wasn't a training program for aerial gunners even back in the States. Bombardiers and navigators were about the same. Charlie knew he was lucky to have Al Stern, not because of any special training Al received, but because Al Stern had natural talent as a navigator. Not to mention the fact that in Al's short skinny frame beat the heart of a man who never gave up, not on himself, not on his crew.

After replacement aircrew, Charlie knew what they needed was ground crew. Mechanics, crew chiefs, radiomen, cartographers, great Jehosophat, for that matter the group HQ squadron could use a dozen trained typists. Sometimes he typed his own mission reports, to save time.

The 19th was operating on a shoestring, and one hell of a frayed, tattered shoestring at that.

"Hey, Charlie! Where the hell you been?"

Charlie turned to see Captain Bart Allen and 1st Lt. Ira West. They were the airplane commanders of the other two operational bombers in his squadron.

"Aw, Colonel Carmichael needed some advice on running the war," Charlie said, shaking hands with his pilots.

"What's up, then, Boss?" asked West.

"Lae."

"Jeeziz," said Allen. "But not Rabaul?"

"Carmichael just said Lae. Of course, you know how that is. We'll get up to Seven-Mile and the whole thing will be changed."

Allen nodded thoughtfully. "Or rained out."

"My No. 3 engine has been acting up again," said West.

Charlie faked a punch to West's chin. "I thought it was your No. 1 that liked to act up."

"Oh, yeah, that one too."

"Let's see if it gets you as far as Seven-Mile before it craps out on you."

West grinned. "Hope so. Don't want to lose an engine over the Coral Sea."

"Yeah, no kidding. OK, it's 1300 now, if we want to reach Seven-Mile before dark we've got two hours. You guys need anything?"

"For once we're good," said Allen.

"Actually, I was kidding about my No. 3. We just changed that engine. All we need is gas and .50-cal. ammo, boss."

Charlie nodded. "OK. You know the drill, so let's get going. Wheels up no later than 1500."

Jimmy Ardana walked into the RAAF Officers Mess, got a beer, and looked around. He almost missed Al Stern's diminutive figure, seated with a couple of guys he didn't know, and some big guy who nearly dwarfed the navigator. He waved at Al, who waved back, and when he did the big guy turned to see who Al was waving at.

"I'll be damned," said Jimmy. He stood looking down at the big guy. "Danny Evans."

"Ardana."

Al looked from Evans to Jimmy and back. "So," he said over the noise of riotous Australians and American aircrew. "You two know each other."

Jimmy sat down at the table. The RAAF officers made room for him with nods. Jimmy stared across the table at Evans, who sat next to Al Stern, who looked from Jimmy to Evans and back.

"Yeah," Jimmy said. "You could say that. You look like hell, Evans."

"Just got out of hospital," Evans said evenly.

Jimmy sipped his beer and looked at Stern. "Al, I thought you guys would be down in Oz for a few days."

"Me too. But that's the Army."

Jimmy nodded. He held his hand out to the RAAF officer next to him. "Jimmy Ardana," he said.

"Billy Watkins," said one.

"Harry Morris," said the other. They both wore RAAF pilot's wings.

"What are you guys flying?"

"Catalinas," said Billy Watkins. "Got a bit of a show on tomorrow."

"Oh?"

"Terribly hush hush, you know. Can't talk about it."

"Great day, pal, I don't want to know about it. I've got enough to do flying P-39s. We've got something terribly hush hush on tomorrow ourselves." Jimmy raised his beer and clinked with the two Aussies.

"Cheers, mate," said Harry Morris. "You don't ask about us and we won't ask about you."

"Deal," said Jimmy, who drank. Then he looked at Al Stern. "And here you guys are. Where's Charlie?"

"Asleep. I think he's getting old. He's twenty-five, you know. Practically one foot in the grave."

Jimmy nodded. Then he looked back at Evans, who was drinking his beer.

"You're pretty quiet, Evans," he said.

Danny nodded. "I hear you have four Japs now," he said. "And you're Boxcar Red Leader."

"I was. What are you doing these days?"

"I'm copilot for Major Davis."

Jimmy nodded. He looked at Danny Evans, and he could see in Danny's eyes something of what had to be going on in his own mind, remembering when Danny was Boxcar Red Two.

What Jimmy didn't see in Danny Evans was the bellicose frat boy that came to Seven-Mile with him last May.

Jimmy said, "I heard Charlie say once that Bombardment is where the Air Corps separates the men from the boys."

Evans blinked. "Who'd he say that to?"

"Guess."

Evans grinned briefly. "What did Captain Davis say to that?"

"Jack allowed that was probably so, but they had to use a crowbar."

The two Aussies looked at each other. Al put his face in his hand and Jimmy saw his shoulders shaking. Evans blinked, puzzled for a half-second, then his face turned pink.

"Oh," he said weakly. "That's disgusting."

He sipped his beer.

The Aussies erupted with laughter. Al put his beer down and took a handkerchief out of his pocket and wiped his eyes.

"Wow," he said. "That stings. You pursuit types really know how to hurt a guy."

"That's the business we're in," said Jimmy. He looked at Evans, who nodded slowly. Jimmy looked at Al Stern. "What are you guys up to?"

"Oh, you know. Dropping bombs on unfriendly strangers here and there."

"Gosh," said Jimmy. "All sorts of terribly hush-hush things seem to be happening tomorrow. Let's stop talking about it. Anyone ready for another beer?"

The next morning Jimmy went with Boyd Wagner to the harbor where the RAAF Catalinas moored. It was quiet and dark. The smooth surface of the harbor reflected the light of the stars overhead. A hint of pink light defined the horizon to the southeast. The hill where most of Port Moresby was built blocked off the rest of the horizon.

A small party stood on the shore by a boat.

"Wagner, is that you?"

"Colonel Yoder, I'd like you to meet Jimmy Ardana, one of my pilots," Wagner replied.

Jimmy shook hands with Colonel Yoder, who was an Army engineer. "My pleasure, Colonel. I understand you build airfields."

"I do, young man. Boyd tells me you shoot down Japs."

"Whenever I get the chance, sir."

"Good! Well, hopefully we'll find a place up north where we can give you a shot at a few more. Boyd, you've briefed Lt. Ardana on our escort requirements?"

"Yes, sir. My boys will be over the beach in relays, four-plane elements at different altitudes. I checked with 19th Bomb Group Operations a little earlier. They're sending some B-17s to visit the Jap field at Lae during the day, today and tomorrow."

Jimmy saw Colonel Yoder nod in the vague light. "All right. Let's get loaded up. Where's Squadron Leader Colleton?"

"Here, sir. Are we ready?"

"Whenever you like."

"Then let's get aboard." Squadron Leader Colleton looked at Wagner. "Morning, Boyd."

"Morning, Snipe. You're still taking T-for-Taffy and C-for-Charlie?"

"That's right."

"You got that, Ardana?"

"Affirmative, Colonel. T-Taffy, C-Charlie. Frequencies as briefed."

"Good. Take off. We'll see you this side of Buna in an hour and a half. Don't be late."

"No, sir."

Wagner clapped Jimmy on the shoulder and climbed into the waiting boat with the other members of the scout party.

Jimmy walked back to the truck. The driver took him back to the Boxcar flight line and let him out in front of his revetment.

"Morning, Don," he said to the crew chief.

"Morning, Jimmy. We haven't been up this early in a while."

"Tell me. How's the *Gremlin* doing this morning?"

"I'm starting to worry about the lubricating oil they're sending us. Looks to me like it's breaking down faster than it ought to."

"What does Chief Halloran say?"

"He growls something about goddamned Stateside supply types and chomps on his cigar. He thinks the tropical heat and humidity is doing it. You know, hell on men ..."

"And worse on Allison engines. Yeah. So what's in the crankcase today?"

"We changed the oil last night. Cross your fingers, boss."

"Swell. Why don't you fly her?"

"Aw, now, Jimmy, I would, but see..."

"You washed out of flight training." Jimmy shook his head, grinning.

"Aw, you know me too well." The crew chief frowned. "Seriously, Jimmy, it's starting to be a problem for the whole group. If Shell Oil doesn't get the thumb out we're going to be in real trouble."

"That's nothing new," Jimmy said. "OK, Don, let's get this show on the road."

From down the flight line came the whine of an energizer. The crew chief helped Jimmy into his parachute and up into the cockpit as Allisons coughed and growled into life.

After two months, the switches and pedals and instruments found themselves under his fingers or feet or eyes. Jimmy started the engine, and the drive-shaft between his feet turned the screaming gearbox driving the propeller. Terraine's warning echoed in Jimmy's mind as he stood hard on the brakes and pushed the throttle forward until the RPM indicator pointed to 3000 RPM. Jimmy let it sit there for a minute, keeping an eye on the oil and cylinder head temp gauges, before bringing the throttle back to idle. He looked at Terraine, who shrugged.

"Like I said, cross your fingers. Maybe the oil is from a good batch."

"OK."

Terraine shut the cockpit door and climbed down off the wing. Jimmy looked left and right, blinked his running lights once and started to taxi. He was the first in line down to the runway, and behind him came his flight.

In minutes they were on the runway, accelerating, then lifting off into the dawn flooding down the airstrip as the sun rose over Bootless Inlet. They circled once, forming up, then took up a heading of 030 and climbed to ten thousand feet.

Jimmy kept an eye on his temps and oil pressure gauges. Engine trouble was no joke. He put it out of his mind and concentrated on the sky and his flight.

Charlie took a deep breath through his oxygen mask and scanned the instrument panel before he looked over at Danny Evans.

Evans didn't impress Charlie as being particularly smart, but the guy had a retentive memory, and, so far, Charlie only had to show him something once. As Charlie watched Evans reached out and made a minor change to the rudder control on the autopilot. Charlie had been watching the gyrocompass slowly changing heading, and was about to tweak the rudder control himself.

Maybe Evans was right to change his specialty from pursuit to bombardment. Charlie didn't know what happened between Jack and Danny Evans when Danny was in Jack's flight. He had the impression Danny wasn't the best P-39 pilot in the world, but that didn't mean Evans was a bad pilot. There was a difference between guys who could fly the hell out of a single-engine airplane like the P-39 or the P-40, and guys who could fly airplanes like the B-26 or the B-17. Unless you were like Jimmy Ardana, who might be one of the few individuals who could bridge both worlds. Jimmy landed *Bronco Buster II* like he'd flown four-engine airplanes since he got out of flight school.

Anyway it looked like maybe Danny Evans might become a good B-17 pilot.

"Navigator, pilot."

"Go ahead, Charlie."

"Al, where the hell are we?"

"Touchy, touchy. We're ninety miles south of the target. I was just about to call you."

Charlie looked to the left and the right at Primrose Two and Three. The other bombers were in good formation. Two was on the left, and high; Three was on the right, and low. Lae was ninety miles north.

Charlie gestured to Evans, who dialed the autopilot to bring them onto the proper heading.

Ninety miles and twenty-five minutes to the target.

"Pilot, bombardier. Coming up on IP in ten minutes."

"Thank you, bombardier."

Charlie looked over at Evans. "OK, Danny. This is a first for you."

"What happens?"

"Look north. Can you see the airfield?"

"I don't see anything but earth and ocean."

"Right. Don't worry about it. Bombardier, pilot."

"Go ahead, pilot."

"Danny doesn't see the target."

"That's OK, Lieutenant," said Frye. "I do. Opening bomb bay doors. Pilot, steady on this heading."

Jimmy shifted his ass on the seat parachute, took a deep breath of oxygen, and scanned the sky all around, above, and below him. Nothing but clouds around them, the jungle below, and the coast ahead.

His radio snarled and hissed on the tactical channel. "...car White ...er, this is T for Taffy, how do you read?"

Jimmy keyed his radio. "T for Taffy, this is Boxcar White Leader, read you three by three."

"Boxcar...der, primary...o'clock."

"Say again, T for Taffy."

"Boxcar White Leader, ...o'clock."

Jimmy sighed. "Say again, T for Taffy. You're being blanked out by intermittent static."

"...eleven...clock, Boxcar White Leader."

"Okay, T for Taffy, primary at eleven o'clock, Boxcar White Leader out."

Jimmy watched the two PBYs alter course slightly to the west.

It was a short flight to Buna Mission. That was a good thing, given the limited range of the P-39. Jimmy's drop tank was almost dry, which meant everyone else was at the point of jettisoning tanks.

"Boxcar White Flight, say your fuel state."

"Lead, Two has two hundred gallons."

"Three has two hundred twenty."

"Four has one hundred eighty."

"Four from Lead, is your aux tank dry?"

"Affirmative."

"Jettison the tank right now, Four. Two and Three, how about it?"

"This is Two, tank will be dry in a couple minutes.

"Lead, Three has a little more than that."

"OK, thanks." Jimmy looked at his clock. White Four, that dumb kid. He should have pickled his drop tank and let someone know about it. The drag of the tank increased fuel consumption. If the tank was empty it had to go. It was about what he expected from White Four, who was another kid straight out of flight school.

"Boxcar Yellow Leader, this is Boxcar White Leader. How's your fuel state?"

Jimmy could make out words in the static, but not the words themselves. The tropics were hell on everything, even radio waves. Static moaned and sizzled in his earphones.

"Hey, Stan, it's Jimmy, you read?"

"Jimmy ... fuel ... hour."

"Stan, say again."

Static crashed.

"White Three from White Leader, do you read Yellow Leader?"

"Not well, White Leader. Something about an hour's fuel."

Crap. An hour was about right for the guys flying low over T for Taffy. Jimmy and his flight had about another half hour. From here it was forty minutes back to Seven-Mile. Yellow Flight barely had enough fuel for five minutes of combat if the Japs showed up.

The mission briefing had the Brickbats launching two flights behind them, Brickbat Blue and Brickbat White. The idea was for the Brickbats to provide cover for T for Taffy and C for Charlie when the Boxcars turned for home.

Jimmy looked west and north. The Zeroes could come from anywhere, even from behind them, but the main Jap bases were at Salamaua and Lae to the west and Rabaul to the northeast. Charlie Davis and his B-17s were headed for Lae to bomb the airfield there. Hopefully that would give the Japs something to worry over closer to home than Buna Mission.

He looked at his fuel gauge and his clock. Thirty minutes and he'd have to lead his flight home.

Thirty minutes.

The Zeros hit Charlie's flight during the bomb run.

"Crew, ball turret. Got six of them little bastards climbing up at us. Reckon they'll be heah in about ten minutes."

"Roger, ball turret, thanks. Tail gunner, pilot."

"Go ahead, skipper."

"Em, anything coming up from Salamaua?"

"Not yet."

Kim Smith rotated the upper turret. Evans looked over his shoulder, frowning, until he saw the gunner rotating on the turntable.

Evans blinked once and turned back to the controls. He rolled his shoulders and settled into his seat, flexing his fingers on the controls. Charlie looked at him, caught his eye and raised his eyebrow. Evans nodded at him.

"I'm OK," he told Charlie.

"I hope so. We're going to have company."

"I saw 'em."

"Pilot, bombardier."

"Go ahead, Bob."

"Boss, bring us right just a hair."

Charlie tweaked the controls to the right.

"That's good, that's good. OK, three minutes."

Charlie saw the Zeros then.

"Zeros, one o'clock low," he called. "Count six."

"Pilot, upper turret, got the Zeros."

"Pilot, ball turret, ditto."

"Pilot, tail gunner, we're clear back here."

Six Zeros. The Japs kept thirty-plus Zeros at Lae and about the same at Salamaua. Why were they only sending six Zeros up?

Maybe they should count their blessings. Six Zeros were bad enough news.

"Pilot, bombardier, that's a good heading. Keep it there. Two minutes."

"Danny, if I get hit on the bomb run, you have to do what Bob tells you to do. Mostly keep it steady, a little left, a little right, that kind of thing."

"OK, Skipper." Danny's voice over the intercom was earnest and deadly serious.

Charlie looked at him again, then the Zeros turned in for their attack run.

Al Stern crouched over the right cheek .50-cal., looking at the approaching Zeros through the little window.

"OK, OK, steady," said the bombardier.

Al steadied his machine gun on the lead Zero and pressed the trigger. The gun roared, tracers flashed, and the Zeros flashed by out of his view as the other gunners picked up a staccato chorus.

"Bombs away," said Frye. "Closing bomb bay doors."

"Zeros passing through four o'clock," came over the intercom.

"Radio operator, pilot. Send to formation, turn to heading 175."

"Roger, pilot, formation turn to 175."

"OK, bombardier, set up the camera. We'll pass over Salamaua in seven minutes."

"Roger, boss, passing over Salamaua in seven minutes."

"Tail gunner has six Zeros climbing at seven o'clock."

"Left waist, got the Zeros. Looks like they're going after the high B-17, passing abeam, now passing overhead."

Al duck-walked across the nose compartment to the left cheek gun, looking out the window. He caught a glimpse of the Zeros passing overhead as the upper turret opened fire.

"Al, give me a hand with this god-blessed camera," said Frye. "The shutter timer is stuck."

Al looked away from the window and bent to help Frye with the camera. He could see the peninsula approaching ahead of them, with the harbor on the west side and the airfield near the base of the peninsula to the east.

Jimmy listened carefully to the radio. The static wasn't as bad now.

"White Leader, this is T for Taffy. Have you heard from the Brickbats?"

"T for Taffy, White Leader, negative, repeat negative." Jimmy looked at his fuel gauge, which told him he'd have to leave in fifteen minutes, and his number four probably had less than ten.

"Ah, roger, White Leader. How long can you stay with us?"

"Six minutes."

"Thank you, White Leader, stand by."

"Roger, Taffy." Jimmy looked across at White Three. "Three, Lead."

"Go ahead, Lead."

"Three, see if you can raise the Brickbats."

"Roger, Lead."

"Four, Lead."

"Go ahead, Lead."

"Say your fuel, Four."

"Lead, Four has about eight minutes."

"Thanks, Four. Two, how about you?"

"About the same, Lead."

"Thanks, Two."

Jimmy looked left at his wingman. He was a steady kid named Ames, who returned the look.

"Lead, Three."

"Go ahead, Three."

"Lead, I got in touch with Brickbat Yellow Lead. He says they're still ten minutes out and wants to know where we are."

"What did you tell him, Three?"

"Didn't exactly want to say in the clear, Lead. I told him to look west of Milne Bay and east of Salamaua."

Jimmy grinned. He didn't know what the Brickbats would make of that, but his own dead reckoning put them midway between those two landmarks. The pre-mission briefing should tell the Brickbats the rest.

"Roger," Jimmy said.

Ten minutes before the Brickbats arrived on station. Jimmy didn't think the eight minutes of fuel Four reported was accurate. The kid was inexperienced and the gas gauges on the P-39s weren't wholly reliable. Five minutes plus a ten-minute reserve, and if the Japs attacked Seven-Mile while the Boxcars were in the landing pattern that reserve would melt in seconds, not minutes. Allison engines drank fuel like crazy when pilots jockeyed throttles in a dogfight.

Crap. He didn't want to leave Wagner and two Catalinas full of brass stooging around on the north coast of New Guinea within easy reach of the Jap Zeroes at Lae and Salamaua.

He looked west and north again. The sky was empty.

119

Empty or not, Jimmy didn't like it. The sky was empty now but in the next five seconds a squadron of Zeroes could appear. Jimmy looked at the distant silhouette of T for Taffy. The PBY Catalina wasn't as well armed as a B-17, but it wasn't exactly an easy target.

Jimmy was a pursuit pilot. Boyd Wagner was aboard T for Taffy, and Wagner was a friend. Jimmy didn't want to leave. It was as simple as that.

It was equally as simple as the gasoline being pulled into the engine and converted into energy to turn the propeller, and *that* simplicity meant there were five minutes to go until the Boxcars had to turn back to Seven-Mile.

Five minutes at maximum conserve. Any more than that and they'd land in the trees somewhere short of Seven-Mile.

God-damned short-legged P-39s.

"T for Taffy, this is White Leader, come in."

"White Leader, T for Taffy, go ahead."

The static cleared magically from the radio.

"Taffy, we're turning for home. Brickbat Yellow Flight reports they are ten minutes out."

"Copy that, Boxcar. The head cobra says get home in one piece."

Jimmy grinned. The "head cobra" was undoubtedly Wagner.

"Tell him I said thanks. Boxcar White Leader, out."

"Lead, Three. We heading home?"

"Affirmative, Three, follow me. Heading 225."

Jimmy led the Boxcars back up and over the mountains with one eye on the sky around them and the other on his fuel gage. They came up over the crest on oxygen as clouds built along the slopes.

"Bogey! White Leader, White Three has a bogey, three o'clock low."

"Three, just the one?"

"Affirmative, Lead, that's all I see."

Jimmy looked at three o'clock low. White Three was right, there was only the one airplane out there.

"Three, that look like a P-39 to you?"

"Does, kind of."

Jimmy watched the P-39. It was two miles away and as he watched the P-39 did a leisurely circle.

"Three, reckon you can find Seven-Mile on your own?"

"Sure. You about to do something stupid?"

"Probably."

"OK. Can I have your booze?"

"If you get there before my tent mates. Go."

"Roger, White Leader. White Two, White Four, follow me."

Jimmy throttled back and pushed forward on the stick, then banked right. He watched for a moment as the other P-39s formed up on White Three and maintained heading for Seven-Mile. Then he looked ahead at the single P-39.

The guy acted like he was all alone in the world. He kept circling like he was enjoying the pretty clouds and the pleasant sights of Papua New Guinea, not varying his altitude or his rate of turn, a sitting duck for any Jap Zeroes that happened by. If he saw Jimmy shaping into an intercept curve he gave no sign of it, just kept up that nice level standard rate turn. Jimmy eased up alongside him, matching the other pilot's rate of turn and speed.

He actually had his head down in the cockpit, as if fiddling with something on the instrument panel. Then he tapped his earphones.

Jimmy pushed the throttle forward a hair and crept up until he was ahead of the other pilot, who abruptly looked up. His eyes went wide behind his goggles. Jimmy pointed to him, at himself, and then in the direction of Seven-Mile. He could still see his flight, heading in the same direction. The other pilot nodded. Jimmy tapped his ears. The other pilot touched his earphone and shook his head. Jimmy nodded in reply and pointed emphatically to himself and then the direction of Seven-Mile.

The guy nodded. Jimmy turned and looked over his shoulder. At least the guy was following him.

He had a look at the markings on the P-39. This guy was a Corncob, up from Australia for area familiarization.

That left some questions without good answers, like what the hell happened that this obviously clueless child was wandering alone up here where he was equally obvious Jap-bait.

It made Jimmy angry.

He looked around the sky. Except for the clouds building on the slopes of the mountains the sky was clear blue overhead and empty, thankfully empty, all the way home to Seven-Mile.

Chapter Five

Golden hands and a penny's worth of brains

"**J**immy, I want you to meet someone. Step in here."

Jimmy walked into Wagner's office. There was another man, a captain in coveralls and the sweat-plastered hair of a pilot who had just taken his helmet off. The captain rose and held out his hand.

"Captain William Allen, this is Jimmy Ardana."

The two shook hands.

"You guys sit down. Jimmy, Allen here is operations officer for the 43rd Squadron with the 35th Fighter Group. I want you to fly with him and his boys and help them get acclimated."

"Yes, sir." Jimmy looked at Allen, sizing him up. Allen returned the look wryly. Jimmy could all but read his mind: *Yeah, I'm a captain and you're a first lieutenant, but you've spent two months up here fighting the Japs and you've got four kills to show for it.*

"Do you have some guys in mind for me to fly with, Captain?" Jimmy asked.

"Call me Bill. You'll call me something worse when you meet the guys I want to saddle you with."

Jimmy looked at Wagner, who smiled and looked up at the ceiling. "If you're lucky, Jimmy, at least they won't be damp from the birth."

Allen looked at Wagner and then back at Jimmy. His eyebrows rose slightly.

"It's an inside joke," Jimmy said drily. "But maybe you can tell me a little bit about these boys."

"They're not bad pilots. Well, I'm not sure about Kellerman. He hasn't killed himself yet, I can say that much. Of the other two, one likes to drink and chase women even more than the average pursuit pilot, and as a pilot, average is probably descriptive. The other one, well, he's got a hearing problem when it comes to being told what to do. Sonofabitch reminds me of an Irish setter I had when I was a kid."

"An Irish setter? Don't know much about the breed."

Allen shook his head. "First-class gun dogs. Some of 'em can outrun a greyhound and all of 'em are pretty good runners. This dog, though, he'd chase birds all day long, but damned if he'd bring 'em to you when he caught one, or if you managed to shoot one. Yell at him, cuss at him, kick him, hell, that damned dog would wag his tail and go running off after whatever caught his attention."

"Swell."

"Bell's a good stick, though, as far as his flying goes. Loves to see how low he can go or how close he can come. Maybe a little too much so. There's skill and there's luck and if you go into that no-man's land between them too often…"

Allen waved his hand in a dismissive gesture. Jimmy looked at Wagner, whose face was expressionless.

"When do I get to meet these paragons?" Jimmy asked.

"As it happens they're coming in later today. I heard you already met Kellerman." Allen favored Jimmy with a sour smile. "Thanks for pulling him off the runway. Anyway, their flight was about an hour behind mine. You'll have a chance to see for yourself."

"OK." Jimmy thought about it. Maybe it wouldn't be too bad.

Wagner leaned back in his chair, puffing on his pipe as he listened. "What's this I hear about Kellerman being called Captain Midnight?"

Jimmy blinked. Captain Midnight was a radio serial hero.

Allen said, "Aw, when Kellerman got back to Townsville, Major Dionne chewed him out pretty good. He speculated about whether or not he got his wings out of the same cereal box as his Captain Midnight decoder ring."

Jimmy scowled.

Wagner laughed. "OK, Jimmy, they're all yours. I hope I didn't hand you more than you can chew."

"What do you mean, Colonel?"

"You already know Kellerman can't fly worth a crap. Tommy Bell can fly, but he likes to fly low. Seems he can't resist blowing laundry off a clothesline, but he'll fly inverted over the treetops if that's all he's got. Mike Shafer's tastes run to chasing women, and, evidently, drinking."

"Tommy Bell likes flying low. Didn't you tell me that ground attack was going to be a big thing?"

"I did. So maybe Bell works out, but he and Shafer sound like discipline problems."

"As far as Shafer goes, Colonel, most of these guys drink and chase women, given half a chance."

"My point is you aren't most guys, Jimmy, and take that as a compliment. Jack Davis wasn't above

125

getting a snootful now and again, but I'm also pretty sure he was true to his girl back home. You have a girl back home?"

"No, sir. A pen pal, I guess. We went to the same high school, but she was a year behind me."

"Oh? She write a lot?"

"I got a letter from her back in May, and another last week. I wrote her back, oh, I guess it was the last week in May. You know what mail is like. I could get a letter today or next month."

Wagner grimaced. "Yeah. I don't hear from my fiancée as much as I might like. OK, Jimmy, take off. Sounds like you've got your work cut out for you."

"Yes, sir."

Allen said, "Ardana, if you want, I'll be happy to buy you a beer."

"Thanks, Captain."

When Jimmy went into the O-Club the first thing he saw was that dumb kid, David Kellerman, sitting with a couple of other guys.

Allen nudged him. "You know Kellerman. That's Bell and Shafer with him. Bell's the one with the brown curly hair. Shafer's got the moustache. Go introduce yourself, and I'll bring the beer."

Jimmy nodded. As he got closer he could hear the curly-haired one talking, while Kellerman and Shafer sipped their beer.

"So there I was, right? That dumbass Captain Swift, leading the flight, you remember him, couldn't find his stick with both hands, am I right? So we're in the break at Archerfield and I can see he isn't lookin',

126

you know, 'cause he's lookin' at the downwind approach. I thought, hell, I can do a yo-yo and be on the deck and back up before the silly bastard looks around. There's this Hudson on the taxiway, too, makes it perfect, just perfect, so I bump the throttle and dump the stick and pull out right over that Hudson's turret, aw, you shoulda seen it through the gunsight! Aw! It was everything I could do not to pull the triggers! It woulda been beautiful!"

Jimmy listened to this from behind the speaker.

"In the break at Archerfield, eh?" he said. He sat down at the table, uninvited, and leaned forward towards the speaker. "And I bet you're Tommy Bell, aren't you?"

"Aw, I didn't know I was famous already! Why, everyone in Australia's gotta know about me and these golden hands."

"Golden hands, eh?"

"Yep, that's right," said Captain Allen. He put a beer down in front of Jimmy and sat next to him. "Golden hands and not a penny's worth of brains. Right, Bell?"

Bell scowled. Allen chuckled.

Jimmy took a sip at his own beer.

"I can fly lower and come closer than any sonofabitch between here and the States," Bell growled. "And you can bet the farm on it."

"So that was you that buzzed my Hudson," said Jimmy. "Two weeks ago."

Bell brightened at once. "Oh, you saw it! Swell! You can tell everyone how great I was!"

"Well, I can sure tell you you're lucky not to be back at Kelly Field, Bell, because if you were you'd get busted into the infantry."

Bell laughed. He said, "Guess I am lucky at that. We're not at Kelly Field, we're at god-damn Seven-Mile Drome, and you ain't my flight leader. Who the hell are you, anyway?"

"This is Jimmy Ardana," Allen replied cheerfully. "Also known as Corncob Blue Leader."

Jimmy leaned back and sipped his beer, looking Bell in the eyes.

"I noticed you were flying No. 4 that day, Bell, so you should be familiar with the slot. It shouldn't be any trouble for you to stay there."

Bell looked at Jimmy, opened his mouth, and shut it again.

"At least you know when to shut your mouth, even if you're a little slow," Jimmy said. He looked at the other two guys.

"Kellerman," he said. "You can't fly worth a crap. Don't know why you're still alive. You, what's your name again? Shafer, right?"

"Yes, sir."

"Shafer, I hear you like booze and broads, not necessarily in that order. That why you went after those wings? You know some kinds of women see those little silver wings and go all weak and gooey from the knees on up? And pilots have a rep for boozing it up, so you feel like you have to live up to it?"

"Well, ah, I …"

"Skip it. No women here and you'll have to go through a lot of beer to get really drunk, from what I'm

128

told. All you have time to do is your job. Fly. Fight Japs."

Jimmy sipped his beer. "That's our job. We fly and we shoot Japs. Don't forget it."

He pointed his mug at Kellerman. "You're Blue Two. Shafer, you're Blue Three. For now. Bell, I almost feel like I'm signing Shafer's death warrant making you his wingman, but if you've seen Kellerman land you know he's not any better."

There was silence at the table, and Jimmy was the only one drinking beer. "So I'm the one who has to take you sorry bastards and turn you into a respectable bunch of pursuit pilots. I asked Colonel Wagner what I did to piss him off. He smiled and told me to think of it as a challenge. It's a challenge, all right. Bluntly, I don't know if I'm up to it. Doesn't matter, though, 'cause those are my orders."

Jimmy looked at them again. He lifted his glass. "Drink up. Tomorrow morning, 0700, you be down at the flight line. We're going to do some air work. You boys ever do spins in a P-39?"

"I have," said Bell. Jimmy looked at him. Bell subsided into his chair.

"How about you, Kellerman?" Jimmy asked.

"Spins? No. Manual doesn't recommend them."

Jimmy nodded slowly. "OK. You're right. The manual doesn't recommend deliberately spinning the P-39. Do you know the proper spin recovery technique for the P-39?"

"Ah…center controls, chop the throttle, nose down when the rate of spin slows."

"Kellerman, don't ever, ever bullshit me again. If you don't know, say so. Ignorance is one thing, bullshit is another. Understood?"

"Yes, sir."

"OK, Shafer, how about you?"

"No."

"OK, then, here's what we'll do. Spin training as part of the air work. Meet on the flight line, 0700. You and me, Bell, we're wheels up by 0720. Shafer, you and Kellerman, review spin recovery procedures, you'll need 'em."

"0700?" said Shafer. "Hell, there's time for another beer."

Charlie Davis bent over the recon photos of Simpson Harbor, Lae, and Salamaua. The photos of Simpson Harbor included the airfields at Lakunai, east of the town of Rabaul, and Vunakanau, south of the harbor.

"I thought we left more holes in those runways," Al Stern said.

"We did," Charlie agreed. "The Japs have been busy filling in bomb craters. No one ever said they weren't industrious."

Al nodded. "Bigger bombs? And maybe time delay fuses. I remember reading something about the Krauts using those in Britain."

"Yeah, but still, it seems like we're doing a lot of bombing and post-holing of runways and it works for a little while, but how much runway does a Zero need to take off?"

"Not a lot, I bet."

"And I bet you're right." Charlie scowled at the photos. "Be a lot better if we could bomb the airplanes."

"Why don't we? Load up on 100-pounders and try for the revetments. How many 100-pound bombs can we carry?"

Charlie thought about it. "Twenty-four."

"So, we have three bombers..."

"Maybe four. I heard from Carmichael. Draper's airplane came out of the shop and he's headed up here."

"So that's 96 bombs. Look here." Al pointed to the revetments and airplane dispersal area on the south side of Vunakanau. "What if we drop in train, one airplane at a time, all along this concentration of airplanes?"

Charlie nodded slowly. "You know, Al, that's not so bad. Hit 'em just after dawn, maybe come in low, say, ten thousand feet to stay above the light flak and improve bombing accuracy."

"Well, if we're wrong we won't have long to be sorry about it."

"You're such a well of optimism, Al."

"It's why you love me, Charlie."

"Yeah, right. OK, let's take it to the other guys and see what they think."

"Hey, Charlie, I thought you were the squadron commander. You know, like, Charlie say, pilots do."

"I am the squadron commander, but I'm not God. Those are smart guys. And just a little leadership lesson here, Al, if these guys think it's their plan, they'll work harder to carry it out."

"I had, no idea you were such a Machiavelli, Charlie."

"Al, I had no idea you read Machiavelli."

"Lots of things you don't know about me."

Charlie shook his head and stood, gathering up the recon photos. "Let's do it."

Draper's B-17, *Didgeriwho?*, came in that evening before sunset. The next morning Charlie looked over at Danny Evans as they sat on the flight deck of *Bronco Buster II*, looking down the runway, illuminated by dim flares, barely visible.

"Jeez," Danny said. He leaned out of his open side window. "I can't see the runway."

"Well, it's no problem. The runway's right there, between the flare pots."

Evans shook his head. "OK, Boss, I believe you."

"Relax, Danny, we've both done this before. Stand on the brakes and give me takeoff power."

"Roger," Evans acknowledged. Charlie pushed on the toe brakes, feeling Evans come in as well.

Evans advanced the throttles to the stops and held them there, watching the gauges, glowing in the light of the ultraviolet lamps while the engines roared and the airframe shook and shimmied.

"Looks good," said Charlie. "Crew, pilot, here goes nothin'."

Minutes later they were climbing out above the hills west and south of the airfield. One by one the other three B-17s made their takeoff runs and climbed out to join Charlie. There was a bit of a moon, enough to see each other but not enough to fly formation. The subject of formation came up during the briefing.

"We going to fly wingtip to wingtip in the moonlight, Boss?" asked Lt. Draper.

"If we do, Draper, I guess that means you're flying the lead airplane," said Charlie. That raised a chuckle. The lead airplane didn't have to worry about keeping formation, because the other airplanes flew formation on the lead.

"Ha, ha," said Draper as the laughter died away. "Seriously."

"No. We'll stay loose until we turn in for the target. You know from the navigation briefing that'll be one hundred miles east of Vunakanau. We'll keep radio silence enroute. I'll blink my running lights twice to signal the turn and once to signal execute. By then there should be enough light to see by."

But the briefing was hours ago and it would be hours before the sunrise.

"Pilot, navigator. Make your heading zero five zero."

"Acknowledged, navigator, zero five zero."

Charlie looked over at Evans, who nodded and set the heading into the autopilot. The formation, such as it was, continued climbing and leveled off at ten thousand feet. They took off on oxygen, as required by the manual, and stayed on oxygen to keep their night vision sharp. Charlie scanned the instruments and looked out the cockpit windows at the stars and the moon. He could see the other three airplanes, shadowy in the light of those same stars and moon.

He looked at the ocean below them. The sea glittered dimly in the moonlight, changing subtly as the waves rose and fell.

Two hours and thirty minutes, then they'd turn left and the target would be one hundred miles ahead.

Jehosophat, flying at night was boring. There was nothing to look at except the instruments and Danny Evans, and that wasn't inspiring. Still, again, Evans was showing more than improvement, he was showing growth.

After that first mission, Evans came to him and asked for operating manuals. Charlie had to tell him he had none, even though manuals for just about everything from loading bombs to navigation were a way of life in the Air Corps. On the other hand, what the pilot of a B-17 needed to know more than anything else was the engines, the Wright R-1830 engines the powered the airplane. And Charlie knew where he could get manuals for those engines, and he pointed Danny that way.

It looked like Danny had done some reading. Charlie could tell from the way he looked at the engine gauges and studied the throttles before moving them to a different setting as the formation continued to climb. Charlie checked the new settings. Either Danny knew what he was doing or he was lucky.

For an hour, then, they flew at ten thousand feet. Nothing changed around them, there was only the even drone of the engines and the hiss of the air over the fuselage. Another hour, the same, and as they came up to the half hour Al Stern called over the intercom.

"Pilot, navigator. Formation turn to heading three-one-five, five minutes."

"Navigator, pilot, acknowledged. Crew, pilot. I'm going to blink our lights to signal the turn. Let me know when the other airplanes acknowledge."

"Right waist, I got two sets of lights blinking."

134

"Tail, two sets.

"Left waist, one set of lights."

"Top turret, what Johann said, skipper."

"OK, thanks, guys."

"Navigator, pilot."

"Go ahead, Charlie."

"Al, give me a countdown from ten seconds."

"Acknowledged, Charlie. That's about two minutes. Just to confirm, you'll come to heading three-one-five."

"OK, Al, new heading three-one-five. Crew, pilot, you heard that."

Charlie looked to the right but there wasn't any sign yet of the sun and the dawn of the new day. He looked to the left and saw nothing but the glimmer of starlight, reflected from the surface of the sea.

"Pilot, navigator. Coming up on countdown."

"Understood, navigator. Crew, pilot, I'm flashing our running lights."

Al counted down from ten, and at "zero" Charlie flashed his running lights once and turned to heading three-one-five.

"Navigator, pilot. Heading good, estimate twenty-four minutes to target."

"Acknowledged, navigator. Thanks."

"Pilot, top turret. Looks like all three Forts followed us into the turn."

"Pilot, tail gunner. Confirm."

"OK, thanks, guys."

Charlie scanned the instruments and the horizon. Ahead it was still night, and there was no sign – yet – that the Japs knew they were coming.

"Tail gunner, pilot."

"Go ahead, pilot."

"Sun come up yet, Em?"

"Peeking over the horizon right now, skipper."

"OK. Crew, pilot, if we can see the sun the Japs will see us soon enough. Be ready."

The sunlight stole gradually over the ocean below. On their right it lit up the peaks and eastern slopes of the hills of New Ireland. Then, dead ahead of them, the peaks south of Simpson Harbor appeared. That meant the formation was above the horizon to any observers on the coast of New Britain, and a Zero could climb from sea level to ten thousand feet in less than three minutes.

"Navigator, pilot."

"Eight minutes to IP, fifteen to target."

"Al, one of these days I'm going to ask a different question."

"What, eight minutes away from starting the bomb run?"

"Good point. I'll take it as a challenge."

Charlie looked left and right. With the light of dawn the other bombers were closing up the formation, with *Bronco Buster II* in the lead, two bombers staggered up on the right, one bomber low to the left, leaving all the guns on each bomber exposed to defend the formation, and no bomber in the path of falling bombs.

Then there was the rising tension as they approached the target, the sensation familiar and new at once, the waiting, the past experience of bullets and cannon shells and flak, knowing what might be, not knowing what would be. Then they were over the coast, and the coast-in point was the IP.

"Pilot, navigator, I see dust trails at Vunakanau."

"OK, Al. Crew, pilot, you heard it. Gonna be busy as hell in about five minutes."

"Pilot, bombardier. Over the IP, opening bomb bay doors."

"Roger, bombardier."

Once Al checked the drift and the forward airspeed for Bob Frye to input into the Norden bombsight he checked the machine guns. Frye was bent over the bombsight, with its telescope peering forward to the target, its angle adjusted automatically by the gyroscopes in the bombsight. As the bomber approached the target, two contacts on counter-rotating drums spun towards each other. When they touched they completed a circuit that dropped the bombs.

"Pilot, bombardier, two minutes."

"Upper turret has bandits, count seven, eight, nine. Nine Zeros inbound!"

"Only nine, who do they think we are? The Navy?"

"Can it, Lefty. That is the Navy, well, the Jap Navy, anyway."

"Swell."

Al crouched just behind Bob Frye where he could get to either of the cheek guns easily. Frye was absorbed in his bomb run, calling course corrections to Charlie. The Zeros turned hard and dove, the three elements splitting to attack the three B-17s on the right side of the formation. Al could see the Japs maneuvering into a steep-angled diving pass, which meant he wouldn't get a shot. He moved back and stuck his head up in the astrodome.

The astrodome was midway between the Plexiglas nose of the B-17 and the cockpit windows of the flight deck. He could see Charlie and Danny Evans looking up and right at the Zeros, and as Al watched Kim Smith rotated the upper turret and elevated his twin .50s. Al looked right and up to follow Smith's tracers. He could see another stream of tracer reach out from further aft as Lefkowicz at the right waist gun fired. Their tracer reached up at the Japs, who were also firing on the B-17, but with the steep angle and speed of the dive the Zeros swept by without either side doing any apparent damage, even though Jap tracer flashed and *zinged* around the bomber. Kim Smith stopped firing, but Al felt the deck under his feet vibrating as the ball turret gunner joined in.

"Pilot, bombardier, steady. Steady. Steady. Bombs gone, closing bomb bay doors."

"Watch out theah, Em, Ah reckon they comin' yo' way," drawled the ball gunner.

"I see 'em, Johnny," the tail gunner replied.

"Crew, top turret, Zeros seven o'clock high."

Al looked where Emmons indicated and saw three Zeros, probably the ones that attacked the high bomber, reefing in a hard right turn to set up a gunnery pass on either *Bronco Buster II* or *Didgeriwho?* flying low off their left wing. Al lost sight of them for a moment.

"Zeros six o'clock level!"

Smith had the upper turret pointed aft. From the rear of the fuselage Al felt the hammering of the tail guns, and in another second Smith joined in. Five

138

seconds later two Zeros swept overhead on the left, with the third on the right. This time Al heard the *ping-pop* rattle of machine-gun bullets riddling the fuselage.

Al looked at his desk. He'd written down the initial return course, and a quick glance refreshed his memory.

"Pilot, navigator."

"Go ahead, Al."

"Charlie, make your heading two zero zero," said Al.

"Crew, top turret, they're forming up again."

"Al, that's two zero zero?"

"Affirmative, two zero zero."

"OK, thanks. Radio operator, pilot. Contact base, tell 'em we hit the target."

"Radio operator, understood."

"Crew, bombardier, they're comin' in head-on." Al watched Frye safe up the bombsight and reach for the nose-mounted .50-cal.

Ahead of them the Zeros roared in to the attack, straight down their throats.

Chapter Six

Spins are not recommended

Jimmy walked down the path to Major Wolchek's tent. Wolchek was seated under the scrap of tent he had rigged to give him some shade, fanning himself with a scrap of aircraft aluminum.

"Give up on the palm fronds?" Jimmy asked.

Wolchek flipped the square of aluminum between his fingers. "Chief Halloran got this for me. Said he was tired of me using a silly piece of vegetable that kept coming apart and didn't seem to be moving any air at all."

"You're lucky he didn't bring you a propeller blade," Jimmy said. "Complete with geared-down Allison engine."

Wolchek laughed. "We need all our Allisons for the P-39s," he said.

He looked at Jimmy. "Wagner tells me you volunteered to go to Buna for PROVIDENCE. Did he say if we're the squadron to go from the 8th?"

"No, sir. Want me to ask?"

"Nah. We go or we don't. We'll probably shuttle squadrons up there for a week or two and bring them back here to rest. But I gather you're going regardless. You taking those new guys with you?"

"Hopefully I'll have a couple of weeks to work with them, Major. Then we'll see."

Wolchek nodded. "Speak of the devil, there they are."

Jimmy looked up the path. Three men in flight gear came down the path carrying parachutes over their shoulders, sweating freely in the tropical heat. They put their 'chutes down and stood in the sun, looking from Jimmy to Major Wolchek. They finally saluted the Major, who returned the salute casually.

"Good morning, gentlemen," said Wolchek. "It seems the three of you come complete with more baggage than your duffel bags, at least according to my esteemed colleague, Major Dionne."

Jimmy didn't miss the scowl that came and went on Bell's face, or the grimace on Kellerman's.

"I've been talking to Jimmy here about you, and I think the best solution is to give Jimmy the power of high and low justice as far as the three of you are concerned. Understood?"

Kellerman cleared his throat. "High and low justice? You mean, like a feudal lord?"

"That's exactly right, Lieutenant Kellerman."

"So, that means he can kill us if he likes?"

"Only if you run from the Japs if I don't tell you to. Then I'll shoot you myself. Right, Major?"

Wolchek fanned himself and smiled. "Absolutely, Jimmy," he said expansively.

He looked at the new guys. "You guys know this is Jimmy the Kid, right?"

"Aw, Major..."

"Now, Jimmy, no false modesty." Wolchek looked at the new guys and suddenly his eyes were hard. "Jimmy here might have four Jap flags on his ship but he can claim five dead Japs. You know why that is?"

The three new guys looked at each other. Kellerman finally said, "No, sir."

"As it happens a Zero shot Jimmy down, and Jimmy's flight leader, a hell of a pilot, by the way, shot the Zero down. So, there's Jimmy and the Jap, both of 'em crashed on the airstrip, right out there. The Jap got out of his airplane and started shooting at Jimmy, who shot him dead with that .45 he carries."

The new guys looked involuntarily at Jimmy's long-barreled Colt revolver.

"I suggest you do what he tells you, when he tells you, or maybe Jimmy the Kid here carves another notch on his pistol. With my blessing. You boys got it?"

Kellerman and Shafer nodded. "Yes, sir," they said in unison.

Bell looked at Jimmy. Then he nodded. Wolchek looked at Bell, eyes narrowed.

"Good. They're all yours, Jimmy. No need to be gentle with them. Go fly."

"Yes, sir!" Jimmy barked. He turned to his new flight. "Follow me."

Kellerman caught up with him. The other two trailed behind. "What are we gonna do?" he asked.

"Well, Captain Midnight, we're going to fly."

"Ah, Jimmy, please don't call me that."

"Might be the only way you ever make captain, but suit yourself, Midnight."

Behind them Shafer and Bell snickered.

"You guys know how people get nicknames in the service?" Jimmy asked, without looking over his shoulder.

"Ah...no," said Bell.

142

"It's usually the most publicly embarrassing and humiliating thing you can imagine. Don't worry, Midnight, your pals will get the nicknames they deserve. Shafer, I hear you like to drink and chase sheilas. So how do you want to be called, Chunder or Sheila?"

"What...? Neither one!"

"OK, Sheila it is. Bell, you're up. I hear you like to fly low. Why is that?"

"Because I can, Ardana. And I like it."

Jimmy didn't look around at Bell. He noted the insolence of the pilot's voice.

Fine.

"You like to fly low, you like to blow laundry off the clothesline. Laundry. Hm. Chinese laundry. China Bell. Tinkerbell. Yup, you're Chinkerbell."

Bell growled. Shafer and Kellerman snickered.

"So what've we got?" Jimmy asked. "Jimmy the Kid, leading Midnight, Sheila and Chinkerbell. Oh yeah. We're gonna scare the living hell out of the Japs, all right. Here we are."

Jimmy put his fingers to his lips and whistled. They were near the revetments and the crew chiefs came out.

"OK, these are your crew chiefs and mine. Let me make a suggestion. These guys will save your life. Be polite. Say please. Bring them beer."

"Ah, beggin' yer pardon, there, Jimmy..."

"I know, Don, I know. Wait. You mean to tell me I brought you guys a case of beer each last week and you're out already?"

"It is kind of hot out here, Boss."

143

"OK. I'll see what I can do. In the meantime, who's got a P-39 ready to go? Other than our airplane, Don."

"Jeez, Mr. Ardana, we're all ready to go," said one of the crew chiefs.

"Good," said Jimmy. "Midnight, go with Sergeant Tomlinson here. We're going to fly in a couple minutes. Be ready."

"Yes, sir, Mr. Ardana." Tommy Sims, crew chief for the yet-unnamed airplane number 81, went to his revetment. Kellerman followed him.

"OK. Sheila, Chinkerbell, go with Kelly and Mowery. Midnight and I will be back in an hour or two. So, get to know your airplanes and your ground crew."

Don Terraine fell in with Jimmy and walked towards *Gremlin II*.

"How's the engine, Don?"

"I've been keeping an eye on the oil, Boss. Holman and I were talking it over. We're thinking if we change the oil every ten hours or so we can avoid the viscosity breakdown."

"Yeah, until we run out of lubricating oil."

"Yeah. Until then."

"OK. The 19th Bomb Group went up to Rabaul this morning. I'm going to take Kellerman and we're going to intercept them."

Terraine nodded. "The airplane is ready to go when you are."

"What about Tommy over there, with number 81?"

"His airplane should be ready. Look, Jimmy, you mind if I ask what's up?"

144

"I don't mind you asking, Don. For now, let's say this flight once more is the home to infants and tenderfeet, and we'll have our work cut out for us getting them ready to fight."

Terraine grinned. "You got more than 48 hours?"

"Oh, I hope so. I really hope so."

"Well, Captain Davis did OK in 48 hours. You will too."

"Thanks."

Twenty minutes later Jimmy taxied out of his revetment. Looking over his shoulder he saw Kellerman nosing out of his own revetment, slowly and cautiously, but at least his movements on the brakes seemed even. Jimmy shuddered, remembering how Gerry...what the hell was his last name, again? Gerry something ... nearly collided with him while taxiing out for their first flight together.

It seemed that Kellerman had the basics down. His ground handling was good, but hell, a P-39 with its tricycle landing gear was easy to taxi. When they lined up on the runway and took off Kellerman was smooth enough, didn't balloon up the way so many low-time P-39 pilots did, horsing back on the control stick as if it were an AT-6 trainer back at Kelly Field. After takeoff Kellerman snugged into a reasonable formation off Jimmy's right wing and stayed there. Jimmy didn't try any sudden moves and Kellerman didn't play the hot dog by moving within a foot of Jimmy's right wingtip.

They climbed to ten thousand feet.

"Corncob Blue Two, this is Corncob Blue Leader, come in."

"Blue Leader from Two, go ahead."

"Move out a bit, Two, maybe a hundred feet. You're my wingman. Watch to the right and astern, I'll watch to the left and ahead."

"Acknowledged, Lead, Two has right and astern."

Drinking beer with Kellerman and his buddies the night before, Jimmy learned that their tactical instruction was limited to such aphorisms as, stay on my wing, keep your eyes open, and don't speak until you're spoken to.

Jimmy decided it was time to preach to them from the Gospel According to Captain Jack Davis.

"OK. Formation is fine for show, but in combat if your attention is on me it isn't on looking for the Japs. So flying formation, especially close formation, is a good way to get us all killed. We'll spread out a little bit. Stay where you can see me, and you can turn in on someone behind me. As for keeping your mouth shut, that depends on what you have to say. If you want to share your feelings about the pretty white clouds, keep your mouth shut. If you see Japs, or any airplane you can't identify, sing out loud and clear until your call is acknowledged. And don't just scream 'Bandits' in a high falsetto voice. Call bandits, say where, identify yourself. The goddamned radio can't tell us where you are. Your call sign will."

So now Jimmy watched Kellerman slide to the right off Jimmy's wing. That way each of them could watch the other's tail.

They stayed at ten thousand feet, headed north, and to the east the mountains of the Owen Stanley Range peaked above them. The ground below them undulated like God crumpled it during the Creation and left it that

146

way, clouds drifting among the peaks, peaks serrated like sharp teeth on a saw, teeth that had already claimed dozens of airplanes.

Jimmy saw them first, four dots in an odd slanted formation off to their right, about one o'clock. He figured the formation made them Charlie's B-17s, but he didn't say anything. He wanted to see how long it took Kellerman to notice them.

"Ah, bogeys! Boxcar Red Two has four bogeys at one o'clock, passing to two o'clock."

"Roger, Two, Lead has the bogeys. What d'you think they are?"

"Don't know, Lead. They're...wait one, are those B-17s? Looks like they've got four engines."

"That's what they look like to me, Two. Right, stay with me."

Jimmy pulled back on the stick and gave the engine some throttle, again watching the oil temp and pressure gauges for the first sign of problems.

At a closing speed of over 400 mph it took less than a minute to confirm the oncoming airplanes were B-17s.

"OK, Two, we'll stay to one side and well away."

"Ah, roger, Lead. Why?"

"They just got back from being shot at. See the one guy trailing smoke? They're likely to be jumpy, so give them some room."

"Ah, roger, Lead."

The formation of B-17s flew past. Once they were close enough Jimmy saw the appearance of a slant line was only from head-on. The trailing B-17s were spaced behind the lead airplane, so from above they'd look like a "V".

Jimmy let them get past and continued over the mountains, still climbing, scanning the sky around them, taking in Kellerman's flying, watching his own engine and fuel gauges. The sky behind the bombers was empty. This time no one followed the B-17s home, not this far, at least.

Jimmy turned to port, watching Kellerman, who stayed with him. It puzzled Jimmy. The guy wasn't obviously ham-handed. He flew like he had some notion of what the controls did.

But that botched landing, and flying in circles with your head down in the cockpit in a combat zone!

When they completed their turn Seven-Mile was dead ahead of them, and Jimmy saw the B-17s peeling off one by one to land.

"OK, Two, let's head for the barn," Jimmy radioed. "You land first. I want to watch at a safe distance."

"Gee, thanks, Lead."

The next morning Jimmy walked down the path to the flight line and was unsurprised to see Evarra squatting across the taxiway from his revetment.

"Hello, Evarra," Jimmy said.

"Jimmy," said Evarra. "Halo. Youpela hunt Jap balus-men today?"

Jimmy grinned briefly. "Not unless they come hunting us. What are you doing today?"

The sanguma man shrugged. "Keep watch."

"Yakirai?"

148

The sanguma man looked at Jimmy. "Maybe," he said slowly. "Be careful."

"Always," said Jimmy.

Jimmy walked across the taxiway to the revetment where his airplane, *Green Gremlin II*, sat.

"Jimmy, why d'you talk to that guy?" Terraine asked quietly.

"Damned if I know," Jimmy told his mechanic. "I'd like to know how he manages to appear and disappear the way he does."

"Yeah," said Terraine. "I noticed that, myself. He'll sit there under that tree for hours, watching us work on the airplane, then you'll turn away for a wrench, one, maybe two seconds, and he's gone."

"He's been around since before I got here, hasn't he?"

Terraine grinned. "Yeah, I remember the way you jumped first time you saw him. He does sort of come out of the woodwork."

"OK. How's our baby?"

"Engine's running pretty good. Changed the oil again. You've got a full ammo load. No aux tank, just like you asked."

"Great. Thanks."

Down the path his three pilots came. Bell swaggered in the lead, followed by Shafer. Kellerman lagged a little behind, hands in the pockets of his flight jacket.

Kellerman stopped to look at Evarra, who regarded him silently. After a moment Kellerman turned away and joined Jimmy and the others.

"Morning, Dave, glad you could join us. Bell, you ready to fly?"

"Any time, any place."

"Good. Go get your airplane. Be ready to follow me in ten minutes. Shoo."

"Gotcha," said Bell. He turned and sauntered on down the line.

Jimmy turned to Shafer and Kellerman. "You two. Think you know how to recover from a spin in a P-39?"

Shafer nodded. Kellerman set his mouth in a thin line and said, "I'm ready."

"Remember this. Rate of spin in the P-39 isn't constant. You need to pick out when it slows. Before that, close the throttle, prop control to low, control stick back in your lap. Wait for the rotation to slow. When it does, full rudder against the spin, push the stick forward, ailerons opposite the spin. You should come out in a half turn. You miss it the first time, wait until it comes around again."

"How long should I keep doing that?" Kellerman asked.

Jimmy put a hand on Kellerman's shoulder and looked him in the eye. He said gravely, "Midnight, you keep doing that for the rest of your life. Or until you come out of the spin."

Shafer found something to look at elsewhere in the revetment.

"Oh," said Kellerman.

"Yeah. If you can't pick out when the spin slows down, the rest of it won't mean shit. But it's pretty obvious, and I'll be close by, watching. I'll talk you through it."

150

"OK."

"Right. Practice the procedure in your cockpit. We'll be back in an hour or less."

A jeep drove up. Wagner was driving. Everyone in the revetment came to attention and saluted. Wagner returned the salute.

"Rest, gentlemen. Jimmy, a word."

Jimmy went to the colonel's jeep. Wagner yawned. "Damn, Jimmy, what's with the oh-early-thirty stuff? You got a mission I don't know about?"

"No, sir. Spin recovery training."

"Spin recovery training," said Wagner slowly. He looked at Jimmy. "Why?"

"Skipper, I figure if you know how to come out of a spin in the P-39, it will boost your confidence in your ability to control the airplane."

"You know deliberate spinning of a P-39 is not recommended."

"Yes, sir."

"OK. Be sure you go over the procedure thoroughly with your boys. Have you been in a spin in the P-39 yourself?"

"Yes."

"Well, you're still here, so you must know what you're doing." Wagner winked at Jimmy and pitched his voice to carry. "Be careful, Jimmy. Pilots we can replace but P-39s are hard to come by."

Wagner put the jeep in gear and drove off.

Jimmy and Bell climbed to 17,000 feet, breathing oxygen through their masks. Jimmy expected Bell to do something dumb, but he stayed on Jimmy's wing like he knew what he was doing.

Which, Jimmy reflected a little sourly, was probably the way of it. Bell could fly the airplane, it was the rest of it he had trouble with.

"Right, Two, throttle back, nose up, let's review stalls. No flaps, she'll stall at about 105 indicated. Get the nose down, give it some throttle, don't try anything until you've got at least 130 on the airspeed indicator, maybe 140. Feel it out. Ready?"

"I'm ready. We both going to do this?"

"Nope. Might be Japs. One of us has to stay fast enough to fight."

"Riiiiight. Here I go."

Jimmy pulled up and went into a turn to keep Bell in sight.

Bell's P-39 slowed perceptibly, slowed more. The airplane wobbled a little, then Bell put the nose down and picked up speed.

"OK, Two, that was practice. Now let's try a spin. Anytime, you're already slow."

"OK, Lead."

The nose of the P-39 pulled up. It slowed, and Jimmy saw Bell kick in full rudder.

The P-39 broke abruptly to the left and dropped its nose, spinning nose down like someone stuck a pin through its midsection and twirled. One turn, two turns; Jimmy watched the rate of spin and saw Bell kick full rudder. The elevator came up and Jimmy saw the ailerons move. Bell's P-39 came out of the spin in one smooth motion, after a half-turn, and Bell accelerated in a dive, climbing back to Jimmy's altitude.

152

"How was that, Lead?"

"It looked just like you knew what you were doing, Two. Try it again the other direction."

Shafer followed Jimmy to 17,000 feet, stalled his airplane, spun his airplane, had to be coached through his first recovery, then did two more successfully.

Jimmy hadn't worried about Bell. He'd been reasonably sure about Shafer, and now there was only Kellerman.

As Jack or Charlie would say, holy howling jumping Jehosophat.

Jimmy decided he'd put Kellerman in the lead position and watch his flying again. Once he got the P-39 off the ground Kellerman wasn't bad. His turns were coordinated, and he didn't fly one wing low or any of the usual neophyte mistakes.

It hit Jimmy, watching Kellerman fly, that the man was someone to whom flying didn't come naturally. Kellerman flew like he'd been taught in training, with technical competence, but not like someone to whom that training led to something else, not within Kellerman's mind and heart.

Jimmy was fifteen years old when his uncle took him flying for the first time. When Uncle Kurt handed Jimmy the controls it all seemed pretty obvious. You pulled back on the stick, the nose went up, push down and the nose went down, rudder pedals, ailerons, it was all straightforward. So straightforward that it surprised Jimmy when Uncle Kurt told him that not everyone could do it straight off the bat.

It surprised Jimmy because it seemed so natural.

He watched Kellerman fly, and Jimmy could see the man flew like a machine might fly, with a certain precision, but the precision was calculated, not spontaneous.

Kellerman didn't know what he was doing. Not really.

For the first time Jimmy felt uncertainty.

"All right, Two," he radioed. "Let's try a stall first."

And there was no fault to find with the way Kellerman entered or recovered from the stall.

"Right, then. Whenever you're ready."

"Here we go," Kellerman radioed.

Kellerman's nose came up, his rudder came over, and all hell broke loose. The P-39 flipped over on its back and spun like a top, nose wavering up and down.

Jimmy chopped his own throttle and put his nose down, turning and diving to stay level with Kellerman. He took a moment and keyed his radio, being careful to pitch his voice to a calm and even tone.

"Dave, how you doing?"

"Ah, Jimmy, I wasn't supposed to pitch over on my back, was I?"

"No. Chop your throttle, prop controls to low. Stick forward."

"You said stick back."

"You're upside down, Dave. Think it through."

"Why did I flip over on my back?"

"It doesn't matter now. Watch your rate of spin. You're spinning to the right, upside down. Be ready to kick left rudder when it slows."

154

Jimmy watched Kellerman's airplane. A spin required the airplane to stall, and to recover from a stall one had to build speed to create lift from the wings. You put the nose down and let gravity take over, or you pushed the throttle forward to increase power to the engine. But as long as the airplane was in a spin no power to the engine would result in acceleration. The pilot had to regain control of the airplane first.

"Jimmy, what do I do?"

Kellerman's P-39 slowed and accelerated. He had missed the first opportunity to break the spin.

"OK, Dave, watch for it, watch for it, you're coming around again, be ready, ready, ready, now, kick it!"

Kellerman kicked the rudder in, but he kicked it the wrong way. The P-39 continued to spin.

Jimmy looked at his altimeter. It read 15,000 feet, and his vertical speed indicator showed he was going down at 3000 feet per minute. Five minutes, then. Five minutes before Kellerman's P-39 smashed into the ocean below them.

By any measure it was a short lifespan.

"Dave, pay attention, you kicked it the wrong way. Ready, ready left rudder, now!"

Jimmy saw Dave's rudder come over, the right way this time, to the left. The rate of spin slowed noticeably.

"Ailerons!"

Kellerman applied ailerons, but in the opposite direction. They counteracted the effect of the rudder. The P-39's nose dipped lower and the rate of spin increased.

155

Jimmy had a moment's image of what it was like in Kellerman's cockpit. The odd screaming whine of the propeller as the wind washed over it in ways the wind wasn't supposed to go, the shuddering and bucking of the whole airplane, the sudden dip and rise of the nose that was felt not only with the eyes, as the horizon sank and Kellerman could see the ocean below looming up, but also in the swooping pit of his stomach that reached up into his throat, and the sudden quickening rotation assaulting his inner ear, the dizziness, the incipient vertigo, the instruments on the panel dancing and unreadable, his feet floating on the rudder pedals aas the g-force varied, the grip of his hands, straining on the stick and the throttle.

The fear. The fear crawling inside him, the fear weakening his bladder, fear's adrenaline leaking into his veins and …

Jimmy shut out the image, like slamming the door to a room on fire. He checked his own horizon, his own instruments, holy Hannah, still 3000 fpm down, 12,000 feet above sea level, less than four minutes to live, less than four minutes.

"Dave, you have to remember you're upside down. You've got plenty of time. Now center your controls."

"Jimmy…"

"Center your controls, Dave, do it now."

Jimmy saw the ailerons, elevator, and rudder move into the neutral position.

The P-39's rate of spin slowed a little. The nose came up, a little.

"OK, Dave, you're doing good. Right, remember, you're still upside down. Stick all the way forward, good, good, that's it. Now, ready with left rudder and left aileron, ready, now! Left rudder!"

Kellerman's rudder came over hard.

"Wait, wait, now!" called Jimmy. "Left aileron, Dave, and control stick in your lap!"

The control surface moved, they moved the right way, and the spin slowed.

A half-turn, and Kellerman was still on his back, but in a coordinated turn to the left.

At 8,000 feet.

Kellerman rolled right out of the turn, still in a shallow dive, gaining speed. Jimmy rolled out of his own turn and pulled up alongside Kellerman.

Kellerman looked across at Jimmy. They were almost wingtip to wingtip, and Jimmy saw Kellerman's eyes, wide and staring.

"All right, there, Two?" Jimmy asked.

"Yeah," said Kellerman. The single syllable was breathless and shaky.

"OK, then. Follow me, we're going up to do it again."

"Jimmy…"

"Two, this is Lead. Follow me."

Jimmy pulled ahead of Kellerman's airplane, advanced the throttle, and started to climb. He didn't look over his shoulder.

Captain Allen waited in a jeep at Jimmy's revetment when Jimmy taxied up from the runway. He waited until Jimmy shut down and helped Jimmy and his crew push the airplane back into the revetment.

When they were done Allen asked Jimmy if he had a moment.

They walked to a tree nearby and sat in the shade. Allen handed Jimmy a canteen.

"Thanks," said Jimmy. He drank.

"We were listening on the radio," Allen said.

"Yeah? Who's 'we'?"

"Oh, me, Steve Wolchek, and Colonel Wagner."

"And?"

"Got a bit tense up there."

"Yup."

Allen gestured down the taxiway. Kellerman and his ground crew were pushing his P-39 back into their revetment.

"Your boy got a little confused."

"He did, but we straightened it out."

Allen nodded. "Out of curiosity, what was your altitude when Kellerman recovered?"

"Eight thousand."

"Damn."

"We still had two minutes and change."

Allen looked at Jimmy, shook his head, and looked down the taxiway. Bell and Shafer stood with Kellerman, who was making twirling motions with his hands.

"Telling them all about it," Allen observed.

"Yup," Jimmy replied.

"You came pretty close yourself."

Jimmy shook his head. "No, not really. Not that time."

"Oh. Right. You had two minutes."

Jimmy looked at Allen. "You mind if I call you Bill?"

"Not at all."

"Bill, two minutes is a long time. Yeah, we were descending pretty fast, but all I had to do was roll out of the turn. So even if Kellerman didn't pull out at 8,000 he could still have made it. Kellerman's only problem is he's not a talented enough pilot to have any confidence in himself. I think I can help him with that."

"Good enough to fight the Japs?"

"That's the whole idea."

Allen nodded down the taxiway. "Well, here come your boys. What's your next move?"

"You got any suggestions? You've known them longer than I have."

"No, not really. They came in with the last batch of replacements. They've been in the squadron maybe two, three weeks. We tried to get them as much time in the airplane as we could. As for the rest, what I told you in Wagner's office is all I know."

The pilots stopped in front of them and looked from Jimmy to Allen.

"Don't look at me," said Allen. He waved a hand at Jimmy. "Lt. Ardana here is your flight leader."

"We're going up as soon as our mechanics check and refuel the airplanes. We'll do a little rat-racing." Jimmy thought for a minute. "A little formation work, first, and a gunnery pass on Daugo Island. Then maybe a little two on two. Let's see. Kellerman, you and me against Shafer and Bell."

The three newies exchanged glances.

"Any questions? No? Good. Be sure you have your crew check your guns and the cannon. We're going up to practice but the Japs could wander by any time, and then the scrimmage turns into the varsity championship. Got it?"

Kellerman nodded. So did Shafer and Bell.

"Yeah, you say that like you mean it. Trust me, you won't know what you're agreeing to, not until you've had Tojo on your ass or dropping bombs on you. Go on, go check your airplanes. Kellerman, hang a minute."

Shafer and Bell exchanged glances and walked off, talking to each other as they went. Kellerman watched them go, then turned back to look at Jimmy.

"Dave, you ever do any dogfighting back in training?"

"Some."

"How'd you do?"

"Won a few, lost a few."

"How d'you feel about that? Losing, I mean?"

"No one likes to lose."

"Yup. You lose a fight out here, you sure as hell won't like it, except you won't be able to bitch about it. You'll be dead. Keep that in mind. You're going to have two jobs. One of them is to keep an eye out for Japs and let me know if there are any around. The other is to stay with me so we can protect each other. Keep those two in mind and we'll do OK. Even against the Japs. Maybe."

"Yes, sir."

"OK, take off."

Kellerman nodded and walked away.

"Since I'm going to be your boss, Jimmy, you mind telling me what you have in mind?"

"Sure. We'll do some low-level formation work first, maybe a practice gunnery pass on Daugo Island. Then we'll try a little dogfighting. You heard what I told Kellerman. I'm going to leave Shafer and Bell to work it out on their own. We'll see how it goes."

Allen grinned. "You trying to sell someone on the virtues of sticking with your wingman?"

"Could be."

The fuel truck pulled up to Jimmy's revetment. The driver helped Jimmy's mechanics snake out the fuel hoses to Jimmy's airplane and begin pumping gas.

"That's my cue," Jimmy said. He stood up and dusted himself off.

Daugo Island was ten thousand feet below. Jimmy looked left and right, checking his flight. Bell was showing off by sticking his wingtip right behind Shafer's, and Kellerman was wobbling a little but keeping passable formation. Jimmy remembered Danny Evans, gyrating up and down and nearly colliding with Jimmy every few seconds. None of these guys were in Danny's league for ham-handedness, which was a relief.

"Corncob Blue flight, this is Lead. That's Daugo Island directly below us. Three, you and Four stay up here. Keep your eyes open, and if you see anything you don't like, get on the radio and sing out."

"Three, roger."

"Four. Gotcha."

"Right. Two, let's go."

161

Jimmy rolled right and kicked right rudder. The horizon tilted, dipped, the ground filled his windscreen. He darted a look to the left and Kellerman was there, where he should be, off Jimmy's left wing.

The west end of the island was their objective. There was a rock and the stump of a palm tree there, and the rock was the aim point. Jimmy reefed into a hard left turn, straightened to head away from the island, then rolled to the right and dove with the west end of Daugo Island in sight.

"You with me, Two?"

"On your left, Lead."

Jimmy looked around. He checked on Three and Four, orbiting above them, where they should be.

The island loomed ahead, spreading out on either side of the windscreen as the range closed. The airspeed indicator read 330 mph.

"Four! Tommy, what the hell!"

Jimmy darted a look up and saw a P-39 diving away from another.

"Four from Lead, get back in position."

No reply.

"Lead, Two, what do we do?"

"Continue the run, Two." Jimmy darted another look up at the diving P-39.

The rock swelled in his gunsight and Jimmy triggered his machine guns, leaving the cannon alone. His tracers reached out and bounced off the rock. Kellerman's tracers whipped past his left wingtip, spraying the beach to the left of the rock.

"OK, Two, move to my right wing."

"Roger, Lead, moving to your right wing."

Four was above and behind them, still diving. *He likes to go low and come close*, Jimmy thought to himself.

Jimmy reefed hard left with his wingtip scant feet above the water, pushing the throttle forward and increasing the RPMs. He looked right to check on Kellerman, who was where Jimmy wanted him, a few feet higher and in less danger of a mistake putting him into the drink.

Bell figured if he came down with the speed advantage from altitude he'd have Jimmy and Kellerman cold, get on their tails, and probably yell something over the radio like *"TakaTakaTakaTaka gotcha!"*

Jimmy eased back on the throttle and cracked his flaps open, tightening the turn. He darted a look back at Kellerman and then up at Bell. Bell was close, speeding up if anything, trying to turn with Jimmy and Kellerman. Dropping the flaps and bleeding airspeed let them turn tighter than Bell could hope to at his speed, but it was a temporary advantage, and Jimmy didn't want to give up too much speed.

He hoped that idiot Bell wouldn't pull too tight in a turn and get into an accelerated stall. This low he'd go straight in.

Then Bell was past them without being able to get into firing position. Jimmy saw his elevator and nose come up. Bell was awfully low, his airplane still sinking towards the ground, but Jimmy judged he'd make it.

"Two, you still with me?"

"Right behind you, Lead."

163

Jimmy reversed his turn. It put Bell ahead of them. Jimmy pushed the throttle forward and closed the flaps. He felt the P-39 accelerate, and there was Bell, bottoming out of his dive, still faster than Jimmy and Kellerman, but close.

Close enough to sink right into Jimmy's gunsight.

"Hey, Bell," Jimmy said. "Look behind you."

Bell pulled up hard, trading speed for altitude. It got him out of Jimmy's sights, reduced his forward motion relative to Jimmy and Kellerman, and put him in position to come down on Jimmy's tail.

"Two, break right, now."

Jimmy broke hard left as Kellerman broke right. "Two, Lead, remember you're my wingman."

"Ah, roger, Lead."

If Kellerman couldn't take a hint like that he'd never be any use in a real fight.

Bell now had his choice of two targets, but Jimmy knew who Bell was after.

"Ah, Lead, this is Three."

"Kinda busy down here, Three."

"What can I do?"

"Stay up there and keep your eyes peeled for Japs, Three."

Jimmy looked over his shoulder at Bell. Bell flipped over and came down, but he'd lost a lot of speed.

Speed is life, and Bell was about to learn that.

"Two, this is Lead. Your guns still hot?"

"Roger, Lead."

"Good. Feel free to shoot at Bell."

Bell broke silence. "Hey, wait a minute! You guys can't shoot at me!"

"Sure we can, Four. We've got machine guns."

"But I'm an American!"

"So are we. You're the one that broke formation and attacked us. What d'you think I should do about that, Four?"

There was silence over the radio. Bell abruptly pulled up and headed back towards Seven-Mile.

"That's what I thought," Jimmy said to himself. "Two, join up. We're headed home. Corncob Blue Four, this is Corncob Blue Leader. Join up on me."

Jimmy could see Bell's P-39 abruptly dive down on the harbor, headed straight for a freighter at anchor.

"Four, this is Lead, join up one me, right now."

Bell's P-39 pulled up abruptly and rocketed over the side of the ship, barely missing the smoke-stack of the freighter. Jimmy saw figures diving off the ship's deck into the waters of the harbor.

"Woooo-hooo!" came over the radio.

Jimmy flipped his guns on, pushing the throttle all the way forward.

"Ah, Lead, this is Two."

"Not now, Two."

"Lead…"

Jimmy gritted his teeth, safed his guns, and pulled back on the throttle.

"Roger, Two."

Jimmy watched as Bell kept climbing. Bell rolled, a well-executed four-point roll, and then he leveled off, turning northwest towards Seven-Mile.

Chapter Seven

Wrongfooted

Jimmy climbed out of his P-39, shrugged free of the parachute harness, and took off his Mae West. He pulled off his helmet and ran his fingers through his sweat-soaked hair.

"You OK, Jimmy?" Terraine asked.

"Yeah."

At that moment a jeep drove up trailing a heavy cloud of dust. Jimmy winced on the inside, because Col. Wagner drove the jeep, and Jimmy knew what was coming.

There was no use trying to evade it, either. Jimmy walked to the edge of the revetment, and when Wagner braked to a stop in front of him he locked up, chest in, shoulders back, eyes straight ahead.

"That's good, Jimmy, you stand there just like that."

It was a tone he had never heard from Wagner. There was something hard in every syllable, as if Wagner bit the sound off at the end. Jimmy gritted his teeth. Wagner looked from Jimmy down the flight line, where Kellerman and Shafer taxied in, and behind them was Tommy Bell.

Wagner didn't speak until the P-39s shut their engines down. Then, in the quiet, he spoke quietly.

"Lt. Ardana, I never thought I would question Jack Davis about anything, but now I begin to wonder if he was wrong about you, and that means I wonder about myself, because I agreed with Jack's judgment. He thought you would make a flight leader. I thought so too. But it seems there is a genuine problem with discipline in your flight. Saying that makes me realize that the words 'genuine problem' aren't sufficiently descriptive. A member of your flight committed breaches of safety that merit forfeiture of flight status. Ultimately, as flight leader, that's your responsibility."

"Yes, sir."

Jimmy wanted to add that he understood that, but he knew it was a time to say as little as possible and otherwise keep silent.

Wagner watched the pilots talking to their ground crew. They started coming up the taxiway towards Jimmy, but stopped short when they saw Jimmy standing at attention in front of Wagner.

"Relax, Jimmy," Wagner said softly. "I'm not doing this in front of your flight."

"Yes, sir." Jimmy went to parade rest, but at the look on Wagner's face he relaxed even further. At least, he felt like he did. But he had to resist that feeling from cadet days, that fear of washing out that he only ever felt once, maybe.

"If I did this in front of your flight I'd have to break it up. Your authority over them would be broken, probably irretrievably. You understand?"

"Yes, sir. I do."

For the first time Wagner looked at Jimmy.

"This is a first-class fuck-up, Jimmy. Wild flying is one thing. We all do that from time to time. But what I heard over the radio was flat-out disobedience of a direct order. What do you intend to do about it?"

168

Jimmy looked at Wagner. "Sir, I'll fix it. It won't happen again."

"All right, Jimmy. You do that. You fix it."

"Yes, sir."

Wagner put the jeep in gear. He looked down the taxiway where the members of Jimmy's flight still waited, watching.

"Damp from the birth," Wagner growled. "Jimmy, I'm not going to ask how you're going to fix this problem. But you find a way where we keep a pilot and a flight leader. That's what I need. Understood?"

"Yes, sir, that's affirmative."

"Very well. Carry on." Wagner backed the jeep up and drove away.

Jimmy felt something he had never felt before. He'd heard about it, but never felt it.

A red mist fell over his eyes.

He didn't know that really happened. His grandfather told him about "seeing red," but Jimmy thought it was just a saying.

Now he saw red and felt what came with it, which was absolutely nothing. There was no feeling, no past, no future, only a sort of present moment narrowed down into what was right before him. The moment stretched out until Jimmy took a deep, slow breath.

Jimmy knew, if he committed murder in a moment like that, he'd feel nothing.

He took another deep, slow breath.

The red receded. It didn't go away, but at least Jimmy felt like he could move without that move being towards his pistol or his knife.

Great God Almighty.

169

He turned to look at his pilots.

"Bell, you come with me." Jimmy started off among the trees.

"Why?"

Jimmy stopped. The red mist threatened to fall over his eyes again.

Then he turned. He took four strides forward, saw Shafer and Kellerman back off, leaving Bell standing alone. Four more strides, and the smug, cocky look on Bell's face wavered.

Then they stood nose to nose. Jimmy looked straight into Bell's eyes, and part of him had to admit that Bell might not be too smart, but he had nerve, because Bell returned the look.

With his right hand Jimmy pushed hard on Bell's chest, knocking him off balance. With his other hand he grabbed Bell's right helmet strap, pulling him forward as Jimmy took a step back, then another, and kept moving. Bell shouted and tried to wrench Jimmy's hand away from his helmet strap. Jimmy tightened his grip, jerked Bell's helmet strap hard, and moved faster.

"Damn it, Ardana, let go!"

Jimmy jerked harder and moved faster. He turned around, pulling a still-shouting Bell with him. When he figured they were far enough away from the tent city he stopped, releasing his hold on Bell's helmet. Bell stumbled and fell to one knee.

"What the hell?" Bell raged. He got to his feet and moved forward, clenching his fists.

Jimmy unbuckled his holster and laid it carefully on the ground.

Bell stopped in his tracks, looking down at the holstered pistol.

Jimmy stood there, looking at Bell.

The moment stretched out. Bell looked at the pistol again.

"Why did you do that?" he asked.

Jimmy took a moment before he replied. Red still overlaid his vision and the blood still sang in his ears.

"My grandfather told me once that when you're mad clear through your judgment isn't the best."

"Yeah? So?"

"So when you're that angry maybe having a pistol at hand isn't the best idea. You pull a trigger, and things happen that can't be undone. So yeah, Grandpa advised putting your guns and knives aside when dealing with a damn fool whose foolishness doesn't merit a lead slug in the belly."

Bell looked from the pistol to Jimmy. "Knife?" he asked.

Jimmy gave him a hard look. Then he reached down and brought the Bowie knife out of its sheath, tied around his right ankle. He laid the knife down on the pistol holster and stood up.

Bell stared at the knife.

"You pack a lot of hardware," Bell said.

"Yeah."

"So, what...ah..."

"What am I going to do? You ever do any boxing, Bell?"

"No."

"I doubt if a fist to the jaw would knock any sense into you, anyway."

Abruptly the anger left Jimmy, leaving him with a cold feeling inside. Bell started to bristle and opened his mouth. Jimmy held his hand up, palm open.

"Shut up, Bell. Better if you don't say anything. Didn't they teach you about discipline, back in flight school?"

"Sure, but that's all bullshit. You're going to get split up in a fight anyway, so why stay together?"

"You're wrong. You stay together not because of some chickenshit rule, but because it makes sense. You stick together so you can fight together. You don't, you break up so you're on your own and it's just you against the whole Jap air force, how long you think you'll last?"

"That's crap, Ardana. I can lick any Jap I come across."

Jimmy shook his head. "You think so? Because I've known a dozen guys in the last two months who thought that. Some of them didn't leave so much as a smoke trail when they went down."

"That'll never happen to me."

"Maybe not. But you break discipline in a fight, it's not just you who gets the chop. If someone relies on you to be there and you aren't, then that's Sheila, or Midnight, or me. All because Chinkerbell thought his shit was so hot he could do anything he wanted."

"God damn it, don't call me Chinkerbell! And that discipline crap is just you trying to tell me what to do!"

"Are you serious? People have been telling you what to do ever since you were sworn in as an air cadet. What's your problem?"

"I don't have a problem!"

"Yeah, you do. You know, Chinkerbell, maybe your hands are solid gold but I wouldn't give you a wooden nickel for that so-called brain you carry for ballast."

"You're right about one thing, Ardana. I've got good hands. Better than you."

Jimmy nodded. "OK. So is your problem that you think you should run this flight because you're a better pilot than I am?"

"You're damned right!"

"Good. That makes this easy. How about a little bet?"

"Bet?"

"Yeah. A bet, a wager, you know what that is."

"Of course I do!"

"Then here's the bet. You and me, right down the center of the airstrip, and whoever looks down on the other guy loses."

"You're kidding."

"I'm betting your life, Chinkerbell. I'm not kidding about that."

"What are the stakes?"

"If you win, what do you want?"

"All right. If I win, I want you to let me alone. I do what I want, whenever I want. You don't tell me what to do, not ever again. Oh, and you have to stop calling me Chinkerbell."

Jimmy nodded. "OK, Chinkerbell. And if I win, you do what I say, when I say, no questions asked. And whoever wants, right down to the mess cooks and the latrine orderlies, can call you Chinkerbell."

"What? Even the enlisted men?"

173

"They can call you Sir Chinkerbell."

Bell scoffed. "You're on, Ardana."

"All right. Go check your airplane. Be ready to go in fifteen minutes. I'll even follow you out."

"You better get used to following me, Ardana."

Jimmy held Bell's eyes until Bell turned away and headed back to the flight line.

Bell called over his shoulder. "Fifteen minutes, Ardana. Enjoy your little world for fifteen more minutes, because after that it's all mine."

Terraine stood on the wing of *Gremlin II*, helping Jimmy buckle in.

"You sure this is a good idea, Jimmy?"

"What's that?"

"You. Mr. Bell. This low-level thing."

"I guess we'll find out."

"Why are you doing it?"

"To beat Bell at his own game."

"I hear he can go real low."

"He can. I've seen him."

"You figure you can go lower?"

"I wouldn't go if I didn't think so." Jimmy frowned. "Don, how did you hear about it?"

Terraine squatted down by the open door of the airplane. "Evidently Mr. Bell told his ground crew all about how he was going to splash you down the center of the runway, trying to go lower than he could."

"Did he." It wasn't a question. Terraine looked at him. "Well, I guess everyone in Port Moresby knows about it by now."

"Probably."

174

"OK. Let's get started."

Terraine closed the door and clapped his hand twice on the cockpit.

Jimmy went through the engine start and before-taxi checklists, then got on the radio. "Tower, Army 557 with a flight of two, request taxi clearance."

"Army 557, roger. What are your intentions?"

"Tower, 557 is conducting a training flight."

"Roger, 557, you are clear to taxi."

Jimmy looked at Terraine, standing near the entrance of the revetment, who saluted and stood to one side.

"So how do you want to do this, Ardana?"

"You put your left wingtip on my right wingtip, go to full throttle, and we'll fly down the runway just like that."

"You're on."

Jimmy called the tower. "This is Army 557, flight of two, request permission for a low-level pass down the runway."

"Ah...wait one, 557."

Jimmy led Chinkerbell in a long downwind until they were flying opposite Bootless Inlet, off the east end of the runway. He looked around. The sky was clear.

"Ah, Army 557, Jackson Tower, you are cleared for a low-level pass."

"Roger, Tower. Chinkerbell, let's go."

Jimmy stood his P-39 on its left wing, pulling gee hard enough to stream vapor from the wingtips, gasping against the weight of the turn, holding it right on the edge of an accelerated stall. He rolled out of the turn on the runway heading over Bootless Inlet. Chinkerbell didn't turn quite as tight and Jimmy fishtailed a little until Chinkerbell's wingtip was opposite his own. Then the two P-39s roared down Bootless Bay with the throttles against the stops and the salt spray spattering their windscreens, lifting over the treetops beyond the beach, and as the end of the runway approached Jimmy didn't try to fly lower than Tommy Bell, he just went down until his ass cheeks started biting into his parachute pack, and then a hair more, and howled down the runway like that. Most of him flew in front of the airplane, calculating the future two seconds ahead as the trees and revetments blurred past them and the end of the runway approached, but part of him could see Bell's wingtip, level with the top of his canopy. Jimmy felt the runway in his mind, scant inches below his propeller arc, and at 330 mph it took less than a minute to traverse. Jimmy saw Bell's wingtip from the corner of his eye, dipping a few inches and rising, dipping a few inches and rising, until they came to the end of the runway and Jimmy pulled up to clear the trees, rolling as he cleared them, an eight-point aileron roll barely above the treetops, the kind of stunt that got you grounded stateside, and in his mirror he caught a glimpse of Bell's P-39, low above the trees and not even trying to follow Jimmy's maneuver.

Jimmy had to admit the sweet, seductive thrill of that kind of flying. It wasn't something he intended to do often, or without some good reason. And it wasn't as if that kind of flying was scary, not really, because hell's bells, if he went in at that altitude and airspeed he'd never feel it, never even have time to say *oh shit* because he'd be dead before the first syllable.

He keyed his radio and was careful to school his voice into a tone of near-boredom. "Jackson Tower, Army 557, request permission to land."

"Army 557, cleared to land."

As Jimmy taxied back to the revetment he noticed mechanics and pilots standing along the taxiway, looking at him. No salute, no wave, just a slightly-stunned look. Jimmy turned and shut down in front of his revetment and listened for a moment to the sound of the engine cooling, noticing the brilliant blue of the sky and the dusty green of the tree leaves. Then he took a deep breath and exhaled sharply before unbuckling and opening the door.

Terraine stood by his wing root and helped him down. He looked at Jimmy with that same slightly-stunned look.

Jimmy frowned. "What?"

"Jimmy, do you know how low you were?"

"No, not exactly. I was as low as I cared to go. I know that."

Terraine shook his head slowly. "I could barely tell you were clear of the runway."

"How about Chinkerbell?"

"Guess that nickname's going to stick with him, now. He was low, but you were two feet lower."

Jimmy nodded. "Good."

"I hope to hell that shuts him up, boss."

"Me too." Jimmy shook his head. "Look, be sure I don't have anything in the wheel wells, will you? And double-check the prop tips and the underside of the wings and fuselage. I might've plowed up the runway a little without knowing it."

Terraine nodded. He grinned. It was weak but it was still a grin. "Yes, sir, Mr. Jimmy Ardana, sir."

Jimmy shrugged out of his parachute harness and walked to the next revetment over. Tommy Bell leaned against the wing of his P-39, and his ground crew was industriously, ostentatiously busy doing nothing Jimmy could see.

"Let's hear it," Jimmy said.

Bell scowled.

"You gonna say I didn't win, fair and square? The bet was to see which of us could fly the lowest down the runway. I had your wheel wells in sight. How about you?"

"I could see the top of your head," Bell acknowledged. The acknowledgment was reluctant and grudging.

"OK, then. You know what to do."

Bell scowled and turned reluctantly to his ground crew. "Guys."

The crew chief, assistant chief, and the armorer turned to face their pilot. "Yes, sir?" asked Mowery.

"You can call me Chinkerbell."

"Beg pardon, sir? I couldn't quite hear you."

"Goddamnit! I said you can all call me Chinkerbell!"

"Yes, sir, Chinkerbell, sir," the crew chief replied.

Tommy Bell stalked off, stripping his helmet off his head in an abrupt motion, head sunk down between his shoulders. His boot heels struck dirt from the

178

ground with every step. He muttered something inaudible but almost certainly profane.

"Hey, Chinkerbell," Jimmy called.

Bell stopped but he didn't turn around. Jimmy could see the pilot's fists opening and closing.

"Could be worse," Jimmy said to Bell's hunched back. "The bet could've been we got to call you Stinkerbell."

Behind him, Jimmy heard stifled laughter. Bell's fists grew tighter, his head sunk fractionally lower between his shoulders. Then he walked forward, down the path to the tents.

"Stinkerbell, Mr. Ardana?" said a dry voice at his elbow.

Jimmy turned to see Chief Halloran standing there.

"Yup," Jimmy replied.

The Chief shook his head. "Goddamned pursuit pilots," he said, and walked off.

Jimmy couldn't tell if the older man was amused or displeased. He used that phrase to express either emotion.

"Mr. Ardana?"

"Yes, Mowery?"

"If it's all the same to you, sir, maybe we won't call Lt. Bell Chinkerbell. Not more than once or twice, anyway."

"If I was a hateful bastard, Mowery, I'd tell you to paint that name on his god-damned airplane. But it's your airplane too, so I won't. But maybe you're right." Jimmy grinned suddenly. "On the other hand, every sonofabitch on this airfield will call him Chinkerbell now."

The crew chief grinned faintly. "I expect you're right, sir. Probably the whole damned Air Corps."

"Look, I asked Sgt. Terraine to go over my airplane carefully. You do the same, hear? Down that low we could blow any sort of debris up into the airplane."

"Yes, sir," Mowery replied. "We'll take care of it."

Jimmy walked back to his revetment.

David Kellerman was standing there waiting for him. "Where's Sheila?" Jimmy asked.

"Went after Tommy."

"Chinkerbell. We don't call him anything else for one week."

"Jeez. Remind me not to piss you off."

"Midnight, he got off easy. After that stunt he pulled? Come on."

Kellerman fell into step beside him as they walked up to Operations. "Well. If you put it that way. I heard Colonel Wagner was going to bust him. Is that true?"

"The Colonel was pretty mad. I was pretty mad, too, but do you know what we were both mad about?"

Kellerman looked at Jimmy. "Why do I think it wasn't because he flew between the masts of that freighter?

"Nah. If he pulled that shit on his own hook, I'd take him down a little, but what pissed me off was I told him, in the clear, over the radio, not to leave the formation, and the stupid sonofabitch did it anyway. Chinkerbell is lucky all that happened is he's got a nickname that he hates that'll follow him the rest of his life. The Colonel was going to take his wings, bust him to private, and make him permanent latrine orderly."

"But he's a good pilot! The Colonel wouldn't do that!"

"He's a good pilot, all right. Not quite as good as he thinks, but good. But there's a difference between being a good pilot, in the sense of the kind of idiot who can fly under bridges and get away with it, and being a good pursuit pilot. You want to tell me what that is?"

Kellerman hesitated, and Jimmy remembered doing the same thing with Boyd Wagner.

"A good pursuit pilot weighs the risks," said Kellerman. "So, what now?"

"What d'you mean?"

"Well, you showed Tommy – I mean, Chinkerbell – he wasn't the only possessor of angel-wings in this man's Air Corps, and I don't think he knew that before. But the point was to make him obey orders. Will that happen now?"

"Yes, I think so."

"Why?"

"Because, Dave, Chinkerbell thought he was so good he was a law unto himself. He thought he could get away with anything. Now he's dealing with the idea that maybe, just maybe, someone is a little better than he is." Jimmy shook his head. "But maybe more important than that, Bell shot his mouth off about the bet. Now everyone in the 8th Fighter Group, and probably every other outfit on the field, knows Bell lost his bet. What do you think will happen now?"

Kellerman grinned suddenly. "Tommy…I mean, Chinkerbell, may be a lot of things, but one thing I've noticed about him, he's a man of his word. I think he'll do what he said he'd do. Especially when doing otherwise would make him a welsher."

"Good. Then that silly stunt was worth it. Maybe he'll start thinking about that, and maybe he'll figure out that I knew I could beat him ahead of time."

"Did you?"

"Hell, yes, or I would've done something different."

Kellerman shook his head. "Jesus," he said quietly.

"What?"

"I don't know if I'll ever be that good."

"You don't have to be as good as me, Midnight. I'm on your side. You just have to be better than any Jap bastard we meet. Chinkerbell either didn't know that, or forgot."

A private trotted down the path and pulled up in front of them, panting and coming to attention.

"Lt. Ardana, sir?"

Jimmy returned the man's salute. "Yes, private?"

"Colonel Wagner's respects, sir, and will you please report to him at once."

"Well, lead on, then, private. I'm right behind you."

"Yes, sir."

"Jeez," said Kellerman. "You still in trouble with the Colonel?"

"Don't know, but if I am putting it off will make it worse. I'll see you later."

"Good luck."

Wagner sat on the veranda of the Operations shack where he had a grand view of the length of Seven-Mile's runway, and Jimmy had the uneasy feeling that

Wagner had been sitting there when he and Bell buzzed the runway. Jimmy came to a cadet-rigid posture of attention, saluted crisply, and barked, "Lt. Ardana reporting as ordered, sir!"

The Colonel returned Jimmy's salute with an expressionless face. He said, "Jimmy, let's take a little walk."

They walked down the path and stood in the shade of a dusty tree. Wagner leaned against the tree and pulled out his pipe. He knocked it out against the tree, reloaded it, lit up, and took a couple of puffs before turning to Jimmy.

"I got an odd phone call from the tower a while ago. Something about a low-level pass. Then I looked up and happened to notice two P-39s going down the runway at a very low altitude indeed," Wagner said. "Want to tell me about that?"

"Colonel, I offered Lt. Bell a wager."

"Oh? Kindly elaborate, Lieutenant."

"Sir, pursuant to the Colonel's directive to correct the, ah, problem in flight discipline that occurred earlier today, I figured that if I showed Lt. Bell that he wasn't the best pilot in the world, even at his own game, it would provide me with moral superiority."

"Damn, Jimmy. I think that's the most words I've ever heard you string together at one time."

"Yes, sir."

"The bet was to see who could fly the length of the runway at the lowest possible altitude?"

"Yes, sir."

"And what were the stakes?" *Other than your lives and two P-39s*, was what the Colonel didn't have to say.

"If I won everyone gets to call Lt. Bell by his nickname, sir. Chinkerbell. Oh, and my word was law."

"I see. And if you lost?"

"Then Lt. Bell could go off on his own whenever he liked. And I would never call him Chinkerbell again."

"Even in the past tense I don't like the terms of that bet, Jimmy."

"Understood, sir."

"You were that damned confident you'd win." It wasn't a question. Wagner knew it was true.

"Yes, sir. I've watched Chinkerbell's flying for the last two days. He's good, Colonel. Really good. I'm better."

Wagner shook his head slowly, and with an unutterable sense of relief Jimmy realized Wagner was laughing silently.

"So, Jimmy, you still think you're a better pilot than me?" Wagner asked. He looked straight into Jimmy's eyes when he spoke. The question was a challenge, but Wagner had the ghost of mirth dancing in his eyes.

"Only one way to find out, sir," Jimmy replied. "But maybe not today."

"Good. It's a wise man who doesn't push the line between skill and luck too hard, too often. You're one of the best pilots I've ever seen, Jimmy, but you do realize you had luck riding with you today."

"Yes, sir."

Wagner nodded. "So, speaking to the wider purpose. That was impressive flying, Jimmy, but did it work?"

"I think so, Colonel. It seems everyone heard about the bet before we took off, and when we taxied back in it looked like most of them were watching."

"All right." Wagner took out a handkerchief and mopped the sweat from his face. "That's good, because we're about to need every pilot we have."

"What's happened?"

Wagner frowned. "I got a phone call from the 22nd Bomb Group operations officer. Seems the 22nd went to Salamaua today and found a whole bunch of Jap shipping headed east from Salamaua. There were enough freighters and barges that it looks like the Japs are going to land somewhere and set up housekeeping."

"You think they might be headed to Buna, sir?"

"Maybe. Who knows? Anyway, so much for Operation PROVIDENCE," said Wagner in disgust. "The Japs still want Port Moresby. They can't come by sea. Buna is a logical beachhead for an attack overland, since it leads to the north end of the Kokoda Track. Which leads here over the mountains." Wagner shook his head. "If that's what they're up to."

Jimmy shook his head. "That Aussie infantry captain said it would take two weeks to walk the Kokoda Track across the mountains. That's without unfriendly strangers taking potshots at you."

Wagner nodded slowly. He was looking at the airfield. "This can't be the only thing they have going on. Remember that airstrip on, what was the name of

185

that island? Something Spanish-sounding, of all the damned things."

"Beg pardon?"

"It was while you were in Brisbane. The 435th Recon Squadron went to this island way the hell east of here, some place at the southeast end of the Solomon Islands called Tulagi. The Japs kicked the Aussies out of there awhile back and decided to set up a seaplane base. Anyway, turns out that Jap engineers are building an airstrip on the island south of Tulagi. Guadalcanal, that's the name. So now there's a seaplane base and soon an airfield in range of our base at New Caledonia, and if the Japs threaten that, they threaten our air route back to the States."

"Guadalcanal," said Jimmy slowly. "Never heard of it."

"Had you ever heard of any of the geography out here before you got to Australia?"

"No, sir. We learned about Hawaii and the Philippines because they're American possessions. If you looked at the map of the Philippines you could see a bunch of islands with strange names to the south, but I don't think New Guinea was even one of them."

"Yeah, well, from the lack of maps and charts of the area I don't think anybody found this part of the world important, except maybe the Aussies and the Dutch."

"Colonel, what about tomorrow?"

"Tomorrow?"

"Yes, sir."

"Depends on what the Japs do over the next twenty-four hours. They could start landing at Buna tonight or tomorrow morning. We might get word from the Aussie coast watchers if that's the case. Otherwise we'll have to find out where the Jap convoy is headed. I'm going to order the group to be ready to go at first light. Even if the Japs haven't landed at Buna we can still catch up with their convoy and maybe have some fun."

"Bombs?"

"Haven't decided. If the Zeros come out to play we might wish we had the fuel."

Jimmy nodded. "In that case, Colonel, I think I'm going to check my flight and my airplanes."

"OK." Wagner hesitated. "Jimmy, about Lt. Bell. If you have any doubts about him let me know. I'll ground the sonofabitch even if he does have good hands."

"I think I can handle it, Colonel, but thanks."

"OK, Jimmy. Carry on."

Jimmy paused on the porch of the Operations shack and looked around. It was quiet for a moment. The slow clack of a typewriter, coming from the room behind him, was the loudest audible noise. So it was calm now, and that would change in a matter of hours, earlier if the Japs mounted another air raid.

Maybe he'd better write to Laura Sue. He'd been putting it off, and who knew when he'd have a better chance.

Hey, Laura Sue,

It's hot and it's humid and you can probably tell that from the blots in the ink. At least it isn't raining, so enough about the weather. Let it suffice to say I wish I was back home if just for a nice cool evening. So if I were there maybe we could go out for a Coke or something. What's playing at the movies? They keep saying we'll have movies here. Maybe sometime. I won't hold my breath.

You know, it's darn hard to figure what to write, but you asked about Evarra, and I know a little about him. He's gotten to be pretty important around here, if only because all the other natives either listen to him or are scared of him. Hard to tell with these folks, sort of like the Sioux back home. They won't let you know what they're thinking, keep the same poker face going the whole time.

Anyway Evarra shows up now and then, and I wish I could figure how he does it. Speaking of the Sioux, I reckon they could learn from Evarra. There's trees around but here and there, more like a park than a forest with any real cover.

The other day we were going up to play when Evarra walked up to me, and asked, if I can remember it right,

"Youpela ranim balus tede? Pait Jap balus-man?" He wanted to· know if I were going to fly and fight the Japs. I guess the locals don't like the Japs dropping bombs on them any more than we do. Besides, even if the tropic scenery and the ocean seas weren't enough to make you think you were in an article in the National Geographic, having the natives around, including a sanguma man like Evarra, would convince you.

You could ask, what's a sanguma man? I don't know much about what these folks believe, but one of our medics is in with the local missionaries – Catholic priests, mostly – and he says they're animists. The whole world is alive to these folks. I don't know what Pastor Williams would say about that, nor what the local padres think about it. It ain't the Way, the Truth, and the Light the way we learned it in Sunday school, but I reckon it's a bigger world than I thought, too. Bigger than Pastor Williams thought, maybe, and I think he believed the Kingdom of Israel was somewhere next door in Wyoming. Wish I could talk to my grandpa about it. He always had a surprising outlook on things.

Speaking of which, my grandma had good things to say about you in her last letter, and I really appreciate you spending time with her. She likes young folks – says it keeps her looking at things different – and she seems to like you, too.

Since I'm writing about you I want to tell you how much I appreciated the picture you sent me. Awful pretty girl in that picture! You sure that's you? Kidding, just kidding! I haven't shown that picture around much. These guys I bunk with are mostly good fellows to have with you in a fight, but not all of them are known for pure thoughts and clean living, not even me, not all the time. I prefer to keep you all to myself.

I'll wrap this up for now, but if you would, next time you see Miss Susan, please give her a hug from me. And keep writing, I'd hate to think of the old town changing without you to tell me what's going on.

Best as always,

Jimmy

Charlie looked at the message flimsy in his hand and didn't know whether to laugh or cry.

He sat in his tent at Seven-Mile, reading the message by the light of a gas lantern. The pale green light made the dark letters stand out in stark relief. The message was from Colonel Carmichael, and stated, in brief, that Carmichael was bringing up as many B-17s as he could get in the air tomorrow morning , including the two B-17s of Charlie's squadron, to strike at the Japanese convoy somewhere off the north coast. Presumably, though, by the time Carmichael could get here, sometime late in the morning of July 22nd, the Japs would have landed wherever they intended to set up a beachhead.

Charlie and his crew went to Vunakanau that afternoon to photograph the airfield while the other two B-17s went south. The Japs sent up a half-dozen Zeros, but after a series of running attacks over a half-hour or so, the Japs did no damage to *Bronco Buster II* and Charlie's gunners didn't do much more than get a few strikes on the Zeros.

Charlie read Carmichael's message again. He expected the RAAF would send Catalinas out to find and shadow the convoy during the night, and by first light there was a good chance the RAAF would know where the Japs were headed.

"Let's see that map," Charlie told Al Stern, who unrolled the map and pointed to Buna. Charlie nodded.

"Why Buna, Al?"

For answer, the navigator pointed to a small dot labeled "Kokoda" about halfway between the north coast and the crest of the Owen Stanley Mountains to the south.

"You think those crazy bastards will attack overland?" Charlie asked. "I hear that so-called Kokoda Track is just a foot trail. Their objective has to be Port

Moresby, just like last May. How do they think they're going to get enough supplies over a foot trail in the damn mountains to support an infantry attack here on Port Moresby?"

"Do I look like Tojo?" Al asked. "How would I know what they're thinking? Maybe they're going all the way to the eastern tip of New Guinea here, over at Milne Bay."

"Yeah. Maybe." He studied the map some more and tapped the point marked "Buna."

"How far is it, here to there?" he asked the navigator.

"Ninety-three miles."

"Jehosophat. That's all? Is it worth it to climb to 23,000 feet if we're only going ninety-three miles?"

"A lot of wear and tear on worn and torn engines," Al said. "Fly in high enough to stay above the medium-caliber stuff. Come east or west of Buna fifteen or twenty miles to set up the bomb run. What'll we do for bombs?"

"Aw, maybe we can get the Aussies to shake loose with a half-dozen or so."

"Not much of a bomb load."

"No, but there's a bit of a bomb shortage up here. We'll do what we can."

Al grimaced and nodded.

Charlie thought for a moment. "Let's lay it out to bomb from 13,000 feet. That'll keep us above everything the light stuff, anyway. If we go in the morning we should come in from the east. Where's that old airstrip the Aussies had up there?"

Al hunted for a moment and found it, near a river mouth and a spit of land poking out into the ocean. It was near the point labeled "Buna Mission."

"OK. That's probably where we'll find the Japs. Maybe they think they can put Zeros there, so it kind of makes sense. Let's plan on taking enough fuel to go from here to Buna and maybe Horn Island if weather moves in and we can't land back here at Seven-Mile. Add thirty minutes reserve. What's that come to?"

Stern read the distances with a plotter, added them up, and consulted his flight operations chart for fuel consumption. "Make it 1000 gallons. We can carry whatever bombs we can cram into the bomb bay."

"OK. I'll talk to Bob Frye and send him over to the RAAF boys, see what they can let us have in terms of a bomb load. Then let's take about 5000 rounds of .50-cal. Start fueling about 0500."

"Sounds right. You want me to walk Danny through the flight planning?"

"Sure. Do him good to work out a weight and balance chart."

"Right. I'll go start setting things up."

Stern hurried off into the gathering darkness. The sun was setting below the mountains and somewhere north of them the Japs might be putting men and supplies ashore on a beach. Charlie felt pretty sure that the Japs were headed for Buna Bay with every intention of mounting their own version of Operation PROVIDENCE.

Charlie bent over the map in the light of the gas lantern. The Japs had airfields at Lae and Salamaua, and both were 120 miles away. Even a P-39 could make

193

that round trip. The airfields at Lakunai and Vunakanau were four hundred miles away, but a Zero could make even that, much less the Jap bombers.

So tomorrow, over Buna Mission, there'd be as big a formation of B-17s as any the 19th had put over a target since the beginning of the war, depending on the abort rate. The 8th would send P-39s. The 22nd, after bombing targets near Salamaua, had returned to Australia. But the RAAF would take a hand, probably with the Hudsons. Their Catalinas were too damned slow for this kind of fight, in daylight, anyway.

There was no one to organize and coordinate the efforts of the different units involved, either. Charlie decided he'd speak to Carmichael about that. Charlie could see how it might go if everyone's efforts could be coordinated. Send some P-39s in high, ahead of the rest of the attackers, and draw the attentions of whatever Zeros the Japs had over Buna. Send the B-17s in a few minutes behind them, and between the B-17s and the P-39s the Japs would be biting their tails, trying to figure out what they wanted to shoot at the most. If there were any P-39s to spare send them in at low level with the B-26s coming in at medium height, say 8000 feet, and the Jap antiaircraft gunners would have the same problem as the Zeros. Just for fun have everyone attack from different directions.

Charlie sighed. No one had managed to put together an attack like that since the war began. Jack told him about the fight over Den Pasar back last February, when the FEAF in Java pulled off a combined attack using P-40s as cover for A-24 dive bombers and a couple of LB -30 heavy bombers. Jack

194

had no idea how the attack worked, though, because his outfit, the 17th Provisional Pursuit Squadron, had been jumped by Zeros. The whole thing turned into a confused mess, and in the end the Japanese kept what they'd been after, the airstrip at Den Pasar, which cut the aerial supply line from Australia to Java.

If the Japs took Buna they'd have a base on the north coast of New Guinea. From an airstrip at Buna they could hit Seven-Mile with hardly any warning, even if a coastwatcher called it in as the Jap Zeros were taking off. Ninety-three miles, Jehosophat. A Jap Zero could leave Buna and be at Seven-Mile in twenty minutes. Of course, the reverse was true for the P-39s at Seven-Mile, but still, things were bad enough.

Charlie picked up his cap and went out to see if he could help Al Stern.

Tomorrow was going to be a rough day.

Chapter Eight

Bloody wars and sickly seasons

A B-17 roared down the runway and climbed out into the dim early morning light. Jimmy wondered if it was Charlie's bomber, but there was barely enough light to make out the runway, much less identifying details like the rider forking his bronc on the nose of *Bronco Buster II.* He grimaced, thinking of Danny Evans, of all the damned people, flying copilot for Charlie Davis. That made him think of his own problem child, yawning and stumbling along the path behind him.

Tommy Bell was at least a good pilot, so if he managed to kill Jimmy it would be because he meant to do it, not because he was too damned ham-handed and stupid to know better.

Kellerman walked beside him, yawning. Jimmy suppressed a yawn himself, blinking the sleep away.

It hadn't been a restful night for anyone. The mechanics were up most of the night, and the burble and rumble of Allisons being run up and tested was enough to keep Jimmy on the edge of sleep and wakefulness until it stopped around 0300. He figured he slept for about two and a half hours, then, before being awakened for the mission brief at 0530.

"What will it be like?" Kellerman asked quietly.

"Confusing," Jimmy replied. "It'll look like everyone in the world is shooting at you, you're going to be lower than you're comfortable going, and if the

196

Zeros show up you're going to wish you were someplace else, almost anywhere else."

There was a cough from behind Jimmy. "You have something to add, Chinkerbell?" he asked.

"Er, ah, sir, no sir."

"Good. Low-level against the Japs will be more fun than blowing some poor lady's laundry off the line."

Bell was silent.

Shafer said, "Wasn't your first mission a low-level attack on Lae, Jimmy?"

"Yup. I had your job, Boxcar Red Three. Only it was my second combat mission, not my first, although the first one wasn't supposed to be a combat mission."

"How'd that go?" Shafer asked. "The attack on Lae, I mean."

"We lost two guys," Jimmy said. "But my flight leader, Jack Davis, got a Zero, and his wingman got a half-Zero."

"How d'you get a half-Zero?" Bell asked skeptically.

"When one guy shoots hell out of it and another guy shoots hell out of it and it crashes right in front of them. In front of witnesses, including me."

"I'm not sharing any kills."

"Can't share what you don't have, Chinkerbell," said Kellerman.

"Shut up," said Bell.

"Chinkerbell, Midnight, you guys go ahead. I need to talk to Sheila."

Jimmy paused to let the other two go on. Shafer looked at him expectantly.

197

"I'm keeping an eye on you and Bell," Jimmy said quietly. "Not for the same reason, though. Chinkerbell, I'm not sure what he's going to do. You, because it's your first time."

"Why did you make me an element lead, Jimmy?"

"Mostly because I think you're steadier than Bell and smarter than Kellerman. Don't prove me wrong and don't let it go to your head. Just do your job and come home in one piece."

"Yes, sir," Shafer said quietly. "I won't let you down."

"Thanks. Just so we're clear, the best way to not let me down is kill some Japs and live to tell the tale. Now let's go on in to the briefing."

Wagner stood at the head of the room. With him was an Aussie officer in baggy shorts and an enormous digger hat with one side turned up. The man wore a holstered revolver and looked lean and fit.

"Gentlemen, quiet down," said Wagner. "Captain McCormick, would you begin?"

"Thank you, Colonel," said the Australian. He turned to look at the pilots. "Gents, it seems the Nips have taken a shine to Buna Mission, about one hundred miles north of here on the coast. Colonel Wagner was there two weeks ago, scouting for airfields. There's a sorry excuse for one, I'm told, near Buna. What the Nips will make of it I've no idea, but it's possible they have Zeros there already, or will soon." The Australian paused. "I've been to Buna myself. It's a fair cow, oh my word. Swamps, mosquitoes, and malaria. If you have to parachute, try to get as far inland as possible first. We have a battalion of infantry called Maroubra

Force up near Kokoda, forty-eight miles inland. A trail leads inland from Buna and passes through the villages of Popondetta and Dobodura. The Nips will probably head south along that trail as soon as they get organized. They may already have sent advanced parties inland. They've had all night to set that up."

The Australian glanced at Wagner, who nodded.

"Thank you, Captain McCormick. Gentlemen, this will be sort of improvised. Some of you will be carrying bombs, since the distance is short. Your targets will be barges and freighters, but if you happen to see heaps of boxes and supplies on the beach, those are acceptable. If by some odd chance you get a bunch of Jap infantry bunched together, which I think unlikely, put a bomb in the middle of them."

Wagner looked at his pilots. He was silent for a long moment. Then he said, "Back last December I was in the Philippines when the Japs landed. The Japs headed inland pretty quick, to the main road that went down the center of Luzon. The Japs can study maps as well as anyone, and once they were on that road they rolled south with everything they had. We slowed 'em down, but that's not going to be good enough now. We have to stop them. Stopping them is up to you guys, so go and do it. That's all."

As they were filing out Bell scoffed. "I've had better pep talks from football coaches. We'll stop the Japs all right. I thought that Wagner was supposed to be hot shit. He sounds like he's afraid."

Jimmy didn't even know he moved until he had a fistful of the collar of Bell's flight suit and jerked him so close he could see the pupils in Bell's eyes widening.

"Shut the fuck up, Bell," he said. "One more word and you're off flight status, and you'll be off flight status because I'm going to beat you senseless. You understand?"

"Jeez, Ardana, is that what it takes to get you to call me by name?"

Jimmy let go of Bell's collar and pushed him away. It was only then that Jimmy saw the two of them stood inside a circle of pilots, all of whom stood with hard, blank faces, staring at Bell. Bell looked around, suddenly wary.

"OK, Jimmy, I got it," Bell said.

Jimmy turned abruptly and went down the path to the flight line. He could hear the blood rushing in his ears and he knew his fists were clenching and unclenching. Behind him he heard mutters and an indignant shout from Bell, accompanied by the unmistakable sound of punches and kicks landing.

Kellerman walked beside him. "Jimmy, shouldn't we stop that?"

"What?"

"Those guys are kind of roughing Chinkerbell up."

"I don't see anything."

Bell yelped.

"Yeah, but I bet you're hearing plenty," Kellerman said drily.

Abruptly Bell was shoved in between them. There was a bruise on his cheek and his flight suit was dirty.

"Next time you open that filthy hole you call a mouth, Chinkerbell, you might want to consider who's listening," said Jimmy. "Not all of these guys are as gentle and forgiving as I am. And every single one of them think Colonel Wagner walks on water."

Bell opened his mouth, looked warily over his shoulder, and shut it again.

"This is me," said Shafer. "See you guys in the air."

He turned into his revetment.

Kellerman nodded to Jimmy at the next revetment. Bell's airplane was in the revetment next to Jimmy's. He turned without a word and went to his P-39.

Terraine stood by the trailing edge of the wing to help Jimmy with his parachute. "Is it true the Japs landed on the north coast, Jimmy?"

"Sure is."

"Should I find some rifles for me and the boys?"

"You don't have rifles?"

"I've got a pistol, like most of the guys."

"They're not going to be here this afternoon, and even if the Aussies don't stop them it'll take at least two weeks for the Japs to walk over the mountains. I wouldn't worry yet.'

Terraine nodded.

"Just out of curiosity, Don, how did you do with a rifle in Basic?"

"I shot Expert."

"Good. Hopefully we won't have to go hunting, but at least we can if we need to."

"You got that right, boss," said Terraine. Jimmy had never heard that note in his crew chief's voice. No bravado, just pure determination. Jimmy punched him gently on the shoulder.

"How's the *Gremlin* doing this morning?"

"I checked the oil. It looks OK."

"Guess we'll see. Let's get this thing started."

Before taking off for Buna, Charlie had another message from Colonel Carmichael. It read, ATTACK JAP BEACHHEAD AT BUNA BAY YOUR DISCRETION.

"Danny, take us up to 13,000 feet," Charlie ordered after they got the wheels and flaps up and turned north. "Heading 058. Make your climb speed 800 feet per minute."

"Roger, pilot, coming to 058, climbing at 800 feet per minute."

"Navigator, pilot."

"Go ahead, Charlie."

"Al, do I need you for this trip?"

"You might need someone on the cheek guns. Or if the weather closes in and we have to divert to Horn Island."

"No sense of humor. I bet you don't even know how long it'll take us to get to Buna."

"Thirty-seven minutes, pilot. That's if you and Mr. Evans keep us on the right heading. Oh, and those are kind of big mountains up ahead. You guys think you can keep us above them?"

"Al, you're such a nag. Danny, you think we can avoid those mountains?"

"Boss, I sure hope so. I don't like flying close to the ground."

"Pilot, left waist. If I get a vote I'm with Mr. Evans."

A chorus of affirmation swept over the intercom. Charlie let it go for a minute, knowing it was his crew's usual way of getting into the groove.

"Crew, pilot."

The chatter died away. "Normally I'd let you guys rattle on, but we'll be near Buna in no time," said Charlie. "No idea what kind of opposition we might face, so keep your eyes open and no chatter over the intercom unless someone sees something important."

A dead-serious chorus of *rogers* came over the intercom. And there it was, Charlie could feel it, the crew drawing together. He looked over at Danny Evans, who looked up from the instruments.

Charlie winked at his copilot, and the quiet, dead-serious Danny Evans smiled for the first time since he joined the crew.

Ten minutes later they leveled out at 13,000 feet, with the peaks of the Owen Stanley Range four thousand feet below. The north coastline of New Guinea was in sight ahead of them.

"Pilot, navigator."

"Go ahead, Al."

"Charlie, make your heading 086 for Oro Bay."

"Roger, Al, coming to 086."

Charlie nodded at Evans, who turned the bomber right until the gyrocompass showed 086. Ahead of them Charlie saw two indents on the coast, little bays or inlets, with the one to the east being Oro Bay. They would maintain this heading until they were almost over the coast, then turn west. When they came over the target they would be traveling parallel to the coastline. That would give them a greater choice of targets. They would turn over Oro Bay, eighteen miles from Buna, and that would give Bob Frye time to set up the Norden sight for the bomb run.

"Pilot, navigator. You got your binoculars?"

"Yeah, Charlie, I'm looking towards the target now. We're too far away to make out any details but I can see smoke."

"Someone hit the target already?"

"No, I think it's from a ship's smokestack. There's not enough smoke for something burning."

"OK, that's probably it. Show it to Bob."

"Skipper, Al and I have been passing the binoculars back and forth. I think I've got a good idea of the coast around Buna."

"Right. OK, gentlemen, we'll be over the coast in a few minutes."

They turned left to 335. Ahead of them Charlie saw a faint smudge of smoke on the horizon.

Buna.

"Pilot, bombardier. We'll call this the IP."

"Understood, bombardier."

Ten minutes.

"BANDITS. Upper turret has bandits, eleven o'clock high, looks like three Zeros."

Charlie looked up and to the left. There they were, inbound but not diving yet, probably checking to see if the B-17 was really alone.

"Pilot, bombardier, opening bomb bay doors."

"Acknowledged, bombardier."

"Crew, here they come!"

Charlie looked up. The Zeros were diving on them.

"Pilot, bombardier, keep it steady."

"Roger, bombardier."

Tracers whipped by the cockpit and ahead of the nose, then Kim Smith in the upper turret opened up. Charlie saw the barrel of the left cheek gun elevate, then Al Stern fired.

Bullets struck aft with a rattle like stones on a tin roof. Charlie heard the waist gunners calling the Zeros passing left to right, then the ball turret fired two bursts.

"Steady, pilot. I see a nice big freighter down there with some barges around it. We're right in line with it."

Flak blossomed around them, bursting above them at first.

"OK, OK. Pilot, bombardier, right, just a hair right. Good, good, hold that."

"Tail gunner has the Zeros coming up astern."

"OK, Em, I see 'em," said Smith. "They're coming in a bit high."

Charlie could see the beachhead. The flak came from a cruiser and a couple of guns ashore. Barges headed to and from the shore to a collection of what looked like freighters. Small boats or barges along the shore discharged men and material.

"OK, five seconds. Steady. Steady...bombs away, closing bomb bay doors."

The tail guns fired, followed a second later by the upper turret. The Zeros flew by overhead, barely clearing the bomber. One of them trailed thin gray smoke. The Zeros kept heading west.

"Navigator, pilot. You guys get any pictures?"

"Yeah, roger, Charlie."

"OK, good. What's our heading for home?"

"Make it 220."

"Roger, turning to 220."

Jimmy looked around the formation of Boxcar P-39s. Major Wolchek had the lead, flying as Boxcar White Leader. Jimmy and the Corncob Blues flew to the right and above the Boxcars.

They passed over the mountains with the north slope rolling down to the coast and the ocean beyond. Straight ahead of them smoke smudged up from a point on the coastline. There was another column of smoke somewhere inland, not far from the beachhead.

The P-39s cruised at 250 mph, and at 13,000 feet Jimmy didn't like that cruise speed at all. The Zero turned on a wingtip at 250 mph, and the P-39 couldn't come close to that kind of performance. The P-39 needed to keep above 300 mph to even begin to be competitive with the Zero. Fifty mph didn't sound like a lot until you tried to reach it with a Zero on your tail.

But at 250 mph it would only be ten minutes to Buna. Jimmy looked around again.

Zeros. The Japs would come down to protect their beachhead. There'd be Zeros around.

"Boxcars, Boxcar White Leader, let's go."

Wolchek's flight started a descent and increased power to their engines. Jimmy was ready for the move and followed smoothly, checking his flight's formation.

Kellerman was on his right as Blue Two. Shafer and Bell as Three and Four were on his left, and all of them were in good formation, close enough to support each other, spread out enough so they had room to maneuver.

Check your fuel, check your gauges, check your weapons. Jimmy's flight, Corncob Blue, carried aux tanks and no bombs, as did Boxcar White flight. Boxcar Yellow and Boxcar Green carried 500-lb bombs. They'd find something worthwhile to bomb and scoot for home before they ran low on gas.

"Boxcar White Leader to Corncob Blue Leader."

"Go ahead, White Leader."

"Jimmy, go to 15 and keep an eye out for Zeros. My flight will circle the target around 10 while the other two flights go in."

"Roger, White Leader. Corncob Blue Leader to flight, follow me."

"Two."

"Three."

"Four."

Jimmy advanced his throttle and pulled back on the stick. At this height the Allison's half-assed supercharging still gave 2000 feet per minute, but that decreased as they climbed. Even so they were at their patrol altitude in a little over a minute. Jimmy checked his oxygen blinker. Below them he could see the other flights descending towards Buna. He glanced towards the beachhead, glimpsed freighters and warships. The warships were firing at the P-39s already, the flak bursting at different altitudes along the path of the inbound Boxcars.

"Bandits! Corncob Blue Three has bandits at nine o'clock high!"

Jimmy snapped over to his left wingtip and looked up. Three, six, nine Zeros.

"Boxcar White Leader, Corncob Blue Leader has nine Zeros inbound, about angels 17, coming from the west."

"Roger, Blue Leader. Nine Zeros at 17."

"Blue Leader to Blue Flight, let's go to full throttle." Jimmy eased back on his stick to gain a little extra altitude and banked toward the Zeros.

One flight of Zeros dove steeply at Jimmy's flight. The others banked left and banked again, angling to intercept the P-39s attacking the beachhead.

"White Leader, six coming your way."

The Zeros came down as Jimmy's flight turned to meet them head-on.

"Blues, pick a target and hold your fire until you're close."

Jimmy picked the lead Zero, holding the pipper over the airplane's canopy. He held his fire as the Zeros started shooting, tracers winking and flashing around them. The Zero was close, too close, and he held the triggers down. The .50s in the nose roared and hammered while the wing-mounted .30s chattered heavily. The 37-mm cannon fired once and jammed. He got strikes around the Zero's cowling and the canopy, then they were past each other. Jimmy looked left and right. All his boys were there and evidently unhurt.

He banked and dove after the Zeros, who were headed down after the rest of the Boxcars. The first six Zeros were already tangled up with Wolchek's Boxcar Whites. The Zeros were curving and swooping, while one element of P-39s dove away. Six Zeros fastened on the other two P-39s, who also dove away, but not until smoke burst from the lead P-39. It shed a wing and tumbled from the sky. The other P-39 twisted wildly and dove vertically, which shook the Zeros off its tail.

"Blue Three, move out to the right, take these guys on the left. Two, stay with me."

"Three!"

"Two!"

The fight got confused. Zeros and P-39s interwove in an aerial basket linked by tracers and laced with smoke and flame. Jimmy reefed in hard and dove down, banking onto the tail of a Zero firing into a P-39. Jimmy fired and got strikes on the Zero's right wing. Pieces flew off and the Zero banked hard to the left.

"Blue Leader, break, break right!"

Jimmy broke hard to the right. Something slammed into the armor plate behind his seat, and machine gun bullets tore into his left wing. He stomped on the rudder and the nose pointed at the ground, speed building rapidly. He looked over his left shoulder and Kellerman was still there. Tracers flew between them and then quit. Jimmy looked to the right and there were the Zeros, three of them falling away behind and to the right.

Jimmy looked at his fuel. Maneuvering with the Zeros at high speed made the Allison engine gulp fuel at a frightening rate. The Zeros broke left and dove towards the other P-39s, down on the deck with dirt and smoke fountaining up from the beachhead where they dropped their bombs.

He pulled out of the dive and rolled left. They were low, and if they were low the one thing they couldn't do was let their airspeed fall off. Jimmy looked at his fuel gauge and gritted his teeth. Maintaining this speed, they could stay maybe five more minutes.

Three Zeros pulled up in front of them, in that impossible rocketing Zero climb, and Jimmy snapped off a burst from his guns that made the Zeros break right but did no other damage.

Then that was it. Antiaircraft fire burst all around them, the Zeros fled to the west, a few trails of smoke marked where airplanes fell from of the sky. To the south Jimmy saw a couple of P-39s exiting the area.

'Two, let's go home," he said.

"Thank Christ," Kellerman said.

Charlie looked up from his report when he heard the snarl of Allison engines overhead. He walked out of his tent and looked up.

The P-39s were coming back. They were in singles and elements, mostly, and one flight of three that either stayed together or reformed on the way back. Several of them trailed smoke and had other signs of damage, shredded ailerons and holes in wings and fuselage.

Charlie watched them come into the pattern and land and taxi up to the 8th's flight line. The first dozen airplanes arrived all at once, then a half-dozen more, and then singles until maybe twenty P-39s in all got back.

He sighed and wondered how the P-39s did over Buna. He had no idea, as usual, how his own bomb run went. They dropped six 500-lb bombs that walked over the freighter and undoubtedly did some damage to the barges alongside, but whether they hit the freighter no one could tell in the geysers of smoke and water thrown up by their bombs. The Zeros came back to play and harassed them until Lefkowicz at the left waist and Smith in the upper turret turned one of the Zeros into a flaming wreck.

Captain Allen came up and saluted. Charlie returned it. "How's it coming?" he asked.

Allen's airplane had an oil pump go out in its No.4 engine. He landed at Seven-Mile while the rest of the 19th Bomb Group went up to Lae.

"We got the engine running, Major. Figured we'd go hit Buna."

"OK. We came at the target from the east. The Japs had ships in the bay. We got flak from the warships and some guns the Japs must have landed overnight. They may have more set up by now. We bombed a freighter but couldn't tell if we hit it. We might have gotten some of the barges alongside the freighter. Three Zeros over the target. By the time you're airborne Carmichael and the rest of the boys should have hit the beachhead. Add to the general confusion and hopefully sink some freighters."

The other pilot nodded. "Did you see the P-39s come in?"

"Yeah. Looked like they lost some guys. That's either bad flak or Zeros or both."

"Right. We'll be careful. What about the rest of the group?"

Charlie shrugged. "They should be here anytime, but you know how that goes. Weather, winds, mechanical problems, change of orders."

"Yeah. OK, see you."

"Good luck."

Charlie watched him go and turned back to his own airplane. On the way in to Seven-Mile the prop governor on No. 2 engine went out. Charlie shut No. 2 down and gave Danny Evans his first lesson in flying a B-17 with one engine out.

Kim Smith stood on a maintenance stand. He was studying the prop governor assembly at the front of the engine.

"What's it look like, Kim?" Charlie called.

"It's a mess, Boss. Bits of gears and metal shavings all over the box. I can't tell about the crankshaft until we get the governor mount off."

"Can you replace the governor?"

"I'm pretty sure they've got replacements in stores here."

Charlie nodded. Without the prop governor, the engine wouldn't maintain constant RPM, and the propeller would go to flat pitch, raising RPMs uncontrollably until the engine came apart.

"All right. You got all that in hand?"

"Yes, sir. If I need anything I'll give you a shout. Give us about two hours."

"OK. Thanks, Kim."

Charlie took off his cap, wiping the sweat from the headband and mopping his brow with his handkerchief.

"Hey, Charlie!"

He looked to the path back to the 19th's Operations shack. Al Stern stood there, beckoning to him.

"What's up, Al?"

"We got a message from the formation. They're on the bomb run. Ten airplanes."

212

"Ten? Wow. When was the last time we had that many airplanes over the target?"

"One of those raids over Balikpapan, back in early February?"

"Yeah, maybe. Damned if I can remember that far back."

Al nodded. "How's No. 2?"

"Kim thinks he might have it ready to go in two hours." Charlie said. "I guess the Colonel didn't have orders for us?"

"No."

"All right." Charlie looked at his watch. It was almost noon. "We can't be out of here before 1400, maybe later. Allen and his boys might be back by then. We go to Mareeba, bomb up, and hit Buna tomorrow from there."

Al nodded. "I'll get the weather at Mareeba and Horn Island."

"OK."

Charlie looked across the runway. The P-39s that made it back from Buna were back in their revetments among the trees. For the moment, it was quiet at Seven-Mile.

Jimmy and Kellerman went up to Operations and met Shafer and Bell on the way.

"How'd you guys do?" Jimmy asked.

Shafer shrugged wearily. He mopped his face with the sleeve of his coveralls. "Damned if I know," he said. "Were there really only nine Zeros?"

"Yeah."

"Looked like a lot more than that. I think I took some hits."

Bell snorted.

"You got a problem, Chinkerbell?" Jimmy asked.

"We coulda had those guys if you'd turned sooner," Bell said.

"Oh?"

"Yeah. Those first three guys, we could've gotten closer sooner if you'd done that."

"OK. You get any strikes?"

"What?"

"Did you even shoot, Chinkerbell? If you did, did you hit anything?"

"Of course I fired!"

"Well, I got some strikes on the leader. Can you claim a damage? Yes or no?"

Bell looked away, scowling.

"Yeah. You tell that to the briefing officer. You fired off a lot of ammo and didn't hit a thing. Do better next time."

Bell shut his mouth.

"Any of you guys know who went in?"

"It was someone in the low flights," Shafer said. "One of the Boxcar Yellows, maybe."

Jimmy nodded. It wasn't the first time he'd seen a P-39 go in.

"Jimmy, can I talk to you for a minute?"

Ed Groves stood there. He held his helmet and Mae West in his hand.

"Sure, Ed," Jimmy said softly. He turned to Shafer. "You guys go on in. I'll be along in a second."

Groves walked away a few paces.

"Who got it?" Jimmy asked.

"Major Wolchek."

"Jesus."

"Yeah."

"Anyone else?"

"Not from the Boxcars. You hit anything?"

"I got some hits. Can't claim more than damage. One Zero left smoking. You?"

"About the same." Groves sighed. "I don't know if Wagner has a replacement in mind. Let's go talk to him about that."

"OK," said Jimmy. "Doesn't that make you acting squadron commander?"

Groves shrugged. "Yeah, for maybe the next ten minutes. Come on."

The Operations shack was filled with excited, chattering pilots, talking as much with their hands as their mouths, while intelligence officers scribbled hurried notes. Jimmy stayed with Ed Groves as they made their way to the corner where Colonel Wagner stood, smoking his pipe. He looked up at Groves.

"Steve went in?" Wagner asked quietly.

"Yeah."

"OK. He was a good man. Ed, I want you to take over the Boxcars for now. That means you'll need an operations officer."

"I brought him with me," Groves said. He put his hand on Jimmy's shoulder. "I thought this character might come in handy."

Wagner shook his head. "Damn, Ardana. D'you even know what an operations officer does?"

215

"Sure. He helps the squadron commander run the squadron."

The colonel shook his head and looked at Groves, who shrugged. "We'll have a little indoctrination session, Colonel."

"OK. Jimmy, Ed knows what he's doing. You listen to him, you'll work out fine."

"Yes, sir."

"Speaking of which, Jimmy, you hit anything today?"

"Just some damage, Colonel."

Wagner nodded. "What did it look like out there?"

"A lot of ships in that bay, maybe thirty or so. Some kind of warships shooting at us, some little ones and a couple of big ones. They had guns on the ground, looked like their usual 25mm and 37mm stuff. Maybe a couple of 57mm guns. Could've been some small arms, but the guys with the bombs can speak more to that. A lot of bomb hits all over the place. One of the ships out in the harbor was smoking, but it might've been smoking before we arrived."

"Any idea how many Japs were ashore?"

"A lot of guys running around like ants down there. Heaps of supplies and a bunch of barges on the beach. I don't know, it was a lot of guys, at least a couple of hundred that I saw, probably more."

Jimmy looked at Ed Groves, who shrugged. "Looked about like that to me," Groves said. "There were some fires four or five miles inland."

"OK. Ed, be sure your boys are ready to go in the morning. It's likely to be a long day."

"We aren't going back up there this afternoon?"

"I'm sending the Brickbats. Tell me, how would you evaluate the Jap fighter opposition? Aggressive? More so than usual?"

"Well..." Jimmy exchanged a look with Groves and frowned. "You know, they didn't seem all that determined. Not like I've seen them be. Not that they weren't ready to collect scalps, but no. Why do you ask?"

"Curiosity as much as anything." Wagner puffed on his pipe. "They tried to come at us by sea back in May, and they were pretty damned serious about it. You guys remember."

"Yeah," said Jimmy slowly. Groves nodded.

"So now they're going to come at us on foot over the god-blessed mountains and what? I hear your buddy Charlie Davis got chased by three Zeros and you guys tangled with nine. This is their big effort to take Port Moresby, and they don't have a patrol in force over the beachhead?" Wagner shook his head. "We know they've got what, at least thirty Zeros at Lae and maybe ten or fifteen at Salamaua? If there were thirty Zeros over Buna we'd have had real losses. It's hard to lose Steve Wolchek, but it could have been so much worse that I wonder why it wasn't."

"What's on the schedule for tomorrow?" Groves asked.

"Oh, tomorrow? Let's see. The 3rd Attack Group is bringing up some dive bombers, the 22nd will stage through here, and I understand the 19th will send another formation of B-17s. So, on and off we're going to have guys heading to Buna all day. The RAAF will probably join in but I've not heard confirmation on that one. Hell, maybe they'll send their Catalinas over during the night, raise some hell among the shipping." Wagner looked critically at the bowl of his pipe, puffed on it until it began to draw again, and pointed the stem at Jimmy. "Plus whatever we can do to help out. Jimmy, you feel like hauling bombs up north tomorrow?"

"Sure."

"Don't be so quick. You haul a bomb up there, you find a target, you drop, you run. You won't have time or fuel for anything else."

"My crew chief asked me if he needed to find some rifles for the rest of my ground crew. I don't want him to have to worry about that. We stop the Japs on the ground and it won't matter what happens in the air."

Wagner's mouth curved into a lopsided grin. "Well, and that is the reality of the situation, isn't it? If the Japs don't get here it won't matter how many we shoot down over Buna. We can bomb hell out of them up there, and as long as we can help the Aussie infantry stop them coming over the mountains, that's what counts."

Chapter Nine

Look at all that smoke

The Corncobs crested the Owen Stanleys, headed for Buna, and descended with the slope of the mountains as they headed for the coast.

Ed Groves was in the lead flight. Today the Boxcars and the Corncobs hauled bombs, while the Brickbats kept climbing. They'd try to reach 19,000 feet before they got to the target area. Jimmy looked left and right and behind and above, then checked his armament panel. The guns and the cannon were ready to go.

Carrying a 500-lb bomb in a P-39 wasn't fun. The airplane changed from a responsive if willful racehorse to a balky nag. The bomb had about the same drag as an aux tank, but it was almost twice as heavy. You couldn't turn with it and you sure as hell couldn't climb with it, and about the only thing the airplane would do worth a crap was dive. It took more power to maintain cruise speed, which meant the Allison drank gas a lot faster. That meant that even though Buna was less than a hundred miles away, the Boxcars would only have enough fuel to reach the target, drop their bombs, and return to base.

Jimmy had dropped bombs once before, at Salamaua last May. He called up the briefing Jack Davis gave them before they left: *keep your eyes open, keep your eyes moving, keep your speed up as you enter and leave the target area, don't get fixated by your target and follow your bomb in, and oh yeah, did I mention to keep your eyes open and moving?*

"Boxcars from Boxcar White Leader, arm 'em up, arm 'em up."

Jimmy took his hand off the throttle and flipped switches on his armament panel. The green light came on signifying that the bomb release was active. He looked left and right, checking his flight.

Bomb the barges on the beach, preferably the ones that haven't offloaded. Don't try to hit the ships in the bay, leave those for the A-24s and the B-26s.

Yesterday there were two or three small fires within five miles of the beach along what Jimmy figured was the track leading up into the foothills and the village of Kokoda. Today the fires of burning villages stretched at least ten miles inland, which meant the Japs were pushing hard and fast to get up the trail and into the mountains.

Jimmy saw ships in the bay, and above them bursting antiaircraft fire. Then there was an explosion on the sea, white water fountaining up near one of the ships. There was another explosion, and a trail of smoke spiraling down from the sky that could only be an airplane stricken by gunfire. The 3rd Attack sent A-24 dive bombers out ahead of them this morning. From the looks of things they were hard at work.

As they closed in on the target Jimmy could hear the chatter from the dive-bomber pilots, broken up with static and distance. Another explosion tossed a geyser of water into the air, and this time dark black smoke followed it. The radio was intermittently loud with static, but for a moment the ether was clear enough to hear a gleeful voice shout "...*look at (skeereeskawk!)*"

By then the P-39s passed the southernmost smoke column from the burning villages. Jimmy looked down as they flew over, noticing Jap infantry among the flaming huts and small buildings.

They followed Boxcar White Leader down low, down barely over the treetops, as they made their run towards the target.

"Hey, P-39s," said a voice over the radio. "Lots of nice barges on the beach, looks like most of 'em are still unloading. Have fun and watch the 25mm stuff, it's murder."

"Thanks, Third," said a voice Jimmy thought was Groves. "We'll try to drop 'em where they'll do some good."

The Boxcars flew low over the track leading to the beach. Jimmy remembered what the Aussie Army officer said yesterday about Buna being swampy. The ground below was dappled with ponds and meandering streams and trees.

From somewhere below a machine gun opened up, twin streams of tracer dancing among them for a couple of seconds, then it fell behind and there was Buna. You could tell for sure because the light antiaircraft, the 25mm stuff, crisscrossed the air with tracer all around. The beach was ahead and on the beach, barges with their ramps down and boxes and bales stacked in front of them.

"Boxcar White has the barges to the west, Corncob Blue take the barges to the east. Strafe the barges in the water, then turn for home."

"Corncob Blue taking the barges to the east," Jimmy acknowledged.

The barges were just ahead. Something smashed into his right wing, tossing him up. Jimmy wrestled the wing back in line and dropped his bomb in among the barges, riding the lift and the improved bite of the controls as the P-39 accelerated, looking quickly left and right to see that his flight was still with him. Over his shoulder he caught glimpses of smoke and fire behind them on the beach. Dust and smoke gouted into the air as their bombs exploded. Tracer reached out from all around them, and he kicked the rudder furiously, looking at a pair of barges coming up fast. He picked the lead barge and snapped off bursts that walked right up to the barge as he triggered the cannon. The 37mm fired six miraculous rounds, and three struck the barge at the waterline as the splashes from his .50 and .30-cal. guns walked over it.

"Corncob Blues, break right, break right, stay low."

Look left, look right, look above and behind; the lead barge was smoking and someone had hit the barge behind it, which was also smoking. As the flight curved around another barge came across Jimmy's path. The 37mm jammed but there was nothing wrong with his machine guns. Tracers reached past him from the left and the right, and someone's 37mm was still working well enough to lob two shells into the barge. Then they were over the beach and exiting to the southeast. Jimmy looked at his fuel, gritted his teeth while knowing fuel consumption shouldn't be too bad on the way home, if the Zeros didn't come out to play.

He looked over his shoulder again. A half-dozen barges burned or smoked along the beach, and he saw at least one barge sinking in the bay and another three smoking heavily. Barge-hunting, hell, if the armorers could figure out how to keep that damned cannon from jamming, barge-hunting might turn into something the P-39 could do well.

"Wow," said Danny Evans. "Look at all that smoke."

Charlie nodded, looking ahead over the nose of the B-17. Then he looked left and right to check the formation.

Bronco Buster II flew as Primrose Four on this mission, which put them in the lead slot in the high squadron. Colonel Carmichael himself flew in the lead airplane, Primrose One, at the head of the formation.

Like the rest of the 19th Bomb Group, the evening before Charlie had been treated to a Colonel Carmichael almost weeping with frustration and rage when he found out that the ten B-17s he put over Buna yesterday, ten bombers carrying a total of 72 500-lb bombs, achieved exactly nothing because, apparently, the lead bombardier released too early and the formation released on his cue. So somewhere to the east of Buna there was a nice tight pattern of 72 bomb craters that did nothing but stir up the swamp and blow down some mangrove trees.

Charlie understood the Colonel's feelings, but talking it over with Bob Frye, his own bombardier, gave him a different perspective.

223

"Wonder what the Colonel's bombardier found to line up on?" Frye asked. "I lucked out, after all, and that freighter was in line with our heading and I had its smoke for an aiming point. Hell, skipper, this isn't like bombing Vunakanau or the docks at Rabaul. A B-17 isn't a dive bomber, after all. You have to have something to aim the Norden at, and without preliminary reconnaissance and some sort of target photos, well, hitting something useful is luck as much as skill."

Now, as the formation flew down the coast west of Buna, Charlie wondered if the formation was about to repeat the same performance as the larger formation turned in yesterday. In short, piss poor. Hopefully they'd hit *something*, but on this course Charlie couldn't even guess what the bombardier in Carmichael's airplane picked for an aim point.

"Bombardier, pilot."

"Go ahead, skipper."

"Bob, can you see what the lead airplane is aiming at?"

"Me? Skipper, when Joey up there in the Colonel's airplane opens his bomb bay doors, I'm going to open mine, and when he drops his bombs I'm gonna flip the toggle."

Charlie shook his head. "Understood, bombardier."

It wasn't Frye's fault. At the mission briefing Charlie raised the issue of formation bombing, and asked if the bombardiers could drop independently. That question had been slapped down politely but firmly by Carmichael.

Ahead of them flak burst, a little low, but the next volley was dead on their altitude. *Yeah, this'll be fun*, Charlie thought, watching the dark deadly flowers.

"Bombardier, radio operator. Primrose One says open bomb bay doors."

"Acknowledged, Sparks."

Behind the flight deck the bomb bay doors rumbled open and the slipstream howled into the fuselage. The flak started bursting inside and around the formation, and Charlie heard shrapnel pinging and rattling through the fuselage. Something smashed through the cockpit window on Danny's side and exited behind Charlie.

"Co-pilot, you OK?"

"Ah, yes, sir. Just startled me."

"Don't worry, you won't get used to it."

"Gee, thanks, pilot."

Charlie grinned even though he felt the adrenaline in his blood. He took a deep breath of oxygen.

"Bombardier, radio operator. Primrose One says to prepare to drop on his mark. Three. Two. One. MARK."

Bronco Buster II carried six 500-lb bombs in the bomb bay. Charlie held the bomber steady as the bombs fell free.

He still couldn't see what the lead bombardier aimed at.

"Bombardier, pilot. What was the aim point?"

"There's a couple of ships close together, skipper, and I think that's what Joey picked to drop on. I think, anyway."

"OK, thanks, Bob. Tail gunner, ball turret, let us know if we hit anything."

"Roger, boss."

"Sure thing, skipper."

"Pilot, radio operator."

"Go ahead, Sparks."

"Primrose One says to head for the barn."

Ahead of them Carmichael's B-17 turned to the south. Charlie followed along as the formation wheeled to the south.

"Pilot, tail gunner."

"Go ahead, Em."

"Boss, there are two freighters with one hell of a lot of splashes around them. Looks like we chewed up some barges but I don't think we hit the freighters."

"You're kidding."

"Wish I was, skipper."

"Well, Jehosophat. OK, thanks, Em."

Danny Evans looked at Charlie. Then he looked back at the instrument panel and checked the gauges. Charlie shook his head.

The B-17 had a reputation for being big and bad and smashing everything in its path, and the truth was that this reputation needed interpretation. The B-17 was a weapon, and like any weapon, had to be employed properly for maximum effect. Charlie had his own opinion about how the B-17 should be employed, and he wasn't sure this mission conformed to that opinion. Because Bob Frye was right, the Norden bombsight was both the strength and the weakness of the B-17 as a weapon. Against moving ships and small targets it would take too many B-17s to be effective, when dive-bombers and fighter-bombers could pick their targets and put bombs on them.

And Danny wouldn't know that, because he wasn't trained to fly bombers the way Charlie had been, almost from the day he won his wings.

"Pilot, navigator."

"Go ahead, Al."

"Charlie, formation is taking up heading 215."

"OK. And?"

"And I don't know. 215 isn't the heading for Mareeba."

"OK. And?"

"Charlie, it isn't even a heading corrected for wind. It also isn't a heading for Horn Island."

"Al, are you trying to tell me the lead navigator is taking us the wrong way?"

"Yes, sir."

Charlie raised an eyebrow. The 'sir' business was a little unusual for Al.

"OK, Al, you've got my attention. What's up?"

"That's the problem, Charlie. The navigation briefing has us on a direct heading from Buna back to Mareeba. That's a magnetic heading of 199."

"What's the wind?"

"I took a drift reading while we set up the bomb run. There isn't any wind, so it's not a wind correction."

Charlie shook his head. A wind from the west could require a course correction of sixteen degrees. Without any such wind, over the 590 miles from Buna to Mareeba, it was a sixteen-degree error in heading that could put them way out of position at a time when they'd have a lot less fuel to look for a landing spot.

And what if a wind came from the east, blowing them further off course?

"OK. Radio operator, pilot."

"Go ahead, skipper."

"Ask Primrose One to confirm formation heading."

"Roger." There was a pause. "Pilot, radio operator. Primrose One confirms 215."

"OK, thanks, Sparks."

Danny Evans looked at Charlie and raised an eyebrow. Charlie shook his head. Without removing their oxygen masks, inadvisable at 24,000 feet, or speaking over the intercom, there was no way to conduct a private conversation. Charlie knew what Danny wanted to ask was some variant of, *what's going on?*

Danny didn't know Al Stern, but Charlie did. And as far as Charlie was concerned, Al Stern was one of the best navigators in the Air Corps, and if Al said the course was wrong, it was wrong.

"Al, what heading should we take?"

"199, repeat, 199."

"Radio operator, pilot. Get me on voice to Primrose One."

"Roger, pilot." There was a pause. Charlie looked over the nose of the bomber at Primrose Two and Primrose One.

"Skipper, I've got Primrose One on voice. Go ahead."

"Primrose One, this is Primrose Four, come in."

Carmichael's voice crackled over the radio. "Go ahead, Four."

228

"Primrose One, recommend we come to a heading of 199."

There was silence for a moment but for the crackle of static. The moment stretched.

"Primrose One to formation, come to heading 199."

Carmichael turned to 199 as the formation turned with him, and droned on over the peaks of the Owen Stanley Mountains.

Charlie settled into his seat.

He was sure that last transmission from Primrose One was only the beginning. Lousy bombing and lousy navigation with Carmichael leading the formation meant there had to be a shakeup in the 19th.

Jimmy sat with Ed Groves in the tent Groves had shared with Steve Wolchek, looking at the squadron papers. Sgt. Dowell sat with them by the light of a gas lantern.

"The truth is, Jimmy," Groves said, "Sgt. Dowell here runs this end of the squadron."

"Respectfully, Captain, that's not quite true," Dowell protested.

"I remember someone telling me that officers might give orders, but it's the sergeants who really run things," Jimmy said.

Groves looked at him, amused. "Who told you that, Jimmy? Last name wouldn't happen to be Davis, would it?"

"Yes, sir, but it was actually Major Davis who told me that."

"That's right. He's West Point, isn't he? Probably make general before the war is over, or full colonel at the very least. If he lives long enough."

Dowell shook his head. "Pardon me, sirs, but maybe we should get on with the paperwork."

"See, Jimmy? Diplomacy, but unwavering focus," said Groves.

Dowell gave an exaggerated sigh conveying unlimited forbearance. Jimmy laughed.

"Let's get to work," Jimmy suggested. "I have a lot to learn."

For the next two hours Dowell brought out requisitions, inventories, engineering reports, officer fitness reports, and other minutiae related to the day to day running of a squadron. Jimmy found it boring and fascinating by turns. The columns of figures at first blurred in front of his eyes, then, when he found that the squadron had on hand only four brand-new Allison engines, still in the manufacturer's crates, the job started to make sense to him.

Don Terraine, Jimmy's crew chief, had grumbled that the engine in Jimmy's P-39 had close to one hundred hours on it. That engine needed to be replaced or undergo a complete overhaul. And if the engine wasn't available, or was being overhauled, then *Gremlin II* was grounded. That meant one less P-39 that the squadron could put over Buna.

"Sergeant, how do we get more engines?" Jimmy asked.

"Here are the forms, sir," said Dowell. "What I hear is the engines are in Australia, but we can't have them."

230

"Are those sonsofbitches conducting inventory again?" Jimmy asked.

"Couldn't say, sir," Dowell replied. "But look at the date on these invoices. And you'll notice this is a fourth request."

Jimmy leaned back. "I wonder how many Allisons we could get in a C-47?" he wondered aloud.

"You thinking about another Colt requisition, Jimmy?" asked Groves.

"Doesn't look like we're gonna get those engines through normal channels," Jimmy said. "Fourth request, my ass. Those bastards are sitting down there with all the cold beer and sheilas they can handle, and here we are at Seven-Mile eating M&V and being bombed and strafed."

Groves sighed. "Dowell, before Jimmy the Kid here goes on a rampage, maybe we could write a letter with a fifth requisition attached, and copy commanding general, FEAF. Maybe General Brett can build a fire under them. We'll get Colonel Wagner to endorse it and if we're having trouble, I bet the other squadrons are too."

Dowell nodded, scribbling a note. "I'll draft the letter for your signature, sir."

When he was done writing, Dowell looked up and said, "Either of you hear anything about this new general coming out to take over from Brett?"

Jimmy looked at Groves. "New general?" he asked.

"What d'you know, Dowell?" Groves asked.

"Just the name. Kenney, George C. Oh yeah, he flew in the last war."

231

Groves frowned. "I think he was running 3rd Air Force on the West Coast. We passed through San Francisco on the way here and I remember seeing his name on some stationery."

"Wagner probably knows something about him," Dowell said.

"When does he take over?" Jimmy asked.

"I don't know, Mr. Ardana," Dowell said. "Pretty soon, though."

"If he takes over tomorrow, do we get new engines the next day?" asked Jimmy.

"I doubt it, Mr. Ardana," Dowell replied.

"Then what good is he?"

"He's a general."

"Then I'll stand to attention and salute if I ever meet him. In the meantime, we need engines." Jimmy brooded, looking at the requisition, and shook his head. "Captain, you think writing a letter will do any good?"

"Who knows? By the way, Jimmy, call me Ed. In private, anyway."

Dowell rose. "Gentlemen, I think we've done all the damage we can for one evening. I'll get started on that letter, and I'll bring the reports for you to sign in the morning."

"Thanks, Sarge."

Dowell left. Jimmy watched him go and turned to Groves. "Ed, why can't I imagine calling Dowell anything but 'Sarge' or 'Sergeant'?"

"Because it's set up that way from the first day of flight school, Jimmy. Who chased your ass all over Kelly Field? Who taught you to march? Who taught you how to make a bed? Who taught you how to stand at attention? Who..."

"All right, all right!" Jimmy raised his hands in mock surrender. "Point taken."

"Here," said Groves. He reached into a drawer and came out with a bottle full of amber liquid and two glasses. "Want a snort?"

"Sure. Thanks. What is it?"

"Label says it's whisky. Do you believe everything you read?"

Groves poured. Jimmy accepted a glass and clinked with him. They drank.

"We're getting new airplanes," Groves said. "Well, sort of."

"Sort of?"

"Ever hear of a P-400?"

"No."

"It's the export version of the P-39, built for the RAF. They didn't like it and sent it back to the Air Corps. It has a 20-mm cannon instead of the 37-mm, and, if I remember right, uses an RAF type low-pressure oxygen system. Other than that, it's still the same old P-39."

"Is that 20-mm cannon more reliable than that damned 37-mm?"

"Supposed to be."

"Flatter trajectory, too. But the airplane is still nearly useless above 15,000 feet." Jimmy scowled. "Holy Jesus, Ed, RAF-reject airplanes and replacement engines held up in the rear for inventory. Who are we fighting, the Japs or the supply folks?"

"Both, I guess."

Jimmy shook his head, tossed off his drink, and stood up. "Guess I'd better hit the rack. See you in the morning, Ed."

"Yeah, see you. Hey, Jimmy."

"What?"

"Steve told me you did some mountain flying, once upon a time."

"Sure. My Uncle Kurt and I did fire spotting in the Rockies and took hunting parties in wherever there was a long flat meadow. Why?"

"If the Japs get to Kokoda they'll be in the foothills of the Owen Stanleys. If they get any further south than that, we're going to be flying in those mountains. You might want to remember any little tricks you picked up."

Jimmy nodded slowly. "That's not going to be any fun, Ed. We're going to lose a lot of guys to the mountains, maybe as much as to the Japs. And we're going to need those god-damned replacement engines, because flying in the mountains wears engines out."

"I can see that. Go get some sleep, Jimmy."

Jimmy sketched off a salute and walked up the path to Tent 7.

Kellerman was sitting on his bunk reading a letter when Jimmy arrived.

"Mail for you," he said, pointing at Jimmy's bunk, where two envelopes lay.

"Thanks," he said.

One letter from his grandma, which made him smile, and one from Laura Sue Gibbons, which made him grin. He opened the one from his grandmother first.

"Well, I'll be damned," he said after reading the first two paragraphs.

"Bad news?" Kellerman asked.

"No, not at all. Just a letter from my grandma. Made a point of telling me about this girl back home."

Kellerman nodded and went back to his letter. Jimmy finished reading his grandma's letter and opened the letter from Laura Sue. He figured the letter he'd written last week was still in Australia, so this letter wasn't a reply to anything he'd sent. It was full of news from home, about people they both knew, boys who had joined up and left town, the new rationing, a comment about the President – Laura Sue was a big fan of FDR – and she ended by saying,

> *I took a job volunteering with the local war bond drive. It's useful work but I'm wondering if I should do something more important. Well, more directly useful than war bonds, but I don't think I'm cut out to be a nurse. I don't mind a little blood come hunting season, but the idea of carrying bedpans doesn't seem appealing.*
>
> *Any thoughts? Anyway, take care of yourself and drop me a line or six whenever you can.*
>
> *Laura Sue*

Jimmy chuckled and picked up his grandmother's letter again to reread the part about Laura Sue: *That young lady took over the bond drive and raised $4000 for the war effort. Right determined, she is. Asked the bond chairman how much of that would go to the Air Corps and didn't like it much when he told her he didn't know, but maybe a quarter of it. She got me aside last time I was in town with your mother and asked us so many questions about you I thought I better let you know. If we were face to face I'd give you the Grandma's wink about that young lady.*

Kellerman set his own letter down and looked at Jimmy. "Must be good news from home."

"Oh, my pen pal raised a lot of money for the war effort."

"That's a blitzkrieg for sure," Kellerman said drily. "Got to be a girl in there somewhere."

"Why a girl?"

"Nobody gets a goofy grin like that over a letter from home unless there's a girl involved. Mom and Dad just don't have that effect."

"Well, there is a girl, but she's just a pen pal. She writes to a lot of guys from home. Building morale."

Kellerman laughed. "Jimmy, you're a better pilot than I am, and you're probably going to end up saving my life again, so let me pay a little of that forward by asking one simple question. Do you know for sure she's writing to anyone else?"

Jimmy blinked. "She said she was."

"Well, could she just *say* she was writing to you and you alone? Did you two date in high school or something?"

"No. I know who she is, but that's it. Doubt I've ever more than said hello to her."

"So, there you are. Now tell me this. If she had said oh, Jimmy, Jimmy, I love you and please wait for me and I'll wait for you or things like that, what would you have done?"

Jimmy thought about that. "I guess I wouldn't have answered her letter."

"Yeah. Now, what do you know about this girl from her letters?"

"She's keeping me informed with bits and pieces about home. How did she put it? So that if things changed it wouldn't be so much of a surprise when I got back home."

"Supportive. Very good. Anything else?"

"She's thinking about doing something for the war effort. Besides raising money."

"Patriotic. Also very good. What else?"

"She talks to my grandmother."

"Mm. So she likes your family, or at least she's smart enough to cultivate them. What does your family think about her?"

"My grandma likes her. Said she was sensible and a hard worker. And right determined." Jimmy hesitated, wondering about his grandma saying she'd give him "the wink" over Laura Sue.

Grandma's wink was a lot of things, but mostly it was amused approval.

"Tell me about your grandmother."

"She's a pioneer woman, and..."

Kellerman held up his hand. "So, hard-working, sensible, plans ahead, all those pioneer values."

"Pretty much. And more."

"And more. Your grandmother's looking out for you, and she wants someone that reflects her own values."

"Ah...I guess." Jimmy thought about that. He grinned. "I love Grandma, but she's kind of, well..."

"Formidable."

"Good word. The family legend is, the day she met my grandfather, she shot him in the leg to keep him from shooting my great-grandfather."

Kellerman stared at him. "Wow. Shakespeare would love your family. Can't decide if it's 'Love's Labor Lost' or 'The Taming of the Shrew.'"

"You an English major?"

"No, history. Mostly English history, so reading Shakespeare kind of gives a spin on that."

Jimmy blinked. His own two years in college were spent studying mechanical engineering, with a little animal husbandry on the side. He read enough English literature to satisfy his professors, but without a lot of interest.

"Why do you like that stuff?" Jimmy asked.

Kellerman shrugged. "Literature and history can tell you a lot about people. I don't say I read your girl or your family right, but I'd be surprised if I were too far wrong. People don't seem to change that much from one century to the next."

"OK. I can buy that." Jimmy studied Kellerman. "I don't get it."

"What?"

"You're a bright guy. How can you be so stupid?"

Kellerman blinked. "You mean, the way I fly?"

238

"For starters."

"I'm doing my best."

"That's what scares me."

"What does flying have to do with intelligence?"

"Everything, since you're a pilot, flying an airplane like the P-39. You've got to be able to put a lot of pieces together at once, turn them into single process. You're making progress. Not enough."

"I see that. Now that you point it out. Not only that, but I see it's something I'm blind to, at least for now. So I need you, Jimmy."

"That's sort of blunt."

"Like you said, I'm a bright guy. I know my limitations. I know how to fight them."

"What do you want?"

"Teach me. Teach me to be a pursuit pilot. Like I said the other day, I want to make a difference. It's not dying I mind so much as the idea of dying without making a difference."

"I can't promise you that. You know where we're going tomorrow. You've seen enough to know it can be a crap shoot."

"Yes."

"OK, then."

"OK?"

"Sure. It's my job anyway. I'm you're flight commander."

"Then what did I spend all this time asking you for?"

Jimmy laughed. "You said it yourself, Kellerman. You're a bright guy, but you're not that bright."

239

From outside the tent came a burst of song. A moment later Shafer and Bell came in. Shafer promptly stumbled across the wooden floor of the tent and collapsed face down in his bunk.

Bell sat on the edge of his. He had a bottle of beer in his hand and he put it to his lips, drinking in great gulps until it was empty. He tossed the bottle out of the tent and belched.

"So," he said. "What have you ladies been talking about?"

Chapter Ten

Little Jap bastards are getting close

Charlie stood in front of Colonel Carmichael's desk, came to attention, and saluted.

"Major Charles Davis reporting as ordered, sir," he barked.

Carmichael sighed with exasperation and returned the salute. "Damn it, Charlie, relax and sit down."

"Yes, sir." Charlie sat down.

"OK, Charlie, spill. Is your navigator that good?"

"Yes, sir."

"Then why isn't he a lead navigator?"

"Then he's your navigator, sir, not mine, and I want to keep him."

"That may not be your choice."

"You're the group commander, sir, but permit me to point out that Lt. Stern and I are a team, like my whole crew is a team. I don't want to lose any of them."

"Even your copilot? You tend to go through copilots."

"Lt. Evans is coming along. I'd like to keep him as long as I can."

Carmichael scowled. "What are you telling me, Charlie? That if I take one man off your crew they all fall apart? That doesn't say a lot about you as airplane commander."

"No, sir, I'm not saying that at all." Charlie thought about it. "You had some good navigators when you commanded the 435th Recon. I heard you weren't receptive to Colonel Connally wanting to shift your

241

navigators around to the 82nd or the 30th. And my crew does a lot of solo recon work, Colonel. I need a good navigator, and I trust Lt. Stern. With my life. With my airplane, and my crew. On every mission."

"Damn it, Charlie," Carmichael started. Then the Colonel leaned back in his chair. He said quietly, "Things are different on this side of the desk."

"Sir?"

"You've made your point, Charlie, and you get to keep Lt. Stern. The truth is you're one of the most valuable officers I have, and sure as hell one of the best airplane commanders, if not the best. There's something you might want to know, though." Carmichael clasped his hands on his desk and looked at them for a moment before looking up at Charlie. "The FEAF is going to be the 5th Air Force, soon, and it's going to have a new commanding general, George Kenney. Ever heard of him?"

"Only by reputation. Been around since the first war. One of General Mitchell's crowd, before and after Mitchell was court-martialed."

Carmichael snorted. "Yeah. He's got a reputation as a real operator. I hear he's in Australia, but he hasn't taken over from Brett, yet. That'll be soon. There's something else that might be soon. Remember when I told you that the 19th would get rotated out?"

Charlie blinked and sat up a little straighter. "Yes, sir."

"Starting in September, is the word."

"Wow."

"Yeah. That brings me to my next point. What happens to your crew when we rotate back to the

States? They'll be broken up for cadre, turned into instructors. And you, Charlie. What d'you think will happen to you?"

"I don't…I haven't thought about it."

"No, you haven't. Because you're too busy doing your job. You haven't had the 82nd more than a week, Charlie, but you're doing a good job. When we rotate back to the States you'll probably get your own bomb group within six months, probably less. So we're going to put crews together and take them apart who knows how often in the next couple of years. You might want to think about that, and now let's change the subject."

"Yes, sir."

"Our bombing on the last two missions was piss poor, Charlie. What can we do about that?"

"Colonel, when we bomb we have to have a point to aim at. That works fine when it comes to bombing docks or factories or even ships at anchor, but not so good on targets that are dispersed or moving."

Carmichael nodded slowly. "What if we had two or three groups? Full strength groups, I mean."

"Sixty airplanes over a target? Jehosophat, Colonel, if we could put sixty airplanes over that beachhead with a full bomb load in each airplane, we'd…"

"We'd what?"

"We'd kill a lot of Japs, burn up a lot of their supplies, sink some ships. Sixty B-17s!" Charlie shook his head. "Seems like a fairy tale. Maybe they'll do it in Europe."

"Maybe. In the meantime, how can we do our job better?"

243

"Stop trying to hit that damned beachhead. Let's put the group over Rabaul, or even Lae and Salamaua. Bomb the hell out of the harbors and airstrips. We're strategic bombers, let's go after strategic targets. That's what we're supposed to be doing."

Carmichael nodded. "Yeah. Wonder if Kenney will go for that."

"You think he's bringing any bomb groups with him?"

"Doubtful. Be nice, though." Carmichael grinned sourly. "So I need to tell General Brett, next time he wants us to go to Buna, that we should go to Rabaul instead?"

"Brett probaby gets his orders from MacArthur. I guess if Brett says go to Buna that's what MacArthur wants, so that's what we do."

"Yeah. So how do we do that better?"

"Let's go through the reconnaissance pictures of the beachhead, see if we can get some idea of where they're placing supplies or bivouacking troops before they send them down the Track. Problem right now is we only have two days' worth of recon photos. I don't know if there's enough information to be useful."

Carmichael nodded slowly. "Or we take the chance of keeping a contingent of B-17s up at Seven-Mile where they can strike the beachhead quickly if a worthwhile target shows up."

"When will we get an adequate stockpile of bombs up there? That might be the one thing that would help most."

"Ask the Navy." Carmichael scowled. "OK, Charlie, why don't you round up the recon photos and

244

see what you can come up with. We'll probably head down there again in a day or two. But we're going to need maintenance on the airplanes before we can stage another maximum effort mission."

"Yes, sir."

Charlie looked at the chart of the north coast of Papua New Guinea and the dozen recon photos spread out beside it. Al Stern and Bob Frye arranged the photos by orienting them with magnetic north as shown on the chart. When they were done they stood and looked at the photos.

"So the problem is finding an aim point, or a series of aim points, that lets us achieve a useful bomb pattern," said Frye.

"That's right," said Charlie.

"Well, hell," said Frye. He looked at the pictures. They showed the same strip of beach, with the little cape to the east of the beachhead and the stream and the strip of land where the Aussies had an airstrip before the war, in among the swamp and the marshy hummocks and the mangrove trees.

"The geography will be constant," said Stern. Frye nodded absently. He looked at the concentration of ships in the bay.

"They have to get close to the beach to unload their cargo," Frye said. "Look. The white lines, those are wakes of Jap barges, going to and from the beach."

"Yeah," said Charlie. "Look. Are those camouflage nets, or trees?"

"How the hell do I know?" Frye asked. "They're close to the beach. Look at the old recon photo, here, this one. There isn't a grove of trees like that. So it's probably camouflage."

"Right," said Charlie softly. "OK. And that picture is from the mission yesterday?"

Frye nodded.

"Sure as hell we didn't hit that," said Charlie. "But that's not the problem. So they're bringing up the cargo from the beach, they're storing it here, how do we interfere with that?"

Al Stern used his thumb to measure distances. "It's about 1000 yards in from the beach," he said. "It was there late on the 22nd, it was there about midafternoon on the 23rd. We could always try to hit it again."

"Take a SW to NE orientation," said Frye. "We could hit that storage whatever it is and continue the bomb pattern out among the barges and the shipping near to shore."

Charlie nodded slowly. "OK. So where's a good aim point? You don't really want the storage depot to be the aim point."

Al pointed to a clump of trees. "You think you can spot this, Bob?"

Frye scoffed. "A clump of trees in among a couple dozen other clumps?"

He studied the other photos. The bombardier frowned and went back to the photos and the chart.

"Well..." he started.

"Yeah," he said after another minute of study. "Maybe. But hell and damnation, Charlie, it's no sure thing. You've looked through the scope on a Norden bombsight. It's not much of a field of view. You pick out what you hope to hell is the aim point, you slave the

246

gyros to it, you open the bomb bay doors, and if you picked the right point you'll put your bombs on target. Otherwise..."

Frye shook his his head.

"You got a better idea?" Charlie asked.

"Sure. Let's go home. Baseball season starts pretty soon. I like the Yankees."

"Dimwit. Everyone likes the Yankees."

Pillars of smoke rose further inland from Buna. Jimmy looked down at the grass strip near a collection of native huts he'd been told was the village of Kokoda, and from the look of the smoke along the trail from Buna to Kokoda, the Japs were more than halfway there. But even at a distance of twenty miles you could see ships in the little bay at Buna, and smoke rose there as well. Jimmy knew the A-24s from the 3rd Attack headed out early in the morning, followed by six B-26 Marauders from the 22nd Bomb Group a half-hour later.

Today the Corncobs were on a barge hunt. There weren't any docks at Buna, nor anywhere for a sea-going vessel to tie up and discharge cargo, so the Japs landed men and supplies using barges and lighters shuttling back and forth from the ships anchored in deep water out in Buna Bay. The Brickbats would stay high and try to keep the Zeros off the Boxcars and the Corncobs.

Good luck with that, Jimmy thought.

Then they were past the smoke and down above the treetops, low enough to send the upper leaves and branches tossing in their wake. The treetops thinned out and they flew over the swamps, and ahead on the trail they saw a column of infantry.

"Corncobs, check the infantry on the trail dead ahead," he radioed. "Strafe 'em as we go by."

A chorus of rogers came over the radio. Jimmy checked his armament panel and climbed a little. A few tracers whipped by. The infantry saw them and dove off the trail, into the bush on either side. Jimmy started firing, working the rudder a little so his pursuit yawed from side to side, raking the trail and the bush. He pulled up and then they were over the beachhead, light flak bursting around them, with the white waves breaking on the beach with the green shallows and the blue ocean beyond.

There were barges everywhere, and the Corncobs split into elements, turning with their wingtips just above the waves, geysers of water kicking up from their bullets as they walked their fire into the barges. Off to Jimmy's right a barge exploded in a globe of dirty yellow fire, with flaming bits arcing up into the air. He found a barge headed towards the beach, coming at it head on, and concentrated his fire into the ramp at the front of the barge. White water danced and spouted around the ramp, tracers ricocheted off the steel, then Jimmy was up and over the barge, looking left to check on Kellerman, a quick glance at his instrument panel, then fired into another barge. They banked right to avoid the gunfire of a Jap destroyer, then they were headed back towards the beach, shooting at the barges again. Thirty crazy seconds and they were back over the beach with tracer flying around them.

"Corncob Blue Leader, Corncob Blue Three is hit."

"Three, this is Lead. How bad?"

"Losing oil pressure."

"Right. Think you can make Kokoda?"

"I'll sure try like hell."

"Go on, then, we'll be right behind you. Four, stay with Three."

"Roger, Lead."

"Blue Two, this is Lead, stay with me."

"On your left, Lead."

Jimmy watched as Shafer headed south towards Kokoda with Bell right behind him. They were beyond the beachhead now and no one was shooting at them, or at least there wasn't any tracer in the air. The Boxcars were buzzing around the beach and the bay. A half-dozen barges burned and the air over the bay was filled with smoke from the burning barges and bursting anti-aircraft, most of it too high. Jimmy looked up and caught a glimpse of the Brickbats flying high cover.

To the south Jimmy saw two airplanes, their olive-drab paint barely visible against the jungle greens, and he turned after them. Shafer and Bell were on a direct course to Kokoda; Jimmy flew back over the trail, looking for any groups of Jap infantry dumb enough to stay in the open where they could be seen and strafed.

"Lead from Two."

"Go ahead, Two."

"See that smoke at two o'clock? Look kind of dense to you?"

Jimmy checked his fuel. "Let's have a look."

The trail wasn't a road, and it meandered with the contours of the land. Ahead of them was a village, and the village was on fire. They climbed to get a better view.

It looked like two bodies of troops down there, slugging it out in the burning village, but the only way Jimmy knew that was from the bodies scattered here and there, and small explosions he figured were from bursting grenades.

"Lead from Two, how can we tell who's wearing the white hats?"

"Damned if I know, Two. See the trail headed north?"

"Roger."

"Let's go down a little way."

Jimmy banked north. The trail to the village was shaded over in places by the trees and bush. Then a stream of tracer swept by them.

"Two, did you see where that tracer came from?"

"Yeah, I think so."

"OK, you've got the lead, put us over the spot. We'll make one pass."

Jimmy eased back on Kellerman's right wing and followed him through a tight turn.

"Up ahead not far...SHIT!"

A dozen ropes of tracer arced and danced up at them. It seemed to come from one spot, and Jimmy nosed over, firing into the trees. It didn't seem to affect the volume of fire coming up at them and in three seconds he was past the Jap machine guns and headed towards the village.

"Two, you OK?"

"I think so. Sorry about that, I wasn't expecting it."

"Roger. Let's get out of here. I've got the lead."

"Roger."

Kellerman slid back on Jimmy's wing and they went south again. In ten minutes they were over Kokoda and circled once over the grass field. A P-39 was off the runway, being pushed by a dozen Aussies, who looked up and waved as Jimmy flew overhead, rocking his wings.

"That's an awfully short field," said Kellerman.

"Yeah, no kidding." Jimmy looked south towards the mountains, but there was no sign of Bell. "OK, I don't like my fuel state. Let's go home."

Bell was waiting for them, which surprised Jimmy.

"Did you guys fly over Kokoda?" he asked.

"Yeah. Looked like Shiela got down OK," Jimmy said.

"I didn't think he'd make it. Little field like that, I wasn't sure a Piper Cub could get in and out of it."

"That's probably how they'll get him back," said Kellerman. "If the Japs don't get to Kokoda first and he ends up walking over the mountains with the Aussies."

"Screw that," said Jimmy. "Come on."

Ed Groves stood in the door to the Operations shack.

"Where's Shafer?" he asked.

"At that little strip near Kokoda," Jimmy said. "He got his ship down OK. When we flew over it the Aussies were pushing it out of the way, so he couldn't have banged it up much."

"Engine trouble?"

Jimmy nodded. "Took a hit over the beach and started losing oil pressure."

251

Groves frowned. "Damn. Wonder if we could get a C-47 in and out of that strip."

"We got a C-47 handy?"

"Maybe. You boys get through debrief, then we'll go see the Colonel."

A half hour later Wagner nodded as Jimmy finished his account of Kokoda. The Colonel packed his pipe, lit it, and puffed on it before answering.

"Let's see if we can find an adventurous C-47 crew, and then we'll get Captain McCormick over here to find out what he can tell us about that little strip at Kokoda," Wagner said. "We can fly some stuff in for the Aussies. How far from Kokoda was that village where you saw fighting, Jimmy?"

"Ten, maybe twelve miles, sir."

Wagner shook his head. "Damn Japs have been coming up the track at about ten miles a day. They could be in Kokoda in another day or two."

The Colonel picked up his phone. "Sergeant Kleist? Yeah, send someone after Chief Halloran. Ask him to get up here quick as he can."

Jimmy said, "You think we can get that P-39 out of there, Colonel?"

Wagner shrugged. "If there's not much wrong with it, and if we have a little time. That's one reason I want to talk to Halloran. Tell me, Jimmy, how's your short-field work?"

Jimmy grimaced. "Pretty good, Colonel. But you know the risks."

"I do. Can you fly that ship out of there?"

"I'll try if Halloran thinks he can fix it."

252

Halloran scowled when the situation was explained to him. "Damn," he said. He took off his campaign hat and ran his fingers through his thinning red hair.

"Damn," he repeated, a little more softly. "Losing oil pressure, but not bad. Engine kept running another fifteen minutes, enough to get the ship down on a short field without any real damage. Sounds like a nicked oil line. If that's all it is, it shouldn't take long to fix. As far as fixing the airplane goes, Colonel, I think we can do it. How are we going to get there?"

"While we waited for you I got in touch with the transport boys. They're sending one of their pilots over. Captain McCormick should be here any time as well."

"And here I am," said the Aussie. "G'day, Colonel, gentlemen. What's going on?"

"What could we pack on a C-47 that your boys at Kokoda might find useful?" Wagner asked. "We have a P-39 down at the strip up there, and we'd like to get it back if we can."

McCormick nodded thoughtfully. "My word, they can use ammunition, food, water, medical supplies, a rifle squad, anything along those lines. When were you thinking about going?"

"As soon as possible this afternoon."

"I see. How much room are you likely to have?"

"We're taking two mechanics, some tools and parts, and an extra pilot. You could put a squad of infantry with all their equipment and maybe a machine-gun team on board, if you like."

"Well, more men to fight means more mouths to feed, and around and around like that. Mind if I use a telephone?"

"See Sergeant Kleist up front. He'll help you out."

"Thanks."

McCormick ducked out the door. Another man appeared, an Air Corps captain who introduced himself as Hill, Harry Hill, and yeah, he flew C-47s. What's the job?

By three o'clock that afternoon Jimmy sat in the after cabin of Hill's C-47 next to Halloran and Joey Twitchell, Shafer's crew chief. The two mechanics had a kit of tools and spares. Wagner's orders were to fix the P-39 if possible, and if not to strip off everything the mechanics could salvage and bring it back with Shafer, this evening if possible, at first light tomorrow if not.

With them in the C-47 was a squad of Australian infantry. Jimmy had dealt with the RAAF often enough, but this was the first time he'd seen Australian Army types. They carried big packs that looked heavy, .303 Enfield rifles, canteens, knives, ammunition pouches, and whatever gear was distributed in the bulging canvas pouches on their belts. Two cases of .303 rifle ammunition were strapped to the cargo plane's deck, along with an odd-looking weapon the squad leader referred to as a Bren gun. Jimmy thought the Bren gun looked sort of like a BAR with the clip on top instead of on the bottom.

It was a thirty-minute trip to Kokoda. The Aussie infantrymen spent it sleeping. Jimmy went up front to stand between the pilots on the flight deck.

The C-47 wound its way between the cloud-shrouded peaks of the mountains. Jimmy looked at the clouds with distrust. In some places, the clouds went

254

right down into the mountain valleys, and some of those valleys were filled with cloud or fog even late in the afternoon. Then they were through the peaks and over the long slope of foothills to the north coast, with the now-familiar columns of smoke stretching away to the north.

The transport plane turned towards the west and started to descend.

"You guys been to Kokoda before?" Jimmy asked.

The pilot nodded. "Yesterday. We carry ammo and rations and medical supplies in and the wounded out."

"What's the strip like?"

"Bumpy. Grassy. Short."

Jimmy reflected on how the pilot bit off the word "short." The C-47 had an enormous wingspan and, reputedly, could take off on one engine from a field with a density altitude of one mile above sea level. Despite its size it looked like it could get in and out of a good-sized cornfield. If the C-47's pilot thought the strip at Kokoda was short, Jimmy wondered about getting a P-39 off.

The C-47 flew over some mountains and there was Kokoda, set in the middle of a valley ringed by mountains. A string of clouds meandered over the valley.

"You might want to go strap in," the pilot told Jimmy. "Like I said, this field is sort of bumpy."

Jimmy went aft and sat down next to Halloran. The pilot throttled back the engines, and the flaps and gear came down.

"Guess we're almost there," Halloran said.

"I'm told the field is bumpy," Jimmy replied. "And short."

He cinched the seat belt tight.

The sergeant in charge of the squad said, "Almost there, then?"

"Yup."

The sergeant nodded. At a quiet order his men woke up, tightened their seat belts, and checked their rifles and equipment.

The C-47 turned, then turned again, and the pilot came off the power to the engines. He steepened his approach and lowered the last of the flaps. The transport slowed. Jimmy looked out the window and saw green jungle rushing past, very close below them, and the engines powered down to idle as the pilot came back on the controls until the nose of the airplane was at a slight up-angle. The main wheels touched the ground, the tail continuing to fly for a few seconds more, and as it came down the pilots applied brakes, gently at first, and then hard as the tail wheel touched. The brakes squealed and moaned and the transport slowed rapidly until it came to a stop.

The flight engineer came back and opened the cargo door.

"Right, then," said the sergeant. "Let's go, lads."

The infantrymen got up and filed out the door. Jimmy and the mechanics followed behind them.

Shafer stood near the tail, smiling up at them. "Hi, Jimmy," he said. "And you brought friends. You guys think you can fix my airplane?"

"We'll sure try, Mr. Shafer," said Twitchell.

"This way, then," Shafer said.

Jimmy jumped down from the door of the C-47 and looked around. The airstrip at Kokoda was covered in grass that came up to mid-calf. The field itself wasn't level, and looked to be sloped, about fifty feet higher at its west end than its east. The valley was surrounded by mountains, and the mountains looked to be a thousand feet higher than the valley floor. It was humid as hell, but at least it wasn't quite as hot as Port Moresby.

"Where's your airplane, Sheila?" Jimmy asked.

"Right over here," Shafer replied. "C'mon."

They walked over to the P-39. Jimmy kept looking at the sky and the mountains. The Aussie infantry squad had formed up and marched off towards Kokoda, carrying the ammunition boxes. Another man carried the Bren gun, with his rifle slung over his shoulder.

There was a flat cracking boom, then another, then a rapid series of four, like distant thunder. Jimmy thought it came from beyond the mountains to the north.

"That been going on for long?" he asked Shafer.

"All day," Shafer replied. "I'm glad you're here."

"I'll bet," said Jimmy.

They reached Shafer's P-39. "You have a look at it yet, Mr. Shafer?" Twitchell asked.

"Looks like some bullet holes around the engine section," Shafer said. "With oil coming out of a couple of them. See how it streaked down the fuselage?"

"Yeah," said Halloran. "Twitch, let's get this inspection panel off and see what we're dealing with."

The two mechanics quickly had the panel off to inspect the engine.

257

"Look here, Chief," said Twitchell. "This oil feeder line is nicked. Still dripping a little."

"Maybe that's it," said Halloran. "Go ahead and replace the line. I'll check for other damage."

"You guys need any help?" Jimmy asked.

Halloran looked at Jimmy. "If we need you we'll holler," he said.

Jimmy grinned and shook his head. "Right," he replied.

He and Shafer turned and walked up the runway. At the end, they turned and looked down the slope along the runway's length.

"Kind of short," said Jimmy.

"Yeah," said Shafer slowly. He kept looking down the runway. "So, taxi up here, run the engine up to maximum, keep the nose up and get off as soon as she'll fly."

"Short-field technique," Jimmy agreed.

"It's my airplane," Shafer said.

"Yeah, and it's your life, too. Want to draw straws? Or flip a coin?"

"Damn, Jimmy, it's my airplane."

"OK. You think you're good enough?"

"Yeah."

"Well, you'd better be, because if you aren't you're going to find out the hard way."

Shafer scoffed. "I can get my ship off the ground, and on back to Seven-Mile."

"All right. But it depends on Halloran and Twitchell. If they say the engine's good, you can give it a try."

258

A series of booms and thunderclaps reverberated across the valley.

"Artillery," Shafer said.

"Little Jap bastards are getting close," Jimmy said. "Wonder where the Aussies are."

"I talked to one of their officers after I landed. He said they were up in the mountains north of here. He pointed up to that pass, there. See it? That saddle with the tall mountains out there to the east?"

Jimmy nodded slowly. "What is that, maybe ten miles or so?"

"Maybe."

"They could be here tomorrow."

"Yeah. The guy I talked to belonged to Maroubra Force. He thought they could hold the Japs, but he didn't sound real sure to me."

Boom. Boom-bump!

Jimmy nodded. He looked at the mechanics, who had their heads inside the P-39's engine compartment.

"What d'you think?" Shafer asked.

"I think I'm glad that C-47 is here," Jimmy said. "I heard too much about infantry fighting from my Dad. He was in the war in Europe, last go-round."

"Yeah? Mine too. Artillery. He was awful happy being an artilleryman, too, after they started moving east and they saw some of what was left behind from the trench fighting."

Jimmy nodded.

He looked down the airstrip. Halloran moved away from the P-39 and waved at Jimmy and Shafer.

The two pilots walked down the runway.

"Mr. Ardana, we're ready to start the engine," Halloran said. "We checked the fuel and I figure there's enough to get to Seven-Mile with some reserve, but not much of a reserve. I recommend that if we start this engine and it looks OK, you should taxi right on up to the end of the runway and get the hell out of here."

"Talk to Shafer," said Jimmy. "It's his airplane."

Halloran looked from Jimmy to Shafer. "Yes, sir," he said. "What do you say, Mr. Shafer?"

"Your advice sounds good to me, Chief. Why don't we taxi up to the end of the runway and run the engine up there?"

"Just be careful, Mr. Shafer. The nose gear on a P-39 is a little fragile, so watch how you taxi on this so-called air strip."

"Sure thing, Chief. Twitch, what do you think?"

"We've been over the engine pretty thoroughly, Mr. Shafer, and checked the rest of the ship. There's some bullet holes, but nothing that should keep you from getting home."

"OK," said Shafer. "Let's give it a try."

Jimmy stood back with Halloran while Shafer climbed into his parachute and into the airplane. Twitchell crouched by the cockpit and watched as Shafer started the engine, ran it for a minute, and started to taxi up the runway at a walking pace. Jimmy and Halloran walked behind the P-39, until it reached the end of the runway and turned facing down its slope.

"You sure about letting him fly this one, Mr. Ardana?" asked the Chief.

"He thinks he can do it," Jimmy replied. "And it's his ship. His, and Twitchell's. What do you think?"

260

"Twitch is a good mechanic," said the Chief.

Shafer looked at them and gave them a thumb's-up. Jimmy returned the gesture. Shafer looked at Twitchell and exchanged a few words. Twitchell closed the cockpit door, thumped the top of the canopy with his palm, and climbed off the wing.

The engine sang power, climbing in pitch as Shafer fed in throttle. The grass behind the P-39 waved and flattened in the slipstream blasting from the prop, and the little pursuit visibly trembled with the screaming propeller and the engine. The power built up to a crescendo, held there for a long second, and Shafer let off the brakes. Almost at once the P-39 started to roll, slowly, the nose gear bobbing on the uneven surface, gaining speed as it went by them. Shafer waved and then looked straight ahead down the strip.

Jimmy found himself holding his breath, watching the pursuit gain speed. Shafer had a few degrees of flap in, and a little bit of elevator to take some pressure off the nose gear, exactly the recommended technique.

Shafer held the airplane on the runway, held it a little past where Jimmy thought he could have started flying, and then Shafer pulled it gracefully off the strip, sucked up the gear and the flaps, and came back down the runway, wagging his wings in salute, before turning to the south.

Twitchell joined them, watching the P-39 gain altitude to clear the mountain.

Jimmy exhaled.

"Amen," said Halloran.

The pilot of the C-47 came up, watching the P-39. "Thought you guys would like to know we'll be here

261

long enough for the Aussies to bring up some wounded, and then we'll get the hell on out of here and back to Seven-Mile."

Artillery rumbled to the north. The sun sank in the west.

"Sounds good to me," Jimmy said. He looked up the north slope of the Owen Stanley Mountains. The crest of the peaks were shrouded in mist or cloud, and the foothills around them marched up in ranks and folds, and among those folds, in the mists and cloud, was the Kokoda Track.

They'd have to start flying up there soon.

Chapter Eleven

Just a ray of sunshine

"**W**ell, Jimmy, it looks good to me," said Terraine. He buttoned up the inspection panel over the Allison engine.

Jimmy sighed. "Yeah."

The mechanic came and stood with Jimmy where he leaned against the fuselage at the wing root of the P-39. They were quiet for a minute. On the airstrip below them a C-47 took off. Terraine nodded at it.

"That's the second bunch of guys from the 8th headed out," he said.

"Townsville?"

"First stop." Terraine grimaced. "Then it's that damned Aussie railroad down the coast to Brisbane."

"Probably that same slow train I came up on," said Jimmy. "Even the passenger cars smelled like they were used to ship cattle."

"Great," said Terraine.

"But then you'll be in Brisbane. Women. Beer. Not as much rain."

"Can't believe I'm saying this, but getting out of this sauna might be as attractive as the women and the beer."

Jimmy chuckled. "That'll last a couple of days. Maybe. Or until you pass a bar or see your first skirt."

"You might be right, Jimmy." Terraine held his hand out. Jimmy took it.

"I don't quite feel right, leaving you and the *Gremlin* here by yourselves," Terraine said.

"Thanks, Don, but get the hell on out and have fun in Brisbane. You've earned it."

"Maybe so. Why aren't you coming with us?"

"Aw, I told Colonel Wagner I'd help these guys with the 35th learn the ropes. You see how green they are."

"Yeah. But most of their mechanics seem to know what they're doing, at least. And Halloran knows their line chief. Says he's pretty good for a new guy."

"New guy?"

Terraine grinned. "Yeah. He joined the Air Corps after the Great War."

"Oh. OK. New guy. But not too new."

"You know Halloran. If the Good Lord Himself was busting wrenches for Halloran, He might be good enough, but only just."

"What's his name?"

"Benchley, I think."

"OK."

A truck drove up and stopped outside the revetment. The driver beeped the horn.

"That's my ride," said Terraine. "Take care of yourself, Jimmy. Good luck."

"You too, Don."

The mechanic grinned and got on the truck. He waved as it drove away.

Jimmy waved back.

He watched the truck vanish in the dust it left behind.

Terraine was in the last echelon of the 8th Fighter Group to leave Seven-Mile. Slim Atkins and the other pilots left yesterday, replaced by personnel from the 35th.

Jimmy looked up at the sky and, in a near-reflexive gesture, looked north to check the clouds building over the Owen Stanleys. In the other revetments, mechanics he didn't know by sight were looking over the P-39s, some as if they'd never seen one before.

A trio of men in mechanic's coveralls walked down the taxiway and stopped in front of the *Gremlin's* revetment. They looked from the P-39 to Jimmy.

"Pardon me, lieutenant," said one of them. "Is this number 557?"

"Yup. Who are you?"

"Well, I'm the crew chief, Ed Hope. This is my assistant, Johnny Gallagher, and the armorer, Andy Brody."

"I'm Ardana, Jimmy Ardana. Glad to meet you."

Hope and his crew walked slowly around the *Gremlin*, taking in the patches in the aluminum skin and the fabric control surfaces. Hope paused when he got to the Jap flags painted on the nose.

"Those yours, Mr. Ardana?" he asked.

"Yup."

Hope blinked and exchanged glances with the other two before resuming his inspection, ending in front of the engine. He took the panels off and looked at the Allison. He nodded.

"Your last mechanic took pretty good care of this airplane," Hope said. "We'll make you happy, Mr. Ardana."

"I'll hold you to that," Jimmy said. "Did the group commander come up with you?"

265

"Colonel Wrixon? No, sir, last I heard of the Colonel, he was at FEAF HQ in Brisbane. I reckon he'll be up in a day or two. I think Major Dionne is acting group commander until then."

"Who's Major Dionne?"

"He's your new squadron commander, Mr. Ardana."

Jimmy nodded. "OK. Thanks, Hope. You fellows make yourselves at home. How do you like the lovely accomodations?"

"Oh, just swell, Mr. Ardana," said Gallagher. "There was a centipede on my cot big enough to shoot with my .45."

"That small?" Jimmy said. "You guys must rate better than us pilots. I did shoot the one I found. It just hissed at me and kept crawling."

Jimmy patted his revolver.

"Jesus," said Brody. "No disrespect, sir, but are you Jimmy the Kid?"

"Shut up, Andy," Hope growled.

"Where'd you hear about that?" Jimmy asked curiously.

"Oh, hell, Mr. Ardana, everyone in the 35th knows about you shooting that Jap on the airstrip. Only the way I heard it first, you stood off a platoon of Jap paratroopers."

"I thought it was a couple of Jap tanks," Gallagher supplied helpfully.

Jimmy shook his head. "Well, my first day here, I was told most of the guys carry pistols because the Japs have used paratroopers before. But no, it was just the one Jap. He shot me down, in fact, while I was trying to land."

"Jeez," said Gallagher. "That happen often?"

"I hope not."

The mechanics grinned. Hope asked, "What's the word on the Japs, sir?"

"The Japs are on the other side of the Owen Stanleys, for now," Jimmy said. "Any of you boys have rifles?"

The three mechanics looked at each other. "Should we get some rifles?" Hope asked.

"If you know how to use 'em, it couldn't hurt."

"I haven't fired a rifle since Basic," Brody said.

"I wouldn't worry about it for now," Jimmy replied. "Even if the Aussies weren't between us and the Japs, it would take the Japs at least a week to walk over those mountains and get here. So we'll know in plenty of time to get ready."

"OK," said Hope.

"Right. I'm going up to Operations. We might get another flight this afternoon."

"By the way, sir, who else is in your flight?"

"Bell, Shafer, and Kellerman."

"Bell? Tommy Bell? The buzz king?"

"That's him."

Hope shook his head. "Mr. Ardana, you watch yourself with that guy. They don't call him the buzz king for nothing. He's mowed half the lawns around Brisbane."

"And blew laundry off the lines of all the rest," said Jimmy. "I heard. But don't worry about it. Bell's under control."

Jimmy smiled to himself at the dubious looks the three airmen exchanged.

"If you say so, sir," Gallagher said.

Jimmy did smile then. "I'll see you guys later."

Captain Allen was at the tent he inherited from Ed Groves. He smiled at Jimmy.

"Kid, you hear Col. Wagner got his orders?"

"What?"

"Yeah. He's headed home."

"Damn. Where is he now?"

"Don't know. Packing, maybe."

"Bill, you need me for anything right now?"

"Naw. You going to try to see Wagner?"

"Thought I might."

"OK. I'll come along, if you don't mind."

"Sure."

They walked up the hill to Group Operations. The Officer of the Day told them Wagner had just left, on his way to the airfield.

"We better hurry," Allen said.

When they got to the airfield they found an impromptu delegation gathered by an RAAF Hudson. It was a motley bunch, mostly pilots from the RAAF and the newly arrived USAAF 35th Fighter Group, but with a few RAA officers and even one or two civilians from Port Moresby.

Jimmy recognized Wing Commander Colleton, the recently-promoted Catalina pilot.

"Where's Wagner, Winco?" Jimmy asked.

"Hallo, Jimmy. Buzz? I should say he'd be here soon. The bloke flying that Hudson is supposed to take off in a few minutes."

"OK. Thanks."

A jeep came down the hill and drove up to the Hudson. Wagner was in the passenger seat. He stood up and surveyed the crowd while a couple of airmen took his bags to the Hudson.

"Aw, hell," he said. "Don't tell me I owe you guys money."

That raised a laugh and a few cries of "Sign this blank check for me, Colonel."

"Hey, c'mon. You know I'm planning on getting married when I get home. Wives are expensive." Which raised another laugh.

"They gonna send you to Europe to kick some Kraut ass, Colonel?"

"Europe? It's the Army. They'll probably send me to Iceland to count geese."

Amid more laughter Wagner waved and climbed down from the jeep, shaking hands and clapping shoulders as he walked slowly toward the waiting Hudson.

Jimmy stood near the door and stuck his hand out as Wagner put his foot on the step.

"Jimmy," the Colonel said, and took his hand. Wagner leaned close to speak and kept his voice low. "You watch your ass, ace."

"I'm not an ace yet, Colonel."

"You will be. Keep your eyes open and your wits sharp, Jimmy, and keep that goddamned Tommy Bell out of trouble." Wagner clapped him on the shoulder, squeezed his hand, and walked up into the Hudson. Jimmy stepped back away from the hatch as it closed.

The pilot shouted "Clear!" from his window and the crowd stepped away from the airplane. The Hudson's left energizer whined, spinning the prop slowly, reluctantly, until it caught with a flurry of pearl-gray acrid smoke, coughed, and roared with power. Everyone stepped further back. Jimmy looked at the windows of the Hudson and saw Wagner looking out, waving. He waved back, and a moment later the Hudson taxied away.

The crowd stood waiting until the Hudson took off, and they waved as it roared past, lifting from the ground with the flaps and the gear coming up, and dwindled in the distance. It turned to the south and was gone.

Jimmy found Bill Allen standing next to him.

"What did Wagner have to say?" Allen asked.

"Wished me luck. Told me to keep Chinkerbell out of trouble."

Allen scoffed. "Good luck with that."

"He's no problem as long as I let him mow the grass around Buna now and then."

"Speaking of which, I hear we have a trip on the board for 1400."

"Figured. What's the weather look like?"

Allen made a pretense of peering to the north at the cloud-shrouded mountains. "Partly cloudy with a chance of rain," he said.

"You're just a ray of sunshine, Captain Allen," Jimmy said.

"I do my best, Lieutenant Ardana. And now I'd like you to meet someone."

"Oh? Who?"

"Why, your new best friend, of course." Allen looked around the crowd and waved. A man who was a little tall for a pursuit pilot waved back and walked over.

"Jimmy, this is Major Keith Dionne."

Jimmy exchanged salutes with Dionne, who then held out his hand.

"Glad to meet you, Ardana," Dionne said. "Heard a lot about you from Allen, here."

"Yes, sir."

"I had a chance to meet with Boyd Wagner for a little bit. He tells me you're the greatest thing since canned beer." Dionne smiled. There was something a little predatory in that smile. "Are you?"

Jimmy grinned back. "As long as you throw in a bourbon chaser, Major."

Dionne laughed. "You call me Keith and I'll call you Jimmy, at least until you screw up."

"And then you'll call me some other things, I reckon."

"Told you the kid knows the ropes," said Allen. "Speaking of which, Col. Wrixon wants to meet him."

"Really? Well, best not to keep the colonel waiting. You two run along. Good to meet you, Jimmy. I want to sit down with you soon and talk about the Japs and our tactics. I'd like your input."

"Yes, sir."

Jimmy followed Allen up the path to Operations.

271

When the 35th relieved the 8th a whole new atmosphere took over Operations. It was the same old grass shack, but now there was a whole new contingent of clerks sitting bolt upright at their desks, busily doing something with papers or files, and a sergeant barking orders over the phone. Allen went up to the Officer of the Day's desk, where yet another captain Jimmy didn't know yet was reading a typewritten report. Allen addressed the OD casually.

"Skeet, is the Colonel in? He wanted to meet Lt. Ardana."

The captain looked up from his report. "Back in his office," he replied. "So you're Jimmy Ardana?"

"Yes, sir."

The captain nodded. "Go on back. The colonel's expecting you."

"Thanks, Skeet."

The partitions and the heat and the ineffectual fans were all the same, but it was like coming home to find strangers had moved in and set their stamp on things you remembered otherwise.

Allen knocked on the door. Someone had removed the sign that said, "Director of Fighter Operations" and replaced it with, "Commanding Officer 35th Fighter Group."

"Come in."

Allen entered the colonel's office with Jimmy in tow. He walked to a spot in front of the colonel's desk, and came to attention. And saluted.

When he saluted, Jimmy figured he'd better come to attention and salute, too. One more thing to mark the difference between the old and the new.

"Sir, Captain Allen and Lieutenant Ardana, reporting as ordered."

The colonel, like the duty officer, was reading a report. He took a moment, marked his spot with a pencil, and looked up.

Colonel Wrixon was older than Jimmy expected, well over thirty, based on the slightly thinning hair and the faint wrinkles at the corners of his eyes and mouth. When he stood up he revealed himself to be medium height and build, with slightly rounded shoulders.

The colonel returned their salutes. "At ease, gentlemen."

Allen took a position of at ease. Jimmy hesitated before doing the same.

"You are unfamiliar with basic military protocol, Lt. Ardana?" Wrixon asked.

"No, sir."

"I noticed you hesitated to come to attention, render a salute, and then to assume a position of at ease. Are you simply slow, then?"

"No, sir."

"Ah. Then perhaps my predecessor was lax in his enforcement of military courtesy. We'll let that stand for now. Lt. Ardana, I wanted to meet you, not only because I like to know something about the men under my command, but to, shall we say, nip certain behaviors in the bud."

Jimmy blinked. Wrixon leaned forward and frowned.

"I can see you aren't very regulation about your personal equipment," he said.

"I don't understand, sir."

273

"That cowboy revolver and what is that strapped to your leg? A machete?"

"A Bowie knife, Colonel. It belonged to my grandfather."

"Indeed. And it seems you have acquired a nickname to go along with your cowboy paraphernalia. Jimmy the Kid."

"I've been called that, sir."

"Is it because of that revolver?"

"Partly, sir."

"But mostly because he shot a Jap pilot dead with it, out on the airstrip," said Capt. Allen. "His first day in combat."

"So I take it you're a fan of this nonsense, Captain Allen?"

"I'm in favor of killing Japs, Colonel. That's what we're here for."

"Indeed it is. But there's a right way and a wrong way to do anything." The Colonel looked Jimmy slowly up and down. "Remember that, Lieutenant."

"Yes, sir."

"Dismissed."

Jimmy was ready to come to attention and salute this time, followed by a crisp about face and departure from the Colonel's office.

They walked out of Operations and started down to the flight line.

"Well," said Jimmy. "That was different."

"That's Wrixon."

"So he's always like that?"

"Nah. Today was a good day."

"Swell. What's he got against me?"

274

"He thinks you're a cowboy. Not the literal kind, but some sort of Hollywood showoff."

Jimmy shook his head.

"What?"

"I *am* a cowboy. The literal kind, not the Hollywood sort. I grew up on a ranch in Montana."

"No foolin'?"

"Honest Injun."

"So the six-gun and the Bowie knife, that's just normal where you come from?"

"Well, not like it used to be, but yes."

Allen shook his head slowly. "Well, I owe you an apology, Kid."

"What d'you mean?"

"I mean I kind of thought you were a showoff, too. I know the story about you shooting it out with that Jap, and then you're one kill shy of being an ace, and then there's the way you brought Chinkerbell into line. I really did think you had a little Hollywood in you."

Jimmy scoffed. "Well, thanks, Bill. You might consider that showoffs get killed, and usually in a loud and spectacular manner, and I've got more regard for my precious ass than that."

"Not even that day you outflew Bell? Showing off or not, Jimmy, that was some razor-sharp flying."

"Especially that day. I won't deny it was fun, but that's not why I did it."

"Well, damn, you're just a grouchy old sourpuss at heart, aren't you?"

Jimmy bared his teeth and growled theatrically at Allen, who laughed.

275

Jimmy let the engine run for a minute, beckoning his crew chief, Ed Hope, to climb up on the wing. The slipstream blasting back from the propeller made conversation difficult, but the intermittent roughness of the engine announced itself with a disconcerting burble that coughed through the exhaust and shimmied in the airframe. Jimmy pointed at the tachometer.

"RPM drop," he shouted. "And check the oil pressure."

Terraine looked at the instruments, shook his head, and made a "cut" gesture to Jimmy. Jimmy shut the engine down.

"Thankfully it started doing that when we were on this side of the mountains," Jimmy told his crew chief.

"You pick up something over the target, Jimmy?"

"I don't think so. Let's have a look."

They took a circuit around the airplane. There was the tiniest streak of oil running from the oil cooler. Hope dabbed at it with his fingers, rubbed them together, smelled the oil and scowled.

"Changed that oil yesterday," he told Jimmy. "Smell that."

Jimmy sniffed the oil on Hope's fingers. "Damn. Smells like something out of an old jalopy's crankcase."

"Yeah. Which you don't want in your engine at 2900 RPM and high manifold pressure."

Jimmy nodded. "So you reckon it's just a bad batch of oil or is it the tropics?"

"Dunno. Maybe both. That's what Chief Benchley thinks. He's going to try to get the supply people to do something about it, but…"

The mechanic shrugged expressively.

"Right," Jimmy said. "So what do you think?"

"I'll drain this crap and replace it. Then I'm going to check the engine and be sure it's OK. But, Jimmy, if our engine oil is going bad this fast sooner or later we'll either run out of oil or we'll start seizing engines."

A jeep pulled up to the revetment. Jimmy straightened up and waved at Captain Allen.

"You have some trouble there, Jimmy?"

"Engine oil breaking down."

"Yeah. Seems to be happening all over. Hop in, I'll give you and your boys a ride up to the ops shack."

"Thanks."

A few minutes later the jeep sped up the taxiway with Jimmy in the front with Bill Allen and the rest of the flight hanging on in back.

"You guys have any luck up there?" Allen asked.

"Bombed something that went ka-boom," Jimmy said. "Actually I think Shiela got that one. That barge, right?"

Jimmy turned to look at Shafer, who nodded and yawned. "Yeah. Musta been loaded with ammo, the way it went up."

"Good."

"Midnight here strafed a couple of others. One of 'em was smoking when we left."

Kellerman waved a tired hand.

Allen looked over his shoulder and grinned. "Damn, that's only the fourth trip you guys have made today. You're all acting like you're tired or something."

"I'm not tired," said Bell.

"That's 'cause you're crazy, Chinkerbell," said Jimmy. "But I will say this, Bill, if we could get those damned cannons to work right, we could really chew up those barges. How many did you get before yours jammed on you, Bell?"

"Four. Four hits, anyway. Two sunk for sure, the other two were listing but still headed for the beach."

"And you, Jimmy?" Allen asked.

"One barge sunk for sure. Got hits on five others, two of 'em were smoking and one was burning all to billy-hell."

"Lot of flak?"

"Don't think any of us took any hits. Midnight, Chink? Shiela?"

"Got a pretty good scare when some 25mm stuff popped off around me," said Kellerman. "I think they were shooting at Jimmy, though."

"Not too bad, then," Allen said. He pulled up in front of the Ops Shack, which now bore the legend "35TH FIGHTER GROUP OPERATIONS" in hand lettering neater than the old sign for the 8th Fighter Group. "So, since I'm now Group Intelligence Officer, consider yourselves debriefed. All told you're claiming four barges destroyed with three probables and eight barges damaged."

"Yeah, one other thing," said Jimmy. "When we headed for home I looked back at the target. Pretty sure I saw a half-dozen airplanes circling over that airstrip the Japs are carving out of the jungle, right where the Aussies said their old strip used to be. We have anyone else out there?"

"Did they look like Zeros?"

"Maybe. Even probably. Single-engined monoplanes, anyway."

"Damn," said Allen. He looked thoughtful, then he looked at his watch. "1637," he said. "Sundown in about two hours. Jimmy, you feel like going back for a look?"

"My mechanic says my ship is down overnight, at least. Got one I can borrow?"

"Steal one from HQ Flight. Just bring it back without too many holes."

"OK. What d'you think? Carry a bomb just for fun? Go in low?"

Allen waved his hand. "I'll leave that up to your masterful sense of strategy, Jimmy."

Jimmy nodded. "OK. Midnight, Shiela, you two go get yourselves some chow. Chink, we're going to head back north in thirty minutes. You up for it?"

"You bet."

It was more like 45 minutes before Jimmy and Bell got off the ground at Seven-Mile, and Jimmy cast a look at the sun in the west as they headed towards the mountains. It was a lot closer to the horizon than he liked. They'd have plenty of light for the attack on whatever the Japs had up at Buna, but he wasn't so sure about landing at Seven-Mile.

Jimmy looked to see Bell sticking tight off his right wing. Bell waved at him. Jimmy stayed below the peaks and wound among them, then descended down the north slope.

Finding Buna was easy enough. There was smoke rising above the beachhead from burning barges, among

279

whatever else had been hit in the course of the afternoon.

"Two, arm 'em up."

"Lead, I'm hot."

"OK. Fly as briefed."

"Roger, Lead."

Jimmy reviewed the plan in his head. Seven miles out from the target, opposite the village of Dobodura where Wagner once hoped to put in a forward airstrip, Bell would split off to the east. Jimmy would attack from the west, and the two of them would strafe and bomb opposite sides of the airstrip, then join up for the trip home.

They leveled out at five hundred feet, bumping the throttle and manifold pressure forward to keep their speed up. Riding the gravity train down from the mountains they pushed 330 mph even with a 500-pound bomb adding drag and weight to the airplane. The speed slowly bled off as they descended to 300 feet over the jungle, but they still topped 300 mph. A Zero might intercept them but it would have to be one lucky, well-positioned Jap already at full throttle himself to have a chance. Jimmy spared a glance at the oil pressure and temp gauges. This P-39 was from HQ flight, but Jimmy didn't know their mechanics, who came up with the 35th. Jimmy was sure they were conscientious and competent, but he wished he were flying his own airplane, tended by his old crew.

The gauges looked OK, though, and when Jimmy looked up he saw Bell waggle his wings and bank sharply to the north. They were low and fast enough that white streamers of condensation curved back from the P-39's wings.

Then Jimmy concentrated on his flying, letting down until he skimmed the treetops, using the pillar of smoke from the beachhead as his guide. In two minutes he pulled hard to the right himself, over the white breakers and the scummy-green looking tidal pond east of the beachhead, and there was the little open space in among the trees. That was the Jap airstrip, and there were no airplanes parked in the open, which was what Jimmy expected. The Japs made mistakes, but not that obvious. They'd had an hour and a half, easy, to get those planes under cover.

Jimmy checked his airspeed indicator. Still showing 300, and at that speed and one hundred feet of altitude, his bomb would travel 1100 feet before it hit the ground, with Jimmy more or less right on top of it. He had the bomb fuzes set for a five-second delay. But, as the armorer told him with the cheerful grin of a man whose life didn't depend on an infernal device, "Five second delay on these fuzes might mean three seconds or seven, Lieutenant."

The end of the runway came up and as he flashed over it he released his bomb, gave it a one-one-thousand count, and pulled hard to the north. As he pulled he saw Bell's airplane, headed down the seaward side of the runway, beginning a hard left turn.

Crap on a cracker, Bell was cutting it close! Jimmy was still in the turn, looking over his shoulder, and Bell was over and beyond the runway as Jimmy's count reached three-one-thousand, four-one-thousand, five-one-thousand, six…

281

Jimmy's bomb exploded, throwing dirt and bits of jungle foliage in a fountain up into the air, and a second later Bell's bomb detonated, followed by a secondary, a great billowing globe of yellow fire and black smoke from exploding gasoline, followed by another, smaller explosion.

"Wooo-hooo!" shouted Bell over the radio. "That'll teach 'em!"

"Good work, Tommy," Jimmy called back.

"What, no Chinkerbell?"

"You keep dropping 'em like that, I'll ease up on you. Some."

"You're a pal, Kid."

"Best friend you'll ever have. Let's try and get home before dark."

What Jimmy didn't expect, after shutting down back at Seven-Mile with the last of the daylight, was to find himself standing in front of Colonel Wrixon being chewed out for an unauthorized and highly dangerous flight.

"No, not a flight," the colonel corrected himself. "A stunt, worthy of a cowboy like you, Lieutenant Ardana."

"Sir, I…"

"Silence! You're at attention, Lieutenant!"

Jimmy shut his mouth, put his shoulders back, and tucked in his chin as he threw his chest out. From the corner of his eye he saw Bell had done the same, but even from that perspective he could see Bell looked confused.

Wrixon continued. "Risking two airplanes at a moment when we have a shortage of pilots, airplanes and parts, not to mention whatever the hell is going on with the lubricating oil! D'you know how lucky you are, Ardana? Lucky those engines didn't seize up on you and leave blood, guts, and feathers all up and down the jungle, a crash scene, I might add, completely devoid of any trace of brains! What is it with you, Ardana? You think just because you've got four Japs and one more with that silly cowboy gun of yours that you're something special? Well? Do you?"

Jimmy remained silent, eyes looking straight ahead.

"Well? Answer me, God damn it!"

"With respect, sir, the Colonel ordered me to be silent."

Jimmy thought the Colonel was about to explode, and at that moment there was a knock on the door.

"Go away!" the colonel shouted.

"Sir, I understand there may be some confusion about Lt. Ardana's mission this evening, and I thought I might help clear that up."

Jimmy recognized the voice of Major Dionne, the Corncob squadron commander.

"You don't want a part of this, Dionne," the colonel growled.

"Respectfully, Colonel, Lt. Ardana and Lt. Bell were on a mission authorized by Captain Allen, as group intelligence officer. Ardana reported sighting Jap planes landing at Buna, and Allen gave permission for them to conduct an armed reconnaissance."

"That's right, Colonel," a new voice chimed in. Jimmy recognized Allen.

The colonel was glaring beyond Jimmy. He was silent for long enough for Jimmy to feel his heart beat five times.

Finally the Colonel nodded. "All right," he said. His voice was low and hard. "All right. But I've got my eye on you, Ardana. Remember that."

"Yes, sir."

"Dismissed."

Jimmy executed a faultless about-face and exited into the hallway. Bell followed him out, and when they were two steps from the colonel's door Bell said, "What the…"

"Hush," Jimmy said. Dionne grinned at him.

"Come with me, you miscreants," he whispered.

The four pilots walked out of the operations shack into the New Guinea night, and kept walking.

"Would one of you sirs kindly explain to me what that was all about?" Bell asked plaintively. "I mean, I thought we did a good job."

"You did, Chinkerbell," said Allen. "What exactly did you do?"

"You tell him, Tommy," Jimmy said. "Hell, today was your day, not mine."

"Well?" asked Dionne.

"Aw, I don't know. You couldn't really see anything except trees on the edge of the runway, so Jimmy and I both dropped our bombs about the middle on either side. I got a couple of secondaries."

"Big secondaries," Jimmy amplified. "Whatever he hit, it was loaded with gasoline. Made a hell of a nice fire."

"That's got to be good," said Allen. "But you didn't actually see any Zeros?"

"Nope."

"Almost sure to be there, though," Dionne mused. "You guys take any damage?"

"I didn't," said Jimmy.

"Me, either," said Bell.

"Well, that's a good end to a good day. You boys come up to the tent. I have some firewater that ain't for the young, and you two are getting old fast."

Chapter Twelve

A grand show of initiative

There was a valley near the crest of the Owen Stanley Mountains. Jimmy held his P-39 in a turn, looking down his left wing at the fog- and cloud-shrouded valley. Somewhere below the clouds hiding the valley, Aussie troops fought the Japanese on the Kokoda Track.

Those were some damned thick clouds. Jimmy scanned the sky and checked on his flight. Kellerman was tucked in off his right wing, and Sheila and Chinkerbell were two thousand feet above, orbiting slowly, watching for Japs.

"Two from Lead, you see anything like an opening in the clouds down there?"

"Looks solid to me, Lead."

Jimmy scowled behind his oxygen mask.

"Lead from Two."

"Go ahead, Two."

"Jimmy, look at the shadows in those valleys. The sun's going to have to come up and burn that fog off before we can see anything."

Jimmy squinted as their turn brought them face to face with the sun, which wasn't far above the horizon. Well, sunlight burned off fog, that was beginning meteorology.

All right, then.

"Corncob Blue Leader to flight, we'll hit the bridge at Wairopi. Follow me."

"Two."

"Three."

"Four."

Jimmy took his flight south over a valley and turned east, following another valley. The coast was visible, but their destination wasn't that far. They passed the village of Kokoda on their left, and by that time the Kumusi River was in sight, weaving through jungle and grassland in silver folds of reflected sunlight. At eight thousand feet they were out of range of machine guns, and so far that was the heaviest opposition the Japs mounted along the Track.

"Three, Lead, you and Chink split off. You two hit the west bank, we'll hit the east bank, come in about fifteen seconds behind us."

"Roger, Lead."

"Two, Lead, we'll hit the pylon on the east bank. I'll go first, you follow behind me."

"Roger, Lead."

Jimmy looked at the river again, and in another minute he saw the bridge. The bridge span had been knocked down time and again, but somehow no one had managed to hit the pylons that supported the span. A crappy little bridge, and as he got closer he could see little ant figures running off it. A stream of tracer reached up from a machine gun. That was bad enough but at least they hadn't brought up any 25mm or 57mm guns.

"Two, Lead, you got the east pylon?"

"Roger, Lead, I'm right behind you."

"Right, Lead's in on the east."

Jimmy checked his armament panel, set it up for bomb-drop, pulled back on the throttle, and nosed over.

One look over his shoulder to check on Kellerman, in trail behind him, and off to his left and behind him came Three and Four.

Then he looked back at the bridge, checked his gunsight, checked his instruments, then concentrated on his bomb run. Another machine gun joined the other, two streams of tracer reaching up at Jimmy. He saw one stream flash by off his right wingtip, the pylon grew in his gunsight, and he reached out and pulled the bomb release.

"One, two," he counted, and pulled up, jinking hard to avoid ground fire.

"Three's in on the west."

Jimmy looked over his shoulder and saw the smoke and dust from his exploding bomb obscuring the east pylon. He saw Shiela drop on the west pylon and pull out just over the jungle.

"Two's in on the east."

By the time Bell called his run and made his drop the 500-lb bombs had thrown clouds of smoke and dust into the sky above the Kumusi River.

"Two, Lead, join up. Three, Four, you guys all right?"

"Three's good."

"Four's OK. I think I hit that pylon."

"Good, Chink, let's stooge around a bit. Keep your eyes open, watch for Zeros."

When the dust cleared Jimmy saw the span was down, but not the pylons.

"This is Lead. I had two guns shooting at me. Anyone see more than that?"

"Lead, Two, same guns you saw."

"Lead, Three, another gun on the west bank."

"Four had three guns. Someone else can come in last next time."

Jimmy looked at the bridge and wondered what a 37mm gun might do to the pylons. The pylons were wood, two feet thick, and that big pylon looked like a toothpick through a gunsight approaching at three hundred mph.

One pass.

"OK, in trail, one pass on the east pylon. Let's see what the cannon will do. Chink, you go in first. Then Three, Two, Lead. Go."

"Woo-hoo!" called Bell. He rolled hard and dove, banking level above the trees. In a moment smoke trailed behind his nose and wing guns. The bullets kicked up geysers of dirt. Watching them Jimmy could tell Bell was too far to the right, and his cannon shells walked into the water, missing the pylon.

"Three, go."

Midnight followed Shafer and it looked like Midnight's shells and bullets walked over the pylon.

"OK, Lead's in."

Jimmy elected a steeper dive angle, got the pylon in his sights, and triggered his guns. Dirt sprayed around the pylon and Jimmy pulled out, flat-hatting along above the trees before climbing up to rejoin. He checked his fuel.

"Flight, Lead, let's head for home. How's that pylon look?"

"Still there."

"Swell."

Jimmy looked over his shoulder. Maybe they'd hit the pylon, maybe not, but it was still standing.

"And, just for fun, gentlemen, there's an unconfirmed report from the 35th Fighter Group that the Japs are now basing Zeros at Buna."

This pronouncement was greeted with silence from the assembled bomber crews. A couple of navigators made brief notes: *Zeros at Buna.*

Charlie figured if the Japs were basing Zeros at Buna, less than thirty minutes flying time from where he sat at Seven-Mile, they either had plenty of Zeros to spare or they were spreading themselves thin. He raised his hand.

"Yes, Major Davis?"

"George, any assessment as to relative fighter strength at Lae and Salamaua?"

"I don't know, Major. I can ask."

"Please do. I don't think I've noticed any particular reduction in the number of Zeros we encounter..." Charlie paused as a derisive laugh spread around the room. When it died away he said, "But I don't suppose anyone has run the numbers on it, either."

The briefer nodded, made a note on his pad, and continued the briefing.

Charlie figured by now he could give this briefing himself, in his sleep. Compass heading to Rabaul. Formation altitude. Likely fighter opposition. Latest placement of antiaircraft guns. Latest caliber of antiaircraft guns observed. Shipping in the harbor, including warships with even more antiaircraft guns.

Weather, ranging from OK to shitty to who the hell knows, it's the tropics.

Al Stern poked him and Charlie started awake, realizing he'd drifted off. "Did I snore?" he whispered.

"No, but you were about to. What's the matter?" Al whispered back.

"Jehosophat, Al, I think I was asleep and dreaming about this briefing."

"I think George said something different about Lakunai airdrome."

"What?"

"I don't know. I was asleep too."

"You do know where we're going, right?"

"Oh, sure. It isn't like we haven't been there before. At least we have company this time."

"Yeah. Maybe." Charlie looked around at the half-dozen crews from two different squadrons of the 19th Bomb Group that represented a maximum effort for this mission, which was to bomb the airfield at Vunakanau.

Then he looked at Danny Evans, who was listening attentively to the briefer and taking notes. Charlie shook his head, but maybe Evans was right to keep track of things that way. Charlie wondered if he and Al were getting a little too stuck in the "old hand" view of things, the yawn, yeah, I been there, what else is new outlook. Besides, this trip would mark the sixth mission Evans had flown as copilot of *Bronco Buster II*, and that in itself was a milestone. Assuming he made it back from this trip.

As they were walking out to the flight line Charlie said, "Danny, I think I might've fallen asleep at the briefing. What did I miss?"

"Well, sir…" Evans began. He looked at his notes as they walked and gave a quick synopsis of the briefing.

It was, as far as Charlie could tell, concise and accurate. He looked at Al, who shrugged and gave Charlie a surreptitious wink.

"OK, thanks, Danny. Let's take a look around the ship and then we'll load up."

A truck pulled up next to their B-17 and the gunners hopped out, reaching back in for machine-guns and boxes of ammo. Charlie waved Danny ahead and stopped to watch, counting the boxes of .50-cal.

"Damn, Lefty, you guys know something about this trip I don't?" he asked.

Lefkowicz grinned at Charlie. "It's Rabaul, skipper. You can never have too much ammo, going up there."

"OK. Johann, Johnny, Emmons, you guys doing OK?"

Johnny shifted his wad of chewing tobacco and spat expertly, then spat again to clear his mouth. "Sorry, skipper. Don't want to take that wad up with me."

"That's right. Can't have you swallowing at the wrong time and puking into your oxygen mask. How 'bout the rest of you guys?"

"Fine, skipper," said Johann.

Emmons nodded, but Emmons rarely said much unless an answer was actually required.

"All right. Good luck, then."

Charlie joined Danny, who stood looking up at the cowling of No. 3 engine.

Which spilled oil in a thin stream.

"Aw, Jehosophat," said Charlie in disgust. He looked around "Smith! Hey, Kim, get over here and let's unbutton this cowling."

The flight engineer trotted over with a small bag of tools and a step ladder. When he popped the cowling fasteners the thin stream of oil become a brief flood that pooled on the ground below.

"Well," said Kim. He stood looking up into the guts of the Wright Cyclone engine, put his hand on an oil line, which promptly came away to his touch, spilling more oil in the process. Smith hastily stuck his finger over the opening.

"Ow!"

"You OK, Kim?"

"Something sharp in there, skipper. We're going to have to fix that broken line and put some more oil in this engine before we can fly. It'll take thirty minutes to fix, and that's if we can find a replacement oil line."

"Jehosophat," Charlie muttered in disgust. "OK. Kim, I'll hunt up the line chief. Danny, you go down to *Didgeriwho?* and tell Captain West he just got bumped. I'm taking his airplane, and if Kim can get that oil line fixed in time he can fly *Bronco Buster II*."

Charlie didn't miss the look Al flashed him before his face closed off into a strictly-business expression. Charlie didn't want to go with anyone but his own crew, for that matter. It wasn't that he didn't trust West's boys. It was just that they weren't *his* boys.

A jeep drove up with Major Madsen, who was in overall command of the mission.

"Bum engine, Charlie?"

"No. 3 pissing oil all over the ramp."

293

"Swell."

"Have you seen Chief Demopolis?"

"He's over with the flight engineer on *My Shiela*. Electrical system fault." Madsen grimaced. "How long to fix your engine?"

"My flight engineer says a half-hour, if we can scare up an oil line."

"Right. We're down two airplanes out of six. I'm going to delay the mission by an hour and see if we can find enough chewing gum and baling wire around here so all six of us can go." Madsen grinned. "That way you don't upset anyone's tender feelings."

Charlie nodded, aware of the small tickle of relief he felt. "OK. Sounds good to me, Mike."

Chief Demopolis was with the flight engineer of *My Shiela*, a well-worn veteran B-17E that once sported the worthless Bendix remote turret. At some time in the past the turret was removed and the resulting hole patched over with sheet aluminum.

"Chief, I see you're busy," Charlie began.

The line chief waved a hand. "What can I do for you, Major?"

"Got a bad oil line in my No. 3 engine. The one feeding cylinder three. Got a spare?"

Demopolis nodded. "Yeah. I got one of those."

The line chief turned to the B-17's flight engineer. "Squid, you square on how to fix that fuse box?"

"Sure thing, Chief."

"OK. Let me hunt up an oil line for Major Davis here. I'll send one of my boys over to help you."

Chief Demopolis had a jeep at the tail of the B-17. He and Charlie climbed in.

"How are you for spare parts overall, Chief?" Charlie asked.

Demopolis said something in a language Charlie didn't know, but the words sounded angry. When the chief calmed down a little he said, "God damn Air Corps. Spend twenty, thirty years counting every nut and bolt and spool of locking wire because that's the peacetime Air Corps for you. Only now we're in a shooting war and that shit just won't do, sir, if you'll pardon my French."

"You sound like a friend of mine. He and my brother had to steal a couple of P-39s from a supply depot down in Townsville, if you can believe it."

"Major, I've got a stack of copies of requisitions back in my office, must be three feet thick, I'm not lyin'. Don't matter how you fill 'em out, they get bounced back as improperly filled out or temporarily unavailable or some other excuse which don't matter 'cause we need the shit *here*, only Supply has it down *there*, and that's that."

"Jehosophat. I'd ask if they knew we were fighting a war up here, but I doubt they care."

"Tell you what, Major, next time I get down to Townsville or Brisbane I'm goin' to kidnap me a couple of those bastards and bring 'em up here to Seven-Mile. Make *them* fly a mission or two or eat this lousy M&V slop and work on these damn airplanes in the god-damn jungle and keep 'em flyin' with spit, chewing gum and baling wire and hell, Major, sorry to unload all my problems on you."

295

"Chief, you fix my airplanes. Your problems are my problems, after all. But it works better for me and my boys when your problems stay your problems."

The line chief smiled and braked to a stop in front of a tent. It was one of the bigger pyramidal tents and even from ten feet away it stank of mildew and whatever that stink was that canvas got when it was stored away for years and pulled out of the hold of a cargo ship after getting salt water all over it.

"Hang on a sec, Major, I think I've got what you need handy. I'll be right back."

Charlie sat there sweating and closed his eyes, just for a minute, just until Chief Demopolis came back.

There was a wail, the ear-piercing bone-shaking wail of the air raid siren. "Aw, Jehosophat," said Charlie. He jumped over to the driver's seat and cranked the engine as Demopolis burst out of the tent, holding a length of pipe. The chief slammed into the passenger seat and another man came after him, tumbling into the back as Charlie put the jeep into reverse and slewed around before putting it into first and heading for the flight line.

Demopolis held his hat on his head and looked up at the sky. "Shit! There they are, Major!"

"Call the clock!"

"Ah, bombers, eleven o'clock high."

"They coming here or the harbor?"

"Can't tell. Where are we going?"

"To the flight line."

"Major, don't you think we should take cover?"

Charlie looked up from the road, darted a look at the bombers, and looked back at the road. "We're good for two minutes or so."

"No offense, Major, but we're not going to fix your engine and get you off the ground in two minutes."

"I want to be with my crew. You guys can share a slit trench with us, there's one not far. We ought to make it with a minute to spare."

"A whole minute? Gosh, why worry?"

Charlie grinned and pushed down on the accelerator to be sure it was on the floor. Then he was on the brake, coming to a stop within twenty feet of the slit trench, and fifty yards from the flight line. Demopolis and his mechanic piled out and rushed into the slit trench.

Charlie stood looking up at the approaching Jap bombers. There was a roar from the runway and a flight of P-39s took off, followed at once by another. Looking up again Charlie saw the bombers were almost overhead. If they were bombing the airfield they'd turn away from their bomb run in the next few seconds.

"Hey, Charlie, you going to join us over here or watch the pretty bombs fall?"

"Relax, Al, I think they're heading to the harbor."

The navigator climbed up out of the trench and joined Charlie. He looked over his shoulder. "Hey, Bob, how long for a bomb to fall from 23,000 feet?"

"Thirty-eight seconds, give or take." The bombardier stood up and sat on the edge of the slit trench, looking up at the bombers. "From time of drop, anyway."

"Well, Charlie, thirty-eight seconds," said Al. "What do you want to do with your last half-minute of life?"

"Guess I'm going to spend it with you, Al. Not what I had in mind for my last thirty seconds."

"What did you have in mind? Just as a matter of curiosity?"

"Oh, beautiful women, good whisky, a nice juicy steak. That sort of thing. You?"

Al shrugged expressively. "Eh. I'll string along with you, Charlie."

From the harbor came the noise of explosions.

"Anybody see Zeros?" Charlie asked.

"Nope," said Stern. "But if they come over I'll race you to the slit trench."

Charlie looked at Al. A memory filled his mind, a slit trench in Surabaya during a Jap air raid, and a dozen Dutchmen dying in front of him when a Zero strafed the trench. With an effort Charlie put the memory back in its box.

"You all right?" Al asked.

"Sure. You?"

"I hate Zeros."

"Yeah."

Charlie could feel the explosions from the harbor in the soles of his feet. He saw the bombers turning away to the north. They continued to the north and after three minutes the noise of the explosions and the tremors in the soles of his feet died away.

"Guess it isn't our last thirty seconds after all, Al," Charlie said.

"That works," Al replied. "So, we going to Rabaul?"

"You're the navigator. What time is it? Can we get to Rabaul and back here by dark?"

Al looked at his wristwatch. "Sure. We're still within the hour delay."

"Swell. Hey, Demopolis! You want to help Smith get that oil line in?"

"Why, sure, Major. Come on, Sturgis, help me get this line on Major Davis' airplane, and then we'll go check the other one."

Major Marsden drove up. "Charlie, you guys OK?"

"Sure. We'll be up in thirty minutes. Right, Demopolis?"

"Absolutely, Major."

"OK. We'll try to take off about 1100h."

"Sort of marginal, Mike."

"I know, Charlie. We can get back here at sunset if we leave then. Any later and we'll scrub."

Jimmy looked left and right, checking the formation of P-39s he was leading south, away from Seven-Mile. It was a motley bunch, made up of whomever stood close to a P-39 when the air raid siren sounded. Kellerman was on his right as Corncob Two, and Shafer on his left as Corncob Three. The other five P-39s were flown by pilots Jimmy knew by face or sometimes by name from the other three flights in the squadron. He wondered where Tommy Bell was.

"Corncobs from Corncob Leader, anyone have any problems with fuel or engines?"

A chorus of negatives came over the hiss-pop of static. Jimmy checked his altimeter; the formation was at 8,000 feet and still climbing.

"OK. Stay sharp, watch for Zeros. Corncob Leader out."

Jimmy looked over his shoulder at the Jap bombers, still three miles above them and headed south. He didn't see any Zeros, but that didn't mean they weren't there. He looked at the rate of climb indicator and his fuel gauge. Short-legged, slow-climbing P-39s.

By the time they were at 15,000 feet Jimmy saw bombs exploding in the harbor, among the shipping and in the town of Port Moresby. At least they wouldn't have to dodge bomb craters on the runway.

"Seven-Mile Tower, Seven-Mile Tower, this is Corncob Leader."

There was silence on the radio. Jimmy wasn't surprised. People were still probably climbing out of slit trenches and dusting themselves off.

He turned slowly to the west, and his radio squawked and screeched with static.

"...der, come in. *Skeereek!*...wer, calling Corncob Leader, come in."

Jimmy keyed his radio. "Seven Mile, Seven Mile, this is Corncob Leader, come in, over."

"Lea...raid...in sight...rogative."

"Seven Mile, you are coming in broken and intermittent, I say again, broken and intermittent. Have Jap bombers in sight, their heading north, estimate fifteen miles, still above my altitude. Seven Mile, do you receive me?"

"Affirm...der. *Skawwwk!* ...tercept?"

300

Jimmy was sure they were asking him to intercept.

"Corncobs from Corncob Leader, new heading zero three zero, acknowledge."

The airplane to airplane communication was scratchy but readable, and one by one the pilots checked in, following Jimmy as he turned north.

The clouds were building over the mountains. The bombers were still visible, between two banks of clouds. Jimmy looked at his altimeter, which read 18,000 feet, and his VSI, which showed a rate of climb of 650 feet per minute. That would only decrease, and it would take at least another seven or eight minutes to climb to 23,000 feet, where he figured the Jap bombers were. They were probably flying at 180 to 200 mph, and at the 165 mph best climb speed of the P-39, the bombers were traveling even faster over the ground.

He looked at his fuel. No one got off the ground with aux tanks, and they'd burned a lot of fuel climbing to their present altitude.

"Corncob Leader, this is, ah, Corncob Six."

"This is Lead, go ahead, Six."

"Lead, my engine is overheating and my oil pressure is dropping."

"Six, head for the barn. Keep your eyes open for Zeros."

"Corncob Six, heading home."

Jimmy looked down. He saw the P-39 dropping down, probably with the engines throttled back for cooling.

He also saw his flight was coming over the beach, with the harbor to their left and the entrance to Bootless

Inlet on the right, with Seven-Mile at eleven o'clock low.

Six more minutes to 23,000 feet. Jimmy did some arithmetic in his head concerning fuel consumption and speeds over the ground. In the end he figured they'd be able to intercept the Jap bombers, but they'd run out of fuel before they could get back to Seven-Mile.

Crap.

"Seven-Mile, Seven-Mile, this is Corncob Leader, come in, over."

"...*skeerrrk-skarrrsss*..."

"Seven-Mile, repeat."

"Corn...der...fuel...ver."

"Corncob Leader from Corncob Seven."

"Go ahead, Corncob Seven."

"Leader, Seven has CHT overheat and oil overpressure."

"Corncob Seven, understood. Head for home. You know what to do."

"Keep my eyes open, roger."

"OK, this is Corncob Leader to flight. Close up, we'll maintain this heading for a few minutes. Watch your gauges."

The radio cleared of static. "Corncob Leader, Corncob Leader, this is Seven-Mile. Jimmy, it's Dionne. How's it look?"

"Waste of time. We're low on fuel and still climbing."

"Return to base. Repeat, return to base."

"Roger, returning to base. Corncobs, this is Corncob Leader, let's head for home."

Charlie watched as Danny started the No. 3 engine. The oil and fuel pressure came up, the CHT rose to operating range. The pilots watched the gauges for a minute, but they behaved normally.

"All right," said Charlie. "Start No. 1. If the rest of them will start we're headed north."

"Roger," said Danny. "Starting No. 1."

Ten minutes later all four engines were running smooth. "Sparks, pilot."

"Go ahead, Skipper."

"Send our letter to Operations, Sparks."

"Sending." A moment later, Sparks said, "Pilot, we've got the go from Operations."

"Understood, Sparks." Charlie looked out the window. To their left Major Madsen's airplane was taxiing out of the line, followed by the next B-17. Charlie waited for the three B-17s of Madsen's squadron to taxi past, then pushed his own throttles forward.

"Tail gunner, pilot."

"Go ahead, skipper."

"The boys following us?"

"Yes, sir. Both of 'em."

"OK, thanks, Em."

Charlie looked at the chronometer. It read 1120. "Navigator, pilot."

"Go ahead, Charlie."

"How's our time look?"

"It's a definite maybe, Charlie."

"Swell. Well, Danny here needs to learn how to make night landings at Seven-Mile."

"We could do it another time, Skipper."

303

"Now, Danny, don't be shy. I'll walk you through it. Besides, we've got to make it back from Rabaul before we need to worry about that."

Danny Evans checked the engine instruments and then scanned the sky above and ahead. Charlie told him looking for Japs wasn't necessarily his job, but he'd flown pursuits long enough to make keeping a lookout a habit. Charlie never said anything about it, other than shaking his head once. But Danny noticed Charlie kept a pretty good lookout himself.

Danny looked out at the formation. *Bronco Buster II* led the low squadron, with Major Marsden's *Bomb Buggy* leading the high squadron. Below and to the right was the expanse of the Solomon Sea, and ahead of them was the coast of New Ireland.

The trip so far was quiet. No sign of Zeros and the Jap bombers were probably nearing Vunakanau.

Danny thought about that. Jap bombers on the ground, a beehive of activity, maybe refueling and rearming but certainly pushing the bombers back into their revetments.

Hey, with a bit of luck maybe they'd catch the Japs with their trousers about their ankles.

Lefty took a deep breath of oxygen and started his scan of the sky again, one hand on the handles of the .50-cal. Browning, the other on the rim of the gun port, but inside, out of the 200 mph wind. He and Johann struggled into their heavy flying gear as the bomber climbed above 9000 feet, the wool-lined jacket and trousers and the shearling-lined flying boots and the heavy gloves and the helmet and goggles. It was hot until they got above 12,000 feet, still climbing into the stratosphere, but after that it got cooler. Lefty knew that at their normal cruising altitude of 21,000 feet or higher the heavy winter flying gear would barely keep him from freezing his balls off.

Until they sighted Zeros. Then he'd be plenty warm, if he noticed it at all.

Lefty took a second or two to admire the ocean and its whitecaps, then the blue sky and the blinding white clouds wherein the Zeros could appear in less than a heartbeat. He looked over his shoulder at Johann, who was doing much the same thing, one hand on his machine gun and the other on the edge of the window, scanning for Zeros. Ahead of them in the fuselage he could see the ball turret rotate as Johnny searched for Zeros.

And this was life.

This was friendship, and Lefty had grown to treasure his friends, and the crew, and the danger that held them all together. It wasn't fun, exactly, no, not fun. Not when machine gun bullets whipped through the fuselage and cannon shells exploded all too uncomfortably close and flak *woofed* and burst alongside them. It wasn't like Lefty didn't know what that would do, he'd seen too many B-17s go down spewing bits and flames and men in burning parachutes to not have a clear idea of that.

But this was his life, and he scanned the sky on the right side of the bomber, and looked at the clouds, and smiled behind his oxygen mask.

Jimmy took off his helmet and ran his fingers through his sweat-soaked hair before he unbuckled his harness and climbed out on the wing of the P-39.

"Saw a couple of guys come back early," said Hope, as he helped Jimmy out of his parachute harness.

"Yeah. Engine overheat and oil pressure problems."

"How'd the *Gremlin* do?"

"She needs a new engine." Jimmy smacked the panel over the engine exhaust stacks. "Don't know how many hours this one has on it, and it's been used and abused."

"You can't get enough power out of it?"

"Not the rated horsepower, anyway. Not so bad on takeoff, but she suffers at altitude even more than normal."

Hope nodded. "Let me see what I can do. I heard back in Brisbane we were supposed to have some new engines coming, but I haven't seen 'em yet."

Jimmy nodded.

A jeep braked to a stop. Major Dionne was driving. "Hey, Jimmy, hop in."

Jimmy climbed in.

"How much fuel did you have when you landed?"

"Maybe one-third. Call it thirty gallons."

Dionne nodded. "We saw you pass over, about fifteen minutes after the raid ended. Looked like you were still climbing."

"Yup."

"Then your boys started coming back with engine problems."

"Yup."

"Real engine problems?"

"Major, I don't know the boys that aborted. I do know we're having all sorts of maintenance issues because we can't get new engines, or spare parts to fix the ones we've got, or even engine oil that doesn't break down. And that last item alone, when you're constantly pushing an Allison at maximum boost and high RPMs, is enough to eat up an engine from the inside out. So if it were me I'd give them the benefit of the doubt."

Dionne nodded and sighed. "Between you and me, that's not what Colonel Wrixon thinks."

"Well, Keith, between you and me, I haven't seen Colonel Wrixon in the cockpit of a P-39, much less over the beach at Buna or anywhere else we've been going lately."

Dionne gave Jimmy a hard look. Jimmy looked back at him, carefully keeping any expression from his face. Finally Dionne shook his head. "Yeah. Be careful who you say stuff like that to, Jimmy. You're already on Wrixon's shit list."

Jimmy nodded and changed the subject. "Looked to me like the Japs hit the harbor. Any strays come our way?"

"No, we were lucky."

"What happened to those B-17s that were here? From the 19th?"

"They cranked up and headed out right after the raid."

"Know where they're going?"

"No. There's six of 'em up here, so probably Rabaul. Or maybe Lae."

307

"We going to go up to Buna today? Or the Track?"

"Jeez, Jimmy, haven't you had enough for one day?"

"No one's said I could go home to Montana yet. Reckon we may as well get on with the job."

"True enough. Get a look at the weather up north?"

"Clouds. More clouds. Gonna rain, but we won't know about weather on the coast until we get there."

"Damn. Wonder what it would take for the Navy to put a submarine up there and send us weather reports now and then."

Jimmy shrugged. "Submarines. I'd be scared to ride one of those things. Imagine deliberately sinking yourself for a living."

The squadron commander put the jeep in gear. "Let's go collect the rest of your urchins and see what the word is."

"OK. Then maybe we can get some chow."

"Is that what you call that stuff?"

"What, aren't you used to it yet?"

"I hope I *never* get used to that slop," Dionne said fervently. "Makes me miss Stateside chow something fierce."

Dionne drove down the line and met Kellerman and Shafer on the way.

"How did your engines behave?" Jimmy asked.

"OK," said Kellerman. He frowned. "Didn't seem to be turning out the power it should have."

"About the same for me," said Shafer. "Been doing that for a couple of days now."

Jimmy looked at Dionne and raised an eyebrow. Dionne grimaced, looking down the taxiway.

308

The Operations shack wasn't working at the sort of tempo Jimmy associated with an imminent mission. The duty officer nodded at them when they entered.

"Eddie, what's the word?" Dionne asked.

The duty officer shook his head. "Nothing on the board. Weather's socked in on the coast."

"Oh? Someone been up there?"

"The 19th radioed the report. Eight-tenths cloud over Buna, tops at 18,000 feet."

Jimmy thought about that. Eight-tenths, tops at 18.

Dionne looked at him. "Jimmy?"

"Looks bad. From a B-17 climbing through 20,000 feet. Doesn't say what the ceiling is over the beach, or what the weather is likely to be here in a couple of hours. Or over the mountains."

"You think we could go?"

"Maybe. Maybe we'd even get away with it. I'm sure the Aussies up there on the Track appreciate everything we do."

"And wish we could do more."

"Sure. Wouldn't you?"

Dionne nodded. He pursed his lips. "Wanna go up there and take a look?"

"Sure. I'll get my boys together and..."

"No. You and me. I want a look at that airstrip you and Bell hit yesterday. But no bombs. With the weather looking dicey we might want the fuel instead."

Jimmy nodded. "Makes sense." He grinned. "You still want to get some slop at the mess tent before we go? Remember, it might get bumpy up there."

Dionne snorted. "You watch yourself, Lieutenant Ardana, or I might just puke on your boots."

The duty officer said, "You sure you want to do that, Keith? Not exactly an authorized mission."

"Sure it's authorized. We're at war with the Empire of Japan, what other authorization do we need? If anyone asks, you can say it's a maintenance test flight. We've been having a lot of engine issues, you know."

Eddie grinned faintly. "Sure. Better run along and get airborne, then."

They walked outside of the Ops shack and looked reflexively to the north, where the clouds were building over the tops of the Owen Stanley mountains.

"Two, maybe three hours?" Dionne asked.

"Before the rain hits? About that. We can land here in the rain if we have to."

"You've done it?"

"Once. It was slippery."

"I'll bet. Go get some chow if you're really hungry, and meet me on the flight line in thirty minutes."

"Yes, sir."

Dionne got in his jeep and drove off. Kellerman exchanged a look with Shafer.

"What's that all about, Jimmy?" Kellerman asked.

"Aw, Dionne wants to stretch his legs, I reckon."

"He could do that in the pattern."

"He could, but where's the fun in that? Come on, let's grab a bite."

The gap between the bottom of the clouds and the tops of the trees on the north slope of the mountains was maybe five hundred feet, with intermittent rain and visibility ten miles or less. A lot less in the rain, and ten miles wasn't a long way at 260 mph.

Jimmy and Dionne formed up with Jimmy in the lead, flying again as Corncob Leader, with Dionne as Corncob Two.

"I've been up there once," Dionne told Jimmy. "You know the area better than I do, so you take the lead."

As they came down the slope Jimmy looked at the shape of the mountains and the hills. Best he could figure they were a little east of a direct heading to Buna, and the coast was forty miles ahead. Ten minutes or less, then, and when they came over the coast Jimmy figured he'd know where they were. He hoped they weren't right over the antiaircraft guns at Buna. Even taken by surprise those little bastards were good shots.

"Ten minutes," he radioed.

Two mike clicks from Dionne answered him. Jimmy looked to the left and the right and scanned the clouds, but that ceiling was still low and he doubted the Japs could intercept them even if they knew exactly where they were. Why should they, anyway? He and Dionne were coming to them.

Jimmy scanned his instruments. Airspeed 260, descending slowly with the slope of the mountains, engine instruments looked good, aux tank about two-thirds consumed. Jimmy frowned. That seemed a little high on fuel consumption. He wondered how Dionne was doing.

Five minutes passed, and a few minutes after that the coast appeared ahead. Jimmy looked left and right again. They were east of Buna, and east of the Jap airstrip. He looked over his shoulder at Dionne and waggled his wings. Dionne nodded and pointed to the

311

left. Jimmy nodded in reply, reefing into a left turn, diving at a shallow angle, leveling out over the trees with the breakers on the beach in sight on the right.

Then there were ships a half mile from the beach, which meant barges, and the little aisle between the trees that was the Jap airstrip popped into view. There weren't any Zeros in sight, not even among the trees on the north side of the airstrip. Jimmy caught a brief glimpse of a patch of burned-out trees on the north edge of the runway, then they were past and headed for the beachhead.

There were barges in the water, going to and from a freighter out in the bay. Jimmy took them even lower, low enough that the spray from the waves splashed up on his windshield. He lined up on a barge and triggered his machine guns, holding his finger on the cannon trigger until they were close, then *punk!punk!punk!* Jimmy let up on the cannon and pulled up slightly to pass over the barge, banking slightly to line up with another one. On his right he had a brief glimpse of Dionne, pouring it into another barge, clearing it just as it burst into flames.

Tracer lashed around them, a 57-mm shell burst on Jimmy's left as he lined up on another barge. Someone fired at him from the barge, a rope of tracer from a light machine gun, and Jimmy saw dozens of muzzle flashes from the barge, hell, it was full of Jap infantry! Jimmy triggered his guns and watched the bullets strike the water in tall fountains, and as they neared the barge he triggered the cannon. The 37-mm shells struck the barge square on the waterline, the .50-cal. and .30-cal. rounds chewed into the Jap soldiers, Jimmy heard a

312

rattle and tinkle of bullets striking his own fuselage, then he was over the barge and there was nothing ahead of him but the bay on the right and the jungle to the left and the tracers racing after him. He looked over his shoulder for Dionne, who was still on his right and joining up now as the tracer fell behind them.

"Two, you OK?"

"Yeah. You had enough fun for one day?"

"Sure thing. Let's go home before it rains."

Danny Evans didn't like flak.

That first mission to Lae in a P-39 he didn't know enough to be really scared, and it was over and done before real fear could kick in. But flying in formation on a bomb run where you had to fly straight and level, after it had been drilled into him – granted for all of two weeks until he cracked up his P-39 and got sent to hospital – that you never, ever, flew straight and level anywhere you suspected the enemy might be present, that was scary.

It got worse when the flak started.

It wasn't like the Japs were subtle about it, either. They started shooting two or three minutes before the formation arrived over the target. Danny could see the flak over Rabaul and Vunakanau right now, a collection of black flowers that appeared suddenly and drifted on the wind, dissipating but replaced by others. Lots and lots of others, and as the formation got closer to the target the flak got darker and denser.

"Pilot, bombardier. Opening bomb bay doors."

Now Danny knew it as a litany, almost a liturgical set of responses between the pilot and the bombardier on the bomb run, broken sometimes by the gunners calling out Jap fighters and their positions. The bomb bay doors opened and the slipstream roared up through the opening, a wind nearly three times hurricane force. They were in among the flak for certain, and the airplane rocked and bobbed in the fierce turbulence of the bursting shells, while shrapnel tinkled against and slashed through the fuselage.

"Steady, steady."

Fire streamed from the bomber in the number two position in the high squadron. It was from the port inboard engine, and it went out in ten heart-stopping seconds, but gray smoke streamed from the engine. Danny saw the propeller had stopped.

"Steady, pilot, steady. Almost there, almost..."

Danny looked at the instruments, checked the throttle and mixture controls, felt the airplane's controls in his hands and feet, the slight pressures as Charlie kept them steady on the bomb run. *Steady, steady...* Danny kept his own hands light on the controls, the way Charlie taught him, light so as not to interfere with the pilot's movements, but ready to take over immediately if Charlie was hit, an eventuality Danny prayed wouldn't happen, because then he'd have to take over. The copilot was sure he could fly the airplane. He wasn't sure he could lead the crew.

"OK, steady," said the bombardier. "Steady...aaand...bombs gone, closing bomb bay doors."

There was a forward push on the controls as Charlie counteracted the tendency of the airplane to surge upward as the bombs fell free. The formation continued straight on for a long minute, then turned to the south. The flak followed them partway through the turn before tailing off.

"ZEROS. Ball turret has Zeros, seven o'clock low, count nine."

"Tail gunner has the Zeros. Count nine."

Danny fought the urge to look over his left shoulder. He wouldn't see anything but the bulkhead aft of the cockpit and the left inner fuselage with all its wiring and cables.

The B-17 that lost an engine on the bomb run started to fall behind. The high squadron slowed to let the damaged bomber stay in formation. Charlie reached out and pulled their own throttles back. Danny looked out to his right, but their own number two stayed in formation. It made him cringe a little, slowing down, but he knew he'd personally be grateful for the cover, and it kept ten heavy machine guns in the formation.

"ZEROS. Right waist has Zeros, four o'clock low, count six."

"Yeah, tail gunner, I've got those bastards too. Six on the right, nine on the left."

Fifteen Zeros, Danny thought. Holy Mother of God.

He flexed his fingers on the controls and hunched his shoulders, bracing himself. Live through the next hour, he thought, live through the next hour and then all they had to worry about was making it over the mountains and landing at Seven-Mile, or maybe Horn Island if Seven-Mile was socked in.

Lefty looked out of the port, training his gun to four o'clock where six Zeros were climbing above their altitude. It was pretty obvious what the little yellow bastards were up to. They'd climb high enough to dive on the high squadron, then turn to attack the low squadron, then climb back to altitude and do it all over again. The Zeros coming up on the left meant the attackers could actually catch the B-17s in a crossfire, if they were willing to risk a collision as they passed through the bomber formation. Lefty figured they'd take that risk. Whatever else you might say about the Japs, nerve and guts were qualities they had in plenty.

He didn't want to be right about the Jap plan of attack, but the Japs weren't stupid, either, not the ones they'd seen.

"Upper turret, Zeros attacking the high squadron."

Lefty couldn't see what was happening but that didn't matter. When the Japs turned their way Kim Frye in the upper turret would let them know, if only because he'd start shooting. He wondered how Johnny in the ball turret and Emmons in the tail felt. They'd called the Japs and watched them climb up above their altitude, and then the Japs passed outside their field of vision. Lefty knew that feeling, that itch of your hands on the machine-gun grips, your thumbs on the spade trigger, crouching down a little to peer through the sights as the little bastards flew outside your area, and all you could do then was grit your teeth and check your oxygen and keep your eyes open while someone else called out the location.

"Crew, upper turret, heads up, Japs coming down. SKIPPER! WATCH OUT!"

316

"Pilot, Primrose Two coming down right on top of us!"

Lefty fought the urge to leave his post and crowd against Johann, who was craning almost out of his window, looking up. Suddenly the B-17 rolled left hard. Lefty clung desperately to the gun mount as Charlie dove into the turn, faster than Lefty had ever known Charlie to throw the big bomber around.

Then past his window and beyond them a wing tumbled, an entire flaming wing from a B-17, gouting flame and smoke from the wing root, outboard engine still running, flaming bits following it down, coming so close that fire touched their right aileron and burned part of the fabric away. Bits pattered and smacked against the fuselage and wing. Lefty saw them hit and bounce off the wing, and something on fire came through the gunport past his face and smashed against the fuselage bulkhead aft. The bomber turned hard in the opposite direction as Lefty looked to see if the flaming debris had caused a fire inside their own fuselage, and he was thrown against the gun mount. Pain blossomed up from his ribs and he felt rather than heard something crack.

The bomber straightened up and Lefty looked around the outside of the airplane. The damage to the aileron fabric wasn't bad, maybe two or three square feet of fabric gone, and he couldn't see any holes in the wing.

"Crew, copilot, sound off!"

"Bombardier OK."

"Navigator OK."

"Pilot OK."

"Upper turret OK."

"Radio OK."

"Ball turret OK."

"Right waist OK," Lefty said, scanning for Japs as he spoke.

"Left waist OK."

"Tail OK."

"Pilot, right waist, we took some debris back here, nothing serious, but the right aileron got scorched."

"ZEROS. Upper turret has Zeros, nine at eleven o'clock, five at two o'clock."

The upper turret opened up and Lefty saw the Zeros at two o'clock, turning hard to dive on *Bronco Buster II*. He crouched down to the rear of the port, aiming up, caught a Zero in his sights, waited, waited, they were close! He squeezed down on the trigger and the .50-cal. hammered out a burst, Lefty gauging the tracers the way Charlie taught him, changing his aim, firing one more time as the Zeros dove past them.

Everyone was firing now, everyone but Emmons, whose guns wouldn't bear on a target. Zeros dove past from above and left, and they were close, really close, and when Lefty followed them down, firing, he was sure he saw strikes on one of them before they went out of his field of fire.

Then there was a respite while the Zeros climbed back up to attack.

It didn't last as long as Lefty thought it would.

"Crew, tail gunner, we got three coming up our six."

"Ah see 'em, Em," said the ball turret gunner.

Emmons fired, the roaring .50s in the tail amplified by the cone of the fuselage. Three explosions echoed up from aft, shaking the fuselage, Jap 20-mm stuff, and tracer flanked them on either side and high.

"Johann, breakin' youah side!" The ball turret fired, fired again, and Johann at the left waist joined.

"Hit 'im! Ah *hit* that sonabitch! He's a-spittin' fire!"

From the corner of his eye Lefty saw the ball turret swivel furiously, hammering away at the Zeros.

"Scratch one, ah *got* that sonabitch!"

"Ball, navigator, I see him, Johnny, he's streaming flame and pieces. Good shooting!"

"Pilot, tail gunner, we took some hits in the rudder. Got some fabric flappin' in the breeze."

"Thanks, Em. Let me know if the fabric starts unraveling."

Lefty looked out to the right and astern, and saw six Zeros climbing above them, heading fore to aft.

"Right waist has six Zeros climbing on the right, headed astern."

Charlie worked the rudder pedals. There was something about the rudder that felt different from a mere loss of fabric. He didn't know what that was, and the fact that he didn't know worried him.

"Tail gunner, pilot."

"Go ahead, skipper."

"Em, when you can take your eyes off the Zeros, look up at the rudder and tell me what you see."

"Fabric trailing back, and...uh, skipper, it looks bent. Like the spine of the rudder has been blown off center. A cannon shell hit right about there, in the stabilizer forward of the rudder."

Jehosophat, Charlie thought. If the spine of the rudder was bent it could come right out of its frames, leaving the airplane rudderless. Not a disaster, maybe, but really and truly inconvenient.

"OK, thanks, Em."

Danny looked at him and then looked forward.

Charlie checked the high squadron, now down to two airplanes, and left and right at his own squadron. Primrose Five looked OK, but Primrose Six was trailing smoke from the No. 4 engine.

"Crew, tail gunner, Zeros turning in to the attack!"

"Upper turret, I've got them. Two groups, three each, five o'clock high."

Charlie looked at the instruments. The gauges looked good.

Then he looked across the cockpit at Danny Evans. Danny's eyes over the oxygen mask were big. Charlie reached over and punched him in the shoulder.

Danny nodded and took a deep breath, facing forward, hands on the controls. The tension didn't leave his shoulders, but their angle changed.

Charlie took a deep breath himself and settled deeper into his seat.

Behind him it sounded like every gun aft of the flight deck went off at once. *Bronco Buster II* vibrated and shook and roared. Tracers flashed by the cockpit and cannon shells slammed and exploded across the left wing. A Zero flew over the wing and tracers from the upper turret lashed it at point-blank range. Charlie saw hits sparkle down the fuselage and the engine, close

320

enough to see sparks and bits of metal fly as Smith's bullets struck. The Zero reared up as dense black smoke and bright yellow fire streamed from the cowling. The wings separated from the fuselage and the Zero exploded. Three more Zeros flew past, and Charlie saw the left cheek gun firing at them.

Charlie looked at the cannon holes blown in the wing and then at the engine instruments. The cannon shells had to have hit the fuel tanks, but it didn't look as if fuel was leaking from ruptured tanks.

He looked at the fuel pressure again, but it was steady.

The guns stopped all at once, and even with the sound of the engines and the slipstream over the fuselage it seemed quiet. Charlie looked up to see all nine remaining Zeros attacking the two B-17s of the high squadron. Kim Smith in the upper turret fired short bursts at the Zeros and Charlie saw the upper turret on Primrose Five doing the same, and the tracers from the tail and ball turret gunners of Primrose One and Three fired on the Zeros.

Primrose One's right wing sparkled with cannon strikes and the No. 3 engine trailed smoke and then fire. Charlie waited but the fire didn't go out, it got brighter. The Zeros split around the high squadron, and one of them fell off on a wing and tumbled out of the sky, no smoke, no apparent damage, probably the pilot hit.

The fire from Primrose One's No. 3 engine got worse. Charlie could imagine the scene in the cockpit. He shut it out of his mind.

Primrose One nosed over into a dive, and Charlie knew what Madsen would try, get up speed in a dive, put the bomber into a slip, and try to extinguish the fire. That meant he'd tried everything else and couldn't put the fire out, and to try this in the face of attacking Zeros meant he figured if he didn't put the fire out it wouldn't matter about the Zeros.

Jehosophat.

Charlie put the nose down. "Primrose Five, Primrose Six, Primrose Two, this is Primrose Four, follow me."

Lefty's first thought when the bomber put its nose down was that they'd been hit harder than it looked like, then he saw Primrose Four on the right keeping formation. The Zeros peeled off and headed to the north, for which Lefty was profoundly grateful, as long as they kept on going and didn't come back. Maybe they'd run out of ammo, which wouldn't surprise him, given the way the Japs held the trigger down when they attacked.

He craned a little out of the window and looked down.

A B-17 was below them, streaming fire from the No. 3 engine, and as Lefty watched the B-17 skewed into a slip to the left. The fire spread out over the wing and went out. The B-17 held the slip for a long couple of seconds and straightened out.

The B-17 leveled out. They formed up with it, and kept descending.

They leveled out below ten thousand. It was warm enough to make the heavy flying suits unnecessary, along with the oxygen masks. Taking the gear off was part of the post-mission ritual, letting the crazy tension from the fight over Rabaul drain out. The cool air at nine thousand feet was something to enjoy, because it would be hot as hell at Seven-Mile. The cool air was nice, but all the way to Seven-Mile, Lefty stayed on his gun, looking for Zeros. You never knew when the little bastards would come out to play, so the mission wasn't over until the engines shut down.

Jimmy and Major Dionne made their report to Captain Allan as the group intelligence officer.

"Three barges, one burning, one sinking, one full of infantry?" asked the intelligence officer.

"That's right," said Jimmy. He'd counted the holes in his P-39. There weren't that many, which surprised him, considering the number of guns firing at him.

A vivid image of the riflemen lined up on the side of the barge, rifle muzzles winking yellow at him, came and went.

"And you, Major?"

Jimmy turned to listen. Turning away from the beachhead he counted fires and barges that were sinking or damaged. There were at least five fires, and one barge down by the stern with its ramp sticking up and men floating around it.

"I think about the same as Jimmy," Dionne said slowly. "No barge full of infantry, a small secondary explosion on one of the barges. Strikes on two others, one of them looked to be burning."

"In all I saw five barges on fire, exiting from the target," Jimmy said. Allan nodded.

"All right," Allan said. "I'll get this typed up."

He left with his notes.

Dionne leaned back on the bench and grinned wryly at Jimmy. "I think you're going to get me in trouble, Jimmy."

"Why?"

"Talking me into a hare-brained mission like that."

"Hare-brained? I guess so. But you're the squadron commander. Why did you want to go along?"

Dionne looked at Jimmy and then down the flight line, where the mechanics worked on their P-39s, repairing engines and sheet metal. A fuel truck pulled up to one of the P-39s.

"I want to lead this squadron, Jimmy," Dionne replied. "I don't mean run it. Any reasonably competent officer can run a squadron. Do you understand that?"

Jimmy remembered sitting near this spot with Ed Groves and Steve Wolchek, before Wolchek bought it that first day over Buna. He nodded, thinking of the forms and requisition requests they went through, the reports they filled out.

"I think so," Jimmy said. "Before they shipped out I was acting ops officer with the Boxcars. It was less than a week, but enough to learn a thing or two."

Dionne nodded. "When I say I want to lead this squadron it means I have to lead guys like you, who has a pretty good idea of what he's doing, to the majority of the pilots who are lucky to have thirty hours or so in the P-39 and less than three hundred hours in their logbooks. That's not easy."

"No," said Jimmy. "I can see that, too."

"And to cap it all off I hear that new general is up here," said Dionne.

"Kenney?"

324

"You know him?"

"Heard of him."

"Anything special?"

"No."

Dionne nodded.

Bill Allan returned and parked his jeep next to them. "You two are in such trouble," he announced portentously.

Jimmy looked at the operations officer, then at Dionne, who shrugged.

"Why?"

"It seems Colonel Wrixon heard you weren't really on a maintenance flight. He wants you both up at Group Ops right now. He seemed pretty emphatic about it."

"See, Jimmy?" Dionne said. "Hare-brained."

"Aw, let's go and take our medicine, skipper."

There was a Ford sedan at Group Operations when they drove up. Eddie James was the duty officer still, but he appeared more motivated and industrious. Jimmy wasn't sure what the duty officer was doing, exactly, but it seemed to involve a lot of scribbling and insertion of papers into dogeared files.

"Eddie, what's going on?" Dionne asked.

"General Kenney," James said in a low tone. "He's in with the Colonel right now."

"The new general? The one taking over from Brett?"

"The one and only," said James, reaching for another file.

"What the hell are you doing?" Dionne asked.

"Looking busy for the general." James looked to the back of the building where Wrixon's office was.

"Wrixon sent for you but I think he has other things on his mind for now. Why don't you guys wait outside?"

Dionne nodded.

Outside on the porch Jimmy looked down the flight line. Coming up the hill was Tommy Bell and a man Jimmy didn't know, a major in a khaki uniform and an aide's aiguillette over his shoulder. Bell was talking enthusiastically to the major.

"Guess that guy is Kenney's aide," Jimmy said. "What are he and Chinkerbell talking about?"

"Guess we'll find out," said Dionne.

"Oh, hey, Major Benn, this is my squadron commander, Keith Dionne, and my flight leader, Jimmy Ardana," said Bell.

Handshakes and sizing up. "I've been talking to Bell here about low-level flying," said Benn. "He tells me he's pretty good, but there's someone better."

"He told you that, did he?" Jimmy asked.

"Something about a bet," Benn went on.

"Yeah, you could say that," Allen said. "I saw it myself."

He turned to Dionne. "That was a couple of days before you got here."

"Wow, the things you miss," said Dionne.

Benn laughed. "Too bad you guys aren't multi-engine pilots," he said. "I'm putting together a squadron, going after ships by skip-bombing from low level."

"What are you going to fly?" asked Jimmy.

"B-17s, to begin with."

"Yeah? How low will you have to go?"

"Not quite sure. We're working that out. Less than a hundred feet, more than fifty. Masthead height." Benn turned to Jimmy.

"It's Ardana, right? I hear you have four Japs, so I reckon you're pretty much a lost cause. Bell here likes to fly low, though, so maybe you'd let me have him?"

"No offense, Benn, but I'm hard up for pilots right now," said Dionne. "I'd be surprised if you couldn't find better candidates who can already fly B-17s."

There was a stir from inside the building, and Colonel Wrixon emerged onto the porch with another man, not very tall, putting a crush cap on his head. There were two stars on each of his shoulders.

"That's my boss," Benn whispered. "Gotta run."

Jimmy came to attention with the other pilots as Kenney turned their way and saluted.

Kenney returned their salutes and turned to Major Benn.

"Bill!" said the general. "Fallen in with evil companions, have you?"

"Aw, they're just pursuit pilots, general."

"Like I said, evil companions." Kenney walked down the stairs, returned their salutes, and held out his hand to Dionne.

"Dionne, General, Keith Dionne. This is my Ops Office, Captain Bill Allen, and one of my flight leaders, Lt. Jimmy Ardana."

Kenney shook hands with Dionne and Allen and turned a considering eye on Ardana.

"Jimmy Ardana, eh? I hear you're a hot pilot."

"I can hold my own, General."

327

"Good! Four Japs? I'd say you can hold your own. When are you adding a fifth?"

"Just as soon as I can get one in front of me, General."

"Better," said Kenney. He clapped Jimmy on the shoulder.

"General, this is Tommy Bell," said Benn. "He likes to fly low."

"Do you?" said Kenney. "You get tired of P-39s, come see me or Benn here. We could use a guy like you."

Benn sighed and rolled his eyes theatrically. "Already tried to recruit him, General. Major Dionne here says he's too short of pilots to lose one."

"And I'm in Jimmy's flight, General. He needs me to look after him."

"You do that, Bell. Good to meet you boys."

The General and his aide got into the Ford and drove off.

Dionne turned to Colonel Wrixon. "Sir, I understand you wanted to see us?"

Wrixon looked at Dionne for a moment, then turned and walked back into the Ops Shack.

Jimmy said, "What the hell?"

"Ah, actually, Major Benn said Kenney heard about that trip north you and Major Dionne took, Jimmy," said Bell. "I guess Kenney told Wrixon it was, ah, how did Benn put it? A grand show of initiative."

"Really?" Dionne grinned. "OK, let's get the hell out of here before Wrixon changes his mind. Guess we're not going to get gigged if the General thinks we put on a grand show of initiative."

Charlie and Chief Demopolis stood looking up at *Bronco Buster II's* bent rudder and its scorched, tattered fabric.

Demopolis pointed to shrapnel holes on the roof of the tail gunner's position. "Your gunner OK?" he asked

Charlie blinked. "He didn't say anything about being wounded. Climbed out of the airplane like he was OK."

Demopolis nodded. "Yeah. I hear he doesn't talk much."

The line chief walked to the other side of the rudder. "Look at that, Major," he said, pointing.

Charlie saw a hole about the size of a man's head, blackened around the edges, at the trailing edge of the vertical stabilizer, right next to the point where the rudder frame was bent.

"Hey, Squid, go get me a ladder," the chief called to his assistant. "We're going to have to look at the rudder hinges, they've probably been stressed pretty good."

Charlie looked to the west, where the sun was setting, and to the north, where rain-laden clouds were coming down from the mountains.

The chief followed Charlie's look and nodded. "Sorry, Major, but the best I'm going to be able to do before it gets too dark to work is assess the damage and figure out the repairs."

Charlie nodded. There weren't any hangars at Seven-Mile. He remembered the big hangars the Dutch had at Singosari, hangars big enough to push a B-17 into and close the hangar doors on, and blacked out so you could work on an airplane at night. Just like the hangars at Clark Field back in the Philippines, and both of those fine installations were in Jap hands now.

"OK. I'll check with you first thing in the morning, then."

Charlie walked away, to where Danny Evans and Al Stern were waiting in a jeep. Charlie got into the front beside Al and yawned.

"Beer?" Al asked.

"Take me to it," said Charlie. "Where's the rest of the crew?"

"Probably headed in the same direction, enlisted style."

"Good for them. Let's go."

The only time the club at Seven-Mile wasn't crowded was when it wasn't open or there was no beer. They went to the bar and got beer and looked for a place to sit down.

Al said, "Over there. Jimmy Ardana's waving to us."

They made their way through the crowd. They let Danny go in front. Even if he had lost a lot of weight he was a big guy, and it was easier for him to cut a path. The place smelled of spilled beer and sweat, old and new, and, if your nose survived the assault, there were undertones of burned oil and aviation fuel, and traces of cordite, burned insulation, and wood smoke.

Jimmy sat with a couple of guys Charlie didn't know, but he figured they were pursuit pilots from the newly arrived 35th Fighter Group. One was a major and the other was a captain.

Jimmy made introductions. "Glad to meet you," said Keith Dionne.

"Likewise," said Bill Allen.

"Saw a couple of your guys come in after us," said Charlie. He looked at Jimmy.

"Now, Charlie, why do you think that was me?" asked Jimmy.

"Because it takes a lieutenant to pull a stunt like that."

Dionne laughed. "I'm wounded, Charlie. Wounded. Although it *was* a lieutenant that came up with the idea."

Charlie shook his head. "Jehosophat, Dionne, don't you know majors should be able to exercise good sense and sound judgment?"

"This from a guy who makes his living flying straight and level into flak and fighters?" Dionne shook his head and pointed to himself, then Charlie. "Pot. Kettle."

Jimmy laughed. "Let's face it. Maybe we weren't nuts the first time we left the ground, but then we kept doing it."

That brought grins and raised glasses. Except Danny Evans, who did grin, but it came and went and he barely raised his glass.

"Where'd you guys go today?" Jimmy asked. "A certain harbor with lots and lots of guns and lots and lots of Zeros?"

Al raised his glass. Jimmy nodded.

Jimmy looked at Danny Evans, who was sitting a little hunched over, staring into his beer. He looked at

331

Charlie and pointed a shoulder at Danny, raising an eyebrow.

"Who's ready for another beer?" Charlie asked. "Hey, Danny, you're falling behind. Drink up."

Danny took his stein and drank until it was dry. "I'll go get another round," he said, and left the table.

"Well," said Jimmy.

"It was a rough one, Jimmy," Al supplied. "We lost a bomber and crew."

Jimmy nodded.

"Just so you know it came apart right on top of us. I actually had to take evasive action to avoid collision."

Al sighed. "It was downright interesting for a minute there."

"First time Danny saw something like that," Charlie said. "Not that it gets any easier. Danny will be OK."

"Yeah?"

"Jimmy, maybe he wasn't a hot P-39 pilot, but he's really coming along in a B-17."

Jimmy nodded. "Good. Except for nearly killing me a couple of times I don't have anything against Evans. And that's past."

Charlie nodded and raised his glass. Jimmy touched it with his. Danny came back with a fistful of steins.

"Gosh, thanks, Danny," Jimmy said.

"These are for me, Ardana. Go get your own beer." But Danny pushed a stein to him and the others at the table, and held up his glass. "*My Sheila*," he said.

Jimmy held up his glass. Dionne and Allen hesitated a half-second before realizing that was the B-17 lost today over Rabaul.

"*My Sheila,*" they echoed.

And her crew, Jimmy thought as he drank.

The night was a long one. The Japs sent intruders over who dropped an occasional bomb while the searchlights speared into the darkness and the flak guns barked and shrapnel rained down out of the sky. It went on for hours and when it was done, dawn was two hours away.

Charlie didn't figure he'd sleep at all, and surprised himself by doing just that, and being shaken awake by a young private.

"Sir. Major, sir, are you awake?"

"I am now," Charlie said. He sat up and swung his feet over the side of the cot. "What is it, private?"

"Chief Demopolis sends his respects, sir, and needs you at your airplane."

"OK. Thanks. My respects to the Chief and I'll be down on the flight line as soon as I shave."

"Yes, sir." The private indicated the still-sleeping forms of Al Stern and Danny Evans. "Shall I wake them up, too, Major?"

"Nah. Let 'em sleep."

"Yes, sir."

The rasp of the razor against his skin was comforting and familiar, and shaving made Charlie feel nearly human, as human as you could feel when you hadn't had a real bath in a week and hadn't changed out of the same uniform in four days.

When he got to the flight line Chief Demopolis was with another airplane, talking to a couple of his mechanics. From the language being employed and the emphatic gestures at an engine with its cowling off, Charlie gathered the Chief was displeased about something.

The rudder of *Bronco Buster II* had what looked for all the world like a wooden splint between the rudder hinges. Charlie frowned, walking around the tail of the B-17, and he realized what Demopolis had done. The splint was two pieces of wood, cut to hold the rudder together, and with three nuts and bolts torqued down to straighten the bent stringer. The splint was between the rudder counterweights, and Charlie didn't think it would do anything good for the balance of the rudder.

Then he looked at the rudder fabric. The tattered portions had been cut off and not yet replaced.

The blasted thing was nowhere near ready to fly.

"Major, I'm sorry to get you out here with the rudder still like that, but I'm in kind of a bind," said Demopolis. He came from behind Charlie.

"Talk to me," Charlie said. He blinked back a yawn.

"Truth is, sir, I don't have a spare rudder or anything to fix the aluminum members of your rudder, not the way it should be done. I did a little improvisation, and got the stringer more or less straight, but while we were tightening the splint the stringer came apart. The splint's the only thing holding the rudder together now."

"Jehosophat," said Charlie. He turned away for a moment and took his hat off, rubbing his head, wiping out the hatband with a kerchief, and put the hat back on before turning back to the Chief.

"So not only that, but you have to do something about the fabric on the rudder."

"Yes, sir. I have an idea about that, but before I started I wanted your input. You're going to have to fly the thing."

Charlie looked at Demopolis. The line chief wore the slightly crestfallen look of a mechanic doing his absolute level best to fix a problem without the proper tools or parts, and very aware that any solution he might come up with could be inadequate.

"We got some heavy canvas weatherproof cloth, like for tent repair. Wrap it around the front of the rudder so it covers the splint, bring it to the back, sew it all up snug, and hopefully it'll get you back to Townsville."

Charlie bit back the "Hopefully?" that tried rising to his lips. He knew what the Chief meant. They didn't want to leave B-17s too long on the ground at Seven-Mile, certainly not during daylight. The Japs might send over more bombers any time.

Or Zeros. Zeros strafing on the deck were worse than bombers.

"The canvas won't rub against the vertical stabilizer?" Charlie asked.

"I'll make sure it doesn't, sir." The Chief hesitated. "Major, I know it ain't exactly ideal…"

Charlie held up his hand. "Look here, Chief, how are you fixed for sheet aluminum?"

The Chief blinked. Then his face cleared and he smiled. "Well, Major, that might work. I can rivet the aluminum to the wood splint and the rudder structure. It won't be pretty but, yeah, I like that."

The Chief frowned and asked, "Sir, you ain't bucking for my job, are you?"

Charlie chuckled. "No way, Chief. I'm just a simple-minded pilot."

The Chief chuckled in return. "I'll get right on it. Maybe an hour after lunch?"

"OK."

Demopolis was as good as his word, and at 1300 Charlie and Danny Evans started the engines, warmed them up for a few minutes, stood on the brakes, and gave the Wright Cyclones full power. Then they stomped on the rudder pedals, first on the right, then on the left, holding for thirty seconds each time, and throttled back.

The line chief crawled up through the tunnel from the nose compartment and shouted into Charlie's ear.

"Major, it looks pretty solid. Maybe a bit of a shimmy, but that could be the whole airframe vibrating."

"Reckon it'll get us to Mareeba?"

"Well, Major, I'm willing to bet your ass on it."

"That's swell, Chief. OK, unless you want to go AWOL you better get off this airplane."

The Chief shook Charlie's hand and disappeared. A moment later he appeared on Charlie's left. Charlie held his hands out his open window, thumbs out, the signal to remove the chocks. A moment later two airmen appeared, holding up the chocks. Charlie waved and turned to Danny Evans.

"Danny, did you feel anything in the rudder pedals? Anything unusual?"

"Shook a little, just like they always do."

Charlie nodded and keyed his intercom. "Crew, pilot. Boys, sit down and strap in. Here goes nothin'."

Chapter Thirteen

Can we put sixteen B-17s over Rabaul?

Charlie liked Mareeba, if only because it was a little cooler than Townsville, and for the fact that it wasn't quite so afflicted with flies.

And there were civilized amenities. Sort of, at least, certainly compared to Seven-Mile.

For example, at Mareeba there was a spare rudder to replace the one Demopolis jury-rigged. Charlie watched as the mechanics wheeled up a hardstand and began the process of fitting on the new rudder. He went to look at the damaged rudder where the mechanic tossed it.

It was a wonder the damned thing stayed together as long as it did, because Demopolis was right, the stringer at the forward end of the rudder had been blown apart. It wasn't that that bothered Charlie. It was how close they came to having the rudder come apart in flight, on the way home from that last mission to Rabaul.

Al Stern came up and stood next to Charlie. "What are we looking at?"

"Something cosmic, Al."

"Cosmic?"

"Demopolis told me the rudder spine came apart when he tried to straighten it. But look here."

Charlie knelt down next to the rudder. The mechanics had already salvaged the sheet aluminum from it, leaving the broken stringer exposed.

"D'you see it, Al?"

"What, right here? Looks like the cannon shell that hit us sprayed some little bits into the stringer. That weakened it."

"Yes. What conclusion do you draw from this?"

Al looked at the stringer, then stood up and walked to the tail of the B-17, staring up at the fresh sheet metal covering the damage to the vertical stabilizer from the cannon shell. Then he went back to where Charlie stood by the old rudder.

"Yeah," Al said. "Cosmic. If you'd had to really stomp on the rudder it could easily have come apart."

"That's right. And if it had? What might have happened?"

"Well...not much."

"No? No rudder, and you say, not much?"

"I have faith in you, Charlie. And I know that trick you do with the engines. What d'you call it? Different something?"

"You're so cute when you play stupid, Al. So not yourself."

"OK. Differential thrust."

"So much faith you have in me, Al."

Al looked up at Charlie. "So far, you've justified it."

Charlie sighed.

"What is it, Charlie?"

"Look at that thing, Al. Like you said, I could compensate. But d'you know how accidents occur?"

"Enlighten me."

"Margin for error. Every step of the way, there's a couple of steps separating you and disaster. Those steps

339

define a margin for error. Losing our rudder would erode the margin for error. One step closer to disaster."

"You're scaring me a little, Charlie. Don't tell me you're starting to believe in luck."

"I do believe in luck, Al. Luck will keep you alive when skill fails."

Al squatted down on his haunches, wrapping his arms around his legs. Charlie knelt down beside him.

"What are you telling me, Charlie?" Al whispered.

"Jehosophat Al, you think I'm infallible?"

"No one asks you to be."

"I know."

"So what are you telling me?"

"I don't know, Al. This was a close call."

"So?"

"So I don't know." Charlie reached out and touched the discarded rudder.

Al nodded. Then he whispered, "Luck runs out, too, Charlie, and you can't count on it anyway. But there's still skill. And ingenuity."

"Yes."

Charlie held his hand out. Al took it and stood up, looking back at the crew of mechanics fastening the new rudder to their airplane.

"Damn, that thing has a lot of patches," Al said.

"All right, here it is," said Dionne. The major looked around at his pilots. "Since the Japs took Kokoda they're fighting their way uphill along the Track. That means from now on we're flying in the mountains and valleys."

340

Jimmy nodded to himself. Flying in the mountains in clear weather was one thing, but the Owen Stanley Mountains were hardly ever clear.

Two days ago Jimmy bought a beer for Harry Hill, the C-47 guy that flew them into Kokoda to rescue Shafer. The C-47s were now occupied trying to drop supplies to the Aussies on the Track.

"But as our Aussie brethren say, it's a fair cow," Hill said. His copilot sat with him. The copilot was a cherub who looked younger and even shorter than Al Stern. Jimmy couldn't remember his name.

"So you've been up there but you haven't been low in among the hills and bonny dales, I bet. Down low the wind does weird shit, changeable as hell, and now and again you get a wind shear that'll make you diddle in your diapers."

Jimmy nodded.

"There's nowhere to land up there, so we tie up the supplies and put parachutes on 'em and kick 'em out the door. Half the time the wind changes and blows the parachutes off the track. So we try to go low enough that doesn't happen, and sometimes that works."

"When it doesn't?"

"Then there's ammunition and M&V and jerricans of water all over the jungle up there, along with parachute silk some enterprising head-hunter will probably turn into loincloths. None of which does the Aussies any good."

"Tell him about Gordie and Pete," said the cherub.

Jimmy raised his eyebrows and looked at Hill, who scowled and bared his teeth.

341

"Those idiots?" Hill said. "Yeah, well, they had big balls, all right, big brass ones, but you know, if your brains and your skills don't match your balls you end up part of a hillside, whatever doesn't burn to ashes. A C-47 isn't a P-39. You've got to think a lot farther ahead in a cargo plane down below the mountain tops. So, yeah, Gordie and his crew got low, kicked out their load, and I hear the Aussies actually picked it up, but twenty seconds after they unloaded they went into a hillside."

"Pete and I were in flight school together," said the cherub.

Jimmy nodded.

"You with us, Jimmy?" Dionne asked.

Jimmy looked at the major. "Yes, sir."

"OK. Take your boys and White Flight, go up to the Track and see what you can do. Now, here's Lieutenant Mortimer from the Australian Army."

Mortimer was another one of those lean, light-haired Australians who looked like they could walk onto a Hollywood set and play cowboys in a Western. Mortimer looked a little older than most of the Royal Australian Army officers that briefed them.

Mortimer looked around. "Right then. Reckon you blokes have heard of Maroubra Force. They've been fighting the Nips all the way up from the coast, an' we've been sending reinforcements up the Track. No fun, that. You're fair worn out by the time you get to the fighting."

The Aussie studied the map Dionne set up. The map was brand new, the fruit of two months of photo-recon flights by P-38s carrying cameras instead of guns.

342

"Well, the lads are about here," Mortimer said. He pointed to the map.

"Here, then, just north of the crest in the mountains. The Track runs on the south side of this creek, see? Eora Creek, that is, an' our blokes are here, somewhere north of Eora, where there's a little rope bridge, nothing so grand as that wire-rope bridge north of Kokoda, mind. Not more'n a couple of logs across the stream." The Australian thought about it for a minute. "Got no idea what it looks like from the air. Down on the track, you're lucky to see a bit of sky through the jungle overhead. But at the north end of the valley there's a bit of a clearing, and a village called Alola, I think it is. It's about two miles north of Eora, an' you can whiz right down that valley from south to north. There's another clearing east of Alola, on the east side of the creek."

Jimmy looked at the map. "Mortimer, how old is the intelligence?"

"You mean, where are our blokes now? Blowed if I know. Up there you're fighting for a trail, and it might be a few feet wide. It goes up and down. It crosses streams. The jungle on either side, well, you're lucky to see twenty yards most of the time. So I'd say anything north of Eora, that's the Japs. Anything south of that, towards the crest of the mountains, that's our blokes. Sorry, chum, but that's the best I can do."

An hour later Jimmy led two flights of Corncobs, Blue and White, over the crest of the Owen Stanley Mountains.

Jimmy didn't mind flying in the mountains, at least on a clear day without a lot of wind. Neither of those conditions applied often in the Owen Stanleys. In the morning the sun had to be high enough to shine into the mountain valleys and burn off the fog accumulating overnight. Often enough it left low-lying clouds behind. Then by the middle of the afternoon the sunlight that burned off the fog lifted moisture into the air and built rain clouds that came down the south slope to the sea late in the afternoon.

And some days it rained for whatever reason the Great Jehovah and the gods of the local tribesmen decreed.

In fact, the only good thing Jimmy had to say about the Jap advance along the Track was that it only took twenty minutes to get to the target area. It wasn't so bad hauling a 500-lb bomb in a wallowing pig of a P-39 over fifty miles.

"Corncob Blue Leader, this is Corncob White Three. I've got smoke at four o'clock."

Jimmy looked to four o'clock. He saw the smoke, and then he saw the cause, as smoke fountained up suddenly from the jungle.

"White Leader from Blue Leader, is that artillery fire?"

"Yeah, could be."

Jimmy checked his fuel, frowned at his oil pressure gauge, and scanned the sky around them. For whatever reason the Japs hadn't sent Zeros over the Track, yet, anyway. But they only had to catch you by surprise once.

When Jimmy looked down again he saw that same sudden billow of smoke from the jungle.

He looked to the north and made out Buna by the nearly-constant haze of smoke and dust that hung over it. The 22nd Bomb Group and some A-20s from the 3rd Attack were hitting the beachhead this morning. About now, he realized, looking at the clock on his instrument panel, and at that moment a column of black smoke began to rise on the beach forty miles north.

So far no one could think of better objectives for a mission than "targets of opportunity along the Kokoda Track." Jimmy thought that was a laugh, because this far up in the highlands the Track was invisible under trees and folds in the terrain.

"Blue Leader from Blue Four."

"Go ahead, Four."

"Lead, I thought maybe I saw some smoke down there, north of whatever it is the Jap artillery is shooting at. Might· be the guns."

"Can you find it again?"

"You betcha."

"OK. Give us a steer."

"Come right about 90 degrees. That should put it about one o'clock."

Jimmy looked around. They were in this area the day before, and he talked to the Australian lieutenant who replaced Captain McCormick, to get some idea of where the Track was.

A village at Alola with a clearing across the creek to the east, on the north end of the valley, leading down from the crest of the mountains, two miles north of Eora.

Looking down at the smoke from bursting artillery, Jimmy made out a clearing, and then a collection of grass huts, so maybe that was Eora, and looking north, he made out another clearing, maybe two miles away, just as smoke drifted above the trees.

"OK, Blue Leader to formation, we'll split up into elements. Two at a time down the valley, put your bombs where the smoke is rising at the edge of the clearing two miles away."

There was a chorus of rogers.

"OK, Blue Two, follow me."

Jimmy peeled off and dove down, flying over the creek at the bottom of the valley. He looked through his gunsight at the little smudge of lighter green clear space in the dark green jungle. They sped over Eora. The valley swept by on either side, with the slopes folding and undulating as they flew by. Jimmy watched the clearing grow and punched off his bomb, counted three, and pulled up, looking left over his shoulder to check on Kellerman, who was right behind him. When they climbed above the peaks Jimmy turned north and looked back at the target. Smoke and dust climbed above the jungle, short of the edge of the clearing.

"OK, Blue Three, you're up."

Jimmy cleared his tail, checked the sky around them, and watched as Shafer and Bell went down the valley and dropped their bombs just inside the tree line.

"OK, White Two, follow me."

White flight came down by elements and dropped their bombs on either side of the dust cloud left by Jimmy's flight.

Jimmy checked his fuel, then looked at his engine gauges and swore. The oil pressure was falling, the CHT was rising.

"Blue Two from Blue Leader, how's your fuel?"

"Plenty to get home, Lead."

"Blue Three, Blue Leader, how's your fuel?"

"Three's good."

"Lead, Four is losing oil pressure."

"How bad?"

"I better go right now."

"OK, head home. Three, go with him."

"Roger, Lead."

"Blue Leader from White Leader."

"Go ahead, White Leader."

"Jimmy, I think I saw some troops down there, running for the jungle."

"Hope they were Japs."

"Me, too. I'm going to stick around a bit."

Jimmy looked at his oil pressure, which was still falling. "OK. I'm losing oil pressure, so I'm heading home. Watch your ass."

"Affirmative, Blue Leader. You too."

"Blue Leader, Blue Two."

"Go ahead, Two."

"I'm losing oil pressure, too."

"OK."

It was a relief to crest the mountains and see Port Moresby in the near distance.

They were over the lower slopes when Jimmy scanned his instruments and saw his oil pressure still dropping. He cross-checked his electrical system and saw the needle on the ammeter flickering.

"Blue Two from Lead."

"Go ahead, Lead."

347

"Two, I've got something serious going on. My radio might fail. You take the lead."

"What's happening?"

"Looks like I'm losing my electrical system."

No reply.

Kellerman moved up off Jimmy's right wingtip. He pointed to Jimmy, then pointed to his earphones and shook his head. Jimmy looked at his ammeter, which was flat on zero.

"Swell," Jimmy said. He looked over at Kellerman and made an "after you" motion with his hand. Kellerman nodded and moved ahead slightly, where he could still keep an eye on Jimmy.

Jimmy looked ahead and figured they were about twenty miles out from Seven-Mile. He could see Three and Four ahead of them, hardly more than dots in the sky.

His flaps and landing gear were both powered by the electrical system. There was a mechanical ratchet crank by his seat, on the right. Jimmy stole a look at it. The crank looked kind of flimsy to Jimmy. He'd give it a try when he got closer to the field, but he had no idea how long it would take to crank the gear down. If his engine quit, cranking the gear down into the slipstream would increase the drag on his airplane, and shorten the distance he could glide in case of engine failure.

The only thing to do was keep the altitude he had. You could always lose altitude.

Jimmy thought about the Allison engine roaring behind his seat. The engine and its supporting framework was separated from the cockpit by a firewall. Some pilots expressed doubts about whether, in a wheels-up landing, the framework would stay in place. If it didn't stay in place, it would break loose and smash Jimmy flat against the instrument panel.

Jimmy pushed the throttle forward and drew level with Kellerman, who looked over at him. Jimmy held his right hand up, made a fist, and lowered a finger, pointed towards the nose with it, and shook his head. Kellerman made a fist, shook it as if trying to shake water off, and pointed to the nose, shaking his head.

"Great," Jimmy said. He had no idea if Kellerman understood him.

He also wanted to be sure that Kellerman landed ahead of him. If he crash-landed on the field and blocked the runway, he didn't want Kellerman stuck in the air.

Crap. It wasn't just Kellerman he had to worry about. Corncob White flight couldn't be more than a half-hour behind them. If Jimmy had to crash-land, no one would wait for the mechanics to strip the *Gremlin* bare. They'd get a bulldozer and plow it to the side as fast as they could make it happen.

Kellerman dropped back, pointed to himself, and pointed ahead. Jimmy nodded emphatically and pointed ahead. Kellerman nodded, gave Jimmy a salute, and pulled away to enter the pattern.

Jimmy looked at his engine instruments.

The oil pressure was dangerously low, and the cylinder head temps were climbing.

He was going to lose the engine.

The only question was when.

But he wasn't that far from the runway, and he was still at six thousand feet.

349

He could make the runway. Could he put the wheels down with that silly-looking crank?

Jimmy flew to a point north of the approach to the field along Bootless Inlet, put the P-39 into a standard-rate turn to the right, and started pumping the crank with his right hand, flying the airplane with his left hand on the stick.

The engine oil pressure dipped suddenly. Jimmy switched hands and closed the throttle and mixture, then turned the ignition to OFF, prop control to FEATHER. The propeller slowed, windmilling in the breeze until it feathered. Jimmy started cranking again.

He could hear the rush of the wind over his canopy and along the fuselage of the airplane. What he didn't hear was the change in the sound of the wind as the gear came down. He kept cranking until he was down to three thousand feet, and he could tell from the sound of the wind and the feel of the controls that his landing gear was still up.

Well, hell.

He was going to have to land dead-stick, and since he didn't have any flaps he'd have to slip the airplane in to a landing.

Jimmy came out of his turn and curved into the final approach over Bootless Inlet. The tower showed him a green light. He was at two thousand feet, way too high and fast, and he fed in right aileron and left rudder to put the P-39 into a slip. The airframe vibrated as the air slammed into the side of the airplane. Jimmy gauged the angle of the slip and airspeed, adjusted it until he was headed directly for a spot near the end of the runway. Jimmy held the slip until his eye told him he was at the right altitude, twenty feet or so above the runway, and centered his controls, pulling back on the stick, bleeding airspeed and altitude. As he sank down he pulled the stick all the way back. As the nose rose he felt the fuselage hit the runway, and he jockeyed the rudder to keep the airplane pointed straight down the runway. The rudder lost effectiveness as his speed dropped. Finally the left wingtip dropped and dug in on the runway, and the P-39 spun twice and skidded to a stop.

Jimmy hit the quick-release on his harness, opened the door, and got out of the airplane. The left door was pointed to the north side of the runway, and he dashed over to it.

After a moment he figured the *Gremlin* wasn't going to explode. He straightened up and took his helmet off. Jimmy took a deep breath and let it out in one explosive rush.

A jeep drove up. Captain Allen grinned at Jimmy from the driver's seat.

"Hey, Kid. You fly a little too low for once?"

Al Stern wiped the sweat streaming down his face and looked critically at the new drift meter. Its predecessor had taken shrapnel over Lae. No spares were available, either from the depot -- the usual story, "don't know until we finish inventory, lieutenant" -- or from salvage. Stern had even considered enlisting Corporal Lefkowicz in a midnight requisition from either the depot or one of the other airplanes and decided against it. The risk of needing and not having the drift meter, when he could work around its absence, versus the risk of being caught, didn't add up.

The installation looked okay, as much as Al could tell. Sweat kept pouring into his eyes and blinking them constantly didn't help. After he checked it three times and felt like he was about to pass out from the heat and the stuffy airless atmosphere in the nose of the B-17, Al decided it was good enough. He'd check it again before they went up to Seven-Mile.

He crawled down the passage to the open nose hatch, swung himself through it, and dropped to the ground.

"Good morning, lieutenant," someone said.

Al turned and straightened to attention. The voice warned him, the voice of an older man but more. Al couldn't quite figure it, until he saw the two stars on the man's collar. Then he added a salute and barked, "Good morning, general!"

The general wasn't much taller than Al, who no one would ever accuse of being too tall. The general smiled and returned Al's salute in an easy gesture that reeked of the casual style of what Al thought of as the "old Air Corps."

"At ease," said the general. He gestured at the B-17. *Bronco Buster II*, eh? What happened to the first one?"

"Came apart on the ramp at Singosari, General," Al said. "Back in February. Kind of a rough mission."

"While you boys were still in Java?" the general asked. He held out his hand. "I'm Kenney, by the way. George Kenney, but you can call me 'General.'"

Al grinned tentatively and took the offered hand. "Yes, sir. Al Stern, General."

Kenney looked up at the nose of the bomber, inspecting the different markings. Aside from the crow-hopping mustang and its rider, row after row of bombs marking missions flown decorated the nose, along with a dozen or so Jap flags marking Zeros shot down as well as a couple of ships, broken in half into 'vee' shapes.

"Damn," said the General. He looked back at Al. "You the navigator?"

"Yes, sir."

"Of course. You're that Al Stern. I should've known."

Al looked puzzled, but Kenney smiled at him. "Among other things, I hear you and I have some of the same fruit salad, Lt. Stern. I got the DSC back in the last war."

"Oh. Yes, sir, but I just did what I had to do."

Kenney's smile got bigger, then faded. He said softly, "Yeah, me too."

The general turned abruptly and started to walk slowly around the bomber. Al could tell, after three steps, that a very knowledgeable old bird indeed was taking in the details of faded and chipped paint, dents, aluminum skin patches, oil leaking from the cowlings of the radial engines, patched control fabric, and all the other little details that told a considerable part of the bomber's history and current state.

After he completed his slow tour around the bomber Kenney turned back to Al and said, "Lieutenant, where's your pilot?"

Al hesitated. He knew Charlie was trying to sleep, after getting into Mareeba early this morning following three days spent shuttle-bombing between Mareeba and Buna. The only reason Al wasn't sacked out himself was the new drift meter. He wanted to be sure it was installed before they had to fly north again.

"Charlie...I mean, Major Davis, is in his tent, sir. We just got back from Buna. Two missions in three days."

Kenney frowned. "Two missions in three days? You say that like it's a lot."

"Well, General, they don't always have bombs for us up at Seven-Mile, so we usually bomb up here, fly to Seven-Mile, top off with gas, hit Buna or Lae and head back here. Unless we hit Rabaul, in which case we stop off again at Seven-Mile to refuel before we come back here. It kind of adds time and miles to a mission."

"I bet. Which one is Charlie's tent?"

"Ah, this way, General."

"Look here, Lt. Stern, if Major Davis is sleeping I don't blame him. I would be too, if I didn't have something important to ask. Which makes me wonder, why aren't you sleeping yourself?"

"Well..." Al explained about the drift meter.

"Major Davis ask you to do that?"

"No, sir. I'm the navigator, it's my job. I just found out about the drift meter after we debriefed this morning. Charlie had already left with Col. Carmichael."

"And you've flown without a drift meter for what, again? A week?"

"Yes, sir."

Kenney muttered something under his breath that Stern couldn't catch, but there was no mistaking the

354

angry look that passed over the general's face.

"OK," Kenney said. "One more item for my checklist. That your tent?"

"Yes, General."

"OK, son, tell you what. I see a nice shady tree over there. My compliments to Major Davis, and I'd appreciate a few moments of his time."

"Yes, sir."

Kenney walked away towards the indicated tree, which was a typically scrubby Queensland version of a tree that cast little if any shade but was better than standing out in the sun. There was a table under the tree, improvised from a crate with a couple of seats, also improvised from smaller crates, around it.

"Crap," said Al quietly. Then he turned and went into the tent.

"Charlie."

I'm trying to sleep, Charlie thought, and tried to say that. But whatever was left of his brain was drugged with sleep and fatigue, and it came out as a mumble.

"I know, Charlie, but you have to get up, there's a friggin' two-star general waiting on you."

Someone shook him again, gently but insistently.

"Aw, Jehosophat, Al," Charlie said. It didn't quite come out as a moan.

"I'm serious, Charlie. You have to get up."

Charlie blinked, shuddered as the light hit his eyes, and blinked again. He pushed himself up to one elbow.

"Here," said Al. Charlie looked up. He took the cup of water Al offered and drank thirstily. Al refilled it for him.

355

"Thanks," Charlie said. He swung into a sitting position. He drank the cup and rose, went to the water bag hanging from the ridge pole, and poured some water into his hand and splashed it on his face, wiping it away with his kerchief. Then he combed his hair, shoved his feet into his boots, and took the cap Al handed him.

"What general?" he asked Al.

"Kenney. George Kenney."

"Jehosophat," Charlie said, and stepped out of the tent. He followed Al's pointing finger and saw a man sitting under a tree, mopping his face with a handkerchief. "Jehosophat," he repeated.

Charlie walked across the company street with Al one half-step behind him, and they both came to attention and saluted.

"Major Charles Davis, reporting to the General," Charlie said.

Kenney rose as they approached, returned Charlie's salute, and held his hand out to Charlie.

"George Kenney," he said. "I've heard some good things about you and your crew, Major."

"Thank you, General."

Kenney looked at Al and smiled. "Lieutenant, I don't suppose I could trouble you for some coffee or tea or something?"

"I'll get it organized, sir," Al said, and headed towards the mess tent.

Kenney watched Al walk away before turning back to Charlie. "Lt. Stern tells me you boys are having supply issues."

"You could say that, sir. Just for one example, Al's

356

my navigator, and he's been trying to round up a drift meter since the last one got shot out over Lae a week ago."

"He told me. I met him coming out of your airplane. Seems that particular issue has been resolved."

Charlie looked after Al and shook his head slowly. "Let me guess. He was installing the drift meter. Which must have just come in, damn it. I told him...."

Kenney punched Charlie lightly on the shoulder. "He's doing his job, Major, and it looks to me like he does pretty well."

"Al's one hell of a good navigator, General."

"That young rascal barely looks old enough to shave. How long has he been with you?"

"About seven months, General. I actually shanghaied him at Hamilton Field last November. He'd just graduated from navigator's school."

"You're kidding. That was taking a chance, wasn't it? And you went out via Wake Island, I'll bet."

"Yes, sir."

"A hell of a lot of open water between here and San Francisco."

Charlie shrugged. "Al got us all the way across the Pacific to Clark Field without a hitch."

Kenney nodded. "I gather not everyone is that good."

"Well, the navigators in the 19th are pretty good, General. Al's the best, but they're all pretty good."

"How about the rest of the crew? Judging from those Jap flags your gunners are doing their jobs, too."

"They are, sir, but a gunnery school would be a good idea. Not one of my gunners, including my bombardier and navigator, has gone through a gunnery course. Me trying to pass along what I learned about skeet shooting back in Connecticut seems thin when you're trying to shoot down Zeros."

"Tell me a little about your bombardier."

"He's good, too, sir, but..." Charlie hesitated.

"Major, one of the things I intend to do is make improvements," Kenney said. "I can do that a lot faster if I know what needs to be improved."

"General, I know you got into trouble a few years back, fighting for B-17 procurement," Charlie said.

"You could say that," Kenney said drily. "Get to the point, Charlie."

"General, you know how these airplanes are supposed to be used. They're strategic bombers, designed to use the Norden bombsight at high altitude. But to use that bombsight properly you have to have an aim point on the ground, and to pick an aim point you have to have some sort of target intelligence. At the moment, we don't have any kind of target intelligence. Without it, we're just rolling the dice without knowing what number we need. Besides which, everyone from General MacArthur to the RAAF and the United States Navy wants the 19th Bomb Group to conduct armed reconnaissance. We do a lot more of that than we do actual bombing of targets."

"You think we shouldn't be using the B-17 out here?"

"I didn't say that, General. We'll do what we have to do, but the B-17 is meant to go after things like factories and railroad marshaling yards. A strategic bomber only has a handful of targets it can hit profitably in this theater. That's the airfields, harbor, and other installations around Rabaul, and whatever airfields and port facilities the Japs put up, like the ones at Lae and Salamaua."

"What about Buna?"

Charlie shrugged. "It's only a hundred miles from Seven-Mile, so the field and beachhead at Buna are under constant attack by the P-39s and the medium bombers. The Japs have some Zeros there, and they cause trouble, but the point is that we can bomb Buna, and the whole Jap supply line from Buna up into the mountains, whenever we like. I have a friend in the 35th Fighter Group. He tells me that, so far, the Zeros stay over the beachhead at Buna."

Kenney frowned. "Now, that doesn't make any sense. The Japs have plenty of Zeros at Lae and Rabaul, don't they?"

"Sure seems like it to us, General," Charlie said.

Kenney looked off into the distance for a moment.

A jeep drove up. Al Stern sat in the passenger seat, carrying a jug and cups. He got out, thanked the driver, and set the jug down on the crate table.

"What have we here, Lieutenant Stern?" Kenney asked affably.

"It's tea, sir," Stern answered. "The cook says he's out of coffee."

Kenney nodded and accepted the cup of tea. He took a sip and grimaced. "Kind of bitter," the General observed.

"Sorry, sir, but sugar is in short supply, too. The cook put some in, but he needed the rest for dinner."

"Of course." Kenney took another sip of tea. "So,

Major, let me be sure I understand. The B-17 might not be improperly employed, but could certainly be better employed, on fixed targets like airfields and port facilities, of which there are only a few in this theater. A lack of target intelligence aggravates that situation. A disproportionate share of your missions involve armed recon instead of bombing missions. And your understanding, from your friend in the 35th, is that the Japs are limiting their efforts at air defense to the near vicinity of Buna."

Kenney looked at Charlie and raised an eyebrow.

"Yes, sir," Charlie said.

"Who is your friend in the 35th, by the way?"

"1st Lt. Jimmy Ardana," Charlie said. "He's a pretty hot pilot. I think he could fly anything with wings. He's a flight leader and has four Japs."

Kenney grinned. "You mean Jimmy the Kid? I met him at Seven-Mile."

"Yes, sir."

Kenney frowned, obviously in thought, and sipped his tea absently. He made a face. "Sorry, boys. I appreciate the hospitality, but this stuff really is pretty bitter. Is it always like this?"

"This is good, General, compared to what we get up at Seven-Mile. The Aussies do their best but the local water is full of all the bugs known to science and a few besides. They put some kind of chemical in it to kill them, but it does leave an aftertaste."

"I was up there a few days ago. It was pretty primitive."

Charlie hesitated. "General, just about everyone has had dysentery, malaria, dengue, and fevers the docs don't have a name for. Except for Al, here."

"Bugs that bite me die horribly," Stern said gravely.

Kenney smiled. Then his face changed. He looked at Stern. "Lieutenant Stern, I need to speak privately to Charlie. Would you mind?"

"Of course not, General." Al stood.

"Thanks for the tea."

"You're welcome." Al saluted and turned away.

Kenney turned and looked at Charlie. "I spoke with General MacArthur when I got to Australia," the General said. "One of the things I promised him was that the 19th Bomb Group would put sixteen B-17s over Rabaul on August 6. Am I going to look like a fool, Charlie?"

"General, respectfully, why are you asking me? Shouldn't you be asking Colonel Carmichael?"

"I will. I know this is putting you on the spot. But I'd like to know what you think."

"Can we do it? Yes, sir, but it's going to mean at least a three-day stand-down for maintenance."

Kenney nodded. "What's been keeping you from mounting full-strength missions, Charlie? Other than armed recon?"

"Maintenance, first and foremost. We can't get the spare parts and other supplies we need, and for every mechanic we've got we could use two more. We left most of our ground crew in the Philippines, and now they're guests of the Emperor, at best."

Kenney nodded. "What else?"

"General, as you pointed out, we're the only heavy bomb group in the Southwest Pacific. I keep hearing the

361

43rd Bomb Group is supposed to join us, but I've been hearing that for about four months now. So, we're the local fire brigade, and the whole damned city is burning, and we could use some help. If we throw three airplanes at a target here, and another couple at a target there, and a half-dozen somewhere else, and throw in long range missions like the one some of the guys flew from Darwin up to the Celebes a few weeks ago, well, hell. I seem to remember being taught that concentration of force is tactically desirable."

Kenney said, "Well, if we put sixteen planes over Rabaul, that ought to qualify."

"Yes, sir. General, if Colonel Carmichael promised you sixteen B-17s over Rabaul in a week, you'll have them. More if we can do it."

Kenney held out his hand. "I suspect we'll see each other again, Major. Good luck."

At lunch, Colonel Carmichael came over and sat with Charlie.

"Charlie, what did General Kenney have to say?"

"Mostly he wanted an overview of how things were going for heavy bombardment out here, and then he wanted to know if we could put sixteen bombers over Rabaul in seven days."

"Yeah. I always heard Kenney was kind of a fireball. What did you tell him?"

"Sir, as far as us putting sixteen bombers over Rabaul, I told him we could do it. I also told him one reason we weren't putting a lot of airplanes out actually bombing targets was because of the recon missions that get thrown our way."

Carmichael nodded slowly. "I doubt he thinks much of the 19th Bomb Group."

"No?"

"No. Evidently MacArthur wants to know why we aren't doing more about Rabaul. MacArthur thinks we're a bunch of kids spouting off about how great we are who ran for their mommas when the war started."

"Did he."

"Aw, calm down, Charlie. We both know MacArthur has never been a fan of the Air Corps. Hell, look what he did to Billy Mitchell."

Charlie frowned. "Yes, sir. Seems like we've been blamed for the shortcomings of others, though, and I won't name those others."

"You're a wise man, Charlie." Carmichael sipped his tea and grimaced. "Hell, we can't even get enough sugar for our tea up here. Half our airplanes are down for maintenance and a few of those will never fly again without a major overhaul at a properly equipped air depot. Know where we can find one of those, Charlie?"

"I hear there's a peach of a depot being built down in Brisbane."

"Me, too. Doesn't help us much, six hundred miles away in the wilds of Queensland."

The colonel scowled and looked out over the airstrip. "Even our flyable airplanes are about worn out. There's only so much you can do with spit and baling wire. Aw, hell, I guess we'll get fifteen or twenty airplanes over Rabaul. If we don't have too many aborts. What about your squadron?"

"I can promise six with confidence. Seven, maybe eight, depending on parts. A couple of new engines

363

would help a lot."

"Wouldn't it just? OK, Charlie, guess we'd better get to work. Let me know your final available airplanes by tomorrow morning."

"Yes, sir." Charlie hesitated. "Colonel?"

"Yeah, Charlie?"

"You know, it doesn't seem like we can fill out a requisition form to the satisfaction of those Brisbane types. Maybe we should round up some airmen with rifles, fly down to that pretty new depot in Brisbane and load up a couple of B-17s with what we need. I bet Demopolis has a list in his head of what he needs the most."

Carmichael looked at Charlie. "I don't know which of us is crazier. You, for making that suggestion, or me, for giving it serious thought for even two seconds."

"I know, Colonel, but it might make all the difference."

Carmichael sighed. He rubbed his chin. "You know, Charlie, if I thought we could get down there, grab what we want, get back here, fix up some extra bombers to take to Rabaul, and then actually hit Rabaul, much less get back, all without being thrown in the stockade first, I might do it."

"Yeah," Charlie said slowly. "I guess we can't actually declare war on MacArthur's G-1 staff."

The colonel grinned suddenly. "But it might be fun at that. Maybe it would be worth a trip to the stockade, if we could make it to Rabaul with the group at full strength."

Chapter Fourteen

The Whole Damned 19ᵗʰ Bomb Group

Heat, stifling heat and humidity. Jimmy lay on his bunk with his eyes closed and sweat running off him, soaking his coveralls and his cot. They'd been back and forth along the Kokoda Track all morning and early afternoon. The clouds were building over the mountains now, and that meant the cloud bottoms over the Track were lower than the tops of the mountains. Since no one fancied confirming the location of a mountaintop by flying into it, that meant they were done flying for the day.

Kellerman was writing a letter, or writing something, judging from the soft scratching of his pen over a piece of paper. He stopped.

"Run out of ideas?" Jimmy asked.

"Listen. Are those engines?"

Jimmy sat up. "Air raid?"

He looked at Kellerman, who sat on his bunk, pen forgotten and poised in the air over the piece of sheet aluminum he used for a writing desk. Kellerman frowned.

"Don't think so," he said. "They don't sound right."

Jimmy sat up, stuffed his feet in his boots, and went to the entrance of the tent. The sound of the engines was something he could feel in his bones, and now he heard the engines as a rising and falling beat, droning, vibrating, and in the distance to the south he saw dots.

Dots in formation, coming from the south.

"B-17s," he said to Kellerman, who stood beside him. "Looks like the whole damned 19th Bomb Group."

"I only count sixteen. Shouldn't there be twenty or so?"

"They have the same problem with maintenance and spare parts we do."

"Wonder what they're doing?"

"Passing through on the way to bomb the hell out of somewhere. Probably Rabaul."

The formation of B-17s flew over the field and the lead squadron peeled away, landing gear dropping down into place. The rest of the formation flew a little further, and another squadron peeled off behind the lead squadron, whose airplanes entered the pattern one by one, coming down to land and taxi off the strip.

It took at least twenty minutes for all those B-17s to land and for another ten minutes the air reverberated to the beat of their engines as they taxied to their dispersal points. Jimmy and Kellerman walked closer to the airfield as the bombers landed, and Jimmy was sure he saw the red silhouette of the rider on his crow-hopping mustang painted on one of them. Jimmy waved as the bomber rolled by. One of the waist gunners waved back.

"Well, that was a pretty good air show," Kellerman said. "I don't think I've seen that many B-17s in one place before, even back in the States."

Charlie and Danny shut down the engines and sat for a moment, watching the other B-17s taxi by in clouds of swirling dust.

"Well, that was kind of exciting," said Danny. "Don't think I've flown formation with that many airplanes since training."

"You did OK for a single-engine guy," Charlie said. "Some rough edges, but not at all bad. You might make a fair copilot some day."

"Gee, thanks, boss."

"Don't mention it. Seriously, Danny, none of us have any recent practice with this kind of formation work. Since the war started I think the biggest formation I've flown in was half this size, maybe less."

"That raid to Balikpapan," said Al Stern, levering himself up from the access tunnel.

"What's a Balikpapan?" Danny asked.

"Town in Borneo with a whopping big oil refinery," Charlie said tersely. "We went up there with, I don't know, how many ships, Al? Six? Seven?"

"Seven," said Al. "We came back with six."

"So we did."

Danny looked from Al to Charlie. "That bad?" he asked.

"Just so you know the, ah, nature of our enemy, Danny, when Primrose One went down on that raid, the crew bailed out. Fair enough, that's war. What isn't war is the Japs shooting up our guys in their chutes."

"That's a true story? I thought it was bullshit."

"It's true. We saw it, didn't we, Al?"

"Yeah. Emmons saw it best. He had a ring-side seat, back there in the tail."

"Damn," said Danny softly.

"So if we don't exactly feel any pity for the little yellow bastards, that's one reason why," said Charlie.

367

He looked out the window at the bombers still taxiing by. He frowned. "I don't know if I've managed what Colonel Eubank asked me to do, though."

Al laid a hand on Charlie's shoulder. They exchanged a look and Al turned and went back down the nose tunnel.

"What was that all about?" Danny asked. "And who is Colonel Eubank?"

"A good man who had some of the lousiest luck I ever saw. He was our CO when the war started. Lost half his airplanes on the first day of the war."

"Oh. We heard in the States it was bad. We didn't hear that, though."

"Yeah, the Air Corps kept it quiet, like the Navy kept their losses at Pearl Harbor quiet. Anyway, after that mission to Balikpapan, we were...let's say we were angry. Gene Eubank told me that, as officers of the US Army, we had to retain our humanity and not become the thing we were fighting."

Danny frowned. Then he shook his head. "Way above my pay grade," he said. "I'll fly the airplane where we're told to go. Good enough?"

"Plenty good," Charlie said. "Come on. Let's see if the chow is still as lousy as I remember. Then we'll find a beer."

"You're on."

Jimmy walked into the O-Club, which was crowded with bomber crew in addition to the everyday cast of pursuit pilots and RAAF types. It was even louder and smokier and smelled more of beer and harder to find anyone in the press than usual.

He thought he heard someone call his name and then he saw a hand waving. He looked closer and saw Charlie at a table with Al Stern and Danny Evans and a couple of other officers Jimmy didn't know. Jimmy got a beer and went to their table.

"Hiya, Charlie," he said. "Al, Danny."

"Jimmy, still in one piece. There's a miracle in action. These guys are with me. That's Ira West and Bart Allen, pilots in my squadron. You guys, be nice to Jimmy. He might be a pursuit pilot but he's handy to have around."

West and Allen leaned back in their seats and looked skeptical. Jimmy laughed.

"Thanks, Charlie," he said. "Look at this crowd. Even smells like bomber guys in here."

"Sweet," said Stern. "And after we took you in and treated you as one of our own, down in Brisbane."

Jimmy sat down. "I guess I shouldn't ask why you guys are here. Anything to do with this new general?"

"Sort of," Charlie said. "Interesting guy. We met him, didn't we, Al?"

"Yep. Little guy, not much bigger than me."

"What, Al, you're a little guy?" Jimmy said. "I hadn't noticed."

Stern rolled his eyes. "Flattery. From a pursuit guy, yet."

"Kenney was up here a few days ago," said Jimmy. "Seemed like an OK guy, except his aide tried to steal Chinkerbell for some low-level attack squadron he's putting together."

"He's got some good ideas," said Charlie. "He literally wrote the book on attack aviation."

"Yeah, but that ain't you," said Jimmy, who didn't miss the look that passed between Charlie and his pilots. "At least, not the way I heard it. You guys are heavy bombardment. Whole different ball game."

Charlie shrugged and drank. "That's true. And I doubt we'll be doing low-level work any time soon."

"But we *have* done it, Charlie," said Al. "You remember, that time up in Sumatra? When we flew down the river to Palembang?"

"Jeez, Al, how can you remember that far back?" asked Charlie.

Jimmy nodded. He waved around the room. "Well, you've sure got the most B-17s I've ever seen at one time out here. Whatever Kenney has you doing you'll raise hell with someone."

"That's the idea," said Charlie. "Who wants another beer?"

A truck took Charlie and his crew out to the flight line before daybreak the next morning. Another truck went past them, headed to a B-17 that hadn't been there the night before.

Charlie couldn't see much in the starlight but the lights of the truck, even half taped over due to blackout regulations, shone briefly on the name of the airplane: *Why Don't We Do This More Often?*

He frowned. He remembered hearing a B-17 coming in late last night and guessed this was it. The crew jumping down from the truck was in shadow. He couldn't make them out in the darkness. Charlie figured it was probably Harl Pease and his crew. On the flight up yesterday their airplane blew an engine and diverted back to Mareeba. Charlie remembered *Why Don't We Do This More Often?* was at Mareeba awaiting overhaul. That airplane wasn't supposed to be flyable, though, to the point of serious debate about turning the ship into a hangar queen and stripping it for spare parts. Pease and his boys must have worked all yesterday afternoon and well into the night to get it off the ground.

A jeep came by with two officers in it. They stopped in front of the B-17.

Charlie turned to Evans and said, "Danny, start the preflight. Get Kim Smith to help you."

"Yes, sir."

Charlie walked down the line, noticing that three officers were gathered under the nose of the B-17. The jeep was parked in front of the airplane, and in the dim yellowish light of its headlamps, he could see Pease, apparently arguing with the other two officers. Charlie recognized the squadron commander, Major Hardison, and the maintenance officer, Lt. Snyder.

Snyder was pointing at the No. 2 engine. "Goddamnit, Harl, you know this wicked piece of crap of an airplane has some fault with its engines and electrical system no one has been able to track down yet."

"It got us here, didn't it? Maybe not the best rate of climb but fuel consumption was OK. A little high, but not bad. This airplane will get us to Rabaul and back."

Hardison said, "Look, Pease, I know this is a maximum effort mission, but maximum effort doesn't mean going up to Rabaul in an airplane that could fall apart before the Zeros even get a crack at you."

371

"Major, I talked it over with my crew. They all want to go. So do I."

The squadron commander walked away from Pease, took his cap off, and stood looking up at the fading stars.

Charlie heard him say, very quietly, "Shit."

Then the man turned back to Pease and said, "All right, Harl, load up. But damn it, you've already pushed safety just coming here in this piece of junk. You see so much as a twitch in your oil pressure or your temps get one degree too high, you abort. That's an order."

"Yes, sir."

Charlie went back to his bomber. He couldn't decide if Major Hardison had made a good decision or not. Charlie wondered what he would have done – would do, no doubt, in the future – and figured the only way to tell would be if Pease made it to Rabaul without aborting.

Danny and Frye were looking at something in the No. 1 engine, which put them about a quarter of the way through the preflight. Charlie pitched in but it was the same old shot-to-hell and patched up B-17 *Bronco Buster II* had been when they first got her at Batchelor Field in Australia last March.

Jehosophat. Every airplane in the 19th Bomb Group was a piece of junk.

Al Stern thought the takeoff that morning was more than normally thrilling. An airplane in the lead squadron ran off the runway into a pile of rocks kept handy to patch bomb craters. Like every other airplane in the group it was fully loaded with gas and bombs, but, doubtless due to divine intercession, it didn't explode. The other airplanes made it off the ground all right, but during the climb to cruise altitude two more B-17s turned back. One of them had a feathered prop, which meant an engine failure, but Al couldn't see what ailed the other one.

The remaining thirteen airplanes climbed to 23,000 feet and formed up. It seemed to Al Stern, looking through his astrodome at the formation, that the bombers were awfully close, but they'd been briefed on that. Thirteen B-17s mounted one hundred and thirty .50-cal. machine guns, and that was a lot of firepower in anyone's book.

Al took a line on the sun with his octant and plotted their position.

"Pilot, navigator."

"Go ahead, Al."

"Charlie, looks like we're right on heading as briefed. We're over the Solomon Sea, two hours to the target."

"OK, thanks, Al."

Al went forward to squat beside Bill Frye. Bill had one hand resting on the grips of the nose gun and was looking around at the formation.

Frye waved a hand at the B-17s around them. Al could practically read his thoughts: *What d'you suppose the Japs will make of all this?*

Al shrugged and shook his head. It was a lot of firepower, all right, but the intelligence briefing said the Japs had three hundred airplanes at the Vunakanau airfield, which was the group's actual target. The scoop was also that the US Marines, sometime this morning, were landing at an island called Guadalcanal, where the Japs were building an air base. The Jap bombers at Vunakanau were in range of Guadalcanal and whatever the Navy had there to support the Marines. So, this mission had an objective other than smashing up a Jap airfield and a bunch of Jap airplanes, worthwhile objectives in and of themselves as far as the navigator was concerned, but keeping those Jap bombers off the backs of the Navy would probably help.

Al was in favor of that, although hopefully it didn't mean getting his ass shot off in the process.

Frye tapped his shoulder and pointed down and to the left.

That was the coast of New Britain, in among the clouds four miles below. Al duck-walked back to his desk and looked at the course he'd traced on the chart. Then he checked his chronometer.

On course and on time. He keyed his intercom mike. "Pilot, navigator."

"What's up, Al?"

"New Britain coast ahead. On course, on time."

"Right, thanks, Al. And?"

"And what? Oh, you mean how long before we get to the target? One hour, seventeen minutes."

"OK. Crew, pilot, if you aren't already on your toes, now is a good time."

Al listened to the chorus of "Rogers" over the intercom, laconic, grim, determined, deliberately lazy, well-known voices.

The crew.

Al turned to check the cheek guns and their ammunition feeds.

Danny Evans looked over the instrument panel and then scanned around the airplane, looking at the other B-17s in the formation.

This was really different from the solo missions or those flown with one or two other B-17s. This was more like what he imagined, back in flight school, a gaggle of bombers in a tight formation, heading off to bomb the crap out of something.

It made Danny realize how much he liked the B-17. He was ham-handed for a P-39 pilot, maybe, but that worked out OK for flying a four-engine bomber. The B-17 was easy to fly and needed just enough more muscle to work the controls that his ham-handedness translated to smoothness.

No, Danny thought, he didn't like the B-17. He absolutely *loved* it. The airplane made him feel like a pilot instead of an impostor.

Danny knew he wasn't the brightest guy in the Air Corps, but the B-17 made sense to him in a way the P-39 never had. First of all, he had room to move around. In the P-39 he was so crammed up that he could barely use the controls, and if he moved a quarter-inch one way or the other he jammed up against the sides of the cockpit. Second, there were people all around him, and even if the only person he saw consistently was Major Davis, he knew Al Stern was there when the little navigator poked his head up into the astrodome forward of the cockpit to take a sun line, and he could hear Kim Smith behind him in the upper turret, and all the rest of the guys were on the intercom.

Danny moved his gloved fingers on the control wheel, wiggled his ass in the seat, and checked the engine instruments again. Behind his oxygen mask he grinned. He'd forgotten how much he liked playing on a team, and a B-17 bomber crew was a tighter, tougher team than any bunch of football players ever dreamed of being.

"BANDITS! Bandits, ten o'clock high!"

Charlie swiveled his head, looking out the upper cockpit window. Behind him he heard Kim Smith swivel his turret to cover the threat.

"Pilot, navigator. Ten minutes to target. Over the IP."

"Pilot, bombardier. Beginning bomb run."

"OK, understood."

Bronco Buster II led the high squadron. To the left and below he could see Carmichael's airplane, in the formation lead slot in the middle squadron, and below and to the far left was the low squadron.

"Ah, crew, top turret, I'm counting at least twenty of the bastards."

"You can count that high, Kim?"

"I used my fingers *and* my toes, Lefty."

Ahead of them Charlie saw flak blossom, below the formation's altitude at first, and reaching higher on successive salvos.

"Yeah, top turret counting twenty-five bandits now, repeat, twenty-five."

Charlie swept his eyes over the instrument panel and looked at his squadron. Everyone had their bomb

376

bay doors open, and he could hear the roaring slipstream coming through his own bomb bay.

"Primrose Two-One to high squadron, let's tighten it up, boys," he radioed over the tactical channel.

The Zeros dove down onto Charlie's squadron. He heard the upper turret give a brief burst, hold fire, and then almost simultaneously Kim Smith and the Zeros opened up on each other, tracers crisscrossing and darting past. There was a brief rattle of bullets striking the fuselage, Al on the left cheek gun and the left waist gunner joined in, and the Zeros dove past them. It took a few seconds for all those Zeros to pass by. As they did Kim stopped firing and the right waist and the ball turret took up the argument.

"Ball turret to crew, looks lahk those li'l bastids are hookin' round to catch the lead squadron from behind. Em, what you think?"

"'Bout right, Johnny. Don't worry, they'll be back."

"Aw, ah'm not worried. They kin take their time, all they want."

Charlie looked below and ahead. The Zeros came up behind Carmichael's squadron, and he could just make out the crisscrossing tracers.

"Pilot, bombardier. Five minutes."

Charlie took his eyes from the lead squadron's fight with the Zeros and looked ahead. He could see Simpson Harbor with a dark boiling cloud of flak bursting above it, and to the south of the harbor he could see the long straight gash in the jungle that was Vunakanau airfield.

377

Two minutes from bomb release they were in among the bursting flak. The Zeros drew off to let the flak guns work. Charlie checked the engines and, from the corner of his eye, Danny Evans. Maybe it wasn't the guy's first mission but this was his first big raid.

Danny looked relaxed and alert. His eyes darted around the cockpit, checking the engine instruments, peering out over the right wing to check the engines, looking up and around to check the other airplanes in the high squadron, then craning a little to look ahead at the target.

It made Charlie a little nervous. He didn't want to lose Danny, not so much because Danny was becoming a good copilot as it was that, well, Charlie didn't believe in jinxes or hoodoos or any of that crap, but he did believe in luck, and the guys that sat next to him didn't seem to have any. He shoved that thought out of his mind.

Shrapnel pinged and rattled through the airframe.

"Pilot, bombardier, one minute, one minute, hold her steady, steady."

Vunakanau vanished below the nose of the bomber. On their left was Simpson Harbor, ringed by volcanos and crowned with bursting flak.

"Pilot, right a hair, just a hair, and...bombs gone, closing bomb bay doors."

The lift of the airplane as it shed the weight of the bombs, the slight feeling of acceleration as the bomb bay doors closed and the drag came off.

"Primrose One to formation, turn for base, repeat, turn for base."

"Pilot, navigator, the formation should turn to heading 224."

"Understood, navigator, formation heading 224."

Suddenly the flak diminished and quit.

"Bombardier has bandits, twelve o'clock low. Looks like they're going for the lead squadron again."

Charlie was looking at Col. Carmichael's airplane, in the lead of the whole formation, and saw three Zeros concentrating on it. There was a flurry of cannon strikes around the nose and fuselage of the bomber.

"This is Primrose One, Primrose One is hit! Oxygen gone, descending!"

It didn't sound to Charlie like an order for the whole formation to descend, but with his oxygen gone Carmichael had no choice but to descend to an altitude where the crew could breathe without supplemental oxygen. He didn't radio an order to pass command of the formation, either, and the whole lead squadron followed him down.

"Crew, ball turret, B-17 in trouble at nine o'clock."

Charlie growled and clenched his teeth. "This is Primrose Two-One," he radioed. "Keep formation with the lead squadron."

"Primrose Two-Two, understood."

"Primrose Two-Three, understood."

"Primrose Two-Four, understood."

"Danny, ease back about two hundred RPM on the turbos, give me 500 feet per minute rate of descent until we see what Primrose One is doing."

"Two hundred off the turbos, 500 descent," Danny echoed.

Charlie looked to the left and below at the low squadron.

There was a B-17 in trouble down there, all right. It streamed bright yellow flame and black smoke from the bomb bay aft, and as Charlie watched something trailing fire tumbled away from the airplane. Zeros whirled and swooped around the B-17. The left inboard engine streamed fire and suddenly the airplane tumbled, Zeros darting after it like wolves snapping at a wounded bull.

The rest of the low squadron was in trouble too. The Zeros that weren't attacking the burning B-17 were going after the remaining bombers. One Zero shed a wing and went down in flames, but a B-17 trailed smoke from the No. 3 engine. Charlie took a last look at the burning B-17, still diving and trailing smoke and flame as it fell behind them.

Poor bastards, Charlie thought. Then he looked around at his own squadron, checked their formation with the lead squadron, which was still descending to get to denser air before the Colonel and his crew passed out.

The next time Charlie looked to the left to check on the low squadron, it was gone.

"Ball turret, pilot."

"Go ahead, skipper."

"Johnny, did you see what happened to the low squadron?"

"They were fallin' behind and went into some cloud a couple minutes ago. Didn't see 'em come out."

"OK. Em, how about you?"

"I saw 'em close to some clouds, skipper, but when I looked back they weren't there."

"OK. Crew, pilot, keep your eyes open for the low squadron. Let me know if you see 'em."

Charlie took a quick count. Sixteen planes at Seven-Mile this morning, thirteen made it to Rabaul, one shot down leaving the target, and now the three planes remaining in the low squadron were missing. Between his four airplanes and the five in the lead squadron, there were only nine airplanes.

Nine out of thirteen that struck the target. If the low squadron ran into something it couldn't handle, like weather, Zeros, or bad navigation, effective losses for this mission, counting the bomber that cracked up on takeoff, were over thirty percent.

Jehosophat.

"Tail gunner, pilot."

"Go ahead, boss."

"You get a look at the target?"

"A hell of a lot of smoke, and I mean a lot of smoke. Big ball of fire in among all the rest of it, like maybe we hit a bomb dump. Maybe a fuel dump, too."

"Johnny?"

"Em's right, skipper. I saw somethin' go off with a hell of a bang, big old white shock wave, just like a bomb dump goin' up. Looked lahk we hit them li'l bastids a good lick, sure 'nuff."

"OK, understood. Thanks, guys."

If at least they plastered the target, that was a good thing. He wasn't sure it justified a thirty percent loss rate, but if they cut down the Jap air strength at Vunakanau, that meant airplanes and bombs and fuel that the Japs couldn't send to Seven-Mile or Guadalcanal.

Carmichael's airplane was hit hard, though, and if he got hit in the oxygen system, he was lucky his bomber hadn't turned into a blowtorch. Charlie had seen that happen. So there was at least one airplane that would need repairs before it could fly again in combat, and the same was probably true of the two airplanes that aborted. Assuming none of the other airplanes were badly damaged, that meant the available combat strength of the 19th Bomb Group was, at least temporarily, cut by fifty percent.

Holy howling jumping Jehosophat. Even if this new general, Kenney, was a miracle worker he was going to have to conjure airplanes out of thin air to perform miracles with. A bitter thought crossed Charlie's mind, and he tossed it out as soon as it did, that the 19th Bomb Group had been asked to work miracles ever since the first day of the war, without the wherewithal to so much as do their jobs.

Concentrate, Charlie, he told himself. *Your airplane is still flying, and you have a crew and a squadron to bring home. So do your damned job.*

Jimmy, like most of the Corncobs, went down to the rock pile to look at the wrecked B-17. They were kept at a distance because, it seemed, every bomb in the airplane tore loose when the airplane came to a sudden and uncontrolled stop.

"The ordnance guys are in there now, taking the fuses out," the MP guarding the perimeter told him.

Jimmy watched for a little while and then wandered over to the 19th's Ops Shack. He was accepted there with nods and joined the group of officers clustered around the radio.

"Where are they?" Jimmy asked.

"Not far from the target," said a captain Jimmy didn't know. "They seem to be on course and on time."

"Any Japs after them yet?"

"Not yet."

Minutes dragged until suddenly, scratchy with static and faint with distance, a Morse transmission beeped over the loudspeaker. The radio operator sat pressing his left earphone to his ear, writing down letter by letter as the string of dots and dashes came over the air. Jimmy caught a letter here and there, and he could always catch the quick *dit-dit-dit* of "S" or the longer *dah-dah-dah* of "O" – he could see the sergeant back at Kelly Field, teaching his class Morse, saying in dry dour tones, that if you can't send anything else you should at least be able to send an SOS – but for the rest of it, especially, the numbers, he didn't trust his memory.

When the message ended the radio operator leaned back and handed the paper to the captain Jimmy didn't know.

"They just hit the target," the captain said. "Heavy flak and fighters. Bombing results good. Heading for home."

"Well, that's something," said one of the other officers. "No word on losses, then?"

"No, sir."

383

Jimmy looked at his watch, which read 1145. The B-17s were off the ground about four hours ago, which meant they'd start arriving at Seven Mile around a quarter of four this afternoon.

He turned to the captain. "Then they should be off the north coast, probably west of Buna, around three this afternoon?"

"About right. The good Lord willing and the creek don't rise."

Jimmy nodded. He stepped to one side and stood in front of the map tacked to one wall of the Ops Shack.

It was a big map, and it had the 19th's route coming and going for today's raid.

"What are you thinking?" the captain asked.

"Not so long ago I shot a Zero down, about here," Jimmy said. He pointed to a spot near Buna. "Major Davis was coming back from a recon mission up to Rabaul. Two Zeros attacked him. My flight leader and I chased 'em off, and I got one of them in the process."

The captain nodded. He pointed at Buna. "We know the Japs keep Zeros here, or try to," he told Jimmy. "And they have Zeros based at Lae and Salamaua. They could try to hit the 19th on the way back."

The captain pointed to the red thread overlaying the map that represented the return route. He indicated the portion of the route lying over the Solomon Sea between New Britain and the north coast of Papua New Guinea.

Jimmy looked at the map scale. "We have to have enough fuel to fight," he said. "That intercept last May

384

worked out pretty well, right about here, 120 miles northeast."

The captain nodded and looked at Lae. He measured the distance from the Jap airfield at Lae to the point Jimmy indicated. "A hundred-thirty miles, give or take, for the Japs," he said. "Less if they come from Salamaua. And they can always land at Buna if they need to."

Jimmy nodded, frowning as he looked at the point marked "Buna" on the map. He and his boys had been over that beach a dozen times or more, including the time Chinkerbell put a bomb into those Zeros sitting on the ground. Even if they didn't count as kills it was useful work.

The returning B-17s would be damaged, carrying wounded, short of fuel and short of ammunition. They weren't helpless, but the Japs would go after obvious cripples, and it was still ninety miles or so back to Seven-Mile, and that route lay over the mountains and the Kokoda Track. Anyone going down over the track north of the crest of the mountains ran the risk of being captured by the Japs, or parachuting into jungle almost as inhospitable as the Japs themselves.

Those weren't risks Jimmy cared for.

"Reckon I'll go talk to the boss," he said.

"In case you go, the formation call sign is Primrose," the captain told him. "Carmichael's airplane is Primrose One. The two formation leaders are Primrose Three-One and Primrose Two-One."

"Which one is Major Davis?"

"Charlie? He's Primrose Two-One."

"Navigator, pilot."

"Go ahead, pilot."

Al grabbed the edge of his desk as a sudden gust of turbulence shook the airplane. His stomach rose and swooped with the airplane's motion, causing him to take a deep breath and wait for a brief stab of nausea to abate. While he waited for the airplane and his stomach to settle down he looked at his chart.

The formation was at 10,000 feet so that Carmichael's crew could breathe safely. The problem caused by that altitude was towering cumulus clouds shutting out the sun, keeping him from taking a sun sight to determine their position. But he could see the ocean below, and at this altitude taking a sight through the drift meter was easy enough, so at least he had a notion of the wind, and he had a good idea of where and when they crossed the southern shore of New Britain.

He was pretty sure his dead reckoning wouldn't be far off.

The airplane swooped, rocked its wings, and yawed again before Charlie could straighten it out.

"Sorry about that, Al. Got preoccupied. Where are we?"

"Should be over the coast in ten minutes. If we are, we'll know we're on course."

"Understood. Thanks, Al."

Al stood up and stuck his head into the astrodome, looking around at the cloud tops ten thousand feet or more above them.

And froze.

"*Bogeys*," he said tensely. "Navigator has four bogeys, twelve o'clock high, and I mean right on top of these clouds."

From the corner of his eye he could see Smith swivel the upper turret and elevate his guns.

"Upper turret has the bogeys. Al, can you make 'em out?"

"Four airplanes, single engine. That's all I can tell."

"Crew, copilot. Those look like P-39s."

Al looked aft to the copilot's position. Evans was craning back, looking through the upper cockpit window.

"Copilot, upper turret. You sure, Mr. Evans?"

"Pretty sure. The wing's wrong for a Zero, anyway. Looks more like a P-39."

"Crew, pilot. Mr. Evans knows more about P-39s than any of us but keep an eye on those bastards anyway. Radio operator."

"Want me to give 'em a call, skipper?"

"Please do, Sparks."

The Corncob Blues were at 23,000 feet, and by Jimmy's dead reckoning they were about where they should be to pick up the 19th Bomb Group returning from Rabaul. There were cumulus cloud tops about two thousand feet below, and the sky was a beautifully, almost painfully, clear blue, with great visibility in all directions.

But no 19th Bomb Group.

"Lead to flight, I got nothing. Anyone see anything?"

"Two, that's negative, Lead."

"Three has nothing."

"Four has eyestrain and no B-17s."

"OK, let's stay on this heading. Keep your eyes peeled."

There was a crackle of static on Jimmy's earphones. "…39s, P-39s at twenty thousand, come in, this is Primrose Two-One."

Jimmy blinked in surprise. "Primrose Two-One, this is Corncob Blue Leader. You have us on visual?"

"Corncob Blue Leader, that's affirmative. We're at your six o'clock low."

Jimmy put his pursuit into a tight right turn and looked down through the canyon of cloud towards the ocean below.

And there they were.

"Blue Leader from Blue Four, tallyho. Nine B-17s at six o'clock low, and I mean low."

"Roger, Four. Primrose Two-One, we thought we'd see if you collected any limpets or other unfriendly types."

"Jimmy? Is that you?"

"Afternoon, Charlie. Bust any broncos lately?"

"You bet. See any Zeros?"

"Don't think so."

"Yeah. Can you stay up there awhile?"

"You know what we can do."

"Roger. Understood. There might be a few more coming along."

Jimmy had seen two Forts come in not long after the 19th left Seven Mile this morning. Given the one

388

that cracked up on takeoff, thirteen, presumably, made it to Rabaul.

He counted the number of B-17s he could see and came up with the same result: nine.

Jehosophat. Jimmy hoped to hell there were some stragglers, but he knew now wasn't the time to be broadcasting over the airwaves this sort of information for anyone to hear, like the Japs at Lae or Salamaua or even Buna.

"Primrose Two-One, we'll keep our eyes open. You guys see anything on the way home, give a shout."

"Affirmative, Corncob Blue Leader. Primrose Two-One out."

Jimmy took a deep breath and blew out through his oxygen mask. Stragglers, not sure how many, couldn't say over the radio anyway. He checked his fuel. Twenty minutes, and he'd have to take his boys and go home.

God-damned short-legged P-39s.

"Three from Lead."

"Three, go ahead, Lead."

"Three, extend to the east. Keep us in sight."

"Understood."

Shafer peeled off to the east with Bell tucked in behind him.

"Two, with me," he radioed, and turned west.

Jimmy figured if they were west and east of the 19th's course they had a better chance of spotting any straggling B-17s. He looked over his shoulder and the other two P-39s were tiny with distance.

"OK, Three, this is Lead, that's far enough. Assume original heading."

"Understood, Lead."

The twenty minutes ran out, and in the high clear sky the Corncob Blues saw nothing but each other, and Jimmy's repeated calls of "Primrose, Primrose" returned nothing but static. They reversed course and headed for home.

Charlie stood with Colonel Carmichael and Major Hardison while the mission debrief went on.

It was a different scene than normal. The young men jubilant at surviving yet one more mission were still there, but there were a lot more of them, and the void left by the missing low squadron was a silent undertone to the questions of the debriefers and the responses from the aircrew.

The film taken during the bomb run had been rushed to the photo lab, but it wouldn't be ready for at least another hour.

"What do you think, Charlie?" Carmichael asked.

"I think we hit 'em pretty good, Colonel. Who got it over the target?"

"Pease," Hardison replied. His voice was thin with fatigue, dry-throated from seven hours breathing pure oxygen. "He did his best to keep up with us, but he lost his No. 2 engine and then his airplane caught fire."

"Anyone get out?"

"No one saw any chutes. I think they went down in the sea. We'll get a better idea when the briefing reports are done."

"I saw some of that," said Carmichael. "Pease and his boys showed fine airmanship."

"I'd like to put them all in for something, Colonel," Hardison said. "Pease especially. Did you know his airplane blew a jug on the way up from Mareeba?"

"It did? What the hell was he flying?"

"That airplane we were thinking about using as a hangar queen if we couldn't get some replacement engines and a new generator."

"Wait. *Why Don't We Do This More Often?*"

"The very same. God damn it. Snyder didn't want to let him take the airplane. It was borderline at best for a combat mission. I should have listened to him."

"Why didn't you?"

"Pease wanted to go. He and all his boys were standing there. He practically begged me to go."

"That's right," Charlie said. "I saw it."

"You did?" said Hardison. He looked at Charlie in surprise.

"I knew someone came in early this morning, not long after midnight. I figured it was Pease because he was the only abort we had on the way up yesterday. What I couldn't figure was where he got another airplane. We pretty much scraped the cupboard bare of anything that could fly as it was."

Carmichael nodded. "That's what I told General Kenney we'd do. Anything we could get off the ground would go on this mission."

Hardison nodded. "Well, I knew that. That's why I let Pease fly. I figured the airplane couldn't be that bad if he got as far as Seven-Mile from Mareeba, and hell, Colonel, all these airplanes are beat-up pieces of junk. It's a wonder we didn't have the whole group abort."

391

Carmichael scoffed. Then he shook his head. Charlie thought it was a tired motion.

"Let's see if we can get Pease the Distinguished Service Cross, at least, and maybe the Silver Star for everyone else in his crew. Those won't be the only citations for this mission, I'm sure."

"Outstanding leadership, airmanship, and persistence in the face of the enemy," said Charlie softly.

Carmichael grinned at Charlie. It was a wry, lopsided grin, but it was there. "Maybe I'll put you in charge of writing the citations, Charlie."

The grin faded. Then, very quietly, the colonel said, "Although it applies to every man in this bomb group."

A corporal ran up to Colonel Carmichael.

"Here's a message for you, Colonel," the corporal said.

Carmichael took it. After a moment he handed the message to Charlie and walked off a few feet, standing with his head bowed and his shoulders hunched in. The corporal looked at him in confusion.

Hardison looked over his shoulder as Charlie read the message: ENROUTE SEVEN-MILE WITH THREE ETA DEPARTURE PLUS NINE. SIGNED LAWTON.

"But it's good news, isn't it, sir?" the corporal asked Charlie.

Charlie looked at the colonel, who still stood with his head bowed.

"The best," Charlie replied.

392

Chapter Fifteen

In trouble, Lead

"**N**ow, the airfield," said Major Dionne. He pointed to a photo on the table. It was Buna, taken from a B-17 at medium altitude. The photo caught someone's bombs exploding in a string along the beach. The pilots bent close or craned their necks to see what the squadron commander pointed at. "We're pretty sure there are Zeros there, but no one has seen them yet except Jimmy here, and that from a distance. So what the Japs might be doing when we don't have an eyeball on them is an open question. It's not a long runway and the Aussies think the ground is too soft and wet to sustain even Zeros, but maybe nobody told that to the Japs."

Dionne looked around. The seven pilots around the table with him were drawn from all three flights of the Corncobs, since the squadron as a whole was down to eight flyable airplanes.

"The 3rd Attack will send a squadron of A-20s over. The idea is they'll arrive when we do. That should confuse the Jap air defense. I'm told the A-20s will cross the coast east of Buna, head out to sea, and turn southwest to approach Buna Bay from the sea." Dionne paused. "Any questions?"

"Sir, what will we do if we meet Zeros?" asked one of the pilots.

"Bishop, how long is a piece of rope?"

"Sir?"

"You're asking me a question I can't answer. Look, remember one thing. Any pilot who hits the beach, causes some damage, and gets his airplane and himself back home more or less in one piece, has done his duty. I'm not telling you to run from a fight. But we're all carrying bombs today, and that means no one has the speed or maneuverability to fight Zeros before we complete our mission. If we encounter Zeros and we have to drop our bombs before we hit the beach, the Zeros have done *their* job, because we can't do ours. Got it?"

"Yes, sir," said Bishop.

"Jimmy, any words of wisdom?"

"Skipper, like you said, we're bombers today. We'll be low and slow until we drop our bombs. Before that, we're vulnerable. After that, three things. As soon as you can, get your speed up. Always keep your eyes open. Stay with your wingman so you can watch each others' tails."

Dionne nodded and looked at his watch. "Thanks, Jimmy. OK, I've got 0815 in four, three, two, one, hack. Everyone on the same time? All right, we take off at 0845, over the target around 0915, the A-20s hit between 0916 and 0920, we're all out of the area by 0925 and back home by 0955. That's all, man your planes and, like Jimmy said, keep your eyes open."

They formed up after takeoff into two flights of four, with Jimmy leading an impromptu Corncob Blue flight, and Dionne leading the formation as Corncob White Leader.

There were clouds to the north of the mountain peaks. At first Jimmy thought the clouds were building around the peaks, but they weren't, they were monster cumulus clouds still building miles beyond the north coast, reaching up to 20,000 feet or more, stretching to the west and the east as far as the eye could see. When the Corncobs topped out over the mountains and began their descent it was obvious that the clouds were some sort of weather front, coming south.

"Swell," Jimmy muttered to himself. He wondered what the A-20s would make of it.

Then they were down on the coastal plain, throttles all the way forward, four minutes from the target.

"ZEROS! Zeros, Corncob White Three has Zeros, seven o'clock high!"

Jimmy looked over his left shoulder and up. There were three dots, high enough to be dots still, but coming down hard. They'd be on top of them in three minutes, maybe less, and the Corncobs were still four minutes away from the target.

One minute for the Zeros, with an overtake speed of 100 mph, to do whatever they wanted. The P-39s, loaded with bombs, slow and sluggish on the controls with the extra weight, wouldn't have much of a chance.

But there were only three Zeros.

"Corncob White Leader from Blue Leader, come in."

"Go ahead, Jimmy."

"Let's spread out a bit, line abreast. When they get close they'll go after one flight. The other one cuts in behind them."

"OK. Take your boys out to the east."

"Roger. Corncob Blues, follow me."

Jimmy turned right and eased his flight out three hundred yards. He took them down to the treetops. The advantage of altitude was lessened when the target was scooting along at treetop level. If a Zero went in pulling out too late trying to match altitudes with the Corncobs, that was fine with Jimmy.

Then it was waiting, while the Zeros dove on them and the beachhead approached, three minutes that let the adrenaline leak into their blood and accelerate their heartbeats, making their teeth grit behind their oxygen masks as they stole looks over their shoulders. The Zeros went for the Corncob Blues. Jimmy watched the Zeros, knowing Dionne had to time it right to slide in behind the Zeros coming up behind them.

Then at the last second the Zeros turned hard into the Corncob Whites, wrongfooting Dionne as he started turning right into the Zeros.

"Blues, break left," Jimmy called, and pulled hard into the turn. White flight broke into elements, wingtips dipping into the trees. The Zeros concentrated on Corncob White Three and Four, tracers reaching out, and it looked like Corncob White Three took strikes along the right wing before the Zeros overshot.

The Japs pulled up hard and leveled out to burn speed off, then rolled and dove on White Three and Four, who were still turning right.

Jimmy pulled his nose up and triggered his machine guns. His flight pulled up with him and for a moment the air filled with tracers. The Zeros broke up and right without being hit. Then they were over the beach with flak bursting around them and ropes of tracer reaching up, and two barges discharging cargo

396

close together made a wonderful target, which disappeared from view as four 500-lb bombs burst around them.

A twin-engined airplane flew past them, and out in the bay bomb splashes grew and towered over a transport. Jimmy looked for the Zeros and keyed his radio.

"Corncobs, Corncobs, A-20s over the beach."

"Blue Leader, break right!"

Jimmy hauled hard to the right, looking back for the Zero as tracer lashed past his cockpit and something pinged and snapped against his fuselage. Jimmy saw tracers fly by to his left. The Zero passed him, pulling up, and Jimmy rolled hard to the left and pulled up, catching the Zero in his sights for the barest moment, touching the gun triggers. The tracers reached out and fell short and Jimmy kicked his rudder and rolled away.

"Blue Two, where are you?"

"In trouble, Lead."

Kellerman's voice was strained and raspy. Jimmy looked over both shoulders and overhead and saw a P-39 rolling frantically with a Zero taking potshots at him.

Another A-20 raced by. Jimmy turned left towards the P-39.

"Keep doing what you're doing, Two, I'm on the way," Jimmy radioed.

The air over the beachhead was lousy with tracer, flak, A-20s, P-39s, and Zeros, turning and dodging, and Jimmy banged his throttle and mixture into war emergency and hoped the engine oil held out. A Zero rushed in front of him, chasing an A-20 whose pilot was yawing wildly to throw off the Zero's aim while his rear gunner fired at the Zero. Then there was Kellerman, jinking wildly, the Zero sticking with him, shooting in short bursts, and strikes twinkled briefly on Kellerman's right wing.

Kellerman was doing it just right, rolling into a turn and then rolling in the opposite direction, using the P-39's higher roll rate to stay out of the Zero's line of fire.

"Corncobs, Corncobs, this is White Leader, head for home."

Jimmy keyed his radio. "Corncobs, this is Blue Leader, Blue Two has a Zero tight on his ass. I'm in pursuit. Someone watch my tail."

"This is White Leader, you're clear, Jimmy."

"Blue Three, Leader, we're right behind you."

The Zero was getting closer to Kellerman, using its superior acceleration in a turn, and once more Jimmy felt Kellerman in his cockpit, trying anything and everything to shake grim Death from his tail, even taking the P-39 right into the treetops, with green fuzz flying everywhere for a heart-stopping second, but the Zero hung onto him tight.

The Zero was small in Jimmy's gunsight, in range, but farther than Jimmy preferred to shoot. He triggered the machine guns anyway, a short burst, pulled the nose up a little and fired again. There were strikes on the Zero's tail and aft fuselage, and the Jap turned on his wingtip and headed northeast to the field at Buna. For a second Jimmy was tempted to follow him, then he looked at his fuel gauge and decided it was time to fight another day.

Jimmy pulled his engine controls out of war emergency and shot a glance at his CHT and oil temp gauges, which were higher than he liked. Still more reason to head for home.

"Blue Two, this is Lead, how you doing?"

"Better now. Thanks, Kid."

"We aren't home yet, Midnight. How's your engine and fuel?"

"Oil's a little hot, fuel's a little low."

"OK. Stick with me, we'll get there." *I hope*, Jimmy thought. Even though he had throttled back his engine was still overheating.

"Blue Three, this is Blue Lead. Where are you?"

"Behind you a little bit."

"Will you take a look at my engine? Looks like it's overheating."

"Lead, looks like maybe a wisp of smoke coming out. Don't see any oil on your fuselage anywhere."

"OK. How are you guys? Fuel OK?"

"Three's OK. How about you, Four?"

"My engine's OK, and so's my fuel."

"All right, then, enough chatter," said Jimmy. "Sing out if you're in trouble."

"Two."

"Three."

"Four."

Jimmy looked back at Buna, but the rain from the cloud front covered it. Looking to the west he could see it went all the way down the coast. Maybe the Jap fields at Lae and Salamaua were socked in, too, and hopefully that meant no Zeros to play with on the way home.

399

So all he had to worry about was this god-blessed overheating Allison engine. Jimmy climbed as gently as he dared while the north slopes of the mountains rose up in front of him, weaving his way in among the peaks to keep his climb speed, and thus the demand on his engine, as low as possible. When he looked left and right his flight was with him, spread out enough to support each other. Then they were past the highest peaks and through the clouds building over them, and there was the coastal plain, with Port Moresby in sight. Ahead of him were the four Corncob White P-39s, and ahead of the Corncob Whites were a handful of airplanes Jimmy figured were A-20s.

"Corncob Blues, say your fuel."

"Two has twenty-five."

"Three has thirty."

"Four has twenty-two."

"OK. Four, you land first. Two, follow him. Three, I'll follow you."

"How's your fuel, Lead?"

"Thirty-one."

"OK, then."

They followed the Corncob Whites into the pattern at Seven-Mile in that order, and for once Kellerman put his P-39 down without bouncing.

After Jimmy made his report to the intelligence officer Major Dionne took him aside.

"Just strikes on that Zero, eh?"

"Got some hits on the tail. Scared him bad enough to get him off Midnight, anyway."

Dionne nodded. "Too bad, though."

"What do you mean?"

"That would've been your fifth."

Jimmy shrugged. "Yeah, and I landed with twenty-two gallons of fuel left. Mixing it up with a Zero at full throttle, I'd've burned that in eight or nine minutes. Not to mention the way my engine was overheating."

Dionne nodded. "Not much sense shooting down a Zero and putting your airplane down in the jungle somewhere. Anyone ever walk out of the jungle?"

"The 22nd Bomb Group had a crew that did that. Took them six weeks."

"Well, I don't think the Corncobs could do without you for six weeks, Jimmy." Dionne grinned.

Jimmy rolled his eyes. "You never know in this game, Keith."

"I guess that's right." Dionne took a deep breath. "Hell. It was a good day. We sank some barges, shot up some Zeros, and everyone came home. I hear even all the A-20s made it back."

Jimmy grinned. "I saw one of those guys come in so low over the bay there was a rooster-tail of spray behind him until he got over land."

"Don't tell Tommy Bell. He'll want a transfer. He might even volunteer for that low-level squadron of B-17s."

"Nah. Tommy wouldn't like B-17s. Not fast enough. An A-20 is a lot sexier than a B-17. For a guy like Bell, anyway." Jimmy grinned. "The A-20 is kind of a neat airplane. I might have to wander over to the 3rd Attack myself and talk to their pilots."

Dionne shook his head. "Jimmy, Jimmy, Jimmy. Don't you know you have to commit to one thing in this life, and be that thing? You're a pursuit pilot, not a multi-engine type."

"Yeah? What about these P-38s we might get one of these days? That's a twin-engined airplane."

"OK. But there's a lot of difference between a P-38, which is a *pursuit*, and an A-20, which, however fast and sexy it is, is still a *bomber*."

Jimmy snorted. "They're both airplanes, aren't they?"

Dionne said sorrowfully, "I see there's no hope for you, Jimmy Ardana. You're just a whore for anything with wings."

"You're damned right, Major Dionne, sir. This job doesn't pay enough otherwise."

Kellerman sat on the edge of his cot when Jimmy got back from the debrief. He held his helmet in one hand and had his face in the palm of the other.

Jimmy threw his helmet and Mae West on his cot and sat down.

"You all right?" he asked.

"Swell," said Kellerman. "Just trying to get that image out of my mind."

"What's that? That Zero sitting on your tail, trying to perforate your precious anatomy?"

"That would be the one."

"Well, he didn't."

"No, he didn't. Thanks to you, Jimmy."

"How did you do before you attracted that unfriendly stranger?"

"Hit those barges with you and the boys. Got caught in the blast and flipped almost upside down.

Recovered and avoided an A-20. The Zero was chasing the A-20 but I think he liked me better. You know the rest."

"Yeah. So you dodged that sonofabitch for what? At least a minute? Kellerman, that's a lifetime in a dogfight. I saw some of it. That guy was *good*."

"You don't have to convince me."

"Look, Midnight, good as he was, you made that sonofabitch work. Hell, think it over. We were in a bad position, tactically. Low and slow. Couldn't dive away. We can outrun Zeros, but we can't do it fast. You have to fly straight and level to accelerate, and you couldn't do that, not with that bastard on your tail. You had to do exactly what you did, roll hard but don't go too far into the turn, reverse and do it over. And you know why we're going to beat the Japs, Midnight?"

"No. Why?"

"Because I was there to save your ass. We work as a team. Did you see how the Japs split up, looking for kills?"

"Yeah."

"What if that sonofabitch had a wingman to cover him? Like you did?"

Kellerman nodded slowly. "Wingman slips in behind you and keeps you busy while his lead finishes me off."

"That's right. Then they both come after me. And that didn't happen."

"No." Kellerman took a deep breath. "Thanks, Jimmy. Again."

Kellerman grinned suddenly. "Hell. You almost got your fifth kill."

403

"Almost doesn't count."

"No. What happened?"

"I got lucky, so you got lucky. I was barely in range, and my first burst fell short. I raised the pipper and got a couple of strikes on him.He turned hard and ran for it."

"How does that happen? That he got scared and ran?"

"I don't think he was really scared. Not really. Aren't you calculating all the time? Thinking ahead?"

"Ah. Yeah."

"Midnight, you're killing me."

"Sorry."

"Start using your brain. You'll live longer. Like that Jap. He took a couple of strikes, maybe knew he was alone, who knows what his fuel was like. Hell, I hit him with the .50s, even at long range those can do real damage to a Zero. So he decided it wasn't a good day to die for the Emperor, and you got to live to fight another day. Good deal all around."

"I guess so," said Kellerman. He grinned and threw his helmet on his pillow. "Damn. I hope I don't have to go through that again anytime soon."

"Me either."

Chapter Sixteen

Starlight, Searchlights, Rabaul – II

Jimmy waved when he saw Charlie and Al come into the O-Club. It was early in the evening and the club was just beginning to fill.

"Where's Danny?" he asked when they got beers and sat down.

"I thought you didn't like Danny," said Charlie.

"I like him fine as long as he's your copilot and not my wingman."

"Why, Jimmy, what a thing to say. Actually, Danny is coming along as a copilot. I let him do takeoffs and landings now."

Jimmy looked at Al, who shrugged. "I can't tell the difference," Al said, sipping his beer. "They're all bumpy."

"I'll put an extra bounce in for you next time," Charlie promised his navigator. Then he turned to Jimmy. "Heard from Jack."

"Yeah? How is he? Is he back home yet?"

"Probably. The letter was dated to the end of June. Jack said he was sick as a dog in Honolulu. Remember he had that fever they could never identify? It came back on the trip home."

"Good. Is he going to marry that movie star?"

Charlie shook his head. "Even Jack has that much sense. Irina is a wonderful girl. He'd be a fool to pass her up."

"Well, then here's to Jack not being a damned fool." They touched glasses.

Danny Evans came in, got a beer, and sat down.

"How do we look?" Charlie asked.

"Got the airplane fueled and ready. You figuring to go about midnight?"

"Sure. So enjoy that beer." Charlie gestured with his own glass. "It's our last. We'll try to squeeze in a nap before we go."

"Same old place?" Jimmy asked.

"Yeah."

"We ought to have a path worn in the sky between here and there by now," said Al.

"Night mission," said Jimmy. "You and the Aussies?"

"No. Recon. Navy probably wants to see what kind of ships are in the harbor."

"I thought we worked for the Air Corps," said Jimmy.

"We do. You heard about Guadalcanal, right?"

"What's a Guadalcanal?"

"Jehosophat, Jimmy, don't you follow the news? The Marines landed there two weeks ago."

Jimmy gestured wearily. "Me and the boys have been flying two or three missions a day for the last three weeks. The Japs at Buna give me plenty to worry about. And Guadalcanal is a long way from here."

"But Rabaul is the center of things. Lets them hit us here in New Guinea or there at Guadalcanal. What my instructor back at the Point called interior lines of communication."

"If you say so. Japs sending reinforcements or something?"

406

"Oh, probably. I heard a rumor the Japs are really giving the swabbies a pasting around Guadalcanal, but you know what rumors are."

Jimmy scoffed. "Guess it doesn't matter anyway, if those are your orders."

"Jimmy, that's all you really need to understand."

"I guess it's good to be useful," said Jimmy.

"I like being useful," said Danny.

Jimmy blinked in surprise. Charlie raised an eyebrow.

"Well, I like to think I'm handy when you need to lower flaps and stuff, Skipper. And Al, here, if we have to go somewhere we've never been, or where no one knows what the weather is, he kind of comes in handy to keep us from getting lost. And Sgt. Frye, he drops the bombs with that fancy bombsight of his. The gunners, golly, don't know how we'd get along without them."

Danny shuddered. "Why, even Jimmy here is useful. Nice to know he'll meet us on the way home, even if he is hoping for that fifth kill."

Jimmy looked at Danny and tried to figure out if he was joking, being sarcastic, or telling the truth, and finally decided it was a little of all three.

"I think Lt. Evans is getting comfortable in his new role in this man's Air Corps," Jimmy said. He raised his glass. "Good for you, Danny."

Danny looked at him. He touched his glass to Ardana's. "Thanks, Jimmy," he said. "That means something, coming from you."

"You bet. You guys be careful, tonight, OK? I don't know what I'd do without my favorite bomber guys to pick on."

"What? You don't like to drink with your squadron mates?"

Jimmy pointed to another table, where Bell and Shafer were encouraging Kellerman to chug a beer, with a couple of other guys from another flight egging him on. The encouragement was loud and fraternal.

"Too noisy for me," said Jimmy. "I like the quiet life."

Charlie laughed. "You sound like Jack."

"He does, actually," said Danny.

Al peered over Bob Frye's shoulder, into the dark night beyond the Perspex nose cone. Then he stood up and looked at the stars through the navigator's astrodome. It was a clear night for once. He shot the stars and worked out their position.

"Pilot, navigator."

"Go ahead, Al."

"Stay on this heading. We're forty miles from Rabaul, which puts us over the target in fifteen minutes. Five minutes to IP."

"OK, thanks, Al."

Bob Frye bent over the bombsight, checking the settings in the UV light. To Al it was still a mysterious ritual, even if he understood the basics, even if Frye taught him which buttons to push. "Just in case," as Frye once told him, in a different world and a different airplane.

Five minutes went by.

"Pilot, navigator, we're over the IP."

"Roger, Al. Bob, you're up."

"Affirmative, pilot."

Ahead of them a searchlight beam speared up into the sky. A half-dozen others followed, weaving slowly, illuminating a thin deck of clouds that looked like it was at their altitude. To Al it was an eerie, uncanny sight, a Hollywood premiere trying to kill him.

"Pilot, navigator."

"Go ahead, Al."

"See that cloud deck over the target? It's about our altitude."

"I see it. All right, we'll descend one thousand feet. Crew, pilot, we're descending to 19,000. Check your oxygen equipment."

"Crew check," Danny called. The litany of positions began, starting with Frye and Al in the nose and moving down the fuselage to Emmons in the tail.

The searchlight beams got closer. Al watched them and took a deep breath through his oxygen mask. It looked like a Hollywood premiere, all right, and that meant it was showtime.

Danny Evans looked ahead of the bomber at the searchlights over Rabaul and grimaced behind his oxygen mask. How did the Japs know they were coming? The word was they didn't have radar. Did they use some kind of sound detection equipment? Or had a lookout on the beach or out on a ship somewhere seen them against the stars? He shook his head. It didn't matter. What mattered was that the Japs knew they were coming.

The searchlights were bright enough that sometimes, if you looked far enough to the side of the beams, you could see the ghostly outlines of the volcanoes and the shore around Simpson Harbor. Look too close and you could only see the arc-light brilliance of the searchlight beam itself.

Behind him he heard Smith traverse the turret. There was a slight vibration in the seat of his pants from the turret motor and the sound of the air flow over the fuselage changed as the gun barrels rotated.

"Pilot, navigator."

"Go ahead, Al."

"Five minutes to target."

"Roger, navigator. Crew, pilot, you heard the man. Five minutes. Keep your eyes open. Ball turret, can you see Vunakanau?"

"Don't see nothin' but dark down theah, skipper."

"OK. Stay sharp, guys."

Danny looked over at Charlie. Charlie sat in the pilot's seat like he was an extension of the airplane, alert, one hand on the control wheel, scanning the instruments and the sky. The instruments fluoresced in the light from the UV lamps, and once you were night-adapted it threw the palest, vaguest green glow over the cockpit, silhouetting Charlie in the light. Danny was sure it silhouetted him, too, and he wondered what he looked like to Charlie.

"OK, pilot, bombardier. Keep it steady, coming up on drop."

"Roger, bombardier."

Danny saw Charlie put both hands on the controls. He followed suit, looking at the instruments to be sure they flew straight and level. It still made him grit his teeth. Not as bad, not anymore. *Straight and level,*

Danny thought. Just like an offensive lineman punching through the defensive line.

The searchlights were close enough now that they lit up the cockpit, even though Danny was sure none of them pinned the bomber. Flak burst ahead of them, way above them in the cloud layer, tentative, ranging shots.

"OK, steady, steady...bombs gone, flares gone. Starting camera."

A storm of wind and glass burst through the cockpit, things whining and smashing, and explosions, *WHAM!WHAM!WHAM!* bursting on the port side, the flashbulb wink of the bursting charge visible as the shrapnel swept over and through the airplane.

Danny felt the wind blowing through the shattered cockpit windows. Except for that it got quiet.

He looked left. "Charlie?"

The pilot slumped forward against his harness. His hands fell from the controls as Danny watched.

"Crew, copilot! Sound off!"

Dead silence over the earphones. Danny realized the silence wasn't the absence of talk but actual silence. The intercom was dead.

Flak burst around them again, further away.

Danny looked frantically left and right. No fire from the engines, no smoke visible in the illumination of the searchlights. He pushed forward on the controls and banked to the left, away from the lights and the flak.

He reached over and shook Charlie. The pilot's head lolled. His hands were limp at his side. Danny kept one hand on the control wheel and checked his oxygen line. The intercom line was attached to it. He

411

was breathing oxygen, he knew he was breathing because he could hear himself taking rapid breaths.

Slow it down, slow it down, Evans! You scrub the CO2 out of your blood and you're done for!

Danny peered at the nose, but he couldn't see anything. When he turned away from Rabaul and its searchlights he plunged the B-17 into darkness, and ahead of him there was only the night and a few stars.

He looked at the gyrocompass, but it was shot out, shattered along with most of the rest of the flight instruments. The magnetic compass was the only thing working.

What was the heading for Seven-Mile? Two zero zero, or something like that? That was true heading, though, and Danny didn't know the wind drift or the magnetic deviation to arrive at a true heading. He put the magnetic compass on two-zero-zero and held the descent, trimming for two thousand feet per minute. His oxygen was fine, but that didn't mean everyone was fine.

Sort it out later. Get down lower where everyone could breathe, and head for home.

Where everyone could breathe.

What if everyone was dead?

"Crew, copilot. Sound off."

Silence, dead silence on the intercom.

Lefkowicz wondered what the hell that turn was for, sharper than the normal turn off target, and diving, too.

412

Then Lefty wondered why he was down on the floor. There was something lying across his legs that shifted when the wings leveled.

He could see the gunport windows in the light of the stars. Otherwise it was pitch black in the waist section.

Lefty tried to sit up and discovered his left arm wouldn't move. Something pricked in his back, several somethings, and shot pain all across his side when he sat up, leaning on his right arm. Lefty propped himself up and felt his left arm with his right.

He almost passed out. When the pain let up he realized there was something grinding in his upper arm, and he felt something wet down his sleeve and his back.

The flashlight. He had a flashlight clipped to his belt. He pulled it out and turned it on. There was a red lens over the light to keep it from blinding people at night. He played it around the waist section.

Johann lay limp next to him. He was face up, and Lefty recoiled from the wounds that gaped from the gunner's boots, up his legs, to his torso that gleamed wet and black in the red light, to what was left of Johann's face.

Shema Yisrael, Hail Mary Mother of Grace!

He keyed his intercom. "Crew, left waist! Johann's hit bad, I think he's dead! Somebody give me a hand back here!"

Silence. The airplane descended, engine note changing as the engines throttled back.

"Crew, left waist, anybody! Skipper! Mr. Stern!"

Silence.

413

Lefty played the flashlight around the waist. The fuselage looked like a sieve, like someone took a shotgun, a whole hell of a lot of shotguns, to a farmer's tin roof. Holes everywhere, ripped and jagged.

Flak! They'd been hit bad!

Lefty traced his oxygen line to the receptacle. The line was still in, his intercom jack plugged in. He unplugged it and pushed it back in.

"Crew, left waist."

Silence. Lefty braced himself and shoved his useless left arm inside his Mae West where he could keep it from flopping around. He almost passed out from the pain again, but when he was done the life jacket was a good makeshift sling. He felt the fingers of his left hand with his right. He could feel them. Thank you, thank you God.

The B-17 was headed down and someone throttled the engines back. That meant someone was alive on the flight deck, alive and on the controls. Lefty looked at the stars out the left window, until he found the Southern Cross. It was low on the horizon at about eleven o'clock. They were headed south, presumably for home.

Lefty looked aft. The damage didn't look as bad back there. He started crawling. Maybe Emmons was still alive. Or maybe hurt and needing help. Lefty set his teeth against the pain and crawled toward the tail gunner's station.

Al lay on the floor with something wet splashing over him. In the green glow of the instruments he saw

414

the silhouette of a head, right over him, and a hand, feebly reaching for the neck.

Bob's hurt!

Al reached up. Even through his gloves he felt something warm.

Blood.

Frye lay on top of him, twitching, trying to reach his throat. Al reached around him, took the glove off his right hand, and followed Frye's arm to his hand, past his fingers, not to smooth flesh but something hot, not warm, and the gushing was rhythmic. An artery. A vein. Punctured or torn but not severed. Al put his finger over the wound and held it.

He could feel Frye's heart beating in the pulse under his finger. Frye's hand came up, touched his wrist for a moment, and moved away.

Al became aware that he was in pain. His legs, he thought at first, but they felt kind of numb and distant. No, the pain was in his back.

He listened on the earphones for Charlie or Danny, or anyone, to call for a crew check.

The earphones were silent.

He couldn't move, not with Frye lying on top of him and Frye's life beating under his fingers. He could just turn his head, looking forward through the Perspex, and the nose cone was starred and shattered. He looked at the fuselage above him.

The astrodome was gone. Wind whistled and roared over the resulting hole. There were a half-dozen gashes across the top of the fuselage, and lots of little jagged holes on either side of the fuselage. He looked over at his navigation instruments. They were smashed.

415

The UV light caused some of the gauges to fluoresce, and you could see the dials were broken.

Al didn't know how long the bomber descended. It leveled out and the engines throttled up.

Someone, Charlie or Danny or both, was alive on the flight deck. Surely they were headed home.

A wave of faintness swept over him. Suddenly Frye's hand was on top of his, holding his finger in place.

"Sorry, Bob," Al said, but he had his oxygen mask on, and the words were muffled behind it.

Lefty made it past the tail wheel assembly and came to the bulkhead aft of it. There was a small door cut in the bulkhead. Getting through it caused him a lot of pain and difficulty, because it was uphill. Lefty managed it, and then he heard the cables in the elevator controls move, and the B-17 leveled out. So there was someone still alive up front, flying the airplane, and that was good. But he wished they'd leveled out while he was making his way uphill.

He kept crawling. In the light from the gunner's windows he could make out Emmons, hunched forward over his guns.

The ball turret gunner and the tail gunner occupied the most isolated positions on the airplane. Lefty often wondered about that, wondered if Emmons had too much time to think and remember back here by himself.

The sides and windows of the tail compartment were riddled and slashed from shrapnel.

Emmons braced himself against the side of the fuselage and tapped Emmons on the boot.

416

The tail gunner didn't move.

Lefty knew there was a dome light, but the switch was near the gun handles, and that was two feet out of his reach. Lefty moved towards Emmons and rose up on his knees. He shook the tail gunner.

Emmons' head lolled when Lefty shook him. Lefty put the glove in his mouth and took it off. He reached up and found the carotid artery, the way Mr. Stern showed him, and felt for Emmons' pulse.

He felt again, not sure he was in the right place.

Nothing.

Lefty looked around the compartment. The damage from the flak was all around, with the holes on the left side punched in, and those on the right side punched out. Lefty got his flashlight out and played it over Emmons and the compartment.

The right side of the compartment was splashed and dark. There was a wet dark pool on the floor. Emmons' body was slashed and ripped, his jacket tattered and torn and bloody.

Lefty turned off the flashlight and sat back against the side of the bomber. He had a sudden memory of Emmons, how they found him after that air raid on Soerabaja, sitting dazed among the bodies of his first crew, crumpled and huddled on the ground around him. Lefty took a deep breath, and another one. He said a Shema and a Hail Mary.

He knew he had to move. He put the images out of his mind. *The crew,* he thought. *Johnny is trapped in the ball turret.* Lefty started crawling forward, over the bulkhead and past the tail wheel into the waist, past

417

Johann's body, until he fetched up against the ball turret.

In the red glow of his flashlight he could see the turret pointed forward, guns trained slightly low. But the thin metal of the turret, only 3/8 inch of aluminum, was slashed and punctured the way the fuselage was. Lefty braced himself against the turret spindle and hammered the turret with the butt of his flashlight.

"Johnny!" he yelled. "It's Lefty, Johnny. You OK in there?"

Johnny didn't answer.

Lefty reached for the emergency rotation lever, unclutched the turret, and cranked the rotation handle until the turret pointed straight down, exposing the hatch into the turret.

"Aw, shit," Lefty said tiredly. Shrapnel had torn hell out of the hatch, and the left side of the hatch as well. The holes in the hatch were punched into it.

Johnny was dogmeat in there. Had to be. Lefty tried to open the turret access hatch and couldn't manage it one-handed. Reluctantly he rotated the turret back into place so it wouldn't interfere with their landing. He started to chide himself for optimism, but hell, someone was flying the airplane, and hopefully that meant they could land, and they might even survive the landing.

He crawled around the ball turret and into the radio compartment.

Sparks was sprawled on the floor. Lefty saw his oxygen mask was off and his chest was moving, but the radio operator lay in a pool of blood. Lefty couldn't tell where the blood was coming from, and then he saw

Sparks had a tourniquet around his right forearm, and he was holding the tourniquet tight. But he had to let it go every now and then to keep the circulation going, and when he did the arteries pumped blood all over the radio compartment.

Lefty crawled up next to him. Sparks looked at him.

"Hi, Lefty," he said. "I figured everyone else was dead."

"You idiot. Someone's flying the airplane."

"If you say so. Maybe it's on autopilot."

"Is it just your arm? You hurt anywhere else?"

"I don't know. I'm kind of numb."

Lefty looked at the tourniquet. The shrapnel had almost torn the hand off, and he could see bone through the hole in the jacket sleeve.

He got the first aid kit. "You want some morphine?"

"No. Hell no. I'm going in and out anyway. You better get up front and see who's flying this bucket. The intercom is out." Sparks gestured with his head.

Lefty didn't know anything about electronics or radio, but anyone could tell Sparks' black boxes were useless from all the holes in them.

Well, that explains that, he thought.

"You going to be OK?"

"I've made it this far. What's wrong with your arm?"

"I think it's broken. Hurts like a bastard if I move it wrong."

Sparks nodded. "Anyone else alive back there?"

"No."

"Shit."

"Yeah."

"How 'bout you, Lefty? You want some morphine?"

"No. There's another kit up front. If I can get Mr. Stern back here to help you, you might wish you had that morphine."

"OK. Go on. Hurry."

Lefty nodded. He levered himself up on the corner of the radio operator's bench. Then he went forward.

Lefty thought the wind was from all the holes in the fuselage. But when he got to the after end of the bomb bay he saw the doors weren't closed. His flashlight shone down into darkness, while the bomb bay doors pointed straight down.

He would have to cross the narrow catwalk over the open bomb bay doors, one-handed.

With however many thousand feet between him and whatever was below, in the darkness.

Lefty hooked the flashlight to the ring on his belt. Then he turned sideways and shuffled down the catwalk, over the empty night, with the red light dancing and jiggling and throwing the shadows of the girders crazily around the flak-slashed fuselage.

Danny thought he was seeing things when he saw the red light.

It got brighter gradually, but it wavered. Once it went out completely, and then came back stronger. He looked over his shoulder.

There was a red light in the bomb bay.

Fire!

420

No. It couldn't be a fire. The color wasn't right, the intensity wasn't right. Danny looked forward, through the starred and shattered windshield, checking the engine instruments for No. 3 and No. 4, then he looked back over his shoulder.

The red light shone almost in his eyes. He blinked and turned away.

"Sorry," said a familiar voice. Danny couldn't put a name to the voice.

"Mr. Evans? It's Lefkowicz."

"Check on Charlie," Danny said. "He's hurt bad."

There was an odd noise and the red light suddenly danced all over the cockpit. There was a cry of pain, then another, and a gasp.

"Lefkowicz!"

"I'm OK. I slipped in something."

The light pointed aft.

"Oh Mary. Oh God."

Danny looked aft.

Lefkowicz was on the floor, pointing his light up into the upper turret.

Kim Smith's body slumped down on the turntable. His oxygen mask dangled from the right side of his helmet, because the left side was gone, along with that side of Smith's head.

"Check on Major Davis," Danny said.

"Are you OK?"

"I'm fine. Don't worry about me."

Lefty stood up slowly, then reached over. He felt for the pulse in Charlie's neck.

"He's alive," said Lefkowicz. "But there's a hell of a furrow on the top of his head. Bleeding everywhere."

"Anything else?"

"I don't think so. Let me check."

Danny looked forward as Lefty played the flashlight over Charlie.

"Looks like a couple of good slashes," Left said. "Bleeding, but I don't think they're too bad. This head wound doesn't look good. It's bleeding like hell. I don't think it's down into the brain but ..."

Danny sucked in his breath and exhaled it slowly. "OK. Look. Can you get down into the nose and check on Al and Bob? And close the bomb bay doors?"

Lefty contemplated the opening under the flight deck leading to the tunnel into the nose compartment.

His arm hurt like hell and whatever was in his back chose that moment to make it feel like someone drove nails into him. He bit back a gasp.

"Yeah," said Lefty. "I'll head that way. Where are we?"

"I don't know. About a hundred miles south of Rabaul. Something like that."

"OK," said Lefty. *Maybe I should've taken some of that morphine*, he thought. "Look, Mr. Evans, Sparks is alive but he's hurt bad. He says his radio equipment is smashed. No one else is alive back aft."

Danny nodded. No radio. No way to ask for a DF steer. Oh hell.

"Right," he said. "Go check on Al and Bob."

Al heard someone gasp in pain. It was the sort of gasp made in response to the kind of pain you didn't believe in, not until it bit into you. Then he saw a red light illuminating the fuselage above him.

422

"Mr. Stern? Al?"

"Lefty?"

The red light got brighter. Al blinked and then Lefkowicz loomed over him, propping himself against the navigator's table.

"Me and Bob are glad to see you," Al said.

Frye held up his left hand in a thumb's up.

"Oh hell. What do I do, Mr. Stern?"

"Get that first aid kit down here. And second, you can damn well call me Al."

"Yes, sir, Mr. Al, sir."

"Polack."

"Hebe."

"OK, OK." Al resisted the urge to laugh. He knew it would come out as a giggle, high-pitched, and the pitch would probably get higher if he let it. He bit back on the impulse.

Lefkowicz got the kit down from its brackets and opened it.

"What do you want me to do, Al?"

"You see where I'm holding my finger?"

"Yeah."

"Bob here has a punctured artery in his neck. I've been holding my finger on it. Only my finger is getting tired, and by the time Bob here can find the spot he could bleed to death. I need you to take my place."

"OK. But I think maybe I need to close the bomb bay doors first."

"You know where the switch is?"

"Yeah. Bob showed me once."

"Go do it."

Lefkowicz crawled over them and went to the bombardier's station. He studied the bombardier's controls for a moment, found the bomb door handle, and pushed it forward.

There was a faint change in the vibration of the floor underneath them. It stopped after a few seconds, but Lefty had already turned back.

"What happened to your arm?" Al asked.

"I don't know. I think it's broken. Hurts like hell."

Al studied Lefkowicz for a moment. "OK. Get yourself situated so you can use your right hand easily."

"OK."

Lefkowicz put the flashlight down. He squirmed and pushed until he was propped against the navigator's desk. He reached out and poised his finger over Al's.

"Just put my finger where yours is?" he asked.

"Yes. You'll know where. If it pumps blood you're in the wrong place. Put your finger next to mine, and when I pull off you come right behind me. Even if you get it right there'll be some blood. Ready?"

"Yes."

"On three. One, two, three."

Lefty slid his finger where Al's had been. There was a brief spurt of blood, dark in the red light, and then it stopped.

Al flexed his fingers. "You OK, Bob?"

The left hand, thumb's up.

"OK. Lefty, what's going on? Who's flying this thing?"

"Lt. Evans. Charlie's hurt. Got a groove in the top of his head that's bleeding pretty bad. I felt his pulse. It was kind of weak, and he's out cold." Lefty paused.

"No one's alive in back except for Sparks. His hand is about torn off, and he put a tourniquet on his wrist. The radio and intercom are gone."

Al shut his eyes for a moment. "Lefty, I need to get up there. Even if I can't do anything for Charlie or Sparks, Danny will need me to navigate for him."

"I see that," said Lefty. "Problem is, Mr. Frye here is lying on top of you, and if you move, it's liable to dislodge me."

"Right. If you had two hands you could hold his head, but that's why this is a problem."

Al thought for a moment. "OK, Bob, I'm going to support your head with my left hand and push myself out from under you with my right. Lefty, you'll have to be ready to compensate. It's not going to be a nice, smooth motion. All right, get ready, here we go."

Al got his left hand under Bob's head and pushed away from him with his right.

Lefty gasped. There was a spurt of blood, not as bad as Al thought, and then Al was able to slowly lower Bob's head to the floor.

"Would one of those pressure bandages help?" Lefty asked.

"I don't think so. I'd be afraid you couldn't keep the right pressure on the artery." Al hesitated. "I'd better go check on Charlie. Do the best you can, Lefty, but we're hours away from home."

Al started to crawl away.

Lefty said, "Al, can't you move your legs?"

"I don't know, Lefty. I can't feel them."

Al crawled up the pitch-dark tunnel. He wished he had taken Lefty's flashlight. He had no idea where his

425

own light was. It was a much different thing, he discovered, crawling along the tunnel using your elbows without being able to use your legs, than it was to crawl with elbows and knees the way they'd been taught to move under barbed wire back in OCS. Pulling himself out of the tunnel and onto the flight deck was another trial of the will, and when it was done he sat on the edge of the tunnel with his elbows on the metal deck between the pilot's and co-pilot's seats.

"Danny!" he yelled.

The copilot looked down at him. "Al. Am I glad you're alive. Come on up here and see if you can help Charlie."

"Love to, pal, but I can't move my legs."

"Oh. Oh, shit."

"Tell me about it. Does the autopilot work?"

"I don't know. Let's see."

Al made out Danny's arm, moving to switches on the center console, under the throttles and turbocharger levers.

"Whaddya know. It works."

"OK. Come help me up."

Danny unbuckled himself and climbed out of his seat. He bent over and helped Al out of the tunnel, and put him against the fuselage on the right side of the flight deck.

"What do you want to do?"

"Can you get Charlie out of his seat so I can have a look at him?"

"Yeah."

"Danny, do you have a flashlight?"

"Yeah."

"Good. Let me have it, then get Charlie out of his seat and lay him on the deck beside me."

Al remembered the first time he saw Danny Evans, back last May. He was a big beefy kid, but being in hospital had taken a lot of that beef off. Al hoped Danny had his strength back. Or enough of it, at least.

Danny crouched by Charlie and released the harness, pushed the straps out of the way, climbed behind the pilot's seat and lifted Charlie out of it, puffing with the effort, and laid him down by Al. Then he handed Al his flashlight.

"OK, Danny. Tell me, what time did we turn away from Rabaul?"

"It was 0400, give or take a minute."

"OK. What time is it now?"

"0455."

Al nodded. "What's our heading?"

"Magnetic heading is 200. Magnetic compass works, but the gyrocompass is out. Don't kow the wind of the magnetic deviation anyway."

"Can you work out our true airspeed for me?"

"Give me a couple minutes."

Danny climbed back into the copilot's seat. Al saw him reach into the leg pocket of his coveralls and pull out an E6B flight computer.

"Danny, I'm going to use regular light. If you're worried about your night vision, close your eyes."

"OK."

Al turned on the light. First he felt Charlie's pulse, which seemed weak to him. He opened Charlie's eyes. The pupils contracted, but the left looked larger than the right.

427

Then Al looked at the wound on top of Charlie's skull. Lefty's description was accurate, an incised wound to and through the scalp. Al saw the white bone of the skull. He felt the edges of the wound, gently, very gently, but the bone of the skull appeared intact.

Al figured Charlie took a hell of shot to the head, and he probably had a concussion, but that looked to be the worst of it. He looked over the rest of Charlie's body as best he could, without finding anything more than some slashes. At least he couldn't see blood pooling under Charlie's body.

"You gonna finish up some time soon?" Danny asked. "I'd like to open my eyes."

"What, you don't like blind flying?"

"Not the kind where I fly with my eyes closed."

Al looked Charlie over one more time and turned off the flashlight. "OK, I've done what I can."

"Thanks. How does Charlie look?"

"Like a guy who took a hell of a knock to the head. I think he's got concussion, but at least he's not bleeding buckets. You know anything about concussion?"

"Yeah, I do. It's one thing you learn about, playing college ball."

"Should he still be unconscious?"

"Depends. We had a quarterback hit pretty hard once. He was out for two hours. You could try waking him up. But watch out, he might puke. Oh. His eyes. They look right?"

"Left pupil bigger than the right."

"That's not good. He needs a doctor."

"Yeah. You got my true airspeed yet?"

428

"You made me close my eyes."

"Well, they're open now." Al slapped Charlie's cheek gently. "Charlie. Charlie, wake up. Wake up, Charlie."

Someone was slapping the hell out of him and screaming in his ear.

Charlie felt the contents of his stomach rising and he turned his head before it gushed.

"Aw, hell, Charlie!"

Charlie opened his eyes. It was dark, but he could see pale phosphorescence. The light wouldn't focus.

"Aw."

"Charlie, you OK?"

"Al." His voice didn't sound right. "What…"

"Don't talk, Charlie. We got hit by flak over Rabaul. You got a hell of a knock on the head."

"Airplane…"

"We're on the way home. I think you have a concussion, though."

"He sure has the symptoms," said another voice. "He's slurring his words."

"Whozat?"

"It's Danny, Charlie. Danny Evans."

"Danny. Alright?"

"Yeah, Charlie, I'm fine. I've got it under control."

"Guys?"

"There's been casualties, Charlie. You don't worry about it now. We're three hours from home at least."

"Al, true airspeed 175."

"Heading?"

"Still two-zero-zero."

Al thought about that. True heading required a correction to the magnetic heading involving the local magnetic deviation and the wind drift. The drift meter was smashed to bits down in the nose compartment, so no way to figure the wind.

Hell, two-zero-zero was close enough.

"How long you been traveling at 175?"

"Sixty minutes."

"Right. Stay on that heading. Are you at least 10,000 feet?"

"More or less."

"Good. That should keep us over the mountaintops. Stay on this heading and airspeed. Two hours. We should be over the south coast of New Guinea by dawn. We'll figure out then if we need to turn left or right."

"Two hours?" Charlie croaked.

"Charlie. Stay quiet and rest. We might need you to help Danny with the landing."

"OK." Charlie felt like the world was spinning, worse than any hangover he'd ever had, and the nausea made him want to curl up in a ball.

But something nagged at him.

Rabaul. Flak. Casualties. Danny flying the airplane.

His stomach rebelled but he'd flushed most of it the first time. A sour, nasty fluid filled his mouth. He turned away from Al and spat it out. He put out a hand to help him sit up. His hand slipped in something sticky.

Charlie pulled his hand back. He looked up in the vague light from the instrument panel.

He knew he was looking at the turntable for the upper turret, but there was something hanging from it, and he suddenly realized it was a body, and that meant the body was Kim Smith's, and this sticky stuff on the cockpit deck was the flight engineer's blood.

Danny looked ahead into the darkness. He took off his headphones so he could listen to the airplane, the note of the engines, the sound of the slipstream over the fuselage.

For awhile he thought he heard muffled sobbing. Then it quieted.

He had never noticed the way the chatter on the intercom, the crew checks, the bickering, the banter between Al and Charlie, the ritual of flying in a bomber crew, depended on the intercom.

And it was silent, and outside it was dark, and the ghostly luminescence of those instruments still working belied the order represented by the numbers on the dials. Behind him were the dead, and around him the wounded, maybe the dying, and ahead of him were the Owen Stanley Mountains, shrouded by the night. When they crossed the coast the runway at Seven-Mile would be east or west of them, and he'd have to decide which. Regardless of his choice, right or wrong, he'd have to land the B-17 by himself.

It came to Danny that after nine trips in *Bronco Buster II* he had seventy hours in the airplane. That was over twice as many hours as he had in P-39s. It meant he had over three hundred flying hours.

Danny sneaked a look at Charlie's logbook once. Some of the entries didn't have hours opposite them and included places that sounded like they came from a geography book, like Palembang and Soerabaja and Singosari. Some entries were scrawled in pencil, smudged and barely legible. But the total carried forward was nearly three thousand hours.

Danny knew that in some circles that wasn't considered a lot. But maybe in other circles the experience of flying an airplane like the B-17, which included attacks by Zeros and flak and the kind of damage to airframe and engines that changed it into a different airplane in seconds, maybe those hours counted for a little bit more.

What was it that little punk Jimmy Ardana kept saying? "It's just an airplane."

And if Jimmy were here he could probably take this airplane and land it just like he landed that Hudson, a four-month lifetime ago.

Danny decided if Jimmy and Charlie could do it, he could by God take a stab at it.

Hell. All that could happen is he might kill everyone, himself included.

"Charlie. Charlie, wake up."

Al kept slapping Charlie's cheek, not hard.

"Wha…?"

"Charlie? Can you sit up?"

"Yeah. Think so."

"OK. Come on."

Al levered Charlie up, using his elbow as a fulcrum on the floor.

"Al. Why onna floor like that?"

"I can't move my legs, Charlie."

"Wha…?"

"I don't know why. I think I smacked my back on something when the flak hit us."

"You OK?"

"I'm either paralyzed from the waist down or it's temporary. Let's hope for temporary. Now, can you sit up like that?"

"Yeah."

"OK. Look, Lefty is down in the nose with Bob Frye. Lefty's holding his finger over Bob's carotid artery to keep Bob from bleeding to death. I need to get down there to help him."

Charlie looked like he was going to puke again. Then he took a deep breath and nodded.

"Yeah. Go. Worst thing I puke on myself."

"OK. If you can get back in your seat Danny could use your help."

"Yeah." Charlie tried to get his feet under him.

"Keep trying, Charlie."

Al turned and crawled into the tunnel, dragging his useless legs behind him.

Lefty felt tears leaking from his eyes.

His broken arm hurt. It hurt like hell, but the finger over Bob Frye's carotid artery was cramping, and it hurt more than the damned arm did.

"Lefty. I'll take over."

Lefty thought he was going to cry or scream or what, he didn't know. He held it together long enough to let Al put his finger over Bob's artery, and then he lay back, gasping, trying to get his finger to unbend.

"Your finger cramped?" Al asked.

"Oh boy."

"And you can't move the other hand at all."

"I can move it, that's it."

"Try bending the finger against the floor. Gently."

It took three tries but Charlie finally levered himself into the pilot's seat. He felt like he'd puke again, so he opened the side window and retched until the spasm passed.

"How far from Rabaul are we?" he asked.

"About four hundred miles."

"Puts us over the north coast. Can you see the mountains?"

"No. Still too dark."

Charlie looked at the clock. It read 0555. Dawn was forty-five minutes away. If they were over the tops of the mountains, that meant they would get to Seven-Mile some time after the sun rose. It would shine straight down the airstrip, which would help.

"Danny."

"Yeah."

"The radio's dead."

"Yeah."

"OK. Fly over the field. That will let them know we're there. Then go straight in to land. If they can't get you on radio they'll figure it's because we don't have a radio. They'll clear the field."

"Yeah."

"You OK?"

"I'm scared."

"Jehosophat. You and everyone else still alive on this airplane. You're doing fine, Danny, more than fine."

Danny nodded. Charlie watched him sweep the instruments and look to the left and the right.

Charlie looked out the window. He couldn't see anything in the darkness but blue flames from the engine exhaust.

"How are No. 1 and No. 2?"

"Fine."

"Fine? All that flak off our left side and they didn't get hit?"

"My mom used to say something about gratitude for small blessings."

"Yeah. Your mom is right." Charlie looked at the engine instruments but couldn't make his eyes focus. "How's our fuel?"

"I think we have a leak in the fuel cells outboard on the left. Otherwise we're good. It might be close but not that close."

"OK." Charlie took some deep breaths. He looked at Danny. "Not a scratch?"

"What?"

"You. You didn't get a scratch."

"I don't think so."

Charlie shook his head. Then he groaned. "Jehosophat."

"Yeah."

Al looked to the left out the nose cone Perspex. Off to the east the faintest line of pink revealed the horizon.

"How you doing, Lefty?"

435

"I'm OK."

"Bob, you OK?"

The bombardier held up his hand with the thumb up.

"The sun's coming up. We'll be home soon."

"Al."

"Yeah, Lefty?"

"Sparks is back in the radio compartment."

Al sighed.

"I know," said Lefty. "He was OK when I left him. But that was two or three hours ago."

Al sighed again. "Right."

"I'll go. You take over with Frye here."

Al thought about that.

He thought that some feeling was coming back into his legs. He thought maybe, maybe, he could twitch his toes.

Maybe.

But he didn't think he'd be able to crawl on his elbows over the bomb-bay catwalk, dragging his legs behind him.

"You know what to do with a tourniquet?" Al asked.

"I think so."

"OK. Let's change over."

"Right."

Lefty crawled up the tunnel to the flight deck. In the last two hours he'd learned about guarding his broken arm. It didn't mean he didn't gasp in pain more than once, but he made it through the tunnel and onto the flight deck.

By the time he reached the flight deck, though, wan red sunlight came through the windows. It wasn't a lot, but it was enough to illuminate Kim Smith's body, dangling in his harness from the upper turret.

Charlie and Danny were occupied with flying the bomber. They didn't notice him, and Lefty didn't say anything. He got his legs under him and got by the turret and through the bulkhead into the bomb bay.

This time it was easier. The bomb bay doors were closed. But shuffling down the narrow catwalk took a long time, and so did worming his way through the bulkhead into the radio compartment.

Sparks looked at him. "Took your damned time," he said.

"Sorry."

"Where are we?"

"I'm not sure. Al thinks we'll be back at Seven-Mile soon."

"Al's alive?"

"Banged up, but yeah."

"Who's flying the airplane?"

"Charlie and Mr. Evans. Charlie got hit, so it's mostly Mr. Evans."

"Anyone else make it?"

"Bob Frye has a hole in his carotid artery. Al and I took turns keeping him from bleeding to death."

"How's Mr. Stern?"

"Not good. Can't move his legs."

"Shit."

"Yeah."

"What about Kim?"

Lefty shook his head. Sparks nodded slowly.

"Shit," Sparks repeated. His voice held the fatigue of a world.

Charlie's head was spinning and his stomach felt like it would turn inside out, and the sun coming up over the horizon made his eyes hurt. He looked out the window in the growing light. They were over a beach, with the mountains behind them and the ocean in front of them. Now the question was, turn left or right?

"You see anything familiar?" Charlie asked.

Danny took a moment answering. He looked out the window and back.

"We're west of Seven-Mile," he said.

"How d'you know?"

"Those mountains in the west look too close."

"OK."

"OK?"

"Yes. I can't see worth a crap, Danny. It's up to you. Take us home."

Danny banked the B-17 to the east, into the sun coming up and showing itself over the horizon.

In five minutes they saw the familiar hill at the southeast end of the bay, then the bay itself and the ships in the harbor.

"Yeah, stay out to sea," Charlie cautioned. "You know what the flak gunners are like over Moresby."

They were past the harbor, flying down the hills at the north side of Bootless Inlet.

By the time they were there a pair of P-39s climbed up from the airstrip and rendezvoused with them. The P-39s ranged up on Charlie's side, throttled back with some flaps. Charlie waved.

The pilot in the P-39 waved back and pointed to his ears.

Charlie shook his head, pointed to his mouth, and shook his head again. Then he retched out the window as nausea hit him.

The pilot in the lead P-39 nodded. The P-39s peeled off, climbed a few hundred feet and took station off the B-17's left wing.

The B-17 came opposite the east end of Bootless Bay. Danny made a one-eighty, turning in to Bootless Inlet, and lined up with the runway.

"OK, Danny, how you doing?"

"I've got it, Charlie. I'll get us down."

"I know, Danny, I just want to be sure the number of pieces bouncing around is held to a minimum."

Danny grinned briefly, which told Charlie what he needed to know.

There was nothing to fault in Danny's approach, and Charlie lowered the gears and the flaps when Danny told him to, and throttled back the engines as they came over the threshold. The B-17 settled to the runway with a solid bump and a rumble of the main wheels. The tail came down and Danny got on the brakes, slowing the B-17.

Two ambulances came out and chased them down the runway as they braked to a stop. Charlie helped Danny shut the engines down, and the airplane was silent.

Jimmy rushed over to the 19th's flight line as soon as he landed and shut down in his revetment, but by the time he got there the wounded and the dead had been

439

taken away, and a dozen men stood looking in awe at what was left of *Bronco Buster II*. He stood for a moment, looking at the airplane, and then looked around.

Danny Evans sat against the left main gear, eyes closed, knees drawn up against his chest. Jimmy walked over to him, but for a long moment Danny didn't react. Then he shook himself a little, opened his eyes, and blinked up at Jimmy.

"I thought that was you in one of those P-39s," Danny said.

Jimmy sat down next to Danny. "That was a good landing."

"How do you know I made it?"

"I could see Charlie had blood on his face. Looked like he was puking. There were holes all over the fuselage and around the cockpit. I figured he'd been hit pretty bad. You looked OK, though."

Danny nodded. He sighed and closed his eyes again. "Charlie was hit bad," he agreed. "Not as bad as some of the guys, but he got knocked in the head with shrapnel. Probably has a concussion, at least."

"Al?"

"He's alive, but he can't move his legs. The medics couldn't find a wound, so they think he got smashed against something." Danny closed his eyes. "Holy Christ, Jimmy. He couldn't move his legs, and he crawled up from the nose compartment to help Charlie. Then he crawled, crawled back down there because Lefkowicz, who had a broken arm, was holding his finger on the artery in Bob Frye's neck to keep him from bleeding to death."

440

"Lefkowicz? He's a waist gunner, what was he doing in the nose?"

"I guess he got lonely. Everyone else was dead in the back of the airplane except Lefkowicz and the radio operator, who's probably going to lose his hand."

"What happened to Frye?"

"I think he'll be OK. Al and Lefty took turns with their fingers in the dike, and the medics fetched a doctor who stitched up the artery and got him off the airplane."

Jimmy shook his head slowly.

"Al told me once about the first *Bronco Buster*," Danny said. "They lost the bomber they'd been flying in a Jap air raid, and the only one available was this shot-up B-17 that came back with a dead crew. They had to wash the blood out of it and patch it up before they could fly it. They did it themselves because there wasn't anyone else, and Charlie wanted to keep the crew together."

Jimmy looked up at the underside of the bomber's wing. It was streaked with oil and jagged rips and punctures. He put a hand on Danny's shoulder and squeezed. Then he walked under the wing of the bomber and around the left side, which looked like some sort of automated ice pick had come along and punched holes in the side of the airplane. Down the after fuselage there was a streak of something dark. Jimmy thought at first it was oil, but it came from the little holes in the underside of the fuselage. It was dried blood, and it was splashed all over the right side of the tail gunner's position. The fin and control surfaces of the tail were slashed and tattered.

441

The crew door on the right side of the airplane was open. Jimmy climbed in.

Blood, blood splashed everywhere, and in the close confines of the waist it was already beginning to stink. Jimmy walked past the riven and shattered ball turret, through the radio compartment, over the bomb bay and onto the flight deck, where there were boot prints in the dried blood smeared on the deck. Jimmy leaned against the copilot's chair and looked around the flight deck, at the wreck of the instrument panel, the smashed windscreen, and the holes in the fuselage that let in rays of light.

The airplane shook and quivered. Danny Evans squeezed through the tunnel from the nose position and crouched with Jimmy on the flight deck.

Jimmy studied Danny's face. Once again he was struck by the change he'd seen, only now there was something more, something you couldn't point to, except you knew it was there. He couldn't imagine what it had been like for Evans when the flak swept the bomber with shrapnel, changing everything in a heartbeat.

He put his hand on Danny's shoulder. Danny turned and looked at him for a long moment.

Then Danny grinned. There was no amusement in his eyes.

"Isn't this where we came in?" Danny said.

Jimmy shook his head and nodded. "Jehosophat," he said quietly.

"What's that mean, anyway? Major Davis says it all the time. So did Captain Davis."

"Seems their mother was kind of strict," Jimmy said. "Southern lady. No swearing allowed. So their dad suggested they do what he did, and substitute 'Jehosophat.' Means the same thing."

Danny nodded. He sighed and looked around the flight deck. "Yeah. Jehosophat."

Chapter Seventeen

Shut up. Keep going.

Jimmy sat in the cockpit of his P-39, watching the engine gauges as he ran the throttle up to full power. His mechanic sat next to him.

The cylinder head temps started rising, then the oil pressure rose too.

"OK, OK, shut it down," said the mechanic.

Jimmy closed the throttle and mixture. The engine coughed to a stop.

"Well, hell," said the mechanic. "I changed the oil and the plugs, Mr. Ardana. Pulled out the oil lines, purged 'em, miked the cylinders to be sure they were still in round, and about then ran out of ideas and spare parts."

Jimmy nodded. He missed Don Terraine, but he wasn't going to tell...Jimmy had to stop and think of the guy's name. Ed, Ed Hope.

"Ed, as long as it's you and me, you can call me Jimmy. Sounds like you've done your best. What does Chief Benchley say?"

"He says these engines are getting worn out. I asked him what else I might try."

"What did he say?"

"He said he'd think about it."

Jimmy thought that was less than helpful, and remembered Chief Halloran, who, like Don Terraine, went back to Australia when the 8th was replaced by the 35th.

Less than helpful or not, Jimmy figured Benchley was right about the engines being worn-out. The best thing to be done for the Allisons in the P-39s was to replace them. A top overhaul in a properly-equipped engine shop might salvage some of them, but these engines had been pushed hard enough and long enough that an overhaul might be a waste of time.

"Maybe he can pull a rabbit out of his hat," said Jimmy.

"I'll check the spark gaps on the plugs," said Tobias.

"I thought you did that."

"Yes, sir, but maybe I missed something."

Jimmy got out of the P-39.

"OK," he said. "But tomorrow morning, overheating or not, we're going to Buna. Have this crate buttoned up and ready to go by then."

"Yes, sir. I mean, Jimmy."

Jimmy walked down the flight line to Tommy Bell's revetment. Tommy and his mechanic had evidently been having a conversation similar to the one Jimmy had with Ed Tobias. Bell stood with his mechanic, who had the cover off the Allison engine and was pointing to something while Tommy nodded.

In a moment Bell shook his head, clapped his mechanic on the shoulder, and joined Jimmy.

"He thinks he can get the engine in shape for tomorrow," Bell said.

"In shape?"

"Well, it'll get off the ground and carry a bomb and a load of ammo to Buna. How fast it will climb or how high it will get, he couldn't say."

445

"Yeah. Guess we'll find out in the morning."

They walked on down the flight line. Shafer and Kellerman joined them, and they stood for a moment in the shade of a tarp stretched between two trees. It struck Jimmy that this was the spot where he and Jack Davis and a couple of mechanics sheltered during a cloudburst, before that first hairy mission to Lae, when Danny Evans got caught in the downpour. And of them all, all the people standing under the tarp that day, he was the only one still here.

Jimmy looked at the members of his flight. Kellerman looked closed in, the way he always did, and Shafer was looking at the sky. Bell had that goofy grin as he looked down the taxiway to the airstrip.

"Guess it's back to Buna in the morning," Kellerman said.

"Unless it rains."

"My engine isn't running right," said Shafer.

"You don't sound worried," Jimmy replied.

Shafer shrugged. "I hear no one has a really good engine. I just hope mine will get me over the mountains and back."

"Ah, hell, we'll just fly between the mountain peaks and skim the trees there and back," said Bell. "No sense wasting all that gas climbing to 15,000 feet. Keep it low."

Jimmy reflected that might not be a bad idea. The highest peak between Seven-Mile and Buna was 8,000 feet high. But the mountains and valleys were like the teeth of a saw, with gaps between them, and flying through the gaps meant they wouldn't have to get higher than 7,000 feet. Maybe. If the clouds and mist that shrouded the mountain passes didn't reach that high.

The engines, the weather, the Japs. The three variables that separated life from death, defined the chances they'd have to take, all to put bombs and bullets on the target and return to tell the tale.

"C'mon, guys," Jimmy said. "First round's on me."

The Corncobs descended from the mountain pass east of Buna and turned to the north, staying at 7000 feet. There were two decks of clouds, a broken layer above them at 15,000 feet, one below them at 4000, and the lower deck extended to the east and west as far as they could see.

Jimmy scanned around them. The plan of the day was to keep a flight of P-39s over Buna at intervals, and theirs was the second such mission of the day.

So it was Jimmy as Blue Leader, Kellerman as Blue Two, Shafer as Blue Three, and Bell as Blue Four, he reflected, the Kid, Midnight, Shiela, and Chinkerbell, against whatever forces the Empire of Japan chose to throw at them.

Jimmy checked his stopwatch and keyed his radio. "Blues, assume heading of 285, that's 285."

"Two."

"Three."

"Four."

They turned to the west.

Jimmy's dead reckoning said they were twenty miles east of the target when they turned.

"Blues, arm 'em up."

"Two."

"Three."

"Four."

"OK, close up. We're going down, nice and easy."

Jimmy checked left and right as the other pilots closed up the formation, then started a descent at 300 feet per minute. There was no way to know how thick the cloud deck was, and Jimmy had no intention of descending for more than ten minutes.

In five minutes the clouds started to thin out, and in another ten seconds they were below the cloud deck. Jimmy's altimeter read 1700 feet.

WHAM! Flak burst directly ahead of him, and Jimmy pushed down on the stick.

"Three's got barges!"

"Three, Four, go get 'em. Two, follow me, we'll hit that pile of boxes on the beach."

Jimmy opened up on a flak gun spitting fat tracers at them. Their bullets went into the gun emplacement, then they were past it. Jimmy tripped his bomb release, and broke hard left. He looked over his shoulder and Kellerman was there, and behind them their bombs exploded among the supplies on the beach.

"Chink, break left, break left hard!"

"Stay with me, Two," said Jimmy, and reefed into a hard left turn.

Three Zeros were hot on Chinkerbell's tail. He was down in the weeds in a left turn, coming around straight for them.

"Four, this is Lead, come straight ahead, right at us. Two, spread out a little."

Jimmy looked up. Shafer was doing exactly the right thing, climbing in a right turn to keep the Zeros in sight.

Then Bell flew right between them and the Zeros were in front of them. Jimmy snapped a shot at the lead Zero, red balls of tracer flew everywhere, and Jimmy saw strikes on the cowling of the Zero. Something smashed into his cockpit and glass splinters flew in with the wind. Something else smashed into his left wing, then the Zero roared over his cockpit. Jimmy saw a lick of fire and smoke from under the cowling. The trailing Zeros split left and right and the one on Jimmy's right trailed fire from the wing.

"Lead, this is Three, we got three more Zeros lifting off from Buna."

"OK, let's get the hell out of here. Four, where are you?"

"Turning your way, Lead. Three, I see the Zeros. They're bugging out, whoa! Wing came off one of them, the other one is trailing smoke."

Jimmy looked around, kicked his rudders to clear his tail.

"Two, break right, now!"

The last Zero was turning onto Kellerman's tail. Kellerman broke right, away from the Zero, who rolled after Kellerman. Jimmy pulled up and rolled inverted, coming down behind the Zero as Kellerman rolled the other direction. The Zero turned with him, sliding out of Jimmy's sight reticle, and fired on Kellerman. There were strikes on Kellerman's P-39 and then Kellerman started rolling and jinking and yawing and the Zero stayed with him, snapping short bursts. Jimmy got

449

behind the Zero and fired. His tracers curled into the Zero and smashed into the right aileron and wingtip. The Zero turned and dove away from Jimmy's fire, shedding its right aileron in the process.

"Two, you OK?"

"Negative, Kid, that sonofabitch got something into my engine."

"Right. Blues, into the clouds, we'll form up later."

Jimmy pulled up, looking left at the Zeros climbing out of the strip at Buna, then they were in the clouds. Jimmy looked to his right and there was Kellerman, sticking tight.

"Midnight, you need me to slow up?"

"No. I'm with you, Lead."

"Three, Lead, where are you?"

"Climbing. Four's with me."

"OK. Three, those bastards might be waiting for us. Heading 233, rate of climb 100."

"Ah, Lead, hope I can keep it right side up."

"Three, just keep the little ball in the turn and bank indicator right there in the center. Think you can remember how to do that? You know, like back in flight school?"

"Hey, Shiela, if you can't just follow me. I can do that."

"Oh, screw you, Bell."

"This is Lead. You guys keep the chatter down."

Then they were in the clouds. Jimmy looked at Kellerman, shrouded and vague in the mist of the clouds, still tucked in tight.

Jimmy's mind raced ahead. The Zeros climbed twice as fast as a P-39 at this altitude. If the Zeros

450

stayed below the cloud deck, that wouldn't matter, but by now the Zeros could be waiting for the Blues above the clouds with a real altitude advantage.

"Hey, Three, don't be too quick to pop up above the cloud deck."

"Yeah, got you, Lead."

Jimmy watched the clock. He figured there was another minute left to go when the clouds thinned and they were above them.

"Lead, Zeros, eight o'clock high!"

Jimmy looked over his left shoulder. The Zeros were at least two thousand feet higher, climbing, but as Jimmy looked the Zeros pushed over and dove at them. Jimmy looked around quickly but there was no sign of Shiela or Chinkerbell.

"Two, let's get into the clouds, stay close."

"Roger, Lead."

Jimmy nosed over into the clouds with Kellerman right behind him and the white mist closed around them.

"Lead, Two."

"Go ahead, Two."

"Kid, my engine is acting up."

Crap.

"How bad?"

"Bad. CHT and oil pressure. Running rough."

"Right. Three, where are you?"

"How do I know? In the clouds."

"You on the right heading, anyway?"

"Affirmative."

"You guys keep going. We'll take care of ourselves."

451

"Ah, Lead…"

"Shiela, don't be stupid. Just go."

"OK. Good luck."

"Two, Lead."

"Go ahead, Kid."

"Midnight, how's your instrument flying?"

"I'm OK."

"Right. Stay in the clouds on this heading. Not too long. You want to pop up before you hit the mountains."

"Kid, why am I getting a funny feeling about this? Where are you going?"

"Never mind, Midnight. Do what I tell you."

"Jimmy…"

"Shut up. Keep going."

Jimmy pulled up above the clouds, pushing the throttle forward. Three Zeros were to his left in a beautiful formation turn, like something from an air show, and coming his way. A fourth Zero trailed behind them, maybe the one he'd damaged. Jimmy turned into them, climbing as they dove.

He aimed for the lead Zero. The two on the flanks couldn't get a reasonable shot at him without turning into their leader. It didn't keep them from shooting, but their tracers flew on either side of him.

Jimmy hadn't fired his cannon yet and waited now until they were close, with the Zero's cowl guns winking and the cannon on its wings spitting tracers, opening fire with his machine guns when he was close. He put his gunsight pipper just above the Zero's nose and his tracers sparked and cracked across the cowling. Jimmy squeezed the cannon trigger and the cannon gave a single *Punk!* and jammed, but that one round was enough. It exploded in the Zero's engine, transforming it into yellow flame and smoky streaming pieces, wings and fuselage separating and tumbling crazily away. The other two Zeros did that spooky tight Zero turn and came around on his tail. Jimmy dove into the clouds and only once they closed over him did he turn left, watching the artificial horizon, staying coordinated and in a slight dive to get his speed up. Jimmy straightened out for a long count of five, leveled off, and pulled up.

He didn't see the Zero he damaged, but the other two were above the clouds to his right, turning away to the south. As soon as he climbed up above the clouds the Zeros continued their turn to come after him. Jimmy dove back down below the clouds.

This time he looked at his fuel and engine gauges. His fuel was getting low and the CHT was higher than he liked. He made a 90-degree turn to the left and pulled up as he leveled his wings. Two Zeros were above him to his left, diving towards him. One of the Zeros climbed up and turned in to get a shot at Jimmy without hitting his mate. Jimmy turned right and leveled out as the Zeros kept coming. The high Zero got hits on his tail and after fuselage, but Jimmy kicked his rudder and the Zero overshot. For one second the Zero was in Jimmy's sights and he fired, tracers reaching out, hits sparkling on the Zero's right wing and fuselage.

Wham! Wham! Jimmy pulled up hard and rolled, looking over his shoulder. Tracer streamed by his canopy and machine-gun bullets stitched a line across his left wing. Jimmy kicked his rudder hard and looked back over his shoulder. Two Zeros were behind him, cutting inside him, he was too slow and he wasn't going to be able to avoid them. Something rattled in the fuselage aft. He looked at his fuel and engine instruments and looked back at the Zeros.

The Zero in the lead started firing.

Jimmy pulled straight up and chopped his throttle all the way back, and as the P-39 rolled over onto its back he kicked the rudder hard right, with the propeller torque, and took his hands and feet off the controls.

The P-39 went into a spin, inverted, doing that bobbing drunken rotation that looked totally out of control, as if there were a dead pilot at the controls of an airplane with seconds separating it from the earth. He could see the Zeros still curving in at him, then he fell into the clouds.

Jimmy tracked the spin as it stabilized, waiting as the nose came around, paused, rose, and started spinning again, all in the pearl-gray light inside of the cloud. Jimmy remembered there was two thousand feet between the bottom of the cloud and the top of the trees.

Two thousand feet, bobbing, spinning, rattling around in his cinched-up harness, and then, just after the spin slowed and the nose bobbed, the P-39 emerged from the bottom of the cloud, and spent another thousand feet until the nose came around again. But Jimmy was back on the controls and as the nose came up again he was ready, rudder against the spin, full aileron left, and the P-39 broke out of the spin still inverted with the trees growing larger, and Jimmy rolled her and pushed forward on the stick.

The P-39 came out of the dive with the green jungle inches beneath him, and as he pulled up ever so gently on the stick he felt a jolt as the propeller tore through the top of a tree. Then he was up above the treetops in a gentle climb and he scanned left, right and above, then banked sharply to left and right to clear his tail. All he saw was the smoke of Buna behind him, and a few dots above and behind him, heading towards the smoke, and that made them his attackers. Jimmy looked around his cockpit; not much was left in the way of instruments. His tachometer worked; the needle and ball tracked his maneuvers; everything else was starred glass and slashed metal. Wind howled through the holes in his canopy. He looked again over his shoulder at the dots making for Buna, and he turned his P-39 east.

The Japs were sure he was dead or they would have followed him through the clouds. That meant they were already anticipating the boasts and brags they'd make tonight over sake at the O-Club, and argue over who got to paint an American flag on the side of his Zero.

Jimmy wondered how much fuel he had left. His eyes darted to the shot-out fuel gauge even as he continued the turn and straightened out just above the treetops, throttling back a little to conserve whatever fuel he had. Not that it made much difference. There was either enough to get home or he'd wind up in the trees somewhere in the Owen Stanley Mountains.

One pass, he thought to himself. *I'll catch them in the pattern with their wheels down and then we'll see.*

Jimmy stayed low, just above the treetops, and kept up his scan. The Zeros came back into view in a ragged formation, two of them, as the smoke column over Buna thickened and towered over his head.

What do I do if they see me now? he asked. He didn't think it was likely. He was directly behind them, miles away still, and they were descending. None of them fishtailed to look over their shoulders and clear their tails.

Jimmy pushed his throttle all the way forward. He had the fuel for this or he didn't, and a few seconds of mental calculation added up to a definite *maybe*. The maybes included whatever damage he heard in the slightly-ragged note of the engine at full throttle and the faint vibration in the airframe that didn't come from the holes left by exploding cannon shells. Maybe he did a little more than chew through some leaves when he came out of that dive, maybe he'd dinged the prop, thrown it out of balance. Maybe the Zeros hit his engine.

The smoke column marking Buna came closer. Jimmy edged down closer to the treetops, scanning all around. The Zeros in the pattern at Buna turned crosswind. It was a short airstrip, maybe short even for a lightweight Zero, and before one Zero could land the one before it in the pattern had to be off the runway.

The Zeros turned on final, sliding down out of the sky. Jimmy closed in. Under the oxygen mask he felt a savage grin baring his teeth. Then he was over the cleared area, and he went lower still, with streams of

456

Jap antiaircraft suddenly arcing around him and over him. Something slammed into his tail. He skidded wildly but the rudder and elevator still worked. The tracer fell behind him.

The last Zero turned on final. It started down but abruptly leveled out. The Jap's landing gear started to come up. *I know you see me, you bastard, and it's too late.*

Then Jimmy was over the runway, lower even than the Zero on final. Jimmy's engine was roaring at full throttle, driving him through the sky at over three hundred mph. A Zero was at the end of the field, taxiing, and Jimmy gave it a burst with his machine guns as he approached. The tracer walked over the Jap, bullet strikes sparkled over the wings and the canopy, and then he was past. Three thousand feet ahead of him the Zero in the pattern was still cranking up its gear. The pilot probably had his hand on the throttle, pushing it all the way forward, maybe trying to arm his guns after securing them for landing. First the pilot tried to pull up, but even a Zero will stall, and then the pilot put the nose down, a little too abruptly, and pulled up again barely above the treetops at the far end of the runway.

Three thousand feet at a combined closing speed of 450 mph went by in five seconds. Jimmy opened fire on the Zero when he crossed over the runway mid-point. The Zero was still trying to get his nose up. Jimmy held the trigger down. His tracers walked all over the Zero's fuselage. The Jap came apart in a smearing comet of red and yellow fire and black smoke, pieces arcing up before falling to the ground in a burning heap. Jimmy flew through the smoke and thought, *sonofabitch! I'm an ace, but no one saw these last two kills but me and the Japs!*

He sped over the end of the runway and turned hard to the southwest, looking over his shoulder at the Buna airfield. Two columns of smoke burned merrily, black billowing smoke at either end of the runway.

Jimmy couldn't see the mountains through the lower cloud deck. and picked what looked like the most familiar collection of hills as his landmark. He cleared his tail and after five minutes he pulled back the throttle and the mixture to economical cruise.

Now it was just a matter of however much fuel he had left in the tanks and the state of health of his engine. He looked back over his shoulder but couldn't see anything other than the horizontal and vertical stabilizers and the engine exhaust stacks. At least there weren't any holes he could see in the stabilizers, and the exhaust wasn't streaming smoke. He inhaled deeply and let it out in a whoof, sudden fatigue washing over him, there and gone in an instant, leaving him blinking and yawning.

He pulled up through the clouds and kept climbing. The foothills were below him and he could see the mountains ahead and above. He passed Kokoda on the right and flew into the pass in the Owen Stanley Mountains. The Kokoda Track lay along that pass, in the up-and-down elevation of the mountains and valleys of the Papuan highlands, and on this side of the mountains the Japs held the Track. Jimmy touched his revolver and remembered something grim from his grandfather's tales of Indian fighting: *when you fight the Sioux or the Comanche, son, keep count of your cartridges and be sure to save one shot for yourself.*

Jimmy figured the Japs made the Comanche look like choirboys, at least from the stories he heard, and he had no intention of testing the truth of the matter. Not if there were any way to avoid it.

There was cloud here and there over the Track. As he approached the first one Jimmy gritted his teeth, fed in some throttle, and flew over the cloud. It wouldn't do to fly into the clouds to save fuel, and then discover the clouds hid a mountainside.

He held the altitude gained and looked ahead. He was still lower than the mountains on either side of him, and ahead of him was a solid wall of cloud, stretching up higher than the mountain peaks, and blocking his way through east and west.

Try to climb and hope his fuel held? Try to scud-run below the clouds, and hope his luck held? Flying through the clouds wasn't an option with his instruments shot out. Getting into a graveyard spiral just led to the scene of the crash, and being a good pilot had nothing to do with it. Being a good pilot in a case like that meant avoiding the situation.

Jimmy started climbing, listening to the sound of the engine, looking all around in case of lurking Jap Zeros. The engine started running rough. Jimmy fiddled with the throttle and the mixture until it smoothed out, but after another minute, as he gained altitude, it started running rough again.

He kept trying different mixture and throttle settings when the engine started running rough until he finally topped out above the clouds and he could see all

459

the way to the south coast and the Coral Sea, the beautiful lovely blue Coral Sea. Jimmy flew just above the clouds, leaning the mixture until the engine started to run rough, then enriching it again, until he figured he had the best combination of throttle and mixture. Then the southern edge of the cloud appeared ahead of him, and below him was jungle and the corrugated hills of the highlands. The south side of the highlands, he noted thankfully. It was downhill now, all the way to Seven-Mile.

His engine screamed and howled and gave a gut-wrenching mechanical screech. The prop jerked to a stop. He looked behind him. Black smoke vomited out of the exhaust stacks.

The oil! The engine oil broke down, stopped lubricating, temperature rose leading to even greater loss of lubrication and pressure until finally the engine seized up. He chopped the throttle and moved the mixture to AUTOLEAN, switching the ignition and the electrical system to OFF.

He trimmed the airplane for best glide speed, quickly, automatically, nose down, keeping the airspeed up. He did *not* want to stall now, but he was going down, and the only question was where within fifteen miles and when within the next three minutes.

Below and ahead he could see a column of smoke, and he figured he didn't want to be around that. Probably Aussie and Jap infantry shooting at each other, and that was an undesirable place to be. Problem was, looking at the smoke ahead, and feeling the airplane in the seat of his pants, the tips of his fingers, and the balls of his feet, calculating all that and the way the mountaintops around him were rising above him, problem was, he didn't think he could stretch his glide to the other side of the smoke.

He'd have to pick a spot and bail out. He reached over and checked the left door. It opened easily but stayed closed with the slipstream. No problem, he'd kick the P-39 into a skid and that would give him enough of a calm to get the door open, or just jettison it.

A couple miles short of and to one side of the smoke, then, not too damned close to the Track, and maybe the damned Japs would have other things on their minds than tracking down a single Yankee aviator.

He saw a little valley coming up. When he flew over the valley he cross-controlled the P-39. It slipped onto its side. Jimmy jettisoned the door, hit the quick-release button on his seat harness, and when he gave the airplane left aileron he rolled out the door and found himself tumbling through the air with the ground and the sky switching places. When he could see the ground he was still over the little valley, so he waited a few more tumbles before he pulled the ripcord.

There was a rustle and a whispering rush of silk. The parachute filled with a sudden *whoomp!* and something yanked him hard by the crotch. Then he was floating through the sky under an umbrella of white silk, and a god-blessed wind blew him away from the valley into the trees. The trees came up with a rush, and Jimmy put his feet together and crossed his arms over his face. He plunged through some light branches, smashed into something solid, bounced and slid off that.

Something hit his head and everything went dark.

461

Chapter Eighteen

The things you hate the most

There was a scream, high-pitched and sustained, and it brought Jimmy out of the darkness. For a moment he was home, listening to the scream of a panther somewhere near. He reached for his pistol. When his hand wrapped around the revolver's grip he came to the present, and darkness. The scream trailed off into a series of hoarse, coughing gasps, and then it rose again, higher and louder.

Jimmy took his hand off his pistol and looked around. A faint orange light glimmered up through the leaves and branches below him. There was nothing under his feet, and he realized he hung from his parachute risers, with the canopy snagged in the treetops above him. His head hurt and a wave of nausea swept over him. He retched. Nothing came up.

Smells hit him. Over a faint smell of wood smoke was the distinct and pungent smell of urine and feces and vomit, and he realized it was from him. He suppressed a groan. When he went into the trees he must have hit his head, and lost control of his bowels.

Before he could react with too much shame and embarrassment the screaming began again, and Jimmy heard odd laughter, almost like giggling, mixed in with the screams.

He retched again. He took a deep breath, then another one, deeper still. It helped. He checked his pistol to make sure the safety strap was in place. He touched the hilt of his Bowie knife. It was firmly in its

463

sheath. Then he went to his parachute straps. Whatever the canopy was caught on, it was solid.

The screams and the high-pitched laughter kept on while Jimmy tried to find his footing. Eventually he had both feet on a solid branch and one hand around another, but it left his body leaning at an awkward angle. With his free hand, he got his parachute knife out and cut through the risers one at a time. There was tension he hadn't realized on the second riser. When it came off he almost lost his balance, even with one hand firmly wrapped around the tree branch. He managed to hold on to the knife and put it back in his pocket.

He stood on the branch and looked down, but all he saw through the leaves and branches was the faint glow of firelight. Jimmy hit the quick-release buckle on his harness and shrugged out of it carefully to be sure he didn't fall out of the tree. Because by now he'd heard bits of speech, a sing-song, oddly musical speech that mixed with the laughter.

Japs. And from the screams and the hoarse grunting gasps they had some poor bastard down there, carving him up in ways Jimmy didn't want to imagine.

Five shots in his revolver, and the bad thing about a Colt single-action, it took time to reload. Any one of those five shots would put a man down, but the fired casings had to be ejected one by one, and the chambers had to be reloaded, one by one. Jimmy practiced reloading a Colt like this one for hours under his grandfather's watchful eye, until Tom Ardana allowed he was as fast as any of the Texas border gunslingers had ever been. Sitting on the front porch he got down to ten seconds. When they tried it on horseback, Jimmy

464

scattered .45 cartridges halfway across the Ardana spread. At best, on horseback, it took him a minute to reload.

He might kill five Japs with his revolver, and he doubted he'd have ten seconds to reload. If he was lucky he might be able to draw the Bowie knife and take one more Jap with him before he was swarmed.

Oh shit. Oh hell. Oh, Jehosophat. He was going to have to get down out of this tree and face a jungle full of Japs. In among the trees and the dirt and the mud.

Jimmy wrapped his parachute harness in loops like a lariat and started down, cautiously, feeling and testing his way. Jimmy had no idea how much time it took, but every foot involved his heart beating in his throat and his pulse hammering in his temples, while the adrenaline in his blood made him shake.

It was a long way down. Eventually the branches and leaves thinned out, and by that time a thin gray light filtered tentatively down from the treetops. The sun wasn't high enough over the mountains to illuminate the ground below him. Wisps of fog drifted among the tree branches all around and below him.

Somewhere during his slow journey down the tree, the screams of whatever poor bastard the Japs were torturing ceased abruptly. The giggling and the talk trailed off into quiet. Maybe the Japs were sleeping, tired from their night of sport.

Jimmy had absolutely no idea what he would do when he got low enough to climb or jump down from the tree. He had to know how many Japs there were, for starters. He had to be careful not to alert a sentry, if the Japs had someone on watch.

There was a sudden gurgling sound below him, followed immediately by the sound of blows, heavy cracks, thuds, and a choked-off scream. Jimmy froze, listening to a long second of silence.

"Right, lads," said a quiet, Aussie-accented voice. "All present and correct, then?"

"'ere's Palmer, Jock," said another voice. "What's left of 'im, the poor sod."

"Christ and all the virgins," said a third voice. "We should have left one of these bloody Nips alive. Or maybe two or three."

"No time for fun," said the voice belonging to the one called Jock. "Let's clean this lot up. Take any food or canteens, check for maps and papers, binoculars, you know the drill. Slim, you're almost out of ammunition. Take a Jap rifle and all the ammo you can carry."

"Right, Jock."

Jimmy cleared his throat and said, "Hey, chums, you reckon you could save one of those rifles for a Yank?"

There was dead silence.

"I'm not a Jap, if that's what you're thinking," Jimmy said. "I got shot down and ended up in this tree."

"All right, come on down, then," said Jock's voice. "But come easy."

"OK. Here I come."

Jimmy climbed down another fifteen feet to a limb where he could jump to the ground. When he stood up he looked at the eight men standing in the clearing.

Clearly, they were Australian infantry, and clearly, they were the worse for wear. Their uniforms, what was

466

left of them, were stained and tattered and streaked with mud. Two of them wore dirty, bloody bandages. Four of them had helmets. The rest were bare-headed. But they all carried rifles, and the rifles were clean, and they were pointed at Jimmy, who was careful to show them his empty palms.

"Well, he's not a bloody Nip, anyway," said one of them.

"Sounds like a Yank, too."

"Got one of those pilot helmets on," added another.

"Good morning to you blokes, too," Jimmy said. The Aussies lowered their rifles slowly.

One of them stepped forward and looked Jimmy up and down, without any expression in his eyes. "A bleedin' pilot," he said. "You up in that tree all night?"

"Yup."

"Reckon you heard everything that went on?"

"Yup."

"Didn't do a damned thing, either."

"Eighty feet up in that damned tree, swinging from my parachute? No, chum. All I could do was listen, the whole night."

The Aussie looked at Jimmy for another long moment, then nodded slowly. "You mean what you said about that rifle?"

"Sure."

"Good-oh, then. Looks like you've got your pick. Take as much ammo as you can. You'll need a canteen, too."

Jimmy nodded.

"Hey, Jock, this little sod is an officer. 'e's got a map case."

"Yeah? Take it along, then." The one addressed as Jock turned to Jimmy. "You get a good look around before you jumped? Think you could tell where we are on a map?"

Jimmy nodded, thinking about the view from the cockpit. "My compass was shot out, but I got a good look at the south coast and the hills around me. I think I can figure it out, even if it's been a long time since I looked at a chart."

"I thought all you pilots had maps and charts."

"You'd think, but no. Not us pursuit types, anyway. Hell, we never get more than two hundred miles from home base."

Jock nodded.

While they talked the other soldiers moved around the clearing. One of them looked through a small pile of gear to one side, Aussie gear by the look of it. There was a poncho in a musette bag, and the soldier spread it over what was left of Palmer, the man the Japs tortured, and weighed the poncho down with Jap helmets and boots.

Jimmy looked at the Jap rifles and picked one up. The barrel seemed overly long, and the wooden stock too light and short. The rifle felt lighter than a Springfield. Jimmy worked the bolt enough to see that the magazine was loaded.

"'ere," said Jock. "This knob at the end of the bolt, that's the safety. Turn it a bit, this way, see?"

Jimmy looked at the bolt. There was a large knurled knob at the end, and he watched while Jock turned it, then turned it back to put the safety back on.

"Thanks," Jimmy said. "Useful thing to know."

"No worries, chum," said the Aussie. "I'm Jock."

"Jimmy."

Jock nodded at Jimmy's pistol. "Doesn't look like Yank issue."

"It isn't." Jimmy unbuckled the strap and handed the Colt butt-first to Jock. The Aussie took it, hefted it, and pointed it into the jungle. His eyes widened.

"Might have to have one of those," Jock said. "Points like your finger."

"That's the idea," said Jimmy. He took the revolver back and put it in his holster.

Jimmy bent to one of the Japs and took the cartridge belt lying next to the man. It came with cartridge pouches, canteen, and a bayonet in a sheath clipped to the belt. Jimmy took the bayonet out and tested the edge with his thumb.

It was razor-sharp.

"Like them bayonets of theirs, the Nips do," said Jock bitterly.

"How long you fellows been out here?" Jimmy asked.

"We got cut off from our battalion a week past. We've been trying to get back ever since."

"How far away are our lines?"

"Not sure," Jock said. "You can hear the artillery, now and again, and when the wind is right, you can hear the rifles going. It isn't far, but we can't get too close to the Track, because the bloody Nips patrol it in force. I don't reckon we're the only mob wandering about in the jungle, either."

The Aussie indicated the dead Japs lying in their own blood. "Like this bunch. Got cut off, doing their bit for the Emperor, trying to make it back. They found poor Palmer over there while he was scouting ahead and likely not looking around the way he should."

The Aussies took the boots off the Japs and threw them into the brush, along with the rifles and packs. Jock looked around, grimaced, and pulled out a compass.

"That way," he said, pointing to the southwest. "Billy, take the point, and keep your ruddy eyes open. You see what happens when you don't."

Jock nodded towards the poncho that shrouded Palmer's body.

"Too right," Billy muttered. He settled his pack on his shoulders and gripped his rifle, walking in the direction Jock indicated.

Jimmy fell in beside Jock. "Before I bailed out of my ship I saw smoke maybe six or seven miles towards those mountains up ahead. Three columns of smoke, not really dense, maybe like straw huts burning."

"Six or seven miles, you say?"

"Yup."

Jock opened the captured map case and spread the contents on the ground. "Mucking Nip bastards," he growled. "This is an army map."

"Aussie army?"

"Too right." Jock laid a compass on the map and aligned the map with magnetic north.

Jimmy looked at the map. "OK, here's Port Moresby, and there were maybe three ridge lines between where I bailed out and the lowlands. I think we're about here. That puts the fires I saw about here. That line of bearing, anyway."

Jock studied the map. He tapped the last ridge before the lowlands. "Know what that is?"

"Other than a ridge, no."

"That's Imita Ridge. Probably the last defensive position in the highlands. Japs break through there, we'll be fighting them on the road to Port Moresby. It's not more than twenty miles from Imita Ridge to the coast."

Jimmy suppressed a bitter thought that began, *if that damned engine had held together for another ten minutes...*

"That's not far."

"No." Jock frowned. "We've seen your lads overhead quite a bit. What have you been doing?"

"Bombing the Jap beachhead at Buna, mostly. Hitting them anywhere along the Track we think it'll do any good."

Jock nodded. Then he folded the map and stood up. "Right. Well, press on, then. Hope you're up for a bit of a hike. No trails here."

"Swell."

Jock smiled briefly. "Reckon you can use that rifle?"

"If it shoots straight."

"Fair enough. We don't usually shoot at any real distance, not in this brush."

"Thirty, forty yards?"

"Sounds right. If we're lucky we won't run into any more Nips, at least until we get closer to wherever the fighting is. How's it going, by the way?"

"The Japs are still attacking, we're still retreating. We've been hitting the beachhead at Buna every day.

471

Doesn't seem like the Japs could get a lot of supplies to their troops at this end of the Track."

Jock nodded. "That lot back there didn't look well fed. How many rounds are in that cartridge belt?"

"Don't know." Jimmy felt the ammunition pouches. "I stuffed them full, because they were maybe half full to begin with."

"Not a lot of rice in the sacks they were carrying, either. Of course, we don't know how long they've been wandering about in the bush."

Jimmy nodded.

A growling drone became audible, rising in volume. A series of rapid explosions jarred the air and the ground underfoot. When the explosions died away the drone of engines continued, growing in volume again. Jimmy looked up, but the treetops overhead were thick enough to shut out the sky. The engines sounded close. More explosions, near enough that the ground quivered underfoot, marched away to the southwest, the roar of the explosions echoing and re-echoing off the mountains around them. Then the drone of engines died away.

"Let's go," said Jock.

The heat of the day hadn't set in, but the humidity made the sweat run freely under Jimmy's coverall. He readjusted the pack. It wasn't heavy, but the straps were unfamiliar, and he could feel them chafing his skin.

The ground underfoot squished. Water welled up around the soles of his shoes, and the sulfurous smell of rotten vegetation wafted up with every step. It made the footing difficult, as bad as trying to walk in loose sand. Having to move vines and creepers and low-lying

472

branches aside while they marched added to the difficult. Jimmy noticed no one had machetes or tried to slash the vegetation with their bayonets. He also noticed that no one spoke, and everyone looked around them, like pursuit pilots watching for bandits.

Jimmy didn't doubt the wisdom of it, but he doubted anyone could see any further than twenty yards in bush like this. The Aussies walked with an easy step. They didn't crouch down but they looked ready to jump in any direction or throw themselves flat at any moment.

After the bombers left quiet returned to the jungle, broken at irregular intervals by screeching bird cries.

Once the Aussies froze, going into a crouch with their rifles at the ready. There was a tense couple of minutes, until they slowly rose and started forward again.

A flat *boom!* echoed around the mountains.

"Jap cannon," Jock mouthed. Jimmy nodded.

It got hotter and no less humid. The booming cannon continued sporadically through the morning. Once there was a rattle, almost like popping corn, rifle and machine-gun fire from a distance. Then it faded away.

Jimmy had been thirsty before but being thirsty between waterholes in Montana during the summer wasn't like this. Sweat ran off Jimmy as if the pores of his skin were water faucets, and he rolled his tongue around in his mouth, trying to get saliva going. The Aussies were marching in the same conditions, and he figured they were carrying heavier loads. He hadn't seen any of them go for their canteens, so he figured he'd try to hold out.

There wasn't a lot in his canteen anyway, and it was probably full of Jap spit. Thirsty as he was, he wasn't thirsty enough to drink that. Yet.

Eventually they came to a stream. They waded across, one at a time, and on the other side of the stream Jock called a halt.

"Take a break," he said. "Fill your canteens before we go on, but be careful, out in the open."

The Aussies dispersed themselves, propping up against the tree trunks, looking for ant nests before they sat down. Jimmy sat down next to Jock, who opened his canteen and drank deeply. Jimmy looked at the Jap canteen and grimaced.

Jock grinned at him. "What's the matter, Jimmy?"

"Don't know that I'm thirsty enough to drink after a Jap. Yet, anyway."

"You'll get there," Jock promised grimly. The Aussie gestured back towards the creek they had crossed.

"Go fill it up," Jock said. "Just look across the way and be sure there's no one watching before you get out in the open."

Jimmy looked at Jock. "You guys aren't regular Aussie Army, are you?" he asked.

Jock grinned lopsidedly. "No. Special Infantry Force. We were on the left flank of our line when we got cut off, trying to hit the Japs in their flank."

"Mm. Would that be like Commandos?"

"Those bleedin' Pom pansies?" Jock grinned. "Might be. Mind you take your rifle."

Jimmy nodded. "Give me your canteen."

"Thanks, chum."

Jimmy took the proffered canteen and walked to the bank of the stream. It ran swift and clear around moss-covered rock. He laid down next to a bush overhanging the bank and dipped his canteen in, rinsing it out before holding it under the water. He filled the canteen and drank most of it and filled it again.

While he repeated the process with Jock's canteen he became aware of a figure in the bushes across the stream. The stream itself was twenty feet across here. Jimmy froze. The water splashed over his arm as he held Jock's canteen under the surface.

The figure came slowly out of the bushes. It was a native, not a Jap. Jimmy relaxed but still didn't move. He'd heard the Japs used native bearers on the Track.

The man looked slowly around, up and down stream, before he waved to someone behind him. Another native joined him, and they knelt by the stream and drank. When they had their heads down Jimmy slowly drew his hand out of the water, put the canteen down, and put his hand on his pistol, ready to flip the strap off.

Another native came out of the bush across the stream and said something urgent. The other two jumped up and all three fled into the bush.

Jimmy crawled back from the bank of the stream and picked up his rifle. He rotated the knob on the bolt.

Crap. Crap crap crap and jehosofuckingphat crap. He really had no desire to get involved in this infantry shit. He didn't want to fight this way. He didn't have any fucking choice at all, and that made him angrier still.

"What d'you see, Yank?" Jock asked.

"Three natives. Two drinking at the stream, and another called them away. They ran off like rabbits."

"Right." Jock looked over his shoulder and made motions with his hands. In a moment, the rest of Jock's squad ghosted into position facing the stream, rifles at the ready.

Another man appeared from the jungle, and when he appeared Jimmy tensed. The man wore a stained khaki uniform and a cartridge belt. He carried a rifle. Adrenaline spurted into Jimmy's veins. He checked the safety on his rifle again. Jock laid a hand on Jimmy' shoulder. Jimmy nodded, still looking down the sights of his rifle.

"Wait for my signal," Jock said. His voice was only just audible over the rush and tumble of the water in the stream. Jimmy nodded again.

The Jap infantryman looked up and down the stream, almost exactly as the natives had, as Jimmy remembered Jock doing. Jimmy studied the man. He stood tense, his rifle held at something higher than port arms, obviously ready to throw it to his shoulder and fire. Another infantryman joined the first, materializing like a spectre from the bush.

A harsh voice called to the first two infantrymen. They said something back, and abruptly a dozen Jap infantrymen appeared from the jungle. One of them wore an odd-looking curved sword and didn't carry a rifle.

476

Jimmy looked down the sights of his rifle. He felt everything fall away, leaving only the moment, only the sights down the barrel of the rifle, with the target picture of the chest of the Jap with the sword. Jimmy could see his face, the moustache over the firm, thin-lipped mouth, the dark eyes darting from here to there. Jimmy curled his finger over the trigger, aware that he had no idea what the trigger pull was, aware that in seconds, seconds or less, he might find out.

Jock's hand left Jimmy's shoulder.

"Be ready," Jock said. Jimmy nodded.

The man with the sword said something and gestured at the stream. The first two Japs nodded and barked a single syllable in reply, then advanced into the stream, rifles at the ready. A dozen more Jap infantrymen appeared from the jungle.

"Fire!" Jock said, and in the instant, Jimmy took up the slack on his trigger, a little more than he thought, and around him Enfield .303s boomed and cracked, and his own rifle joined the chorus. Over the sights he saw his round take the Jap with the sword. The man spun around and crumpled into a heap. Jimmy worked the bolt, looking for a target, and briefly caught another Jap in his sights. The man was running back into the jungle. Jimmy fired and the man stumbled and fell.

The two Japs in the stream were caught and chewed by bullets from several rifles. Jimmy worked the bolt on his own rifle, looked for another target, and found nothing. The Japs were down and if any survived they were running into the bush.

"Right, lads, let's get the hell out of this," said Jock, pitching his voice to carry. He clapped Jimmy on the shoulder.

Jimmy grabbed the two canteens and his rifle and ran, following Jock and the others into the jungle away from the stream. They ran for ten minutes, until Jimmy gasped for breath and Jock called for a halt. While Jimmy gasped he handed Jock his canteen.

"For a Yank you're a real cobber," Jock said.

"Anytime, pal."

They waited for five minutes, looking back along their trail, until everyone's breathing slowed.

"Right, come on," said Jock, who consulted his compass. "Sammy, take point. We're heading this way."

"Good-oh," said Sammy. He rose and walked off into the bush.

An hour later they came upon the Kokoda Track.

It was obviously the Track. Native bearers walked past, guarded by Jap infantry, with Japanese soldiers staggering under enormous packs alongside the natives. Off to the southwest came a distant burst of gunfire and artillery.

Before the Aussies came on the Track Jock had them crawling on hands and knees through the bush, because the Japs were shouting orders and calling to one another, and the noise was audible from two hundred yards out.

It scared hell out of Jimmy to be this close to that many Japs. From where he lay under another bush overlooking the trail he counted at least a hundred, with more coming from the northeast. If he had a radio, if he

478

only had a radio, he could call the Corncobs to rain bombs and bullets and shells on the Japs, who were obviously the supply train for the troops fighting to the southwest. They could hear the guns going from that direction, but Jimmy couldn't tell how far away they were.

Jimmy looked to the left and the right. He was with eight Aussies. Even if they were some kind of commandos, odds of 20-to-1 weren't realistic. They could shoot from this vantage point, cause casualties and confusion, but Jimmy figured any good ambush needed a good escape route. They didn't really have one, other than maybe fading into the bush and letting the Japs run by, assuming the Japs were that stupid.

It didn't seem like a smart assumption to Jimmy.

After ten minutes of watching the Track, Jock signaled them to move back into the jungle. They stopped in a tiny clearing and squatted down, clutching their rifles.

"Nips behind us and Nips in front of us," Jock said. He pitched his voice just above a whisper, barely enough to carry, lost sometimes in the rumble of cannon to the southwest. "Miles to go to reach our lines, an' before we get there, we'll probably have to go west to turn the Jap flank."

"That's a fair cow," said one of the soldiers. He squatted down on one leg with the other out to the side.

There was silence for a moment. The Aussies looked around them, listening.

"That stream where we scragged those Nips is close to the Track," Jock went on. "Too close, maybe.

They'll be sending watering parties over all the bloody time."

"Nothing for it, then, and that's dinkum," said Slim. "We'll have to press on."

"Too right," Jock replied. He took out his compass. "We'll head towards the west southwest for a bit, an' see when we get close to that stream."

He looked at Jimmy. "Any idea on the terrain ahead of us, Yank?"

"A ridge of some sort up ahead, other side of where I saw the smoke."

Jock nodded. "Well, that makes sense. Most of these fights up here, you defend a ridge, the Japs come around one flank or the other, an' you got to fall back before they get too far up your arse an' cut you off. You can't fight along the bloody Track with the bush on both sides, because you can't see a ruddy thing in the jungle an' no one knows where anyone is. So you fall back to the next ridge or hill an' dig in."

Jock rose and started off. Jimmy and the rest followed him.

The rumble and crack of the guns never quit. As they went slowly through the jungle Jimmy noticed he could tell two different sounds from the guns, the nearer WHAM of the cannon firing, and the distant *boom!* of the shell exploding.

Jock called a halt every half-hour to rest. Before the second break they came across a stream, crossed it one at a time after studying the jungle ahead of them, and refilled their canteens. As they sat listening to the jungle and the artillery Slim said, "Those Nip guns couldn't be far, Jock."

"I know. Any idea?"

Slim shrugged. "The way sound goes in the jungle, and among all these ruddy great mountains? They're close, chum, but other 'n' that I've not a clue."

Slim listened for a moment and pointed to the southeast. "That way, I reckon. They'd have to be close to the Track, wouldn't they? Can't move the bastards through the jungle, an' the ruddy shells for the guns have to come down the Track."

"Climb a tree," Jimmy said.

Jock looked at him.

"Pick one of these trees and climb to the top, see what you can see," Jimmy said. "Take a compass with you so if you see smoke from the cannon you can get a bearing on it. Or on whatever the Japs are shooting at, which will tell you where the lines are."

"Well, I know you can ruddy well climb down," Jock replied. "How are you at climbing up?"

The Aussie smiled at Jimmy. The others chuckled.

"Swell," Jimmy growled. "Give me your compass. Got any binoculars?"

The compass Jimmy put in a zippered pocket of his coveralls. He slung the binoculars by their strap around his neck. He handed his pack and rifle to Jock, took a long drink of water from his canteen, and started climbing.

"Better take this pig-sticker along, Yank," said Jock, offering him the Jap bayonet. "Besides cutting your way through vines an' such, you sometimes find snakes up there."

Jimmy took the Bowie knife from its sheath and showed it to Jock.

"Well, right you are, then," said Jock, grinning. "Careful you don't chop the tree down with that thing, eh?"

"Stay out from underneath," Jimmy warned. "I might drop something."

The climb was hard at first, because the branches lower down were far apart. Twenty feet up it got easier, as much as climbing up a hundred-foot tall tree full of ants, vines, flowers, centipedes, and small branches that slapped you in the face, all against the force of gravity, ever got easier. At least, Jimmy thought, there weren't any snakes. As he neared the top the main trunk branched and splayed and reduced in diameter until Jimmy was concerned it wouldn't bear his weight. He moved around the top of the tree and finally found a place where the leaves and branches thinned out and let him see to the south.

Shells burst on a hillside that was part of a ridge running more or less east to west. Jimmy took a compass bearing on the ridge where the shells landed.

Artillery barked to his left. Jimmy shifted the compass and took a bearing on the smoke drifting up from the cannon fire. He couldn't see the guns themselves, but he waited, watching, and in another minute the guns fired again.

Jimmy triggered the stopwatch on his aviator's chronograph as the guns fired and waited for the shells to burst on the ridge before stopping it. He looked down at the stopwatch. The second hand was at 19 seconds. Slowly and carefully Jimmy climbed back down the tree.

Jock sat at the foot of the tree, but none of the others were visible. The Aussie read Jimmy's look and said, "No sense bunching up and giving the Nips an easy target, eh? What did you find out?"

"What's the muzzle velocity of those Jap artillery pieces?"

"Why?"

"Because the flight time is 19 seconds."

Jock blinked. "Well. Don't know the elevation of the gun, but the muzzle velocity is probably 1200 feet per second. Makes the range, I don't know, 4-5 miles."

"That was fast."

"I was in the Artillery for a while."

"Well, the ridge with the fighting bears 225, while the guns are about 130."

The Aussie blinked. "Then we're maybe four miles from the ridge. Useful to know, Yank. You like being a pilot? We could use a bloke like you. You can shoot straight and use your head."

"I love being a pilot, Jock, and I'll be honest, this whole infantry thing makes me want to crap my pants. I did that once already, when I went into the trees after I bailed out."

Jock grinned. "Don't worry, Jimmy. I feel the same way, once or twice an hour when we're out in the bush like this."

The grin faded. "I did crap my pants, once."

"That's supposed to make me feel better?"

"Sure. We're all just a bunch of crappers, out here in one bloody beaut crapper."

"Then let's get the hell out of here."

"No fear, cobber. 225, you say?"

"Yup."

Jock stood up and handed Jimmy his rifle. "Why don't we head about 235, then? Maybe we can avoid running into any more bloody Nips."

"Sounds good to me."

"We'll make for Imita Ridge," said Jock. "If the lads don't hold them there we may as well head on down to Port Moresby."

Jimmy fell in with the Aussies, walking the way they walked, slowly, rifle in hand, brushing the bush aside, and trying to breathe in the humid, fetid jungle air, with the rattle of rifles and the *boom* of artillery to accompany their march. And they heard the airplanes, the P-39s and the A-20s, strafing and bombing along the trail, and Jimmy gritted his teeth and set one foot after the other, senses straining to see the Japs before they saw him.

He hated the jungle with every step, every one of the thousands of steps he took, all the way to Imita Ridge.

"Hey. You Lt. Ardana?"

Jimmy opened one eye, reluctantly. He saw an American Army captain in fatigues, carrying binoculars and a map case.

"That's me."

"You want a ride back to Seven-Mile, Lieutenant?"

Jimmy blinked. He was tired, tired in a way he never had been in his life. When he and Jock and the Aussies made it past the Japs and into the Aussie lines it was after four days of walking through dense bush, up and down hills, going without water for too long in the jungle heat, and eating weevil-infested Jap rice they boiled over a hatful of fire in a can the Aussies called a "billy." Rice didn't go far towards filling the hole in a man's belly after a day of that kind of marching.

"Yeah," Jimmy said, finally.

Jock lay next to him with his hat over his eyes. "Leaving us, Jimmy?"

"Looks like, Jock."

"Remember the poor bloody infantry when you get back to Seven-Mile."

"Too right, chum, and that's dinkum."

"You've picked up some bad habits, cobber, and that's dinkum too." Jock sat up and held out his hand. Jimmy shook it. "You watch yourself, Jimmy, an' if you decide you don't want to fly anymore, you've got a home with the Special Infantry Force."

"Thanks, Jock."

The American captain held out his hand and helped Jimmy up. Jimmy reached back for his rifle and the equipment belt.

"Souvenirs?" the captain asked.

"Sort of," Jimmy replied. "We aren't home yet."

Artillery landed not far away, and a machine gun *tat-tat-tatted* in the distance.

"Guess not," said the captain. "Come on, I've got a jeep."

Jimmy walked with the captain. He looked back once. Jock was asleep again. The rest of the squad never even stirred.

"I'm Paul Whittaker, by the way. I'm on the staff with the 522nd Infantry Regiment. They sent me up here to look things over. Just in case."

"In case what?"

"The Aussies might not hold. We're getting ready to send a regiment up here to help out."

"Good. These blokes could use our help."

There was a jeep in front of the Aussie brigade command post. A colonel Jimmy recognized vaguely from the debrief he and Jock attended last night came out.

"So, Whittaker, found your little lost angel, have you?"

"Yes, sir."

"Right, then." The colonel stepped around the jeep and shook hands with Jimmy. "Good luck, Ardana."

"Thanks, Colonel."

The colonel to Whittaker. "You look after this lad for us, Whittaker. He's part Australian now, you know."

"Sure thing, Colonel."

"On your way, then."

The colonel turned and went back into the tent.

Captain Whittaker got into the jeep and started the engine. Jimmy put his rifle into the back of the jeep and got into the passenger seat.

Whittaker turned the jeep and started off down the vaguely-defined track, slowly, mostly in first gear with the engine whining on the downhill grade. He stopped now and again to let troops heading up to the line pass by.

Jimmy found himself going in and out of sleep. His head nodded on his chest, then they'd hit a bump and he'd start into wakefulness.

Finally, they came to an open stretch. Whittaker shifted into second gear.

Jimmy said, "How did you hear about me?"

"That Aussie colonel, Palmerston, told me about you."

"You know anything about what's going on with the 35th Fighter Group?"

"Is that your outfit? I don't know much about the Air Corps. Sorry."

Jimmy nodded. "That's OK. I appreciate the ride."

"My pleasure. So, what happened to you?"

"My engine packed up over the Track. I bailed out. Those blokes back there found me, and we walked out together."

"I gather it was a bit more than that."

"Yeah."

Whittaker looked at him, and Jimmy recognized the look. Today was probably the first day the captain had even been close to combat, and he knew he'd get closer, a lot closer than that, before too very long.

"Are you that Ardana I heard about?"

"Don't know. What did you hear?"

"That you got five Japs, plus the one you shot dead on the airstrip."

"Thought you didn't know anything about the Air Corps." Jimmy's brain was sluggish, but the number 'five' finally registered.

"Five? They said I had five Japs?"

"Yeah, that's right."

"Are you kidding me?"

"Why would I?"

"Because I didn't think anyone saw those kills. How'd you hear all this?"

"There's only one officer's club at Seven Mile. I was there last night, drank some beer, heard some stories. I bought drinks for some pursuit guys."

"Yeah? Who?"

"There were four of them. I don't know their names, really. They said they were Midnight, Shiela, Chinkerbell, and some guy they called too new to have a name."

"You're shitting me."

"Why?"

"That's my flight. Well, it was, anyway. What did they have to say?"

"About you? You mean, Jimmy the Kid?"

"Crap."

Whittaker grinned. "Well, I must say, you're not as big as I expected."

Whittaker's grin faded. "Is that the pistol they were telling me about? The one you shot that Jap with?"

Jimmy looked at his .45 Colt. It was splotched with rust and needed cleaning badly.

"Well, it's my pistol. And don't ask me what it was like, Whittaker. I shot that sonofabitch because he was shooting at me."

"Sure."

"Tell me about Chinkerbell."

"Well, he seemed to really think the world about you. I thought he was in love or something."

"Yeah? What about Midnight?"

"Mostly he sat back and drank beer and listened to what, Shiela? And Chinkerbell? Anyway, he listened while the other two told stories and the new guy leaned forward like he was drinking from his momma's teat."

"Yeah, sounds about right. So Chinkerbell called himself that?"

"Sure. What's it mean, anyway? Chinkerbell?"

"It's a term of esteem."

Whittaker looked at him. "Oh. Yeah. Sure."

Jimmy looked at the jungle on the side of the track, so Whittaker couldn't see him grinning.

They came around a curve in the road, passed another battalion of infantry marching up the Track, and there was the southern coastal plain, and by God, he could see airplanes in the pattern at Seven-Mile, and the sparkling blue of the Coral Sea beyond the shore.

On down the dusty road past native villages and over rivers with bridges that didn't look like they'd take a man's weight, much less a jeep carrying two men, which they sped over without a bobble. They passed men going up to the front, men in ambulances, and trucks heading down to Port Moresby to resupply. Jimmy slipped in and out of a doze, and when he woke up a little they were further down the road, and things had changed. He looked in the mirror and saw the thunderheads building over the Owen Stanley Mountains.

An airplane roared overhead. It was a P-39, overhead and gone in an instant, with three others in its wake, followed by another flight of four.

Almost home. He went to sleep and woke up again when the jeep pulled up in front of the familiar grass and palm-frond Operations Shack.

"You good from here?" Whittaker asked.

489

Jimmy got out of the jeep and picked up his rifle. "Yeah. Thanks, Whittaker. Good luck."

"You too."

The captain drove off, leaving Jimmy standing in front of the palm-frond and open window structure that housed Group Operations.

Jimmy turned to look at the airfield. The same patched, part macadam, part steel mat, beat-to-hell airstrip he'd left days ago. He still wasn't sure how long ago that was.

A flight of P-39s taxied onto the strip, ran their engines up, and took off in twos.

Jimmy smiled. He was tired down to his bones, but he smiled anyway. God Almighty, it was good to be home.

Jimmy slung the rifle over his shoulder and walked into the Operations Shack.

He didn't see anybody he knew. As he stood inside the doorway everyone stopped in their tracks, staring at him. Jimmy realized he looked like hell, with ten days' worth of beard, filthy, without a hat or his helmet, his coveralls stained and tattered, a Jap rifle over his shoulder and a Jap bayonet on his belt.

"Ah...can I help you?" asked the sergeant at the desk.

"Who's the Officer of the Day?" Jimmy asked.

"I'm the Officer of the Day," said a captain. Jimmy looked him up and down. The man was in fresh khakis that hardly looked broken in. "Who the hell are you?"

"First Lieutenant Jimmy Ardana," Jimmy replied. "Who the fuck are you?"

Jimmy set the rifle down and took a step towards the man. He stepped back.

"Captain Leonard Johnson," the man said hastily.

Jimmy nodded. "Well, Captain Leonard Johnson, who's in charge here? And where's Major Dionne? Or Captain Allen?"

"Major Dionne got wounded. He's in Australia. Allen's commanding his squadron for now."

Jimmy nodded. "Colonel Wrixon still in command?"

"No, he got transferred to HQ 5th Air Force. Colonel Langston is commanding the group now."

"Good. Maybe the Colonel could spare me a few minutes of his time."

"Well...sure, but what for?"

"For one thing, I want to know what the hell happened to the Corncob Blues. My flight."

"Tenn-hut!"

Jimmy came to attention, a bit wearily, as everyone else in the Day Room snapped to.

"Rest, gentlemen," said a new voice.

Jimmy looked at the man belonging to the voice. He was youngish, but not exactly young. Older than Buzz Wagner, anyway, and suddenly Jimmy felt old. It was the middle of September, 1942, and he'd only been here since May and maybe the last week counted for a year for every day. Jimmy looked at the youngish colonel and saluted.

"Lieutenant James T. Ardana, reporting for duty, sir," he said.

Made in the USA
Las Vegas, NV
07 August 2023

75779787R00284